Quartet

four tales from
the crossroads

by

George RR Martin

Edited by Christine Carpenito

The NESFA Press
Post Office Box 809
Framingham, MA 01701

To Leslie Kay Swigart
Another one for the bibliography

Contents

GEORGE R.R. MARTIN
by
Melinda M. Snodgrass

As I look over the four pieces which constitute *Quartet* I realize that in a sense they mirror their creator's life. There is George R.R. Martin the critically acclaimed, and award winning author of *Skin Trade*. There is the writer in the wilderness period as George searched for the right project, and therefore a treat for the reader because they will get to see a piece of an, as yet, unpublished novel *Black and White and Red all Over*. There is the Hollywood mogul Martin of *Starport* and then there is the critically acclaimed, award winning *and* best selling author of *Blood of the Dragon*. The only thing missing here is the *Wild Cards* period. But I've been there for all of the periods so I'll fill in any blanks.

There is only one place to start in an analysis of George—with his formidable talent. I have several friends, all far more knowledgeable in the ways of English literature then myself, who have said that they think George is one of the great writers of the twentieth century. With three more books to come in his *A Song of Ice and Fire* I expect that will continue well into the twenty-first century. All I know is that George has kept me up far too late for far too many nights as I have obsessively read his books and stories.

The next thing you notice with George is his wit and his humor. Anytime I'm in George's company he makes me laugh. Even when I've come to him to mourn some particular loss or grief in my life George has always managed to find the absurd lining in the looming clouds, made me laugh, and made me decide that I can crawl back to the computer and go on. You have glimpses of George's wit in his characters. Popinjay, the wise-cracking private detective in our *Wild Cards* series. Ned Cullen in Black and White, Willie the put upon werewolf in the *Skin Trade*, Tyrion of the rapier wit and cutting repartee in *A Song of Ice and Fire*. What all these men have in common with their creator is that they are "speaking men." Words are their tools and their weapons, and wit is their armor. They are delightful, and every time I read their stories I hear George's voice.

The charm and the wit are the surface for all of these characters, but dig a little deeper, and you'll find the thread of melancholy which runs through all of them. They all understand that the world is not a fair and wonderful place. That often terrible things happen to the best of people. That good people often do evil things, and that no human is totally good or totally bad.

And that for me is George's greatest gift as a writer. You can't just jog complacently along in one of George's books assuming that the heroes will be noble and the villains will be bad. This is an intricate dance, and people succeed and fail without reference to the state of their souls. Sometimes George's characters display great nobility and bravery. Sometimes those characters are even the heroes. Sometimes his heroes are tempted and succumb. And at all times his characters are frightened because men and women who feel no fear are lunatics, and George isn't interested in madmen. He wants to explore the range of human emotion, and he wants you to explore it with him.

This fascination with humans is what led to the creation of *Wild Cards*. George had been a comic book reader since childhood, and while he loved the glittering, colorful, bigger then life world I suspect that George really wanted to explore how it felt to be a superhero, and how a superhero would function in a "real" world.

That is certainly where he led his writers as we explored what would really happen if people suddenly became endowed with super human powers. The truth is most of us wouldn't put on long johns and go fight crime. We would continue to be bankers and teachers and firemen, and we would try not to frighten the children and the horses with displays of our powers.

The other truth that George made us face is the reality that being the strongest man in the world is ultimately meaningless unless you possess a core of human decency and integrity. That doesn't mean that you won't blow up the Empire State building. It means that you will show courage in small ways that have nothing at all to do with facing physical danger. Rather that you are willing to stand by a friend, or care for an ailing spouse.

I have always said that George creates real people, and places them in real situations within the framework of real worlds. Then I realized that wasn't quite accurate. There are many writers whose grasp of physics and biology and geology are far greater than George's. They will never have double moons out of phase, or an orbit that doesn't adequately explain the seasonal shift on this or than make believe planet. And you know what? I don't give a damn. I would far rather read one of George's books because it will take me on a journey which gives me insight into myself and my life.

George is the ultimate humanist. He values human beings and their interests above technical detail. He's not interested in technology; he's interested in its impact on people. You will never find pages of explanation of light speed engines. None of it's real and he knows that. He goes back to his center, the heart of his work—his characters.

George brought his values to Hollywood, and the result were luminous episodes of *Twilight Zone*, and *Beauty and the Beast*. In a town where power, money and image is everything George gave voice to the lost and disenfranchised. His creations on *Beauty and the Beast* included Mouse, and Winslow and the unforgettable Dragon Man. While on the *Twilight Zone* he brought the work of friends and fellow writers to a broader audience with his adaptation of Roger Zelazny's *Last Defender of Camelot*.

So we come to George the man, not the writer. George writes about honor, duty, loyalty, friendship, and they are the foundations of his life. He always attempted to share his good fortune in Hollywood by reaching back to the world of science fiction and fantasy, and getting writer's books and stories optioned. He also reached back and extended a hand to any writer who wanted to attempt the transition. I am one of those writers.

I knew George when I was a practicing attorney, and miserable in my chosen profession. George and other writers in New Mexico brought me into their circle, and made me realize I wanted to live in a world of ideas and stories not briefs and billable hours. I made the transition from lawyer to prose writer. It was during those years that I assisted George in editing *Wild Cards*, and wrote my stories, and under his tutelage became a much better writer. Then nine years into my new profession George reached out once more, and offered me the chance to tackle Hollywood.

The transplant took, and during George's Hollywood years we worked together on a pilot for NBC, and an adaptation of the *Wild Cards* series for Hollywood Pictures. Then George walked away, and returned to his home in Santa Fe, and his first, true love—books. The result is the magnificent series *A Song of Ice and Fire*. I miss George a lot when I'm lost in the pavement jungle of Los Angeles being asked to lose the character moment and put in another action sequence, but I would never wish him back in Hollywood. The images that wash across a television or movie screen give us pleasure, but it's an ephemeral creation, art as a soap bubble. What George has created and will continue to create are monuments that will endure for generations. They are also ripping good stories. They'll make you laugh and they'll break your heart.

So go and join in George's songs. And enjoy.

Melinda M. Snodgrass
Bernalillo, N.M.
Dec. 14, 2000

Introduction to
Black and White and Red All Over

In some alternate timeline, my fifth novel was published in late 1986: a huge, sprawling, picaresque historical fantasy called *Black and White and Red All Over*, the tale of three rival yellow journalists chasing Jack the Ripper through the wonderland and horrorshow that was New York City in the 1890s.

In that world, I never went to Hollywood, never wrote for *The Twilight Zone* or *Beauty and the Beast*, went on from my fifth novel to my sixth and seventh and eighth. A few of those later novels were sequels to *Black and White*. I had in mind other stories that would pit Kate Hawthorne, Henry Munce, and Ned Cullen against each other in search of a big black headline. In this other world, those books were written and published.

In the real world, alas, *Black and White and Red All Over* was never completed. Nor did it ever see print...until now.

((And for you who are about to read this, a warning—this is an **unfinished** novel. It stops virtually in mid-sentence, and there is nothing even remotely resembling a resolution to be found here. Proceed at your own risk.))

Black and White was based on a real incident: the brutal, Ripper-like murder of a Bowery prostitute called Old Shakespeare in 1891, only a few years after Thomas Byrnes, New York's celebrated superintendent of police, had boasted that Saucy Jack would be caught within thirty-six hours if he ever tried any of his nonsense in New York City. The Old Shakespeare murder was a huge sensation in its day, and half the city was convinced that the Ripper had come to town to take up Byrnes on his challenge. *Suppose he did*, I thought to myself. That was the beginning.

I researched the book for more than year before I began to write it. I read every book on Jack the Ripper that I could find, collected dozens of old books about New York City in the last century, studied biographies of Pulitzer, Hearst, and the wonderfully mad James Gordon Bennett, Junior. I immersed myself in the period, the same way I'd once immersed myself in the antebellum Mississippi to write *Fevre Dream*. In late 1984 I sat down in front of my new Televideo 802, booted up WordStar, and began the first chapter.

All through the first half of 1985 I pounded away. I wrote to my friends that Black and White "looks to be my biggest book, and certainly my most complex. I've got three protagonists and three narrative lines, I've got a conspiracy so complex and convoluted and strange no one will be able to figure it out, and just in the chapters written to date I've got Teddy Roosevelt, William Randolph Hearst, James Gordon Bennett, Pulitzer's Golden Dome, the Gopher Gang, bucket-shops and dives, corrupt policemen, whalebone corsets, gay girls, the Silver Dollar Saloon, ornate yachts, the Sultan Abdul the Damned, cynical city editors, the suffrage movement, child prostitutes, swipes, Coney Island freak shows, and the immortal Elephant Hotel, not to mention yours truly, Jack the Ripper, a dead whore (or is she?) named Old Shakespeare, and lots of snazzy Victorian fashions... [Still to come] are smoky opium dens, Humpty Jackson and his graveyard gang, Joe Pulitzer himself, decadence in Newport, upper-class sadism and lower-class brutality, the owl mausoleum, Professor Wedge's aerocycle, Captain Boyton's rubber suit, Master Mesmerist Simon Rajos, Sebastien King of the Rats, the lost subway, skullduggery in the sewers, tong wars, Clubber Williams, white slavery plots, rogue elephants, and Monk Eastman and his Squab Wheelmen...it's more fun than fucking a monkey, and right now I just don't believe how fast and how *well* it's going...

I was so lost in the 1890s that I hardly noticed the storm clouds gathering over my head in the here and now.

The Armageddon Rag, my previous novel, had garnered rave reviews and been nominated for a World Fantasy Award, but its sales had been dismal, especially in paperback. The *Rag* had been a rock 'n roll novel, part mystery, part horror, and part mainstream. My publishers had hoped that it would appeal to anyone who remembered the music and madness of the Sixties, but it hadn't worked out that way.

Also, every chapter in the *Rag* began with a brief quote from a rock song, and the process of obtaining the necessary permissions to use all those lyrics proved far more expensive and time-consuming than I had anticipated. I spent six months on that alone. I had moved to a new house as well, and then spent most of a year doing my research on New York, the yellow press, and Jack the Ripper, with the result that I was running very late. The *Rag* had been written in 1982 and published in 1983. Ideally, I should have had my fifth novel out in 1984, and a sixth delivered and scheduled for 1985 publication, a seventh partially written. Instead, the summer of 1985 found me maybe a quarter of the way into *Black and White*, and under increasing financial pressure. *The Armageddon Rag* advance had gone into my new house, and it was clear there would be no royalty checks. I had run out of money and started living on credit.

The vast majority of writers in our field sell their books before they write them. They draw up a proposal, or perhaps write up a few chapters and an outline, and have their agents shop them around. If some editor likes the proposed book, a deal is struck, contracts are drawn up, deadlines are set, a portion of the advance is paid on signing, and only then does the book get writtenI had never worked that way. I have never liked working from outlines, and I have never liked deadlines. I preferred to write my novels first, and then ship the finished books off to my agent, Kirby McCauley, for marketing. *Windhaven*, the collaborative novel I wrote with Lisa Tuttle, had been somewhat of an exception, since we sold it on the basis of two novellas published in *Analog*, but my three solo novels had all been completed before an editor ever saw word one of any of them.

But in the summer of 1985, it became clear that I no longer had that luxury. The bills were mounting up, I had a mortgage to pay, and there was no way I was going to finish *Black and White and Red All Over* quickly enough to meet my obligations. I would have to sell the book based on the two hundred pages I had already written. A portion of the advance would be paid on signing the contract, and that would give me enough income to live on while I completed the novel. So I printed out the first two hundred odd pages (the very ones you're about to read) and sent them to Kirby.

I knew that the commercial failure of *The Armageddon Rag* was going to take a toll, of course. I was prepared to take a step backwards, to accept an advance significantly lower than the one I'd gotten for the *Rag*.

I was *not* prepared for was no offers at all. But *Black and White* hit a stone wall.

Poseidon Press had published my previous two novels and held an option on this one, so they saw the pages first. My editor liked a lot of what she read...but not enough to make an offer. Her readers complained that the plot was too hard to follow. Nor did they like my three-headed hero. If I were to drop two of the three protagonists and tell the whole story from the viewpoint of Kate Hawthorne, Poseidon would be interested. Otherwise, no.

I liked Kate well enough, but I liked Henry Munce as well, as I *loved* Ned Cullen, the yellowest yellow journalist of them all, handsome, dashing, clever, and a cad to the core. Besides, much of the fun of the book was going to arise from the interplay between the three reporters. I meant for their paths to cross repeatedly, as they clashed, connived, conspired, shared drinks and leads, misled each other, raced and fought on land and sea, and traded insults, bullets, and lies. There would be double crosses, triple crosses, flirtations and seductions, wild goose chases and desperate flights from the Squab Wheelmen. But if I were to limit myself to a single protagonist — and the most naive, well-meaning, and ethical of my trio at that—I would lose much of that. The book that Poseidon was asking for might well have been a good one, but it was not the book I wanted to write.

I decided to take *Black and White* elsewhere. I was certain some other publisher would make an offer.

I was wrong.

Months passed, and so did the publishers, one after another. Many editors said nice things about the book, but no one bought it. Kirby kept sending out the pages, and they kept coming back. All sorts of reasons were cited for the rejections. I was known as a science fiction writer, but this book wasn't science fiction. They didn't know how to market it. The plot was confusing. It was too much like Doctorow's *Ragtime*, or it wasn't enough like Doctorow's *Ragtime*. They didn't know how to promote it. The story was hard to follow. It fell between stools. There was no audience for this kind of novel. It wasn't literary enough. It wasn't commercial enough. It wasn't like my other novels. It wasn't like *any* other novels. They didn't know how to publish it.

Had I *finished* the novel and offered it as a completed manuscript, I have no doubt I would have sold it. I knew what I wanted to do, and I knew I could do it. But the editors saw only the first two hundred pages of what would likely have been a thousand page book; a beginning without a middle or an end.

You can sell a hard SF book or an epic fantasy with chapters-and-outline, because those are established commercial genres. But when a book blurs genre lines or defies conventions, you stand a much better chance with a completed manuscript. Looking back, I wonder whether anyone would have bought *Fevre Dream* or *The Rag* had I tried to sell them off proposals. Like *Black and White*, they were hybrids, not easily categorized. My fatal mistake was trying to sell the novel before I had finished it.

And yet, even so...

In 1994, Random House published *The Alienist*, a novel by Caleb Carr about a newspaper reporter hunting down a serial killer in New York City in the 1890s. Carr did not use the Old Shakespeare case, his killer was not meant to be Jack the Ripper, and the tone of his novel is darker and less fanciful than mine, but we were drawing on a lot of the same material, and I remain convinced that many of readers who bought *The Alienist* might have been just as enthused about B*lack and White And Red All Over*. As I watched *The Alienist* climb higher and higher up the bestseller lists, I was sorely tempted to send a copy to every editor who had passed on *Black and White*, with a little note that said, "Too bad there's no audience for this sort of book." I resisted the impulse nobly.

I never officially abandoned *Black and White and Red All Over*, but without the prospect of a contract, I found it hard to work up the necessary enthusiasm to continue. Besides, my need for income was growing ever more desperate. So when a couple of other offers came along from out of the blue, I leapt at them.

One was from a television producer named Phil DeGuere, who'd optioned the film rights to *The Armageddon Rag* a few years before. CBS was reviving *The Twilight Zone* with Phil as the Executive Producer, and he offered me the chance to do a script. I'd never written for television or film, had never *wanted* to write for television or film, but I figured I had to take a swing at it. Around about the same time, I also got a call from Betsy Mitchell, who had recently joined Baen Books. Betsy had been at *Analog* with Stan Schmidt when that magazine published a number of my Haviland Tuf stories, and she asked if I was interested in doing a collection of my Tuf stories for Baen. I was, of course.

I did not have enough stories for a book, but that was no problem. I would write some more Tuf tales, sell them to *Analog*, then sell the collection to Betsy, and I'd write the script for *Twilight Zone* as well, and all that would keep me afloat until the end of the year. By then Kirby would surely have found a publisher for *Black and White*.

So I wrote "The Plague Star" and the S'uthlam triptych, assembled the Tuf collection, and delivered it to Betsy. I wrote the script for *The Twilight Zone* too, though not the one I had originally started out to write. That freelance script begat a job on the show as a staff writer, and I went out to Los Angeles in 1986, figuring I'd work on the show for a season or two, and then come back home and resume work on my novel. We continued to try and sell *Black and White and Red All Over* all through 1986 and 1987 and well into 1988. Finally, exhausted, I put the pages in the drawer.

Baen published *Tuf Voyaging* in February, 1986, as a novel. My fifth novel, some say… though I've always counted *Tuf Voyaging* as a short story collection. If the asteroids are the broken remains of a lost fifth planet, as some would claim, *Black and White and Red All Over* will forever be my fifth novel, lost and broken.

Will I ever finish it? Perhaps, if the fever takes me again. But it won't be the same book. After so many years the story has gone cold, and I no longer remember half of what I was intending. Nor am I the same person I was in 1985.

Still…maybe…the time and place still fascinate me, and when I glance over these pages I can see Ned Cullen's wicked smile again, and hear the deep bass growl of that solemn dwarf Henry Munce. So maybe one day you will find out who died in that cheap hotel room in 1891, and why, and who the Ripper really was.

Stranger things have happened…

Black and White and Red All Over

PART ONE

April, 1891

On that damp April morning Ned Cullen started his day with a glass of cheap champagne gone flat, a cup of cold black coffee, and a murder.

It was still pitch dark outside, a hour shy of dawn, when he arrived at the East River Hotel at the corner of Catherine and Water Streets, the champagne bottle tucked somewhat absently under his arm. He stood in the street for a moment, looking rueful and a bit rumpled, his bowler askew, his cravat loosely knotted, his hands shoved deep into the pockets of his charcoal grey trousers, a few stray locks of black hair hanging down across his forehead. The moonlight etched his shadow across the gutter; a poised, slender shadow, sharp-edged and black, altogether too pretty a shadow to be wasted on a gutter, especially in this neighborhood.

The saloon on the ground floor was closed for the night. Ned went around to the Water Street door and entered a short dark hall. From the outside, the building had looked decent enough, a solidly-built four-story edifice of red brick, but the interior was as squalid and filthy as Ned had anticipated. He didn't mind. Squalor and filth lent a little color to the write-up, and even the waterfront was much to be preferred to darkest Africa or some godforsaken battlefield, and there was nothing to be done for it anyway; the Commodore was implacable. Ned went down the hall and up a narrow flight of stairs. The office was on the first floor landing.

Eddie Fitzgerald came scrambling out of his chair when the door opened. "Mister Cullen," he said. "Thank God. I don't know what to do."

Ned put his elbows on the counter and smiled. Ned Cullen had the sort of smile that charmed men out of their money and women out of their clothes; a warm, easy, comfortable smile, with a tiny curl of insouciance at the corner of his mouth and just the barest hint of irony gleaming deep in those brilliant emerald-green eyes. Transformed by his smile, his clean-shaven, boyish face lost its look of mildly perplexed cynicism and became almost innocent. It was a good face, Ned knew. His thin, straight eyebrows were marvelously expressive, his nose straight, his fine dark hair a black Irishman's glory; Ned liked to say it was as black as the Commodore's past, though he never said that at the office, where Bennett's white mice heard and reported all. In twenty-six odd years on earth, Ned Cullen had never met anyone half as handsome as he was. He thought it was all very amusing.

"I'll tell you what to do," he said to Eddie Fitzgerald, as he removed his bowler and set it on top of the hotel register. His motion was assured and elegant, as graceful as Ned himself. "First, find us a couple of glasses."

"Glasses?" said Fitzgerald.

Ned sloshed the champagne bottle. "Waste this and I'll break a fat man's heart," he said. "Diamond Jim would never forgive me. Come on, come on." Eddie Fitzgerald stared for a moment, and then produced two chipped tea-cups from behind the counter. Ned carefully divided the champagne between them. "To murder!" he said, as he raised his cup. He drank and made a face. "Flat, ah well. Why, not drinking, Eddie? A time like this, a man can use a drink."

"I, I don't think, I don't," Fitzgerald said. The red-haired clerk was young, barely nineteen as Ned knew from previous acquaintance, and his nerves were showing; the boy's broad cheeks were a confusion of freckles and pimples, all damp with sweat. Ned squelched the impulse to ask him if corpses always made him break out. Eddie kept glancing out the office window as if he expected the sun to come vaulting over the rooftops any second. With trumpets.

"I'll drink it," Ned offered. He finished off the second cup. "Now, you have a body for me, don't you?"

"Yes," Fitzgerald said. "Upstairs, I'll show…"

"Good. And how about some coffee?"

"Coffee?"

"Black. Strong and black. The coffee first, then the body, I think that's the way to go about it."

"But Mister Cullen, she's upstairs, she's…"

"She's dead," Ned said. "She'll still be dead after I've had my coffee, Eddie. She isn't going anyplace."

"Someone else might find her."

"Eddie, you're not thinking clearly. Remember the hour. All the sensible folks in New York City are in bed sleeping at this moment. Superintendent Byrnes is asleep, he won't be paying you a call. The mayor is asleep. Doctor Parkhurst is asleep and so is the Archbishop. Your sister is asleep, your mother is asleep, and your father is so drunk he's dead to the world. Even my editor is asleep, and my night editor has been asleep for going-on fifty years now. And the few folks like you and me, with more spirit then sense, why, they're in bed too, even if they are not sleeping." He raised a sardonic eyebrow. "You're safe. Trust me"

"What am I going to do?" Fitzgerald said.

"You're going to pour me some coffee," Ned said. Fitzgerald stared at him helplessly. He turned around, found half a pot of coffee left from the night before, poured a cup for Ned. It was black and strong enough. It was also thick and bitter and cold. Ned smiled with resignation, and drank it down wincing.

"There's enough for another cup," Fitzgerald offered, sloshing the pot about.

"What, waste time drinking coffee, when I could be inspecting a dead whore?" Ned said.

"She's up in 31," the boy said. "I'll show you."

"Do you know who she is?" Ned asked. "Let me see your register." He lifted his bowler.

Fitzgerald turned the book around. "Here," he said. "I can't make it out." The register was a big greasy leather-bound book, its pages smudged and dirty. On the top of the page, someone with a heavy, child-like hand had penned in "Thursday, April 23, 1891." Ned studied the signatures. There were more names then rooms. To judge from the turnover, a good many guests preferred toenjoy the dubious comforts of the East River Hotel for only an hour or two at a time, which didn't surprise Ned Cullen in the least. He went down the list until he found room 31, then tried to puzzle out the signature. "Well, that first name is definitely C. I've always found one-letter names very suspicious. The rest of it—Nicolo, I think. Or perhaps Nicolls. Or something along those lines. And I have the motive too, Eddie. Penmanship. Penmanship like this is definitely a capital offense," he said, tapping the register with a well-mani-cured finger.

"I think that's the man she was with," Fitzgerald said.

"Aha," said Ned. "Did you see him?"

"No. Nor her neither. I was off for a bit. Mary Miniter took over the office for me."

"Mary Miniter?"

"She's the assistant housekeeper. She was here last night."

"Anyone else?"

"The bartender downstairs. Samuel Shine."

Ned nodded. "Well, let's see what we've got, shall we? I'd sooner face a corpse than more of your coffee."

Fitzgerald nodded. "It's on the top floor," he said. Ned could see him trembling.

They went up two more flights of stairs, Fitzgerald leading. It was the corner room. Six rooms on the floor, all the doors closed. The boy tiptoed. "Quiet," he cautioned in a whisper. "I got four people on this floor."

"Only three now," Ned corrected.

Fitzgerald swallowed, gestured weakly at the door before them, half-turned.

Ned put his hand on the door to number 31. It was open. "You don't have to come in," he said. "Just give me a few moments to look around." Fitzgerald nodded.

Ned Cullen walked inside and closed the door behind him.

The darkness smelled of gin, urine and blood. The hardwood floor beneath his feet felt sticky. For an instant gooseflesh pimpled Ned's arms. He reached into a vest pocket, produced a match, struck it one-handed against his palm. The shadows danced, and awful things leapt out at him. Red. Lots of red. That shape on the bed, turned away from him. The bed was pushed up against a wall. Ned moved closer, lowered his flame.

Stale champagne and bitter coffee roiled in his stomach. The ancient, sagging mattress was soaked, still damp to his questing fingers. The body was on its right side, facing the wall, where dark splotches spread across the faded wallpaper. Her right arm was twisted around behind her back, and her clothing had been pushed up over her head, leaving her exposed from the armpits down. The skin of her back—wrinkled, pallid, puffy—bore a bloody mark, two intersecting lines, like an X or perhaps a crude cross, lightly carved into the flesh. Below that, near the base of her spine, began a much deeper incision, its edges wet and raw, like two fat red lips. The cut went up over her hip, around to her stomach. She had been opened from abdomen to breasts. Her intestines spread across the soiled, damp sheets like a nest of dark, slimy serpents.

"Jesus," Ned muttered. An eyebrow arched. This would be great copy. "Yankee doodle Ripper," he said, tasting the sound of it. He liked it.

Gingerly, Ned lifted her skirts to get a look at her face. If she was beautiful or famous, so much the better. He had no luck there. She was old, wrinkled, and hideous, as he might have expected in a place like the East River Hotel. Her coarse gray hair was matted with dried blood. Well, he could say she had been beautiful once. *The ruins of a once lovely face, bearing the coarseness and pain of years lost to gin and shame*, that would work just fine, or maybe he could play up her age, *she looked like someone's sweet old grandmother*, provided granny was a cheap waterfront tart, no, the readers wouldn't care to think about their grannies getting disemboweled, better to stay with the the the idea of beauty ravaged by sin.

He noted deep bruises all around the scrawny throat just as the match began to burn his fingers. He blew it out, slipped it into his pocket.

Now, the question was, how to play it? The police would have to be notified, of course. For something like this, Byrnes would certainly come sniffing around himself. And the reporters would come with him, the whole yapping pack. Ned could break the story first in the *Herald*—but that could get him in trouble. Inspector Byrnes didn't always appreciate journalistic enterprise, and would want to know how Ned got the story so early. And for what, one beat? He'd be a one-day sensation, and afterwards he'd be doing drudge work along with everybody else, reporting police efforts to solve the crime. And Byrnes would solve it, Ned had no doubt of that. He remembered the Whitechapel killings a couple years back, when Byrnes had stood up before the assembled press of New York City and boasted how he'd have the Ripper in jail within thirty-six hours if old Saucy Jack ever tried a killing in New York.

In the blink of one of his sly green eyes, it all came to Ned Cullen. Maybe because of the champagne, or maybe because the room's slaughterhouse smell intoxicated him. The sharp smell of blood reminded him of the sweetest perfume he knew, the scent of fresh black printer's ink when the *Herald's* presses rolled.

Stay out of it.

Let Reick give the story to Henry Munce. Let Byrnes investigate and produce a Ripper, let Munce write it all up dutifully. Ned would bide his time, and then, when the man was sentenced to swing, he'd step in, smiling, elegant, eloquent, and solve the crime, point out the real killer, absolve Byrnes' poor doomed catspaw. Even James Gordon Bennett himself would have to sit up and take note of that.

Outside the room, Eddie Fitzgerald was waiting nervously, shifting his weight from one foot to the other. "Well?" he said.

Ned looked serious. "I think she's dead," he said.

"What am I going to *do*?" Fitzgerald asked. "Are they going to blame me?"

"Blame you? Why? Did you do it? If you did it and want to confess, I'll get you page one, right next to the personals."

"*No*," Fitzgerald said, horror-stricken. "I didn't—I wasn't even here, I just found her."

"I know," Ned said. "Never mind. How did you come to find her, by the way?"

"Mister Francis," the boy said, his voice kept low. "He came in drunk, wanted a room, even though the night was half gone. Paid me in pennies. He counted out twenty-five cents into my hand. I took the money and showed him up to his room. He's in room 33, right there." Fitzgerald pointed.

Ned walked down the dingy corridor, idly inspected the door to room 33. "Yes," he said, "fine. And?"

"Well, after Mister Francis went inside I was turning around and I happened to see that the door to 31 was open, just a little bit. So I went down to check, see if maybe they'd left. A lot of times they steal things from the rooms, and sneak out in the middle of the night. I knocked, really quiet, and the door opened and I went inside and I saw." Fitzgerald suddenly had trouble getting the words out. "Your shoes."

"You saw my shoes?" Ned said.

Fitzgerald pointed. "Blood. You've got blood on your shoes.

Ned looked down and grimaced. Sure enough, the boy was right. "Damn it," he said. "That won't do." He pulled out his handkerchief, but it was silk, almost brand new, and he hated to ruin it. "You wouldn't happen to have a cloth of some kind, would you, Eddie?"

Wordless, the boy handed him his own pocket handkerchief. Ned leaned back against the door to room 33, lifted each foot in turn, and wiped the blood off his shoes quite thoroughly. "You don't want to be found with a bloody handkerchief," he said to Fitzgerald when he was done. "I'll dispose of it for you."

The boy nodded. "I have to go to the police."

"Certainly," Ned said. He smiled, put his arm around Eddie's shoulders, and escorted him back downstairs. "But you don't want to tell them the story you just told me."

"I don't?"

"You'll get in trouble. They might even arrest you, try to blame you for this awful thing. It's been hours since you found the body, right?"

"Maybe an hour," the boy said.

"Hours," Ned repeated. "They'll want to know why you didn't come to them right away, they'll say you were involved, that you were just trying to cover up for somebody."

"No," Fitzgerald said. "I was, I, I was just confused. I never had anything like this on my shift before. I didn't know what to do. I thought you'd know, Mister Cullen, you work for the *Herald* and reporters know all about murders, and you been seeing Mary Elizabeth and all."

"Your sister's a fine girl," Ned said, "and she'd be heart-broken if they hanged you, Eddie, so listen to what I'm telling you. What you've got to do is find the body all over again. What happens here if one of your guests sleeps a little late, eh?"

"Well," said Fitzgerald, "if they aren't out by nine or nine-thirty or so, I go around and roust them."

"Fine," said Ned, "so, what you do is go back, and finish your shift, and when the time comes you take yourself upstairs to roust that lag-a-bed in room 31. Knock very loudly. She won't come to the door, of course. If she does, tell me at once, I'll want an interview." Ned smiled, but Fitzgerald didn't seem to see the humor in the remark. "Finally, open the door and go in. When you find her, let the whole world know. Run away, run downstairs, make noise, shout, scream bloody murder. Only appropriate under the circumstances. Maybe you should shout, 'The Ripper, the Ripper!' No, that would be gilding the lily. Just go to the police at once. And whatever happens then, stick to your story about how you found her. Don't ever let on that you really went up there *hours* earlier, or that I came by. Don't mention me at all."

"Aren't you going to write it up for the *Herald*?" the boy asked. He sounded a little disappointed.

"Eventually," said Ned, "but not until I catch the monster who did this. Until then, I'm not going to talk to anybody about this. Why, I won't even tell my editor. The *Herald* will probably send another reporter down here, a little man by the name of Munce. Don't worry about him. You'll be interviewed a lot, Eddie. Your name will be in all the papers. You'll even get to meet Inspector Byrnes himself. So whatever you do, be careful, and don't mention me.

"Why?" Eddie demanded bluntly, as they walked back into the office.

Ned smiled. "Can't you figure it out? This is the Ripper, Saucy Jack, old Leather Apron himself, come to take up the Superintendent on his challenge. The police aren't going to catch him. Scotland Yard couldn't catch him, could they? Byrnes won't do any better. So it's up to me." He grinned and turned on all his charm. "The *Herald* will find him, Eddie, but you can't let him know that we're after him, or he might skip town. Understand?"

"I don't know," Fitzgerald said.

Ned looked wounded. "Eddie, your family would be awfully hurt if you were blamed for this. And Inspector Byrnes, he's got a terrible Irish temper. When he finds out you went to the press instead of the police, he's sure to try to frame you up for this. He once said if the Ripper came to New York, he'd be clapped in jail within thirty-six hours, so he's got to arrest somebody, doesn't he? I don't want to see you get in trouble."

"You don't want to get yourself in trouble, you mean," Fitzgerald said.

"Me?" Ned laughed. "Eddie, Byrnes and I are friends. Besides, I work for the *Herald*. You can't hurt the *Herald*, everyone knows that. No, it's you I'm thinking of."

"All right," the boy said. "I'll do what you said."

"Good," replied Ned, smiling. Behind Eddie Fitzgerald, the sun was breaking over the rooftops; a big, bright, gorgeously red sunrise it was. Ned thought it promised to be a beautiful day.

PART TWO

November, 1895

The card read, "Mister Hearst would be pleased to have you call."

Henry Munce handed it to the man in the outer office of the *New York Morning Journal* on the second floor of the Tribune Building, along with his own calling card, which said very simply, *Henry Munce, Journalist*. At once the man was on his feet. "This way, sir," he said respectfully, ushering Munce through the wooden gate, back down a corridor, and up a flight of stairs to Mister Hearst's private office on the third floor.

It was a large office, though not an especially grand one, the building being old and rickety and the *Journal* merely a poor tenant of the respectable, dignified, Republican *Tribune*. The furnishings, all lovely and no doubt expensive antiques, helped to lend the room a certain grandeur, however. Busts of Lincoln, Jefferson, Franklin, and Julius Caesar stood on marble plinths along one wall. Beneath a massive oil painting of Napoleon in an ornate frame was a vast desk whose carved wooden legs gleamed from the diligent application of oil, polish, and sweat, but the leather throne behind it was empty. "Mister Hearst will be with you in a moment," the secretary said. "Please be seated." He took his leave, keeping the door open behind him.

Munce leaned on his walking stick.

"Hullo, Henry," said a familiar voice.

Henry Munce turned. "Sam Chamberlain," he said. His voice was as gravelly as the coal in a teamster's wagon, as deep as the mine that produced it. "Heard you were back in New York."

Chamberlain slid the book he had been perusing back into its place. "Willie lured me out west to the *Examiner*, and now he's lured me back." He smiled urbanely. Sam Chamberlain was a very urbane man. He was tall and elegant, a fashion plate in costly British tweeds and a colorful flowered cravat, wearing a monocle in his eye and a fresh gardenia in his lapel. "He's a difficult man to say no to. Every time you try, he offers you more money. You'll enjoy working for him, Henry."

"I have not yet accepted employment here," said Henry Munce, "nor has a position been offered."

"Henry Munce!" said a high-pitched voice from the doorway. "I want you to write for me."

Sam Chamberlain smiled. "Henry," he said, "I'd like to present William Randolph Hearst."

"And I am Henry Munce," said Henry Munce. He tucked his walking stick under an arm, and held up his right hand.

Hearst came forward eagerly. Dressed in shirtsleeves, with a brilliant red silk cravat knotted very sloppily about his neck, his blond hair in mild disarray, this tall, slender young man with the high voice and the pale blue close-set eyes looked nothing like the publishers Henry Munce was accustomed to dealing with—nothing like the patriarchal Dana of the *Sun* with his flowing white beard and fierce manner, nothing like profane, blind, nerve-wracked Joseph Pulitzer who ruled the *World* by proxy from his soundproofed yacht, and certainly, definitely, emphatically, nothing at all like James Gordon Bennett the younger, the absurd tyrant and scoundrel whose prolonged self-imposed exile in Paris did little to lift his heavy hand from the reins of the *New York Herald*.

But Henry Munce put small stock in appearances; there were those who might say he himself did not look like the greatest crime reporter in the world.

Hearst tossed the proofs he had in hand down onto his cluttered desktop, looked down, and gave Munce a firm, strong handshake. "I published your dispatches often when Sam and I were out in San Francisco, putting out the *Examiner*. At times I was sure you had to be three people. By Henry Munce. I learned to look for those words. I trust Sam implicitly, and he tells me that there's no better man in New York for covering crime and the underworld, the dark side of the city."

"No better man anywhere," Munce said curtly.

Hearst smiled. "Yes. I'd be delighted to be able to run those familiar words *By Henry Munce*, in the *Journal*. I plan to make this paper the talk of the town. I want the very best people. You're with the *Times* now, Sam tells me. No one reads the *Times*. I venture to say it'll be dead within two years. Come write for me, and I'll double whatever you're getting over there."

"I am a dwarf," Henry Munce rumbled.

He had, of course, been a dwarf all his life, but Henry Munce had never let it stop him. He stood a bare inch over three feet tall, but no one could easily overlook Henry Munce. His body, small and twisted as it might be, was as thickly muscled as that of any strongman in Barnum's circus. Every night, when his working day was done, Henry Munce returned to the room he let in Mrs. Peabody's boarding house on Bleeker Street, stripped to his underthings, and lifted weights for an hour, sometimes two. He had been doing it for most of his thirty-nine years on earth. Under a brown checked jacket of indifferent and unfashionable cut could be found extraordinarily broad shoulders and a chest like a keg of nails. His arms were solid iron, and his stunted legs, as twisted as the limbs of a gnarled tree, shared all the strength of that hard, corded wood. His heavy, scuffed workingman's boots had iron toes, and his broad face was covered by a thick wild beard, the beard of a Biblical patriarch or an anarchist with a bomb, a beard composed in equal parts of hairs black as wrought iron and gray as the winter sea, a beard that flowed down past his frayed wingtip collar to lay against his striped shirt, a beard that covered his cheeks and square, jutting jaw completely and grew out well past the tips of his ears and offered such a spectacle of hair gone mad that many a man, upon meeting Henry Munce for the first time, somehow overlooked the fact that Munce's broad domed head was entirely bald and shiny.

William Randolph Hearst sat on one corner of his expensive antique desk, looking a little uncertain. "Yes, Mister Munce," he said, "Mister Chamberlain had mentioned something in that regard when he recommended that I engage you."

"A dwarf, Mister Hearst, and not fond of dogs!" said Henry Munce, pounding the bottom of his walking stick on the floor. It made a very satisfactory and emphatic sound. Munce's walking stick was like Munce; short and thick. He had ordered it made specially for him, and it was just the precise length to reach from his hand to the ground. There was nothing slender or elegant or fashionable about it. It was made of black iron so wide around that even Munce's huge hand could not encompass its shaft entirely, and inside it was hollowed out and filled with lead. Henry Munce had practiced with it many an hour, until he could shatter a man's kneecap with a single crushing blow. The head of the walking stick was shaped in the likeness of a particularly large, bloated, and obscene owl, with blood-red garnets for its eyes. Munce leaned upon it now. "Not fond of dogs," he repeated loudly, "and dogs are not fond of me."

"Dogs," said Hearst. He sounded frankly perplexed. "No. I see. Or I don't. I don't understand."

Elegant Sam Chamberlain came across the room and seated himself in one of the antique chairs facing the publisher's desk. "He's talking about the Commodore," Sam said, amused. He took out his monocle and began to polish it with a handkerchief.

"Bennett?" said Hearst.

"Henry was once fired by a Pekinese, W.R." said Chamberlain. "Tell him the story, Henry."

Henry Munce stared up at William Randolph Hearst. His brow was a thick ridge of bone, his deep-sunk eyes were gray and gloomy. "By Henry Munce," he said. "Yes, Mister Hearst. No doubt you saw those words on many a dispatch out in San Francisco. I am the best crime reporter in the world. I know the criminals and the gutter scum, the rat-pits and the hell-holes, the opium dens and the bucket-shops, the secret ways, the dark places of the city. No one else knows them as I do, not even the police, and certainly not my so-called colleagues. You are correct, Mister Hearst. No one reads the *Times*. I am not employed there by choice. For more than three years, I was with the *New York Herald*. You are familiar with the *Herald*, of course."

"The greatest newspaper in New York, until Pulitzer moved in," Hearst said amiably.

"The greatest newspaper in the world," corrected Munce. "And I was their greatest reporter. Everyone in the city reads the *Herald*. In France they follow the *Paris Herald*, yet even there the New York edition has one attentive reader. Mister James Gordon Bennett the younger, editor, publisher, and proprietor of the New York Herald. Mister Bennett read those words, By Henry Munce, far more often than you. Three times he cabled instructions that my salary be raised. He was most pleased with me. Yet, of course, we had never met."

"Bennett likes dogs," Hearst suddenly remembered.

Henry Munce would not be rushed. "One day, in the spring of 1891, the city editor at the *Herald* received a cable from Bennett in Paris. This was not unusual. I recall the time well, Mister Hearst, because I was then at work upon a most interesting case, the gruesome murder of a whore called Old Shakespeare in her pathetic lodgings, and I had scarcely begun my investigations."

"A sensational murder!" Hearst said with enthusiasm. "Why, we ran stories on that in the *Examiner*, didn't we, Sam?"

"I recall a headline or two," Chamberlain said dryly.

"Headlines that might have been more numerous had Henry Munce completed his researches," said Henry Munce. "To be called away at such a time, in the midst of such a story, I found most vexing, yet called away I was. Bennett's cable instructed me to come to Paris immediately. When Bennett sent such cables, there was nothing to be done but obey. I proceeded to Paris by fast steamer. Nor was I permitted to travel alone. Bennett, to save a few dollars, denied me the pleasure of solitude and arranged for me to share a stateroom with another *Herald* reporter who had been also been summoned, a man I detest, a thoroughly frivolous, cowardly, drunken, lecherous fraud named Edward Fitzhugh Cullen."

"Ned Cullen!" said Hearst.

"You have heard of him," said Henry Munce.

"Certainly," said Hearst.

"Entertain no thoughts of engaging his services if you wish to engage mine," said Henry Munce.

Hearst frowned. "See here, Munce, I won't have you telling me who I can hire and who I can't hire. Cullen is a splendid reporter, and I want the best for the *Journal*..."

There was a loud thump as Henry Munce stomped his walking stick against the floor. "No," he said fiercely. "You want the best, Mister Hearst, so you want nothing to do with Ned Cullen. The man is a n'eer-do-well and a liar. You may hire whom you choose, of course, but Henry Munce will never again lend his talents to any newspaper that pays a salary to Edward Fitzhugh Cullen."

"What happened in Paris?" Hearst asked curiously.

"We reported to the offices of the Paris *Herald*, and then to Bennett's home on the Champs-Elysees. Bennett was not to be found. Bennett had forgotten about us and gone yachting. The editors had no assignments for us, no arrangements had been made for our salaries, and no one seemed to have any idea of what to do with us. We were forced to take lodgings and wait for instructions. We waited for two weeks. I occupied myself exploring the sewers and catacombs of Paris, acquainting myself with the Parisian underworld, and improving my French. Ned Cullen occupied himself with a number of Parisians. At last a cable arrived. We were to proceed to Marseilles at once, there to meet Bennett's yacht. We proceeded to Marseilles, where we found the yacht in port. At the quay we presented our credentials. Ned Cullen was taken aboard at once, while I, Henry Munce, the greatest crime reporter in the world, after three years of faithful service, was denied the right to board. I was told I must shave my beard."

"Shave your beard?" said Hearst.

Sam Chamberlain chuckled. "The Commodore permits only clean-shaven men aboard his yacht."

"I refused to shave my beard," said Henry Munce. "The *Namouna* set sail without me. I proceeded back to Paris, where I found another cable from Bennett awaiting me. Report to him in Naples, it said. I traveled to Naples. The *Namouna* was in port. I presented my credentials, and once again attention was drawn to my beard and my way was barred. As the ship left without me for a second time, I spied Ned Cullen on her deck. He lifted a glass of champagne to me in mock toast.

"Later that week, as I made preparations to return to America, I received instructions to travel to Greece and there report to Bennett's yacht for a third time. To my eternal dismay, I committed an act I rue bitterly to this very day. I shaved, and did as Bennett bid me."

"Did you board the yacht in Greece?"

"I did indeed. There I was ushered into Bennett's presence, by none other than Ned Cullen himself, who inquired sweetly as to how I had enjoyed my grand tour of Europe. Bennett was waiting for me. He is a tall, rigid man, and I was greatly annoyed to note that he wore imposing gray mustachios waxed at the ends. When I entered his suite, I was at once surrounded by a pack of small yapping dogs, principally Pekinese and Pomeranians. These dogs loved Ned Cullen. They surrounded him, barking and fawning, rubbing against his trouser legs, leaping up, rolling over in delight when he stooped to pet them. Only two of the pack deigned to notice me. They growled at me. One nipped at my hand. At that time I did not carry a walking stick. A pity. Bennett looked me over superciliously. 'The dogs do not like him,' he said, as if I were not in the room. I was left without a reply and Ned Cullen grinned at my discomfiture. Bennett looked directly at me. 'You are a dwarf, sir,' he said. I admitted this was the case. 'My editors have failed to inform me of this, and they will hear about it. The dogs do not like you. You are discharged.' I was left entirely speechless for a moment, but finally I summoned my wits, reminded Bennett of the excellent service I had rendered the *Herald*, and inquired the reason for my pre-emptory discharge. 'Why, the dogs do not like you,' he said, 'and I will have no dwarfs on the *Herald*.'"

Hearst chuckled, then fell silent abruptly as he noticed the look in Henry Munce's eyes and the way the little man was tapping his walking stick on the floor. "Well, Mister Munce," the young publisher said, "here on the *Morning Journal* I leave the hiring and firing to my editors rather than my pets, and I have no love for Bennett myself. Do you know, when I first determined to come to New York and show them how to put out a newspaper, I was looking for a property to acquire, and I was told that the *Herald* might be for sale."

"You were misinformed, sir," said Henry Munce. "Bennett will never sell the *Herald*."

"So I discovered," said Hearst, "but I did not know it at the time. Now make no mistake, I mean to make the *Journal* into a great newspaper, but at present it is nothing better than a foot in the door. The *Herald* is already a great newspaper, so naturally I was interested in acquiring it. Relying on the misinformation I had been given, I cabled Bennett and asked the price of the *Herald*. I received one of his famous cables in reply. Do you know what it said?"

"I do not."

"'Price of *Herald* three cents daily. Five cents Sunday. Bennett.' I am not a man who takes kindly to insults. So you see, you and I have a common goal, and Sam has his grievances with Bennett too, as you know. I say, the devil with the man, and I intend to drive his costs up and his circulation down and keep him awake at nights wondering what I'm planning next. I'd be thrilled if you would join us."

"At what salary?" Munce asked.

Hearst glanced at Chamberlain, who slipped his monocle into his eye and smiled. "He's good, W.R.," said Chamberlain.

"One hundred dollars a week," said Hearst. "That ought to show you how highly I value your talents. It's what I paid Ambrose Bierce to write for the *Examiner*."

"I require one hundred and one dollars a week," said Henry Munce. "I am better than Ambrose Bierce."

Hearst laughed. "Wonderful!" he said. "I like your spirit." He climbed off the desk. "Now, what shall we set you to? We are in a war here, Mister Munce, the devil we are. We are fighting Bennett and Pulitzer and Dana for the people's affection, and we must win it and win it quickly, for the rich and powerful of this city know us for their implacable enemy and will crush us if they can. We've started turning the *Journal* around, but there's a long way to go, Mister Munce, a long way. We need stories that the *Herald* and *World* don't have, big exciting stories, sensational stories, stories that startle and amaze! What can you give me, Mister Munce?"

Henry Munce stared at William Randolph Hearst with his deep, dark, gloomy eyes, and said in his coal-rumble voice, "The usual, Mister Hearst. Sex and death."

"Wrong, Mister Munce," Hearst said, amiably enough but with a certain iron in his voice. "The usual is not for the *Journal*. Let the other papers cover the usual things in the usual ways. Our task is to report the unusual! Astonish them, Mister Munce! Can you do that? Can you help me set this town to reeling? I will give you one hundred and one dollars a week, and a free rein for your undeniable talents. What can you give me, Munce?"

Henry Munce considered for a long moment, his powerful hands knotted about his walking stick, before looking Hearst directly in the eyes. "I can give you Henry Munce's greatest story, Mister Hearst. I can give you an innocent man, wrongly convicted for a murder he did not commit. I can give you police malfeasance at the highest levels. Give me time and freedom, sir, and I can give you Jack the Ripper."

"Look," Kate Hawthorne said to the doctor.

The child could not have been more than four or five, but she was no stranger to the establishment. The proprietor, a huge foul-smelling man in a red flannel shirt and filthy apron, took the battered tin bucket from her small hands with a grunt. "And what'll the old man be wanting tonight?" he asked.

"A quart of swipes please," the girl said. She had to stand on her toes to peek over the edge of the rough-sawn wooden bar.

"Swipes it is," the barkeep said. "Two cents, Annie."

She opened her fist and there were the two pennies; she'd been clutching them so tightly her palm was white. The barkeep took the money with another grunt, turned, and dipped her bucket into the big wooden tub behind the bar, filling it to the quart mark. "Here you go, and off with you," he said.

Her hands slipped when she tried to take the bucket from him, and some of the murky brown liquid sloshed out over the rim before the proprietor could steady it. "Here, careful, you've lost two swallers now, and if you spill any more, your old man will be in yelling that I didn't give him full measure. See that he don't, hear?"

Timorously, Annie nodded, and edged toward the door, holding the pail with both hands and carrying it as carefully as if it had been full of priceless pearls.

When she was gone, the barkeep looked around for other custom, found none, and made a round of the upended barrels that served for tables in his establishment, gathering up abandoned glasses and mopping up spills with a bar rag pulled out from under his belt. Here and there he found unfinished drinks; half of a stale beer, a swallow of raw whiskey, a full tumbler of gin left by the elbow of a drinker who'd passed out in the corner. He carried them all back behind his crude plank bar, where the beer barrels were stacked in tiers from the floor to the low ceiling, festooned with old election placards. One by one he emptied the drinks into the swipes tub before depositing the glassware in a basin of dirty water for rinsing. He used his rag to soak up the brown puddle the girl had left behind and squeezed it out over the swipes, twisting it hard and grunting until he'd gotten every last drop.

Doctor Humphrey Crittenden turned away. "Appalling," he said to his companion. "And people *drink* that?"

"Swipes is the specialty of the bucket-shop," Kate Hawthorne told him, "a sort of house wine, if you will. Elsewhere you'll hear it called all-sorts or dog's nose, but it's the same noxious brew. There's no waste, doctor. Everything goes into the tub. Beer, whiskey, wine, gin, water. Last week I saw a man put out his cigar in a half-glass of beer. The beer still went into the swipes tub, although I'll grant you that the barkeep was fastidious enough to remove the butt before pouring in the rest. The doctors who practice down in the tenements tell me they've had patients go blind from drinking swipes, but the poor continue to drink it."

"The taste must be unspeakable," the doctor said.

"They aren't looking for a fine bouquet. They're looking to get drunk. It's cheap. There's nothing cheaper, and if you have only a penny or two and need the oblivion of alcohol, there's nothing for it but swipes." She nodded toward the glass of water that sat before him on the barrel. "Are you certain you won't have something stronger than that, doctor?" she asked. "Shall I ask to see the wine list, perhaps?"

Doctor Crittenden's deeply lined gray face twisted in a rueful smile. He was a severe man, a man used to authority, but here in the squalor of the bucket-shop, he was obviously out of his element. "Katherine," he said, "if you are attempting to shock me with this irreverence, you'll have no success. I am a physician, and not wholly without experience of the world. I am not your mother." He pushed away the tumbler of water. "I've lost my thirst," he said, "but I see that your own thirsts are undiminished."

"My thirsts?" Kate Hawthorne stared at him frankly with large gray-green eyes. The soot dabbed across her pale forehead with the forced artlessness of badly-applied makeup could not entirely distract from her youth—she had celebrated her majority less than a year ago—and an aura of health and strength that was in conspicuous contradiction to her torn, soiled cloth-

ing. She was a creature of contradiction. Aside from the soot, her skin was too
fresh and pink and clean to fit with the coat she wore, a shapeless brown thing
with two buttons missing from the front. She had no grime caked beneath
her nails, so recently trimmed to the quick, and her smooth white hands,
though bare of jewelry, were also bare of calluses and showed no trace of the
red rawness that comes of frequent vigorous scrubbing with cleap lye soap.
She wore a ragged skirt and covered her head with a soiled green kerchief, but
the thick auburn hair beneath had been pinned up carefully at the back of her
long neck, and still smelled very faintly of good soap and French perfume.
"What thirsts are those, doctor?" she asked, in a voice far too educated for the
bucket-shop.

"Your thirst for melodrama, Katherine," he said.

"I prefer to think of it as a thirst for justice."

"Justice?" Doctor Crittenden was amused. "Is that the point of this transparent masquerade, my child?"

Kate's flush was a warm pink touch beneath her high cheek-bones. "I'm
not a child," she said curtly, "and I'll thank you not to patronize me." Behind
her, the door to the bucket-shop slammed open and a group of sailors came
in, calling for drink. Doctor Crittenden eyed them warily, then leaned forward and lowered his voice, though his tone was no less scolding. "You are
still thirty years my junior, and if you do not wish to be treated as a child, you
had best stop behaving like a child." He adjusted his spectacles.

"By which you mean I had best stop working, and return to serious adult
concerns, the social calendar and summers in Newport." She smiled at him.
"What am I doing in the tenements, when I could be holding court on Mamie
Fish and Harry Lehr? Why am I trying to write stories for the common press
when I might be composing love sonnets?"

"Speaking of poetry, perhaps you've heard that Stephen Blackwood is
back in the country."

Kate had been expecting that revelation. "Mother phoned me at the *World*
the day before yesterday to give me that urgent news. She tells me that Bess
Vanderkellen has been flirting with him shamelessly and will most certainly
steal his heart away unless I come home at once. Bad enough that I insisted
on exposing myself to vulgarity and danger, worse that I was disgracing the
Hawthorne name, but to lose the chance of a match with a Blackwood! Honestly, the news was so frightening I scarcely knew whether I ought to faint or
stop the presses."

"Sarcasm ill becomes a woman," the doctor said. "I'm sure your mother
had your best interests in mind. I seem to recall that you were quite taken
with Stephen not so long ago."

Kate felt her face grow warm. "Not so long ago for a man of your years,
doctor," she said, "but an eternity for a romantic young girl. I was an inno-

cent of seventeen, I had read too many novels, and Stephen at twenty-five seemed fabulously gallant, strong, masterful, and all the other things a maiden's white knight is supposed to be. He was my brother's best friend, a yachtsman, a poet, and the finest horseman I had ever seen." She smiled. "I think I loved those beautiful matched grays of his even more than I loved Stephen. Do you remember them?"

"Byron and Shelley," the doctor said. "Fast as the wind."

"I heard he sold them to some man in Chicago when he went off to Europe," Kate said. "I could never forgive him for doing either. All the rumors about him, about how he gambled and drank and fought duels, those never disturbed me, they only made him even more romantic. I could even forgive the attentions he paid other girls, since I knew I should have him eventually. But leaving me like that, without so much as a goodbye, that broke my heart." Kate smiled. "But that was a long time ago, doctor. I was seventeen, and romantic. I am now twenty-one and I have a purpose in life, and that purpose is certainly not Stephen Blackwood. Explain that to my mother the next time you treat one of her spells, if you would."

"You could do much worse than Stephen, you know. He is a dutiful and energetic young man, and strong enough to curb this perverse spirit of yours and make a good wife of you.

"And if I do not care to have my spirit curbed?"

Doctor Crittenden changed tacks. "Your mother misses you frightfully."

"I know. There is no one to help her plan the theme of the autumn gala."

"You've grown to be a willful young lady, Katherine," Doctor Crittenden said.

"I shall take that as a compliment."

"It was not intended as one. Your mother, it's true, cannot see far beyond the horizons of society, but I'm a broad-minded man, and I'm perfectly willing to accept the idea of a woman occupying herself in some constructive way in the years before marriage. I have seen how valuable properly trained female nurses can be to those in my profession. I have even encountered female physicians. If you wished to pursue a calling appropriate to your sex and station, I would be the last to discourage you, but instead you...you are..."

"This is a new age, Doctor Crittenden. A new century will soon be upon us, and women must play a part in making it a better century. Nellie Bly has gone around the world alone for Mister Pulitzer, and you would have me chaperoned whenever I walked down Fifth Avenue.

"Nellie Bly," Doctor Crittenden said sharply, "is a shanty Irish girl, and you are a Hawthorne. Your dear little Nellie wed Robert Seaman earlier this year, you know. Seventy years old if he's a day, and worth several millions. She knew her opportunity when it presented itself, and she did not hesitate to give up her crass occupation, such that it was. I will not dignify journalism by calling it a profession."

"That was her choice. I will not squander my life in play when there is important work to be done. Look around you, doctor. Surely you cannot condone this?"

"This?" Doctor Crittenden asked. "My dear, you must be more precise. What is it I cannot condone? Swipes? Bucket-shops? Alcohol? The tenements? Poverty?"

"All of it," Kate Hawthorne said crisply.

The doctor shrugged. "The poor will always be with us," he said, "but Christian charity demands that we do what we can to alleviate their suffering. I dare say I do my part."

"Do you?" Kate challenged him. "I know the local mission could make excellent use of the services of a physician. Perhaps you could donate one morning a week?"

"It may surprise you to know that I did such service when I was younger, and my practice was not as demanding. I am not as unfamiliar with these sad streets as you might think. I dare say I did some good, led a few away from drunkenness and sin, saved some of the little ones from an early grave. I was never so naive nor so vain as to think my efforts made any great difference, however. Nor will yours."

"I believe otherwise," she said, "as does my employer."

"Your employer," Doctor Crittenden said acidly. "An unscrupulous Jew. His only concern with these people is that they have two cents to buy his despicable newspaper.

Kate Hawthorne bristled. "He's as Christian as you are. Some might say more Christian."

"Your mother tells me that this...this *profession* of yours does not carry with it a salary, or wages of any sort, an arrangement that strikes me as ingeniously Hebraic."

"I'm on space," Kate said defensively. "Every paper in New York starts new reporters on space, even those dry, tired sheets that you and mother prefer to read, doctor. I do not want for anything. Father left me an independent income."

"I was executor of his estate," Doctor Crittenden said, "and I am familiar with the terms of his will. Your father had a keen business sense, but at times he could be stubbornly romantic and soft-hearted. He bequeathed you a share of his estate to keep you secure and comfortable, so you would not be forced to wed in haste for financial reasons. He would be aghast to think his legacy had plunged his beloved daughter into a life of disreputable scribbling. Geoffrey Hawthorne had no patience with the vulgar press and its radical ideas."

"The father I remember delighted in radical ideas," said Kate. "He increased his wealth tenfold with radical ideas, and he read the vulgar press every morning.

"For the shipping news!" Doctor Crittenden insisted.

"To find out what was going on in the world. He had no use for society either, although he let mother do what she would. Well, father is dead, in any case, so his views are scarcely of relevance, are they? If you must berate a Hawthorne about misuse of father's legacy, you might go visit Jeremy, provided you can find him, and discuss that yacht he wrecked and his stable of racehorses."

"Your brother is an unlucky young man, and perhaps a bit of a wastrel, but this attraction to the sporting life is not unusual among men of good family. In time, I'm sure it will pass. In any case, he does not go about dressed as a shopgirl."

"I would hope not," Kate said. "And no shopgirl would dress as shabbily as this, for fear of discharge. Shopgirls are not patrons of bucket-shops either. I'm supposed to look like a ragpicker's daughter."

Doctor Crittenden smiled tolerantly, removed a cigar case from the inside of his immaculate jacket, selected a cigar, cut off one end with his pocket knife, and lit up. Then he leaned back in the rickety wooden chair to regard her through the dim haze of the bucket-shop, as his smoke darkened the atmosphere still more. "Katherine," he said, "I've known you since you were a babe in arms, and I've known your family since my own childhood. You've young, my dear, and tender-hearted as well. It is a attribute of your sex. Women are notoriously sentimental about the unfortunate. Your sentiments do you credit, but they are misplaced. If these people live in hell, it is a hell of their own making. You don't know them as I do. You see the little ones coming in here with their buckets, and your woman's heart breaks. When I was much younger, I might have felt the same, but I've lived long enough to see those little ones grow up, to see what becomes of them. The wretched man who sent his daughter, that dear little girl, in here for that bucket of swipes, that man could easily be one of the selfsame lads whose life I saved twenty years ago. Yes, saved his life, and for what? His little daughter will be selling her virtue on the streets in ten years, perhaps in five. Really, my dear, these people are different from those you grew up with."

"I know," Kate said, "they are poor."

Doctor Crittenden sighed. "Were it only so simple," he said. "Your naivete would be charming were it not so inevitably doomed. What do hope to accomplish by this quixotic crusade of yours? What can you possibly do for these people?"

"I can expose the conditions under which they live."

The doctor smiled. "I see. And do you seriously suppose that a few articles in a yellow sheet that no decent family would allow into its home can possibly make any difference whatsoever? Even if you were able to persuade them to run your articles, that is, which I note you have thus far been singularly unable to accomplish. How many of your pieces have they accepted now, dear? Ten? Five? No? Two?" He shrugged. "Well, never mind, you are a talented girl and no doubt Mister Pulitzer will see that eventually and take some little thing. And then what? The Jew will sell a few more papers, your mother will have a faint, and you may upset the sensibilities of a few people of quality who will chance to see these writings of yours, but—"

"That is my hope, doctor," Kate said intently. "It is only when people are disturbed that any reform takes place. Nellie Bly exposed the conditions on Blackwell's Island in the *World*, and the outcry caused numerous improvements to be made. It was Mister Steffens of the *Evening Post* and Mister Riis of the *Evening Sun* whose writings led to the downfall of Byrnes and Clubber Williams, and accomplished the recent police reforms."

"Nonsense," said Doctor Crittenden. "It was Doctor Parkhurst and Mayor Strong and the new police board, if you want the truth. I assure you, men of the world have a very good idea of what goes on down in these awful places. They simply do not care to have their noses rubbed in it. And of course, most ladies would not care to know these things you're so eager to divulge. Women are made for finer things, yourself included. You've become a most handsome young lady, but this is no place for you." He waved his cigar airily at the filth of the groggery.

The bucket-shop was filling up now, as the dark fell outside and men filed in after a day of work. "Look at these people," the doctor said. The sailors were drinking beer in the far corner, their tables noisy with rough laughter and pungent oaths. One of them had appropriated the chair of the man who had passed out, dumping its occupant upon the sawdust-covered floor; the fall had not disturbed his drunken sleep. A haggard ragpicker in a slouch hat was standing at the bar, drinking raw whiskey and talking to the barkeep, while at his elbow a ancient, bone-thin prostitute tried to wheedle him out of a drink. "A wee touch of gin will do me," she was saying, her entreaty loud and shrill enough to cut through the din to where they sat. She smiled for him, showing three crooked black teeth. A much decayed red bonnet that might have been costly a dozen years ago sat crookedly atop her thinning gray hair. "I can't do it w'out a drink of gin," she said.

"Buy 'er some swipes, Alfie," called out a younger man from the center of the room. He was tall and wiry-strong, with a full red beard and flaring side-whiskers, and Kate was startled to see that he was wearing a policeman's jacket, though it was several sizes too small for him and filthy with coal dust. Around him clustered a half-dozen young toughs, smoking cheap cigars and drinking from buckets of stale beer. One of them was staring at the doctor with open hostility. Another of that company, a thin twisted young man with a persistent cough, noticed Kate's glance and beckoned at her. But most of them had eyes only for the trollop and their formidable, red-haired friend. "Here," he was shouting, "I'll go half, buy 'er a quart and it's a whole play we'll be getting." He took out a penny and flicked it toward the bar with his thumb. The barkeep snapped it out of the air, as the low, smoky cellar shook with laughter.

"I won't do it for no bar wipings," the prostitute told them. "Gin. I wants me gin."

The ragpicker at the bar showed a mouthful of green teeth and produced a second penny. "That dried-up old purse of yours ain't fit for swipes even, but you can still talk, I'll pay for a bit of that."

Doctor Crittenden frowned. "Katherine," he said, "you ought not be seeing this vulgar display. It's time we took our leave."

"Sssssh," she said, with a sideways glance and a discreet finger to her lips. "I want to hear what's happening."

The doctor sniffed. "They're paying the slattern for, um, they're buying her virtue, my dear, as if she had any left. It is the oldest profession, and it's nothing an innocent girl like you needs to see or hear."

"Gin," the old lady shrilled. "I won't do it but for gin. did it before kings and queens, I did, once." Again the cellar erupted in laughter. "And I drank me champagne too, and I won't do it for swipes."

"Katherine," Doctor Crittenden said, "I must insist."

"*Quiet*," Kate implored him. "There might be a story in this." When he started to reply, she determined to shock him into silence. "Can't you see it's not her damned virtue they're buying?" she said.

The doctor blinked. "Really, that sort of language…"

"Language?" Kate Hawthorne said. "You think that's language? Our printers have taught me language a good deal more choice than that, and the Colonel can make even the printers blush. When I have the opportunity to meet Mister Pulitzer himself I expect to receive a truly advanced education in profanity." She smiled sweetly at him. "So *please* shut your mouth right now, doctor, so I can spare you the benefits of my learning." She turned her attention back to the bar.

The whore was still insisting on gin, Kate saw, but none of the men was willing to pay the price, one by one they were losing interest and turning back to their private conversations, and the barkeep was looking impatient. Kate Hawthorne rose from her seat. "I'll buy you a glass of gin," she proclaimed loudly.

The bucket-shop fell suddenly silent. The tall redhead in the policeman's coat laughed. Doctor Crittenden grabbed her arm. "Katherine, for the love of mercy, some sanity."

She took out her coin purse, found a dime, tossed it to the barkeep in a most unladylike fashion. "Gin," she said.

The ragpicker poked the old prostitute. "There now, do it, g'wan with you, do it."

But the old woman waited until the barkeep had produced an unlabeled jug and poured a half-tumbler of clear fluid. Her hands shook as she drank half of it down in one long swallow.

Then she smiled her three-toothed smile, nodded happily at Kate, and proclaimed, in a huge and suddenly resonant music-hall voice, "A little water clears us of this deed. How easy it is then!"

Everyone laughed, even the huge proprietor, whose swollen gut shook beneath his sweat-stained red flannel shirt with the violence of his mirth. "Y' ain't saying I water the gin, are ye now?" he boomed.

"Consider it not so deeply," she said to him, her theatrical voice startling from such a gaunt, shrunken chest.

"Haw! Listen to her go on," someone shouted.

"Give us the good parts now," another called out.

She faced him. "Come you spirits, that tend on mortal thoughts, unsex me here, and fill me, from the crown to the toe, top-full—"

"I'll fill you, all right," the ragpicker shouted, to lewd guffaws. He reached over and tried to grab a shrunken breast through the thin layers of much-decayed silk she wore, but the old woman backed nimbly out of his reach. "Fill me from the crown to the toe, top-full, of direst cruelty!" she screeched at him. "Make thick my blood! Stop up th' access—"

That was the occasion for more laughter and shouted comments.

"—th' access and passage to remorse, that no compunctious visitings of nature—"

Guffaws ran around the dim cellar.

"—shake my fell purpose, nor keep peace between th' effect and it. Come to my woman's breasts—"

"Go on now, Alfie, she's beggin' for it," shouted out the tall red-haired man. The ragpicker grinned.

"—to my woman's breasts, and take my milk for gall, you murd'ring ministers."

"Here, no name-calling now," the barkeep warned.

The old lady spread scarecrow arms wide in a flamboyant gesture. "Come, thick night, and pall thee on the dunnest smoke of hell, that my keen knife see not the wound it makes, nor heaven peep through the blanket of the dark, to cry, HOLD, HOLD."

The bucket-shop erupted in raucous laughter, catcalls, shouts, and jeers of derision. Kate Hawthorne stood quietly erect for a moment, and then began to applaud. She clapped her hands together until the rest of the tumult had quieted, and all of them were looking at her. The old whore clutched up the tumbler of gin and emptied it. There were tears in the corners of her eyes.

"What is it?" Doctor Crittenden asked. "Why are you looking at her that way, Katherine? So the old slattern knows a few lines from the Bard, I fail to see…"

"Doctor, if you'd be so kind as to escort me to Park Row," Kate Hawthorne said to him, all business now, anxious to get to the morgue. The old clippings would still be on file; she had to check, to make certain she remembered it all correctly, it had been four years after all, she'd only been a schoolgirl, sneaking into her father's study to peek at the newspapers she was not permitted to read, so much livelier and more interesting than the dust-dry *Post* her mother favored.

"Gladly," said the doctor, "but I do not understand—"

"That woman," Kate told them as they made their way toward the exit. The air outside was cool with a hint of frost, and smelled dimly of raw sewage, but it tasted wonderfully fresh and clean and brisk after the smoke and alcoholic stench of the cellar, and Kate Hawthorne took in a healthy lungful of it with a pleasure that was almost joy.

"What about that woman?" Doctor Crittenden asked. "The noxious atmosphere of the tenements is harmful to the lungs, Katherine, you ought not inhale it quite so vigorously."

"What did you think of her Lady Macbeth?"

"Abysmal," the doctor said. "She shouts the lines instead of delivering them. To be fair, I suppose she might be considered like the dancing bear, it being most remarkable not that the bear dances poorly, but that he dances at all."

"I thought her performance was astounding," said Kate, excitement in her voice. If her memories did not play her false, she would have the story that would make her as well known as Riis, or Stanley, or Munce, or even Nellie Bly. It was all she could do not to skip down the sidewalk.

"Astounding!" the doctor exclaimed as they hurried down the streets, past darkened alley mouths and crowded stoops where thin young children stared at the doctor's rich clothing.

"Astounding, astonishing, and incredible!" Kate said, skipping a step, half whirling, and smiling at him. "Considering, my dear doctor, that she has been dead for four years now!"

"Owls?" said Ned Cullen, raising an eyebrow.

Sarah nodded as she fluffed the pillows behind her, pulling the sheet modestly up to her chin. "On my breasts. What do you think of the idea?"

"It's, ah, intriguing." Ned got out of bed, poured two glasses of champagne, handed one to her, and climbed back in by the ornate brass footboard so he could look at her. She was a pleasant sight to wake up to. "Give me a moment to consider it. And you might want to lower the sheet, too. I know you're modest, dear, but if I'm going to help you decide about your owls, I really ought to have a good look at your breasts now."

Sarah blushed and said, "You've seen them often enough, Mister Cullen," but she did as he asked nonetheless.

Ned sipped from a champagne glass and leaned back against the footboard, the cold brass pressing against his naked back as the deck beneath gently rocked the Commodore's huge featherbed. He smiled at Sarah as she sat there, nude, surrounded by pillows and bed clothes. She really did have lovely breasts, he thought, definitely her best feature, very full, hardly sagged at all, and he loved her nipples—broad, upturned nipples of a soft rose color that grew erect whenever he looked at them. They were getting hard now, in fact, and Sarah was blushing again. When she blushed, her bosom turned as red as her cheeks. Ned ran his bare foot along the inside of her leg, and tickled her navel with his toe. "Owls," he repeated bemusedly. Although, come to think on it, her breasts were so round, he could see how a good tattoo artist could do up her whole torso as an owl. The breasts could be the bird's eyes, big round owl eyes with wide rose-colored pupils, and he could tattoo feathers all over her skin, and put the beak down there, bright yellow with the soft pink showing inside when she moved her legs, a nice touch, although hair on a beak, he wasn't sure about that, she'd have to shave. Ned drank some more champagne and decided not to mention the idea.

"Well?" Sarah asked. She cupped her breasts in her hands and looked down, studying them. "Should I do it?"

"Owls are very attractive," Ned said carefully. "Your breasts are also attractive, however, and I understand tattoos are difficult to remove. I think I would leave your breasts just as they are.

She looked disappointed. "I thought Mister Bennett would like the idea. Two little owls on my titties, and he would spend more time with me. Suzanne has an owl tattoo on her inner thigh, you know."

"Does she really?" said Ned, who had seen the tattoo in question on numerous occasions, usually when the Commodore was spending a night with Sarah. The spanking-new *Lysistrata* had much better accommodations than Bennett's old, cramped, 900-ton *Namouna*, and the Commodore kept three palatial suites, one on each of the yacht's three decks, for his own personal use. He stored a mistress in each of them. Ned's own cabin was rather spartan and cramped. Fortunately, he did not have to spend many nights there.

"Yes she does, right on her thigh, she told me so," Sarah said, "and she's the Commodore's favorite. You know how he feels about owls."

"He loves mutton chops too, Sarah, but I wouldn't advise you to get yourself grilled."

"You're not being serious," she said. "He loves owls, and he's never paid much attention to my bosom."

"Well, yes," Ned Cullen admitted, "though I'm sure he cherishes your breasts as much as I do. Still, there is a point to be considered here. I'm partial to champagne and printers' ink, but that doesn't mean I'd care to have them mixed together, if you take my meaning." He swung his feet out of bed, and stood up on the cold hardwood deck.

"I think owls would look nice there," Sarah said, touching her right breast lightly. She took on a pouty expression, grabbed the sheet and covered up again.

Ned smiled for her as he dressed. "Well, perhaps I'm the wrong gent to ask," he said. "After all, if you get these owl tattoos and Bennett starts spending all his nights here, where would that leave me?"

Sarah looked at him. "Oh. I never thought of that."

Ned arched an eyebrow as he pulled on rumpled trousers. He'd have to get back to his own cabin and change before meeting Bennett for breakfast. "No, you wouldn't think of me," he said with just the tiniest hint of bruised feelings in his voice.

"Are you jealous?" Sarah asked.

Ned sighed. "I can't help it if I'm selfish, Sarah. I'd rather have a naked breast in hand than any number covered with owls that belong to the Commodore alone. Never mind about me, however. You have to think of your own advancement." He buttoned up, and left her with that thought as he ducked out into the passageway.

Sarah could be a delight, but there were times when he wondered about her, Ned reflected as he hurried back to his own cabin on the lower deck. She was so emotional. Suzanne, now, was another matter; dark and sloe-eyed and witty, and best of all, she preferred things uncomplicated. And there was Clarise, the French actress on the upper deck, but Ned stayed clear of Clarise. Not that she wasn't exquisite, or that he wasn't attracted; the Frenchwomen he'd sampled during his cruises with Bennett had all been wonderfully uninhibited, and he doubted that Clarise was an exception. Still, actresses were so damned unpredictable, and besides, Clarise had once mentioned that she was writing a book.

After a quick bath and a change, Ned proceeded up on deck. It was a beautiful, bright, sunny morning, crisp and clear; off the port side of where the *Lysistrata* rode at anchor a picturesque Greek village clung to the slope of the rocky hillside. The Commodore had not yet risen, but Clarise was already at breakfast with two of the guests. Bennett's friend Captain Candy, who insisted on introducing himself as "Candy of the Ninth Lancers" and whom Bennett fondly called "Sugar Candy," was spreading marmalade on toast and listening to the over-animated conversation of the fat young bachelor that the *Lysistrata* had taken on in Athens. The Commodore was always asking people aboard on whim, especially if they happened to be wealthy and American.

This fellow's parents had known Bennett in Newport, Ned gathered; that didn't stop the man from being an insufferable boor.

Ned took his accustomed seat to the right of the Commodore's place — Bennett liked to have his secretary handy, in case he was in the mood to do business over breakfast—and opened his napkin with a smart snap. Clarise gave him an enigmatic actress's smile. The talkative American ignored him (a secretary was only an employee, after all) and burbled on, directing his conversation toward Clarise. He seemed to be trying to impress her, a singular lapse of judgement, in Ned's opinion.

"A bracing morning," Ned said to Captain Candy with a radiant smile. A steward approached and he ordered eggs, kippers, and toast.

"I hope you enjoyed a restful night, Mister Cullen," Sugar Candy said.

"Snug and warm," said Ned. "Why?"

"So you'll be prepared for a busy day," Sugar Candy said. "The mail caught up with us." He gestured crisply with his fork.

Ned looked over his shoulder, and stifled a groan. A small launch had tied up to them, and the sailors were hoisting up one canvas mailbag after another, piling them all over the decks. Most of it wasn't even for the Commodore; the bulk, Ned knew from past experience, would be advertising copy and letters addressed to the Paris edition of the *Herald*. But sometimes when the Commodore went cruising, he left orders for all the mail to be forwarded on to him, and then Ned had to sort through it and send ninety per cent of it back. Of course, there was that time Bennett just hadn't been in the mood to deal with correspondence, and had ordered Ned to throw all the sacks into the Gulf of Lyon. That had been an invigorating morning's work.

There were compensations, though. The papers would be there too; two weeks' run of the *Herald*, both the New York and French editions, and probably healthy bundles of the other New York dailies as well: the *Tribune*, the *World*, the *Sun*, even moribund sheets like the virtuous *Evening Post* and the dying *Times*. The Commodore liked to watch the competition, to make sure none of them was exceeding the *Herald* in any respect. Ned was most anxious to get a look at some more numbers of the *Journal*, which was definitely displaying a lot more vigor since it had come into the hands of that profligate Californian. He was buttering his toast when he heard a chorus of yaps, the sound of many pairs of small scampering feet, and the Commodore's brisk, heavy tread, and James Gordon Bennett the younger made his appearance.

This morning the Commodore was dressed in a sporty hounds-tooth suit and vest of impeccable cut. His features were as stern as those of any judge. Bennett had eyes like blue ice, crystalline and cold, beneath heavy brows. His hair, parted in the middle, swept back from a high lined forehead. Beneath a prominent nose was a great gray dragoon's mustache, its waxed ends turned up slightly. He was tall and slender, with a brisk step and an imperious manner, and quite fit considering that he had spent most of his fifty-four years on earth consuming prodigious amounts of alcohol, creating scandals and sensation wherever he went, spending his money in a fashion that was capricious, unpredictable, and eccentric, and indulging himself on every occasion in lovely showgirls and rich food in a style to which Ned Cullen could only aspire.

Suzanne was on his arm, lithe and dark and petite. Around them swirled a pack of small dogs: a half-dozen playful Pekinese, a trio of Pomeranians, two small Cocker Spaniels, and a single surly Chihuahua,

The canine sea swept up around the table, sniffed out Ned, and immediately surrounded him, jumping up against his leg, licking his hand, bouncing and barking and climbing over each other to get at him. "The dogs certainly do like you, Ned," Bennett said. Suzanne smiled at him as the publisher seated her.

"They know how much I like them, Commodore," Ned said with a straight face. He leaned over to pet them, and surreptitiously plucked out the pieces of raw liver he was accustomed to secrete in his trouser cuffs and fed them to the nearest and luckiest animals. The rest of the dogs had to content themselves with sniffing his boots; the cabin boy, on Ned's standing instructions, rubbed a small quantity of meat juices, procured from the galley, into the leather every night while he did the polishing.

The pack finally wandered off when they noticed that one of the stewards was filling a row of bowls with chopped meats and Vichy water. The Commodore's dogs drank nothing but Vichy water; the *Lysistrata* carried a large supply.

Bennett ordered eggs and grilled mutton chops for himself and a breakfast steak for Suzanne, who had a better appetite than any other woman Ned had ever known, and then turned to his guests. "I see the mail has reached us. Cullen and I will have to deal with it after breakfast, I suppose. My apologies, gentlemen, ladies. The *Herald* is a jealous mistress." He glanced at the pudgy American. "I trust you enjoyed your first night aboard the *Lysistrata*."

"Most definitely," the man said. "I had never thought to find such luxury aboard a steam yacht. It is like staying in a first-class hotel, if I might make the comparison. And the service has been of that same standard, except for a few small lapses."

"Lapses?" Bennett said. The waxed ends of his mustache quivered just a bit as he frowned. "What lapses might you be referring to, Jeremy?"

The American shrugged. "The steward was not entirely satisfactory," he said. "I left instructions to be woken promptly at eight, and it was quarter past before he called. And my bath was not tepid. I specifically requested that the bath water be tepid. Not too hot or too cold, tepid."

"I see," Bennett said. Ned saw the look in those bright blue eyes and suppressed a smile. "Tomorrow," the Commodore continued, "you will be awakened at the stroke of eight, and your bath will be delivered to your state-room.

"I don't want to be any additional trouble," the man said.

"No trouble," said Bennett. "Is it, Ned? No trouble at all."

"None at all, Commodore," Ned said, permitting the smile to break at last.

"When we have taken aboard the mail," Bennett said, "we will be making sail for Turkey. I have a mind to pay a call on the Sultan."

"Turkey?" the American said, startled. "I had not planned to go to Turkey."

"You must change your plans, then," Bennett said, cutting into a mutton chop. "You will enjoy Turkey, Jeremy. The Sultan is a friend of mine."

"I see. Well, certainly, then," Jeremy said, obviously taken with the idea of consorting with Eastern potentates.

Ned was attracted to the idea himself, actually. They had paid a call on Bennett's friend, the Sultan Abdul the Damned, once before, some two years ago. Abdul was a odd fellow, a dark little ferret of a man who skulked about his huge palace in a perpetual state of terror, moving his bedroom every night to make it more difficult for imagined assassins to locate him. He and Bennett spent the visit reclining on silken pillows, drinking and holding long conversations in French, while stone-faced bodyguards hid behind every drape and secret panel. Left to his own devices, Ned befriended one or two of the palace eunuchs and pumped them for as much information as he could about the Sultan and the court. Bennett would never permit anything critical of his friend Abdul the Damned to appear in the *Herald*, of course, but the day might come when Ned Cullen was employed by someone other than the Commodore, and it was always an excellent idea to provide for contingencies.

Besides, one night when he was with Bennett and Abdul, taking dictation for a cable to New York, Ned had gotten a brief glimpse of two harem lovelies peering through a latticework around the edge of a drawn curtain, and that smoky vision had lingered in his memory, filling his dreams with wide dark eyes full of innocent lust, silken veils hiding tender treasures, jeweled navels in dusky, gently-rounded bellies, exquisite soft curves that beckoned to be stroked, and secret warm places that cried out for his hand. Given time and opportunity, Ned was certain he'd be able to figure out a way to gain access to the harem.

For the rest of the meal, Ned let the conversation swirl around him, interrupting his daydream of harem pleasures only long enough to note how pleasantly Suzanne was smiling at him, how fresh Clarise looked in the morning light with the austerity of the mountains behind her, and how incessantly fat Jeremy was talking. Sugar Candy, no doubt bored to tears by the American's prattle of Newport and Fifth Avenue, excused himself early, just as Sarah was arriving at table. Bennett himself listened politely to it all, wearing a grim smile.

Afterwards, the guests dismissed, Bennett and Ned repaired to the Commodore's office, a large airy room on the top deck, cluttered with furniture and papers. Bennett seated himself behind his spacious desk and took out a long, sharp pencil and several sheets of eggshell-blue stationery graven with owls. Ned had one of the stewards bring in the first mailbag. He cleared a space on the large table along the port wall, emptied the mail, and began to sort through it, while Bennett went through the most recent run of the *New York Herald* and made notes.

They worked all morning, while the *Lysistrata* got underway for Istanbul and the Golden Horn. As Ned had anticipated, ninety per cent of the mail would just have to be sent on back to Paris when they made their next port of call. He carefully set aside the handful of letters that Bennett would want to deal with personally, and tried not to yawn as he called for the second sack.

"I've written out a few cables," Bennett said, as he came up behind Ned and peered down over his shoulder. He thrust out a sheaf of the eggshell-blue stationary. "Here, have these sent immediately. What's that?" He took up one of the cables Ned Cullen had set aside, from the managing editor of the *Herald* in New York. "Ah, good," he said. "The list."

"He's a new man," Ned said of the managing editor, not quite sure why he was defending the idiot.

"Editors," Bennett snapped. "Think they run the newspaper, Cullen. Nonsense. Anyone could be a managing editor. I could pick a copyboy or a printer, or even a man off the street, and they'd do as good a job as these overpaid fools." He was looking over the cable, which was simply a long list of names.

Ned Cullen knew what was coming next. Just before they had gone to sea, the Commodore had decided that the Paris edition of the *Herald* needed the services of a young feature writer who had recently distinguished himself on the New York edition, and he'd snapped off a cable summoning the man to Paris. His new managing editor, however, had cabled back, pleading that the man was indispensable and could not possibly be spared from his duties in New York. Ned recalled the look on Bennett's face when he had received that cable, off the coast of France; it had not been wholly dissimilar from his look when young Jeremy had complained about the temperature of his bath water. Bennett had promptly cabled back to New York, requesting a list of all the indispensable men on the *Herald* staff.

And now the list was in hand. "Will you be replying, sir?" Ned asked him.

The Commodore nodded. "Certainly," he said. He waited until Ned had picked up paper and pencil. "Cable this to my managing editor," he said crisply. "Sir. Discharge following immediately." He read every name on the list he had in hand, and closed with, "I will have no indispensable men in my employ. Bennett."

"I'll send it out at once," Ned said.

"Good. I'm going up to the bridge. Go through the rest of this" — he waved at the letters, cables, and newspapers— "and inform me if there's anything else that requires my attention." When the office door had safely closed and Bennett's footsteps had receded down the hall, Ned Cullen grinned, put down his pen, and said, "Good thing I'm so easily replaced." He had no illusions on that score; Bennett's secretaries came and went, though Ned had lasted longer than almost any of them except good old SamChamberlain. He pushed the mail aside, found a few of the New York papers, swung his boots up onto the table, leaned back, and began to read.

Some forty-five minutes later, his feet hit the deck again with a thump as he sat up suddenly. "Here now," he said, "what's this?" He spread the paper out before him. It was a two-week old number of Joe Pulitzer's *New York World*, and the story was in the third column of the first page.

MURDER VICTIM BACK
FROM DEAD

Old Shakespeare
Alive and Well

Seen Drinking Gin
in Bowery Dive

World Asks, 'Who
Did Frenchy Kill?'

East River Hotel
Mystery Deepens

"I'll be damned," Ned Cullen said. "She didn't look very lively the last time I had the pleasure of her company." A thought struck him. He got up and went over to Bennett's desk and sorted through the *Herald*s until he'd found the issue for the same day. He went through it carefully, page by page. Then he looked at the number for the day before and the day after. Nothing. Nothing at all.

"Beaten by the *World*," he said. He glanced at the by-line. "Beaten by a woman, too."

James Gordon Bennett the younger hated nothing so much as when his *Herald* was outshone by one of the competing dailies, and he had never had much love for old Joe Pulitzer, who had elbowed Bennett aside to claim the greatest circulation in New York. The Commodore would be furious. And he'd also be helpless; since he'd just fired all of his best and most experienced reporters, the *Herald* would continue to look bad on this one.

Unless...

Ned thought about Sarah's breasts and Suzanne's big dark eyes and Clarise and her enigmatic smile. He thought about featherbeds, the salt air, the warm breezes of the Mediterranean, about champagne and good food, about the harem of Abdul the Damned. Being Bennett's personal secretary had its charms, no doubt of it.

On the other hand, Sarah was about to tattoo owls on a perfectly good set of breasts, the whole business of sneaking about by night was perilous, he was weary of liver in his trouser cuffs and boots *au jus*, there was all that mail to sort through, and if they caught you sneaking into the harem you were speedily admitted into the ranks of the eunuchs, no waiting period required. And then there was Bennett.

He might as well admit it, Ned thought. He missed the city, missed the clatter of hooves on cobbled streets and the rumble of iron wheels, the palaces along Fifth Avenue and the shanties up around the Dakota, the shouts of newsboys and oyster vendors, the hicks from Pittsburgh and Cincinnati pressing their noses to the glass to watch the *Herald*'s presses roll, all the myriad ladies proper and im-, starched Gibson girls and shanty Irish roses and debutantes in jewels and whalebone corsets and the big-eyed tenement sweethearts, nights full of champagne and beefsteak in the Tenderloin, and endless days in hot pursuit of one story or the other. Murders, scandal, sin, sex, fads, follies, corruption, crusades, and then at the end that marvelous moment when he held the *Herald* in his hand, the ink still wet, and there it was, sharp and black on the crisp white paper: BY NED CULLEN.

And on this one, he had a edge; he knew something the rest of those poor hacks didn't. If Bennett approved, he could be back on the streets in two or three weeks

Ned Cullen gathered the *World* and the *Herald* up under his arm, and set off in search of Bennett, whistling "Battle Hymn of the Republic" as he went.

The policeman was running full out, heedless of the other pedestrian traffic on Broadway. He had lost his hat some time back, and his light-colored hair was in a state of wild disarray. The street lights, dazzling Brush electric arc lamps whose hard white brilliance was painful to look at directly, bathed the sidewalks with a cold radiance that turned the fleeing patrolman's face ghostly white. The top two buttons of his jacket were undone. He had his nightstick in hand, and as he plunged down the thoroughfare, panting and sweaty, he gave a good swack in passing to a fat businessman in a derby and striped suit who was too slow to get out of his way. The man grunted with pain and shock, his little pig eyes bugging in astonishment, but the policeman was past him before he could utter any protest.

Outside of one fashionable dance hall, a cluster of young dandies called after him, but he sprinted by with not so much as a glance in their direction. His long face was damp with perspiration and as white as if he had the very devil on his heels.

As the blue-jacketed form raced away down the sidewalks, the well-dressed young loiterers heard shouting and glanced back in the other direction just in time to see the second runner come around the corner at the cross street, hopping unsteadily on his left leg as he made the turn. "Stop that man!" he shouted in a high, piercing voice. "Stop him, I say!" He did not pause to see whether anyone would obey, but came charging down Broadway in hot pursuit, a snorting bull of a man waving a fashionably slim black walking stick. Chunky and heavyset, with a thick neck and broad shoulders and a big barrel chest, the policeman's pursuer was dressed like a gentleman, in a dark brown suit and vest well-matched to the color of his carefully parted hair and square, bushy mustache. His long heavy overcoat, trimmed with a fur collar, was unbuttoned down the front, and flapped vigorously against his legs with the energy of his running.

The fat man who had gotten a lick of the policeman's night-stick turned angrily toward the stocky newcomer and tried to arrest his progress. That was a misjudgment; the runner bowled right into him, roaring, and the fat man squealed as he was rudely deposited upon his buttocks. The other staggered but kept his feet, recovered himself, and leapt nimbly over the corpulent businessman on the sidewalk, losing only a step or two. "Stop him, you hear!" he shouted in that high voice, and ran on.

"They're doing it wrong," quipped a slightly drunken young wit standing in the doorway of a saloon on the other side of Broadway. "The cop is the one supposed to run to the rear and shout, 'Stop, thief.'" He laughed at his own joke. Across Broadway, the fleeing policeman darted down a narrow alley between two dark buildings. His pursuer came hard after him, twenty paces behind.

Henry Munce did not crack a smile. "Pardon me," he said, stepping around the would-be wit. Swinging his heavy iron stick, he crossed the street at a brisk stroll, reached the mouth of the alley in time to see the bullish man vanish into the shadows, and proceeded smartly to the next cross street. It was quieter and less traveled here, and the shadows lay thick; these side streets had not yet been blessed with Brush electric arcs and the blinding white light of progress. Henry Munce looked about carefully, and nodded with approval when he had ascertained that he was indeed alone. Halfway down the block he reached the mouth of another alley. He stepped into a particularly thick patch of darkness to its side. A moment later he heard the sound of running footsteps.

He waited until the sound of boot leather pounding hard against pavement was right on top of him, and he could discern the gasping wheeze of the policeman's breath. Then Henry Munce stepped out of the dark and delivered the beak of his iron owl directly to the policeman's right shin with a single short, economical swing. The man squalled in distress and pain, lost his footing, and flew headfirst to the pavement. His nightstick clattered off an alley wall, and he hit with a sickening crunch. In a trice Munce was on him.

When the well-dressed man with the bushy mustache came puffing up, looking somewhat the worse for wear for his run through the maze of alleys, Henry Munce was seated comfortably on the prone policeman's buttocks, his hands clasped around his walking stick, a huge black cigar smoldering in his mouth. "Commissioner," he rasped, "I am Henry Munce. You wished to speak to this man."

"By Jove," the police commissioner puffed, obviously out of breath. He stopped, broad chest heaving with exertion, and studied the astonishing scene before him, his small dark eyes hard with intensity. Reaching into his vest pocket—one of the buttons was gone, no doubt popped off during the chase—he extracted a pince-nez which he fitted carefully atop his nose. A few strands of brown hair were plastered to his broad forehead by sweat. He pushed them back in place with his hand. Blinking, he lifted up the tip of his slim walking stick as if he were about to poke Munce to determine if he were real, and then hesitated as if it had occurred to him that such a poke might be considered impolite.

"By Jove," he repeated, "a dwarf. And you've got the wretch." The ruddy face broke into a most amazing smile. The commissioner's famous teeth were square and dazzling-white and very large, and his laughter was a boisterous snort. "Good work, Mister Munce, good for you! A bold dwarf, well, and a citizen who knows his duty!"

"A reporter," said Henry Munce, "at work on a story." Smoke from his cigar eddied about his face.

"A reporter?" said the commissioner. The high, clipped voice had a sudden note of wariness in it. He craned around over his shoulder. "I had a reporter with me when I started out tonight, Munce, but I believe we lost him quite a ways back. Jake does not have much endurance, I'm afraid." He gave another bark of laughter. "Not as spry as you are, Munce. He'll hear about this, no doubt."

"No doubt," said Henry Munce. He knew big, shaggy Jacob Riis, who had been regularly accompanying the new police board president on these nocturnal inspections and writing up their exploits for the *Evening Sun*. A good man in his way, but soft of heart and soft of body. Munce sucked in on his cigar and blew a thick cloud of foul-smelling cigar smoke up at the commissioner, who broke out in a fit of coughing.

The patrolman beneath Henry Munce gave a piteous moan. "Let me up," he said. "I think my nose is broke."

Henry Munce removed the cigar from his mouth and looked up at the commissioner. "Your pleasure?"

Waving his hand vigorously to clear the air, the man said, "Oh, I suppose you might as well get off him. We've run him to ground now, eh?"

Munce spit on his thumb and the forefinger and squeezed out his cigar. It died with a hiss. He replaced it in the pocket of his black woolen overcoat and got to his feet. The battered policeman rolled over. A rivulet of blood ran from his nose, looking black in the dim alley light, and his uniform was torn where he had scraped his knee bloody against the pavement.

"Get up, get up," the commissioner barked. "Take your punishment like a man. You're a disgrace to the force. Drinking on duty, and then running like that. Shows all the backbone of a chocolate eclair. Did you think you'd get away, and then I wouldn't be able to find you out? Ha!" From inside his coat, he produced a pad. "Your name now, and don't try to lie."

"Beekman," the policeman said. "Nathaniel Beekman, sir." He was quite young, Henry Munce saw; no doubt terrified when the president of the police board himself came down upon him, all spectacles and teeth. "I was only taking a rest and having a small beer," he said weakly. "I'd been walking the beat and my feet was tired and my throat was dry, Mister Roosevelt, I didn't mean no harm."

"Don't you dare whine at me, Beekman! Excuses, that's all. And that young woman who was undoing your uniform, what's your excuse for her?" He put away his notepad and tapped the tip of his stick on the policeman's chest, where the two top buttons of his jacket were still hanging open. "Lurking around a saloon door, beer in hand, consorting with women of ill repute, don't pretend you're innocent now, I saw it with my own eyes. Go on, get out of here. I'm bringing you up on charges. Go home and pray you aren't fired. Go on." His stick flicked toward the street, a curt and pre-emptory dismissal.

"Yes, sir," the patrolman said. His Adam's apple bobbed up and down as he swallowed his pride. "I'm sorry, Commissioner." "Get out of here now," snapped Theodore Roosevelt. The cop backed into the street and then was gone, walking off as quickly as he could. Roosevelt looked down at Henry Munce again and flashed his famous smile. "The boy did lead me quite a chase. We left old Jake wheezing in a gutter somewhere. If I hadn't been toughened up by my years out West, I might not have been fit enough to catch him. Still, it was a good stroke of luck you happened along, Munce."

"Henry Munce does not happen along," said Henry Munce.

Roosevelt looked at him. "What's that?"

"Your habit of prowling the nighttime streets and surprising policemen who are derelict in their duty is well known. I was informed that you would be in this precinct tonight."

"Informed," Roosevelt said. "By whom?"

"Henry Munce has his sources. Knowing you would be prowling hereabouts, I made it my business to be in the same vicinity. There is a matter I wish to discuss."

Roosevelt was still preoccupied by the idea of someone informing on his movements. "If it was Jake, I'll have it out with him. You reporters all—"

"It was not Jake Riis," Munce said brusquely. "Enough of that. I wish to talk."

"Munce, if you want an interview, you can come to my office on Mulberry Street like the rest of them."

"I prefer not to call on you in your office," said Henry Munce. "I am a dwarf, sir. I am noteworthy. Your own face is well known. Earlier this week I came upon a peddler selling celluloid dentures fashioned to resemble your teeth. Each came equipped with a whistle. 'Get your Roosey Teeth,' the man cried as I passed, 'Get your Roosey Teeth and scare the coppers.'"

"I've seen them," Roosevelt said, with a slightly strained smile. "Very pretty."

"Were I to visit your office, or meet with you in a restaurant or other public place, my height and your features could not hope to go unremarked. Our conference would be noted. Other reporters would be curious as to why you conferred with Henry Munce, would suspect that something of consequence was afoot, and might be prodded to efforts of their own that could interfere with my plans. And it is well known that you have cultivated friendships with Jake Riis of the *Sun* and Lincoln Steffens of the *Post*. I would not have them alerted that Henry Munce has embarked on a new investigation."

"Riis and Steffens have been of great help to me in my fight to reform this city's police," Theodore Roosevelt said. "Why should I keep them in the dark about you and whatever this investigation of yours concerns?"

"You are in my debt," Henry Munce said.

"Why," said Roosevelt, "I would have caught the boy in a block or two even if you hadn't taken a hand."

Henry Munce shrugged; it was nothing to him if the police commissioner wanted to deceive himself. "You will say nothing to Riis and Steffens because silence will be in your best interests, sir," he said in his deep, growly voice. "The proposition I have for you will rebound to your credit as well as mine."

Roosevelt coughed, then smiled. "Well, then, out with it, Munce. Let's hear this proposition of yours."

"Walk with me," said Henry Munce.

"Gladly," said Roosevelt, setting off at a sharp clip. "An alley is no place for us, eh, Munce? Back to Broadway!"

"No," said Munce. "I am not partial to the glare of our electrified streets. Discretion is best served in shadow and gaslight. And I prefer a slower pace." They emerged onto the street and Munce turned left. Roosevelt checked his own headlong stride and paced restlessly alongside.

"You have a man in prison in Sing-Sing," Munce began. "His name is Ameer ben Ali, but he was popularly known, in the press and on the streets, as Frenchy. He is innocent of the murder for which he has been convicted."

"Frenchy," said Roosevelt. "I recall the case dimly. It was a number of years ago, Munce. An Arabian."

"Algerian," said Henry Munch.

"I will not say that all of these foreigners are thieves and murderers, but most of them certainly are, and I don't propose to let one free to prey on good Americans just on your say-so. The scoundrel probably deserves to be right where he is now."

"I believe he was deliberately framed by Superintendent Byrnes and Inspector Williams," said Henry Munce.

Teddy Roosevelt stopped dead. "Clubber Williams?" he said. "Now that's of a bit more interest. Go on."

"The case was bungled," Henry Munce said. "I suspected that in 1891, when I first covered what was commonly referred to as the Old Shakespeare case or the East River Hotel murder, but I was called abroad suddenly, and had no time to confirm my suspicions. Recently, I have gone back into the files, and my certainty is greater than ever. Bungled, sir, bungled! Even the corpse is not who she was alleged to be, if the *World* can be believed. An old whore, found brutally hacked apart, was said to be a cheap waterfront tart known as Old Shakespeare, so called because she claimed to have been a famous actress once, and would recite the women's parts from various of Shakespeare's plays in return for a drink of gin. Very well, we had no reason to question it, but now the *World* asserts that just such a woman, as alive as any of her class can be said to be, is haunting the stale beer dives and bucket-shops of the Bowery. Who was the victim?"

Roosevelt snorted. "Well, so one degenerate old woman was confused with another by the common press. This city is infested with these women, Munce, we have thousands of 'em, and most of them have forgotten their real names. If this Frenchy was responsible for the atrocity, does it matter who the wretched woman was?"

"Perhaps," said Munce, his dark eyes straight ahead, boring into the waiting night as they walked, "and perhaps not. But Frenchy murdered no one, I am convinced."

"Why?" said Roosevelt. "Byrnes was involved, you say? Well, he is no friend of mine, and he was wise to retire before I could bring him up on charges, but for all our differences, the man was no fool, Munce. He had been a police officer for a long time, yes, a long time. He knew what he was about."

"Thomas Byrnes was a great detective," Henry Munce said. "He was as much a master of his art as I am of mine, and the criminal element feared and respected him. But he was also a proud man. Recall his Whitechapel boast. Reflect on how closely the East River Hotel killing resembled the crimes of the Ripper. Byrnes needed to arrest someone quickly to live up to his words. One need not be Henry Munce to look over the contemporary newspaper accounts and the evidence presented at the inquest and trial and see clearly that Byrnes, unable to find the obvious chief suspect, the man at whom every clue pointed, the man whom the police searched for diligently for over a week and *never found*, acted in desperation and arrested the most convenient man. It was then necessary to convict him, and this Byrnes did, by ignoring all the testimony that pointed to other possible suspects." Henry Munce stamped his walking stick hard against the pavement to punctuate his statement.

"You have the advantage of me," said Roosevelt. "I do not recall the fine details of the case.

"Had not expected you would," replied Henry Munce. "The murder took place on the night of Thursday, April 23, 1891, or the predawn hours of Friday the 24th. The night clerk discovered the body that morning when he attempted to roust what he thought to be a late sleeper. Consider this, sir. The hotel was a notorious house of assignation for prostitutes of the lowest class, and the victim had not been alone when she took lodging that evening. The night clerk, one Eddie Fitzgerald, was away from the desk when they signed the register, but a woman named Mary Miniter, employed there as assistant housekeeper, saw the man who accompanied the whore when she took their money. She described him fully to the police. He was said to be a slender man in his thirties, under six feet in height, wearing a dark brown cutaway coat, black trousers, and a derby with a dented crown. His clothing was decent but well-worn. His nose was long and sharp and he wore a very heavy mustache of light or sandy color. Mary Miniter had the impression that he was a foreigner."

"Bully for her," said Roosevelt, "the police rarely get such detailed descriptions." He swung his stick jauntily as they walked. "How does this dovetail with the description of Frenchy?"

"It does not," grumbled Henry Munce. "Ameer ben Ali is tall and lean, with sallow dark skin, coal black eyes, and black hair. His nose is aquiline, and prior to his arrest he affected a full beard. But even Byrnes did not suggest that Frenchy was the man described by Mary Miniter. Frenchy arrived at the East River Hotel alone during the hours between midnight and dawn—"

"The very hours of the murder!" Roosevelt interrupted.

"True, but of no import," said Munce. "Using the name of George Francis, a man he had robbed at knifepoint some months earlier, Frenchy rented a room for the night, paying Eddie Fitzgerald with twenty-five pennies. Fitzgerald gave the Algerian room 33. The woman thought to be Old Shakespeare was sharing room 31 with her client. This client, the mystery man, was never seen to leave, but was most definitely gone in the morning. I assure you, Mister Roosevelt, that Byrnes searched for him vigorously. *Vigorously*, sir! He was the obvious object of suspicion."

"Yes, certainly," Roosevelt said. "Go on. You've piqued my interest, Munce."

"In the first few days of the investigation, while the search for the man with the dented derby and sandy mustache was being pursued, police and press both turned up additional evidence against him. Bloodstains were found on the trap to the roof, indicating that the killer had escaped over the rooftops. This would account for why neither Fitzgerald nor Mary Miniter saw the man depart. Even more telling was the testimony of a man named Kelly who was night clerk at the Glenmore Hotel, a cheap lodging house on Chatham Square. In the middle of the night, Kelly claimed, a man in a brown coat closely fitting the description given by Mary Miniter entered and asked for a room. He seemed nervous and agitated. As he leaned against the desk, Kelly noted that his right hand was all bloody. He studied the man more closely and spied bloodstains on his collar and coat sleeve and two splotches of blood on his right cheek as well, although this alone would hardly be considered noteworthy in that neighborhood. When the clerk demanded payment in advance for a room, the man admitted that he had 'not a cent.' Kelly then told him the hotel was full up, but before the man turned to go he asked if he might use the washroom. Kelly refused, and told him the washroom was for hotel guests only, and the bloody man went back out into the night. He had a slight accent, according to Kelly."

"Very incriminating," said Roosevelt. "It would seem they had the culprit dead to rights."

"Obvious," said Munce. "Byrnes would no doubt have agreed as well, but a problem arose. He could not find the suspect. Numerous people had seen a man with the murdered woman *before* the crime. Two other prostitutes, Mary Healey and one Lizzie the Angel, had seen them that very night, as had a sailor named Isaac Perringer, and the barkeep of the saloon downstairs, Samuel Shine. Yet no one had seen this man at all afterwards. Clubber Williams and his men turned out hundreds, went door to door through the fourth ward, checked every cheap lodging house night after night, even passed the word among the criminal element, and all for naught. Finally, on May 1, Byrnes charged the crime to Frenchy, who had been arrested days before along with Mary Healey, Mary Miniter, and several others who it was thought might be concealing useful information that could be coaxed from them with Byrnes' famed techniques of interrogation."

"What?" said Roosevelt. "Just like that? Surely there must have been some reason, some evidence?"

"An abundance of evidence," Munce said gloomily. "Another saloon keeper said she had seen Frenchy and Old Shakespeare together days earlier, arguing. Frenchy was known to carry a knife. Blood was found on his underclothing and on the blanket and chair in room 33. A scraping was made of the dirt beneath his fingernails, and it was announced to be composed of decaying cheese, corned beef, and cabbage. These were precisely the foods Old Shakespeare had made her lunch on, Byrnes said. The source of this intelligence was said to be the coroner. The killer had pulled out the victim's intestines, much in the manner of the Ripper, and it was suggested that this was how Frenchy had gotten these remains beneath his nails. The most telling single piece of evidence offered by Byrnes, however, was a trail of blood leading from room 31 to room 33."

"A trail of blood?" Roosevelt said. He snorted.

"The Algerian did not conduct his case well," said Henry Munce. "He spoke no English on some days, and spoke it passably well on others. He was given to violent outbreaks and calling upon Allah in court. Allah was as unhelpful as his lawyer, in the end it was the trail of blood that undid him. Byrnes claimed that the victim's last patron was just that and no more, that he left the hotel after satisfying his lusts, and therefore had no bearing on the case. The bloodstains on the roof were utterly forgotten, and night clerk Kelly of the Glenmore was never called into court to give testimony. After the whore's partner had departed, Byrnes suggested, Frenchy stole down the hall and butchered the sleeping woman for reasons of his own, most likely monetary. The court found him guilty of second-degree murder and sentenced him to a life in prison. The day after the conviction, Byrnes gilded his lily by announcing to the press that he had evidence in his possession that Ameer ben Ali had been in London during the Whitechapel murders, leaving unspoken the suggestion that Frenchy was indeed Jack the Ripper. This evidence, however, was never produced." Henry Munce thumped the side of a lamp post as they rounded a corner, producing a dramatic ringing sound, and said, "There you have it, sir."

"Well," said Teddy Roosevelt. "A bully tale. Very enlightening, Munce. I agree, the case against the Arab is hardly convincing, but there would seem to be some evidence."

"Nothing that cannot be accounted for save the trail of blood," Munce said. "Cheese and corned beef, weeks old and rotten, might be found under the fingernails of half the Irishmen in Manhattan. As for his bloody clothing, the Algerian claimed he had been in a fight that evening. Fights are more common than corned beef along the Bowery and the waterfront. The blood on the roof trap bespeaks a hurried escape, but Frenchy left the East River Hotel openly the next morning, and returned to his room the following night, was in fact in and out constantly until his arrest. And what of the agitated man with the bloody hand who sought a room at the Glenmore? No. Ameer ben Ali is gutter sweepings, but he is not the killer." He stopped abruptly, in a pool of light cast by a flickering gas lamp, and looked up at his companion, his gloomy eyes pools of shadow beneath his thick brow. "She was slain by Jack the Ripper, sir!"

Roosevelt stopped too, and stared down at Munce through his pince-nez. "The Whitechapel killer? The same man? Unlikely, Munce. Outlandish, in fact."

"Henry Munce does not propose outlandish theories. With or without your help, I intend to give proof to my words. I give you fair warning."

"Warning?" said Roosevelt. "You're giving me *warning*, are you? You're an impudent little man. No one talks to me like that, Munce."

"Henry Munce speaks as he pleases and says what he will. What I require from you can be easily stated. It is my certain belief that the police have extensive files on the investigation Byrnes conducted in 1891, the full contents of which were never given over to the public. I wish you to get hold of these files and turn them over to me. It must be done surreptitiously. I would also ask for whatever morgue photographs of the victim might exist. These will be useful in helping me establish the true identity of the dead woman, a fact that may or may not be of importance. You should arrange to put this information into my hands as soon as possible. Afterwards, should any of my competitors come nosing about in search of the missing files, you may simply inform them that the notes and photographs have been lost, or deny that such ever existed."

Theodore Roosevelt was staring down at Munce incredulously, his small dark eyes growing hotter and hotter. "How dare you?" he snapped. "Do you take me for Clubber Williams, little man? I was made president of the police board to clean up this city, not to carry on the corruption! No friend of mine would dare suggest that I would even consider such a proposition!"

"I am no friend of yours, Roosevelt," Munce said. "Do not mistake me for Riis or Steffens. They are idealistic fools and they love you for the knight they think you are, even while you use them ruthlessly to further your swollen ambitions. Henry Munce is no man's sycophant, and he sees you clearly, sir, clearly. You are a vain, posturing man, but you are shrewd enough to realize that I can be of great use to you."

In the unsteady gaslight, a flush could be seen creeping up the commissioner's thick neck. "You," he said, "you, you—"

"You will, of course, get full public credit for Henry Munce's solution," Munce said. "The public will believe you broke the case, freed an innocent man, captured Jack the Ripper, and rectified the corrupt bungling of Superintendent Byrnes."

Roosevelt glowered fiercely through his pince-nez, tapping his stick in an staccato rhythm against the pavement. "What's this?" he demanded.

"You heard me," Munce said curtly. "I want those files, but I am under no illusions that you will provide them to me merely for the sake of justice. Henry Munce pays his debts."

"You amaze me," Roosevelt said. "What foolery makes you think I need your corrupt schemes?"

"You are not a popular man," Munce said. "You are beloved of Dr. Parkhurst and his congregation, no doubt, but to the most of the public you are the man who arrests saloon owners, f lower-peddlers, bootblacks, and ice dealers alike when they sell their wares on Sunday. The Germans depise you, the Irish hate you, you are poison to the saloon keepers and, soon now I think, you will be a liability to your own party."

"The law is the law," Roosevelt blustered. "It's not for me or any policeman on the beat to decide which laws he'll enforce and which ones he'll ignore."

"The blue laws are hated, and as you have forced the police to enforce them, you are hated as well. Deny it if you will, but you are the most unpopular man in town, and it will write an end to your political career. Do you think your colleagues in the party will stand by you when your star is eclipsed? Even your police board will turn on you. Four men sit on that commission, and already the others have grown weary of reading about you in the headlines, listening to your speeches, hearing jokes about your teeth and your spectacles, and deferring to your every decision. They will turn against you, and soon too, and where will you be then?"

Roosevelt laughed. "The board? Your cynicism is misplaced, little man. They are solidly behind me, every man of them, and good men too."

"Even Parker?" said Henry Munce.

"Andrew Parker is the best of them," said Roosevelt, "my right hand, as brilliant and efficient as any man in government."

"So Christ said of Judas Iscariot," Henry Munce grumbled, knowing the comparison would appeal to Roosevelt. "In contrast to your own swelling unpopularity, Thomas Byrnes is still revered and loved. He is the genius detective, the great inspector, the man who established the deadline to keep sneaks and dips and robbers off Wall Street, who singlehandedly solved countless celebrated crimes. Even the criminals loved Byrnes, because he let them know where they stood. The day he retired, Fifth Avenue and the Bowery both trembled and mourned. The Lexow investigation forced out Clubber Williams and dozens of others in disgrace, but Byrnes' reputation remains unblemished.

"Henry Munce can change that. I shall snap this case like a cord of rotten wood, and when my researches are done, Byrnes will be known as a corrupt incompetent who jailed an innocent man to cover his own bungling, and you will be the forceful reformer who came along years later to clean up his mistakes and right the wrongs he committed in the name of justice. Moreover, you will be forever known as the man who caught the Ripper. The Ripper, sir! Infinitely more notorious than any criminal ever jailed by Byrnes. It will be your redemption. Every newspaper in this nation and England will reprint my dispatches. The fame you will achieve courtesy of Henry Munce will be more than enough to see you elected mayor, governor, senator, whatever you might wish."

"Well," said Roosevelt, hesitantly. Then he smiled. "By Jove, it might actually do that! Whatever I might wish? These are challenging times, Munce, we are in desperate need of real leadership, of men of insight and ability who are equal to the challenge. I could do great good, I'm sure of it."

Henry Munce stared at him in silence, leaning his weight on his thick owl-headed stick.

"A few files," Roosevelt mused. "What harm could come of it? There has been an injustice here, the more I reflect on the things you've told me, the more certain I am of it. You're a bold man, Munce. I like that, we need bold men." He slashed at the air with his walking stick. "Daring! We need men of daring, who have the courage to be true to their principles. I am a keen judge of men, and I can tell that your cynicism is a pose, sir! You are as hot to do the right thing as I am, we have that in common." The police commissioner beamed now, and the teeth gleamed.

"Believe what you will," said Henry Munce.

"I'll do it!" Roosevelt said. "That miserable little man in Sing-Sing, and the real killer still out on the streets, well, I have no choice, do I? We have a bargain, Munce, you'll get your files." He adjusted his pince-nez. "But what's in it for you, Munce? What does Henry Munce get out of this?"

"A story," said Henry Munce, as if that said it all.

PART THREE

December 1895

From bad to worse, thought Kate Hawthorne. "You have no idea where he is?" she snapped. She had her notes clutched tightly in one white-gloved hand, all the names carefully copied out in an elegant longhand from the yellowed clippings in the *World* morgue. "He was the night clerk here four years ago. Eddie Fitzgerald."

"Said I didn't. Don't." Rotund and near-sighted, the little man had a smile that Kate found greasy and repugnant. "Been here six months. Don't know him."

"You must keep records?" Kate said.

The clerk laughed.

"Fine," Kate said crisply, glancing at her notes. "In that case, I'd like to speak to Mary Miniter."

"Who?" His lips were wet and his teeth green.

"Mary Miniter. The assistant housekeeper."

"Don't know no Mary Miniver. Housekeeper ain't got no assistant. This look like the Waldorf?"

Kate pressed her lips together. The Fourth Ward Hotel—they had changed the name since 1891, though perhaps not the sheets—looked nothing like the Waldorf, that she could agree to readily. "Where can I find Mary Miniter?"

The man shrugged. "Damned if I know."

"The housekeeper," she said, consulting her notes again. "Her name is Mary Cochran, correct?"

"Wrong," he said. He seemed to be enjoying discomfitting the reporter lady, as he called her. Having learned quickly that women disguised as ragpickers seldom got their questions answered respectfully, Kate had donned her city room clothes: a simple woolen suit in navy, with big sleeves and puffed shoulders and the ruffled flare of a peplum at her fashionably trim, corsetted waist, over a high-collared white shirtwaist crisp with starch. Her bell-shaped skirt brushed against the bare, dusty floorboards of the office, a small fedora was pinned to her auburn hair, and she had laid her soft leather handbag next to the register.

"What is the housekeeper's name?" she asked.

"Sally, we call her. Chinee girl. Works cheap."

The office door opened behind her and Will Worth came in, struggling with his camera and ungainly tripod. He was a big soft man with a moon face and ginger-colored mutton-chop side-whiskers; on Park Row, they called him Willie Worthless. "I got the pictures of the room," he said.

"Pictures?" the clerk said, his smile curdling quickly. "You didn't tell me you were going to take no pictures. You paid a nickle to look at the room where that terrible thing happened, but that don't entitle you to take no pictures."

"Oh," Willie Worth said meekly. "How much to take pictures?"

"One dollar," the man said, smirking. "One dollar American. For pictures.

"Willie, get your hand out of your pocket," snapped Kate. "He's been totally useless and we're not paying him another penny.

"Not my fault I don't know them people you been asking about," the clerk complained. "You got any more names wrote down there? Maybe I know the next one."

Kate Hawthorne looked at her list. "Samuel Shine tended bar in the saloon downstairs."

"Oh, him. Him I know." He favored her with his greasy smile again.

"Well?" Kate prompted.

"Ain't seen that dollar," he pointed out.

"How about Mary Healey?" Kate asked.

"Sure, I know how you can find her."

"Lizzie the Angel?"

"Her too. I know 'em all."

"I see. What did Lizzie do here, since you know her so well?"

"She, uh, she was the assistant night clerk."

"Goddamn," Kate swore. She wadded up her notes, and jammed them violently into her small leather handbag. "You don't know any of them, and I'm not going to pay you for your wretched lies." She turned to Will Worth. "Should I bother looking at the room?" she asked him.

"It's just a room," Worth said. "Someone was sick in there. You can still smell it. You can see some bloodstains on the wall, but they're kind of faded now. Brown. Maybe they're just dirt."

"Oh, splendid," Kate exclaimed in disgust. "Come on, we're leaving." She walked briskly from the office. The clerk's shouted protestations chased her down the stairs and through the dim hall. Will Worth followed behind like a huge soft puppy, until he banged his tripod up against a doorjamb. Kate pushed ahead, out of the building; she needed a breath of fresh air.

At this hour of the morning, Catherine Street was all astir with noise and activity. She could hear a distant roar of steam and the pounding of great hammers from the boiler factory around the corner on Water street, and columns of smoke as dark as a black knight's plume rose up from its stacks into a gray sky. A swarm of small, dirty children swept past her, shrieking with glee and breathing hard, intent on some wild game. At the cross streets two teamsters were screaming at each other, one in Italian and one in raw gutter English. They looked almost twins, with their slouch hats, grimy hair and furious red faces. Their wagons, one laden with coal and the other with barrels of beer, sat blocking all traffic while they argued. All four corners were occupied by saloons, Kate noted. She watched the people going in and out, the gaunt wiry men with dirty faces, the obvious drunkards, the gang toughs, the children with their tin buckets, the whores young and old, alone or in male company. She watched them and she let her anger build, waiting for Will Worth.

"This is infuriating," she told him when he finally emerged behind her. "First the police tell me that all the files are lost and now all the witnesses have vanished mysteriously." Kate considered that for a moment, with the beginnings of a speculative gleam in her gray-green eyes. "Vanished mysteriously," she repeated. "Perhaps I could write something about that."

"A tenement lodging house," Worth said, "hell, there's nothing mysterious about it, Kate. People don't work for long in these kinds of places. It's been four years."

"So all we have is a photograph of a four-year-old bloodstain?" she said. "A bloodstain that could just as easily be simple filth?"

"We can say it's a bloodstain," Will Worth pointed out. "The color won't matter none."

"The Colonel will not be happy," Kate said. She was not very happy herself. This story had started off splendidly. The first article of hers they'd used, on page one, with her name right there in black and white, she couldn't have asked for more. Even Nellie Bly hadn't started off on the front page of the *New York World*. Of course, her mother had been mortified and Doctor Crittenden had telephoned to tell her that her prose was too good for the tawdry subject matter, but Kate didn't give a damn, they were finally taking her seriously. The *World* had noticed her, and the world could not be far behind. Sitting behind the massive city editor's desk, the Colonel had stroked the underside of his formidable handlebar mustache and smiled at her, a huge smile on a huge man, as he told her to go out and get the rest of the story.

And in the two weeks since that golden moment, Kate Hawthorne had worked day and night and come up with exactly nothing.

She'd gone back to the bucket-shop where she'd found Old Shakespeare, this time with Will Worth and camera in tow, intending to photograph the supposedly-dead woman and interview her about her demise. The barkeep pretended not to know who Kate was talking about until she paid him, and after that all he could say was that sometimes she came in and sometimes she didn't. That night she didn't. Kate stayed until legal closing, which was enforced punctually for perhaps the first time in bucket-shop's history, a backhanded tribute to the power of a crusading press, Kate thought. But it was small comfort.

They were back the next night and the night after. Kate saw a man get sick on swipes and Will Worth's camera was stolen, but nothing else was accomplished. A few people knew Old Shakespeare, but no one knew her real name, and no one knew where she lived, and no one knew how she could be found.

Kate Hawthorne was proud of her resourcefulness. After three futile nights and a half-dozen talks with the Colonel, she broadened her search. For a week she visited more bucket-shops, saloons, groggeries, and stale beer dives than she could count or remember, though most of them were of the character that Kate wished most devoutly to forget. She kept quiet, bought stale beer and pretended to drink it, tried to eavesdrop without drawing attention to herself. She heard nothing of use, and while she saw dozens of toothless, gray-haired prostitutes whose condition tore at her heart, none of them were Old Shakespeare, and worse, when she bought them drinks and tried to question them, none of them even *knew* of Old Shakespeare. Didn't these people read the *World*?

By then the story had died. Dana, who never missed a chance to sneer at the competition, had suggested in the *Sun* that it was only another case of "Jew Pulitzer" printing a sensational lie and had challenged the *World* to produce this gin-guzzling corpse it claimed to have unearthed. The other dailies were thunderous in their silence, though Kate knew damned well they must have sent out their own men to find Old Shakespeare after Kate's story had run. Maybe one of them *had* found her. Maybe the woman was in an uptown hotel room right now, under wraps, drinking gin from a bottle and telling her life story to some man from the *Herald*. The *Herald* men were notorious for things like that.

Meanwhile, the *World* was running stories about the bicycling craze, Turkish atrocities somewhere or other (there was no beating the Turks for a good atrocity, the Colonel liked to say), and cannibalism in New Jersey, and the Colonel no longer smiled when Kate entered the city room. She tried to redeem herself with stories about the dreadful living conditions she'd witnessed in the tenements, but it had been no use. The Colonel had read her work in a stony silence and then barked out her name in a thunderclap bellow as big as he was. "What the hell is this?" he'd roared at Kate when she'd come running.

"My story," she'd said.

"Your *story*?" the Colonel said. "Well, maybe it's a story, but it damn well isn't news." He looked down at the handwritten sheets. "Let's see, you say here the Bowery whores dress poorly and have no teeth. Is that news, Caldwell?"

"Hell no," Caldwell had snapped back.

"The tenements are not pleasant places to live. That news to you, McCarren?"

McCarren cackled with malicious glee.

"Merciful god, says here there's sickness in those buildings, and little children don't have enough to eat, and some of these rotters drink too much and beat their wives bloody. Stop the presses, let's print an extra, eh, boys?" The Colonel looked around as laughter erupted from all sides.

Kate had turned bright red and stood very still, her lips pressed tightly together, bound and determined not to let her humiliation show. When they finally stopped laughing at her, she said stiffly, "I'll turn in my resignation if that what you're asking for, Colonel."

"Kate," the Colonel said, "if I damn well wanted to get rid of you, I wouldn't ask for your goddamned resignation, I'd fire your ass and before you could turn around you'd be out scraping your bustle off Park Row. Why in the name of hell should I fire you? You're on space, as long as you keep turning in copy like this we don't have to pay you one goddamned cent of Mister Pulitzer's money." He took her story firmly between two large, pale, soft hands and ripped it in half. Then he looked up and saw her grim face and sighed from deep within his massive three-hundred pound body. "It was well written," he said. "Ten years ago, it might have made great copy, but we've all read Jake Riis' book. What was that title?"

"*How the Other Half Lives*," Kate muttered.

The Colonel folded his hands together. His brown hair was parted in the middle and slicked down, the thick flesh of his neck squeezed out over his stiff winged collar, and he had dark circles of sweat under his arms, but his eyes were not without kindness. "Be grateful the old man is in Europe on the yacht," he said to her. "I'm damned gentle compared to him. Now, hell, I wouldn't have taken you on, even on space, if I didn't think you could do the goddamned job. Give me *news*, Kate. News is something I don't already know. Go after this Old Shakespeare business from another angle, damn it. But don't write me any more goddamned stories about how the poor don't have much money! You got that?"

"Yes, Colonel," she'd said, and she had actually left the city room feeling strangely encouraged. As stinging as it had been, the dressing-down was a sign of progress, Kate thought. She had seen the Colonel give the same, or worse, to a half-dozen other reporters in the weeks that she'd been in and out of the city room, but he had always treated her with a certain reserve and deference, like a child, or a delicate lady. Now he was treating her like a reporter. She went back on the streets determined to *be* a reporter.

And where it had all gotten her? Nowhere, she reflected bitterly. All all the police files were lost, it appeared that every single witness in the case was gone as well, and the bricks of the East River Hotel were as frustrating and incommunicative as its staff. Again she would have to go back to the Pulitzer Building and the Colonel empty-handed.

"Aren't you coming?" Will Worth asked her. He had walked several paces up Catherine Street, his camera and tripod perched on one pudgy shoulder, before he had noticed that Kate wasn't keeping up with him.

"I suppose so," Kate Hawthorne said with resignation. She caught up to him. "Quickly now, Willie," she said bitterly, "home to the Colonel, to take my medicine like a good girl." She started off down the sidewalk at a brisk pace.

It was only a short walk from the East River Hotel, or the Fourth Ward Hotel, or whatever they were calling that dismal place this week, to Park Row, where the *World* stood head-and-shoulders above the other newspaper buildings that lined the busy street. Convenient from a reporter's point of view, no doubt, but Kate appreciated the symbolism of the location as well, a symbolism that Mister Bennett had sacrificed when he moved his *Herald* way uptown to its proud isolation on what they were now calling Herald Square.

For Kate, it seemed as though the heart of the metropolis beat at Park Row and Printing House Square; at times, standing by Ben Franklin's statue or looking down from the golden dome, Kate almost fancied she could hear it pounding. City Hall Park and the seats of county and city government were right across the street. Broadway ran past the far side of the Park, and met Park Row just to the south, and to the north Park Row turned into Chatham Street and shortly crossed the Bowery, and there you had it, Broadway with the sunlight by day and the blaze of electricity by night, its paving stones ringing with the clatter of hooves and all manner of fashionable footsteps, and the Bowery in the perpetual shadow of its overhanging elevated tracks, where the noises were the rattle of crowded cars upon the tracks and the hiss and roar of the steam engines that pulled them, where the facades of the old buildings that housed the street's endless stale-beer dives and dime museums were black with smoke and soot, and cinders drifted down like pigeon droppings onto the shabby coats of the men and women below. Broadway and the Bowery, sunlight and shadow, the two faces of the city, and the press was right between them, close to both, where it belonged.

And to the east, the eighth wonder of the world, the Great Bridge to Brooklyn, climbed high into the sky upon its massive stone towers, its broad roadway stretching away over the East River, the wonder of all who beheld it, one of the great triumphs of humanity...and yet, with what Kate Hawthorne thought grim irony, some of the worst crimes of humanity festered in the dingy five-story tenements that stood in the perpetual shadow cast by the looming stones of the Great Bridge.

Close by the foot of the Bridge, the Pulitzer Building rose sixteen stories above Park Row, crowned by a high cupola with a golden dome and a flagpole. The other reporters told Kate that Joe Pulitzer had put it up on the site of a fancy hotel that had once refused him admittance. Only five years ago it had been the tallest edifice in the city. It was still one of the proudest. The golden dome caught the first rays of the rising sun at dawn, and blazed with reflected sunlight all day. From that lofty eyrie, the *World* men could see far up the bay and across to Brooklyn, could look down on City Hall, could watch the elevated trains running north and south, and could see at a glance the champagne lights of Broadway and the swipes-soaked darkness of the tenements. From there, Joe Pultizer could spit on the *Sun*.

Kate could see the *World* by the time she and Will Worth reached Chambers street, the golden dome looming over the low rooftops of the tenements, gleaming even beneath a cold iron-gray December sky, and as always the sight stirred her romantic sensibilities. For Kate Hawthorne, the *World* was aptly named, and that high golden dome sparkled with meaning: all the adventure of life, all the glory and riches of the world, everything high and bright and fine, art and intellect and dreams of love and truth. All the nobler human aspirations stirred beneath that cupola, she thought. Dana said of his *Sun* that "It shines for all," but his light was flickering now, and if justice lived anywhere in the sprawling, dirty, clamorous city it lived beneath the golden dome, where blind Joseph Pulitzer lifted the scales.

The sight was an inspiration to Kate Hawthorne, now as always; it restored her and filled her with new determination and a sense of excitement that made her blood run hot. But around her swirled the ceaseless stream of humanity, shouting, swearing, running, pushing each other aside, looking down at the gutter, blind to the tall golden promise that stood so close before them. "What do you think it's like for them, Will?" she asked the photographer. "How do you imagine they feel, living like this and looking up every day and seeing it?"

"It?" he said.

"The golden dome," Kate said. "Do you think it inspires them? Or does it infuriate them instead? Does it represent justice to them, or the worldly wealth they'll never have?"

"Them?" Will Worth said. "Who do you mean, Kate?"

Kate Kawthorne gave a vague wave at the crowded, noisy street scene. "Them," she snapped, irritated at his dullness. "All of them, Will, any of them. The poor. The teamster there." His wheels had locked, he was swearing a blue streak in a language Kate didn't even recognize. "That vegetable man." A turnip-seller, Italian from his look, with missing teeth and an ingratiating smile. Lacking a horse, he was pulling his small wagon himself. "The newsboy." Holding up the *Morning Journal*, read all about it, strange case of bigamy, man with six wives. "Those toughs by the alley." The oldest was maybe twelve, the youngest half that age, Kate could

hardly tell the boys from the girls. "The old woman in the horrid wig."
It was horrid, some kind of frightful horsehair, dyed bright yellow, and
the woman wearing it might have been forty or even thirty, but she looked
eighty. "The man in the policeman's jacket, there, ducking down that
alley." But he was no policeman, Kate saw at a glance, the jacket was
much too small and one sleeve was had been ripped off, and under it he
had a bright red flannel shirt.

Kate stopped dead, frowning. She knew him. Didn't she? He was
gone now, vanished down that alley, but she *had* known him.

"They don't think about it, Kate," Will Worth was saying. "They
were born here, they're just used to it. Most of them probably don't even
notice it any more."

"What?" Kate said. She hadn't been paying attention. "Of course,"
she blurted. "The bucket-shop! He was the one who put her up to it!"

"Who? What?" Will said, confused. He stopped beside her.

"I've got to go after him," Kate said. "I'll see you back at the *World*,
I have to talk to that man."

"Him? Who? Shouldn't I go with you? Just to protect you?" Kate
had already started toward the street. She stifled the impulse to tell him
that he would be about as useful in a dangerous situation as would her
mother. Less, probably; her mother at least had a withering stare and a
caustic tongue. "I'll be fine," she shouted, and that was all the time for
shouting she had, as she hurried across the street with as much speed as
she could manage.

The alley mouth her quarry had vanished into was a brick archway
between a cellar groggery whose sign proclaimed, "ALL OUR DRINKS
3 CENT," and a five-story tenement house. Passing under it was like
entering a tunnel; the buildings pressed closely, shutting out the light,
and the passage was fragrant with the smell of the sewer. Kate gathered
up her courage and the hem of her long skirt. Hiking it several inches
above her ankle, presently clad in a high patent-leather button shoe, she
took a deep breath and plunged on through, wading through an inch of
indescribable filth and several yards of dimness before passing under another
brick archway into a tiny courtyard.

Brick buildings, pockmarked by blind windows crusted over with dirt,
hemmed her in on every side, and a maze of clotheslines intersected overhead, crossing each other up, down and sideways in a web of poverty, drooping beneath the weight of countless flannel shirts, union suits, baggy trousers,
and faded cotton skirts. The cobblestones of the courtyard were slimy with
sewage, and from the ancient well at its center thick, noxious fumes rose like
steam into the cold air. Everywhere she turned, Kate was confronted by closed
doorways, cheap paint flaking from the gray wood. She saw only one way left

open; a pair of slanting doors down to some dank cellar were agape in the darkest angle of the courtyard.

Kate Hawthorne moved toward them. A dozen stone stairs, wet and crumbling and slippery, led down into the dark. From somewhere below, she heard rough male voices. The only word she made out distinctly was one she was not supposed to know. Again she hesitated. Her mother would be aghast to think of her going down into some cellar in the tenements, chasing a man she hadn't even been properly introduced to. Did she really know what she was getting into? Then she thought of what the Colonel would say if she went back to the *World* without a story. She went down the stairs with a bravura she did not really possess, and stepped out into the basement.

An ancient kerosene lantern, hung from a sweaty pipe that ran along the ceiling, swung slowly to and fro, bathing the scene in an unsteady light that made the shadows shift and sway. A half-dozen men were crowded around a scarred table, peering down intently into a wooden box, and talking to each other in loud voices. "He's a big son of a bitch, he is," proclaimed one of them, a skinny, stoop-backed man in a much-patched black suit. The cellar smelled of beer and blood, and several of the men had obviously been drinking. They were so intent on whatever they had in the box that none of them seemed to notice her.

"Excuse me," she said loudly.

All conversation stopped. They looked at her. A short, grizzled man with big pop-eyes gaped at her. "Hih," said the skinny man in black. Kate wasn't certain if he was laughing or blowing his long, hooked nose. "Looky, boys," he continued in a thin nasal voice. "A Fifth Av'noo lady's come to play with the Gophers."

Kate ignored him. "I want to talk to you," she said crisply to the man she had followed, the brawny young man in the torn policeman's jacket. The lantern light found gold and orange highlights in his dirty hair and full red beard. "We've met before," Kate told him.

The comment provoked a storm of nasty laughter. "Met her, did you, Mike?" smirked the man in the black suit. "Hih. And here she comes crawlin' back for another taste."

"Shut y' mouth, Slyne, or I'll be shuttin' it for you," Mike said bluntly. He looked at Kate. "Yer lyin' through y' damned teeth, " he said. "I never met you."

"It's the clothes," Kate said. "I write for the *New York World* " she said, "and I was in disguise when we last encountered one another. Think back to the bucket-shop on Cherry, several weeks ago. I bought Old Shakespeare her gin."

Mike gave her a long, hard scrutiny, looking her up and down with a frakness that would have made her blush a year ago. "Jesus, Mary, and Joseph," he said. Then he laughed.

Slyne turned and plucked up the wooden box from the table. "Lemme show her what we got, Mike," he said. He came toward her with long gliding strides, clutching the box to his chest. "Fifth Av'noo ladies like furry little things, don't they? You can write us up in y' paper, hih." That was definitely a laugh, Kate had decided, although an altogether nasty little sound, *hih-hih-hih*, made more of malice and mucous than of merriment. He thrust the box toward her.

Kate Hawthorne had a pretty good idea of what was in that box, but she was damned if she was going to let him frighten her. She stepped forward boldly to meet him halfway, and peered down into the box at the biggest rat she had ever seen, a greasy black wharf rat the size of Sultan, her mother's pampered white tomcat. "It's a very handsome rat," she forced herself to say, impressed by her own aplomb.

Then Slyne started going *hih-hih-hih* as if he were choking to death, and the rat tried to climb out of the box to get at her. Its tiny yellow eyes brimmed with hostility, and it scrabbled at the sides of its prison with soft pink paws that looked almost like little hands, its hairless pink tail lashing from side to side. Slyne was tilting the box, and for one horrid moment Kate thought he was going to dump the creature down her bodice. She backed off, fighting desperately for her composure. Slyne followed with long mincing steps, *hih-hih*ing every inch of the way as he backed her toward a corner.

But then suddenly it was Slyne whining and backing away, bent over his rat, and the man in the policeman's jacket, Mike, was pushing at him roughly, and cuffing him with his fist. "No, Mike," Slyne was saying. "Hih, just a fun, Mike, hih hih, no harm to 'er, hih."

Mike shoved the thin, stooped man up against the cellar wall, took the big hooked nose between thumb and forefinger, and twisted it painfully until Slyne began to squeal. "You're just the boy for fun, Slyne. Ain't that so? Ain't it god's truth?"

"Hih, hih," Slyne said, with an ingratiating grin, bobbing his head in agreement, all the time sheltering his rat with his scrawny arms, as if he feared Mike would do the creature in. "I likes me fun too," Mike said. "I been thinkin' it'd be jolly if you was to yam that rat of yers." The other men in the cellar were grinning at each other in anticipation.

"Oh no, Mikey," Slyne said. "No, I'm going to sell 'im to the Rat King, Mikey, he's a big son of a bitch, betcha I get me dews for 'im, I do, hih."

Mike gave Slyne the back of his hand hard across one thin, stubbly cheek, snapping his head half-around. The sound of the blow was a sharp crack that made Kate wince. "Eat 'im," Mike said, in a voice that left no room for appeal.

Slyne was shaking badly. Averting his eyes, he thrust one skinny hand down into the box. Something thumped and there was a furious scrabbling

sound, but when he pulled his hand out Slyne was holding the rat by its long
pink tail. In a blink, the creature had climbed up its own tail and fastened its
claws on Slyne's hand, but he gave his wrist a hard snap and sent it swinging
again. Then he lifted it up over his head.

"Open y' damned yap, or it'll bite off y' boke," called out the pop-eyed
man.

Kate could not watch any more. "*Stop it!*" she shouted.

They all looked at her, startled. Mike smiled. "Y' heard her, Slyne," he
said. "It's lucky y' are. Out of here." He turned around. "All of y', out of here."

Quick as if he were a rodent himself, Slyne thrust the rat back into its
box, tucked it under one long black-clad arm, and scrambled for the stairs so
fast that Kate had to hurry to get out of his way. The other men did not linger
long behind him. Kate Hawthorne felt Mike looking at her. "Thank you,"
she said awkwardly, looking back over her shoulder, at the coal bin in the
back, toward the furnace, anywhere but at him.

His walk was half swagger and half rude grace. He came over to her and
inspected her again from up close before pulling out a chair, sinking down
into it, and kicking his heavy-shod feet up on the table. "So y' come to talk to
Mike," he said, lacing his fingers together at the back on his head.

Kate was still feeling a little shaken, but she took hold of herself firmly.
"I'm searching for Old Shakespeare," she said in a businesslike voice. "That
night in the bucket-shop, you seemed to know her. If you can lead me to her,
I'll pay you."

"Sure, you'll be payin' me, is it?" He seemed to find that amusing. "What's
y' name?"

"Katherine Hawthorne," she said, "of the *New York World.*"

"Well, Katie, pleased t' make yer acquaintance," he said, a sly smile gleaming through the red hair of his beard.

"You have the advantage of me," Kate said.

"That's right," he said. He laughed.

"I mean," said Kate, "what's *your* name?"

"Mike," he said.

"That's all?" Kate asked, with a hint of annoyance in her voice.

He shrugged. "Irish Mike," he said, "or Mike the Gopher, or Mike the
Hammer, or Red Mike, or Hoolie. Take y' pick."

"Red Mike," said Kate, "will do nicely, I suppose. Do you know where
Old Shakespeare is?"

"Maybe I do," he said, "and maybe I don't."

"I offered to pay you for whatever information you have."

Red Mike shook his head. "Jesus, Mary, and Joseph," he said. "You think
I need rhino?"

"Rhino?" Kate said, confused.

"Money," Red Mike explained, as if he were talking to a particularly stupid child. "Now, if I were wantin' whatever you got in that bitty little leather bag there, I'd take it off y', and there wouldn't be much you'd be doin' to stop me, would there? Y' see this coat I'm wearin'?"

"A policeman's jacket," Kate said.

"Now, did y' think the crusher just up and gave it to me, on account of me sweet face?" He laughed. "I took it off him, and he didn't like it one bit, I'm tellin' y'. Tried to hit me with that little stick o' his, for all the good it did 'im. The coat means I'm a Gopher, a real Gopher, not like them." He waved his hand casually at the stairs that led up to the dingy courtyard, dismissing his erstwhile companions.

Kate Hawthorne knew that she might be naive where the ways of the tenement streets were concerned, but she was damned if she was going to stay that way. "A Gopher," she said. "That's some kind of a gang, isn't it? Like the Bowery Boys?" She had heard of the Bowery Boys. She had even seen a play about them once.

"The Bowery Boys," Red Mike said, "ain't been around for years and years, but any damn cop knows the Gophers."

"Why do they call you Gophers?" Kate asked, curious.

Red Mike swept his hand around, at the dim cellar, the kerosene lamp, the coal and the darkness. "This is the why of it, Katie. I hear gophers like it under the ground, where they can be gettin' about dark and secret. When the crushers come lookin' for one o' our boys, we know a few things too. I could show you a place or two, girlie."

"I'm sure you could," she said dubiously.

"Y' got all kinds o' tunnels down there," he said, with a gleam in his eye. "Tunnels and sewers and cellars and all kinds o' secret ways. You got rats down there make Slyne's little pet look like nothin' at all, I'm tellin' you, rats big as Irish wolfhounds, Katie. Ask the Rat King if you think I'm lyin' to you. But it ain't all bad, no. I got me a secret place down there, a real sweet place. Someday maybe I'll be showin' it to you, if you're nice to Red Mike." He smiled.

There was a story in this, Kate Hawthorne realized suddenly. Would this be something the Colonel would already know? Surely not. A gang of rogues who robbed policemen for their jackets and hid underground to escape arrest? *Like the furtive beast from which they take their name, the Gophers thrive in the dark winding ways beneath the earth, and come up only by night to work their violent deeds*, she thought, although she'd really need to find out a little about their violent deeds before she could write the story. That would make the Colonel smile, Kate was sure of it. And if there was some way she could get Red Mike to tell her more, or even a way to penetrate the gang the way that Nellie Bly had penetrated Blackwell's Island, why, there was no telling how big a story this might be!

But her train of thought reminded her that she had a more immediate assignment to worry about, and that this rude, arrogant, uncouth man in the torn's policeman's jacket was her last hope, her only possible lead. "I must speak to Old Shakespeare," she said. "Will you tell me where to find her or not?"

"Well, maybe she don't want to be found by the likes o' you," Red Mike said.

"Then you do know where she is?" Kate snapped.

"Sure." He grinned, and ran his thick fingers back through that tangle of red hair.

"You won't tell me?"

"Now, don't be hearin' things I didn't say, Katie. I just said I didn't want y' money, that's all." He stood up and stretched lazily. She could see the muscles flex under the tightness of the blue jacket. "Even when I saw y' that other night, dressed in rags and all, I was thinkin to meself, 'Mike, that's one bleak molly over there'."

"One bleak molly?" Kate echoed.

"That means I like the way you look, Katie," he said. He took a step toward her, smiling. "Bleak as they come, and I'm bettin' you're sweet and warm under all them posh things you're wearin' there."

Kate Hawthorne edged backward toward the stairs. If he really came after her, she was suddenly aware, there was no way she could hope to outrun him, dressed as she was, and no way she could possibly overpower him either. Briefly, she found herself wishing that Will Worth was with her after all. Or better yet, her mother. "Keep away, I warn you," she said. She opened her purse, thrust her hand inside, and brandished the small leather handbag threateningly. "I've got a revolver in here," she said.

"Do you now?" Red Mike said. ""Then you'll be wanting to show it to me, won't you?" He came closer.

"Don't you dare lay a hand on me," Kate said loudly. "I'm with the *New York World*."

Surprisingly, he stopped. "Well," he said. "And I wouldn't be wantin' the whole world after me, would I? Besides, I'm not that sort, Katie. I like the mollies free and easy." He taunted her with a crooked grin. "What I'm thinkin'," he said, "is maybe I could give you what you want, and you could give me something that I want."

"What?" Kate Hawthorne said suspiciously.

"I never mowed me a fancy harp like you before," he said.

"I don't know what you said," Kate Hawthorne told him, "but it sounded filthy."

Red Mike made a smacking sound with his lips. "A kiss, Katie. A kiss and I'll be tellin' ya where to find the ginny cow."

"A kiss," she said. She felt the blush beginning to creep up her neck. Her mother would have been shocked speechless, but Kate had read all of Victoria Woodhull's speeches, and she had tried her first kiss six years ago, in the gardens outside their cottage in Newport. His name had been Harold Vanderkellen and it had been anything but a transcendent moment, but Kate had conducted other, more successful experiments since. Stephen Blackwood knew quite a lot about kissing, and she remembered Mrs. Astor's spring ball, when he'd trapped her in a corner for a brief moment and hinted darkly that there were other things he might teach her as well, if they ever got the chance. Less than a month afterwards, he was gone to Europe.

Kate looked at Red Mike. He was a gangster, a cruel, hard-handed, semi-literate lout, probably a killer too, but in a certain rude, uncouth way, he made her think of Stephen, though he had no hint of the sullen moodiness the Blackwoods so often displayed. She reminded herself of all the dangers and indignities that Nellie Bly and Henry Stanley and Richard Harding Davis had been forced to suffer in pursuit of their great stories. If they could do it, so could Katherine Hawthorne. "All right," she said. "One kiss, and you tell me."

"Done," said Red Mike. He opened his arms and stepped toward her, grinning.

Kate Hawthorne poked him in the chest with a finger. "Stop. No one said anything about an embrace, or any sort of touching. Just a kiss. And not until you've told me what I need to know. I don't trust you."

Red Mike crossed his arms. "You're hard as you are bleak," he said. "Well, so be it. She don't want to be found. She heard that she got herself written up in that paper o' yours, and it put the fear in her, I hear. But she ain't far from here. Ask about her down to Bloody Meg's on Hester street."

"Bloody Meg's," Kate repeated. She smiled. This was exciting. A few years ago, she'd never have dreamed that she'd be going into dives with names like Bloody Meg's, hunting for corpses who refused to stay dead. "Thank you."

"Glad t' help y', Katie," he said. "And me kiss?"

"Stand right there," she said. She pointed at a spot on the floor. "And close your eyes."

"A hard one," he repeated. But he did as she told him, grinning all the while like that cat in Mr. Carroll's children's story. Kate felt a certain dryness in her throat. She swallowed, and then leaned forward quickly and gave him a kiss full on the lips. He smelled of tobacco and beer and the coarseness of his beard tickled her skin.

When his lips opened under hers, Kate pulled back in alarm. "Stop that. That's enough. You've been kissed."

"It's sweeter with some velvet in it," Red Mike said. "But I'd be no gentleman t' complain, would I?"

"We both got what we wanted," Kate said, backing away.

"You'll be wantin' to see me again," he told her, cock-sure. "Come up to Mallet Murphy's place on Battle Row and ask for me. "That won't be necessary, I'm sure," Kate said, as she climbed up the stairs.

"That's where you're wrong, Katie," he called after her, "that's where you're dead wrong."

Outside in the candle-lit dimness of the church, some elderly nun was droning her penance much too loudly. Her mumbled Hail Marys echoed through the hushed stillness of the empty pews, rising and falling like the tide of some prayerful sea, broken only by the sound of her rosary beads clicking together. The quavering voice penetrated even into the confessional, making it difficult for him to concentrate on the whisperings at hand. Fortunately, it was all the same old thing, so not much concentration was necessary, but if she went on much longer like that, she was going to give him a splitting headache. Maybe that was something to be desired. It was hot and stuffy in here, and a headache might help keep him awake.

Close at hand, the soft whispering stopped. He gave her some penace, a rosary or ten, and repressed the urge to instruct her to say them quietly. As she left the confessional with a swish of fabric, he moved to the other side of the booth to deal with the next one, waiting in the second curtained alcove.

He slid back the wooden panel and peered through the black gauze— he'd cut a little slit in the cloth, just in case he didn't recognize the voice—and there she was. Suddenly he felt a lot better. By now his eyes had grown accustomed to the dark, and he knew her face at once by the faint light that leaked in through the curtain. The pious solemnity of her expression could not change that generous mouth, and the severe nun's headdress that hid her ears and hair did nothing at all to disguise her full cheeks and robust color. The years had faded her freckles some, but the pug nose was still the same.

When she heard the panel rasp open behind the cloth, she clasped her hands together in the attitude of prayer and lowered her eyes—lovely big green eyes, he remembered, innocent, trusting, warm—unwilling to look at him even though he was quite invisible in the darkness behind the gauze. "Bless me, Father, for I have sinned," she whispered, and she began to tell him her transgressions.

Ned Cullen listened attentively until she got thoughts. "Impure thoughts," he interrupted, "are best gotten rid of by impure deeds.

The nun's face came up sharply and she blinked, as if she could not have heard right. "Pardon me, Father?"

"Impure deeds," Ned repeated. "That's your penance, Sister. Far more diverting than the rosary. Come see me in the rectory after confession is over."

Her mouthed opened in a tiny shocked oh, and her clasped hands flew apart like two doves flushed from cover.

Ned Cullen chuckled softly.

The nun's face suddenly grew suspicious. "You're not Father Flynn," she said in an urgent whisper. "Who's in there?"

"Not so loud, Mary Elizabeth," Ned said. "It's me. Ned."

"*Ned*!" she repeated, much too loudly.

"Ssssh," he said. "Quiet."

"Ned Cullen," she said, but quieter, quieter. "Of course it's Ned Cullen. Damn you to hell." The nun made a fist. "What have you done to Father Flynn?"

"Me? Why, nothing. He was called away suddenly to perform the last rites for a poor dying man. I saw the whole thing, Mary Elizabeth. Awful. A full team of horses, and then the wheel crushed the life right out of the fellow. God only knows how long the poor soul can keep on breathing. Fortunately, once I'd impressed the urgency on Father Flynn, he was ready to leave at once. I even lent him my cab." Ned smiled. "That hack had no sense of direction, though. By now the good father might be up in Harlem, for all I know. Wouldn't surprise me a bit."

"What are *you* doing in there?" she demanded, if you can demand in a hoarse whisper.

"Well, Father Flynn did put up a little sign that there would be no confession today, but I couldn't let that happen, could I? The whole neighborhood knows that the sisters from St. Henry's convent cleanse their soiled souls here every week. I always thought I had a vocation. I never thought you did, though. Black and white aren't your colors, Mary Elizabeth."

Mary Elizabeth was trying very hard to look angry and shocked, but the thin hint of a smile kept breaking through despite everything she could do. "This is a mortal sin, Ned Cullen," she whispered. "You'll burn in hell for this. And I'm Sister Joseph now."

"Sister Joseph?" said Ned incredulously. Thinking of Mary Elizabeth as a Joseph was harder than imagining Sarah's breasts covered with owls. "I think I prefer Mary Elizabeth," he said.

"How did you find me?" she asked.

"Your neighbors were always very helpful. Mrs. Callahan seems to know what's become of everyone in the building, except your damned brother. I was sorry to hear about your father."

"I'll believe that, Ned Cullen, just as much as I believe you were in love with me four years ago. It was you killed him, you know. When he found out what you'd done to his daughter." "Don't be cruel to me, Mary Elizabeth," Ned said, with hurt in his voice. "I went through a lot to find you again. I had to listen to Mrs. Callahan for over an hour before she'd get to the point, and then I had to track down your convent, and then I had to face your Mother Superior. She reminds me of Bennett on a bad day, though I dare say the Commodore would look better in a habit. Any sacrilege that's been done here is squarely on her head. She wouldn't let me see you." Ned winced. "What sort of lies did she hear about me anyway?"

"Nothing but the truth, Ned Cullen," the former Mary Elizabeth Fitzgerald said sternly.

"The truth? That's a foul blow. In any case, I've paid for this conversation with suffering. It's stuffy in here, Mary Elizabeth, and those nuns have the most boring sins I've ever heard, except for the Mother Superior. She has no sins at all. So be kind to me."

"What do you want? And don't tell me you've come back because you love me. I'm not eighteen any more." Sister Joseph scowled at him through the gauze.

"You're cute when you get angry," Ned said. "I can't lie to a nun. I have to find your brother."

"Eddie?"

"How many brothers do you have? Eddie."

"Oho," she said. "If I weren't a bride of Christ—"

"Christ is a lucky man," Ned interrupted. "The Lord's gain is my loss."

"—if I wasn't a nun, I'd tell you where to find Eddie," she said. "But I can't have a murder on my soul. Father Flynn is too old to hear those sorts of confessions. It's his heart." "Listen to me," Ned whispered, putting urgency in his voice. "I know your brother has it in for me, but I have to find him, regardless of my personal risk. I owe it to him. This is for his own good, Mary Elizabeth. If I don't find him, the police certainly will."

"The police?" she said skeptically.

"Don't you read the papers?" Ned asked. "That old woman who was ripped up in his hotel four years ago, they've just discovered she wasn't who they thought she was. And the police have lost all the files on the case, or so they say." He raised an eyebrow. "They're looking into it again, don't you see? On the sneak. They want your brother and when they find him, it will go badly for him. They know he lied to them."

Sister Joseph squawked with indignation. "He lied because *you* told him to lie, Ned Cullen! He trusted you and it just got him in deeper and deeper. You told him not to worry, that you'd take care of everything, that you'd solve the case, and Eddie believed you just like I did, both of us must have been soft in the head, because two days later you were gone with nary even a goodbye and when I called the *Herald*, they said you were off to Europe, and by then, what was Eddie to do but stick to his story? He was sick about it. They blamed that man Frenchy and Eddie knew he didn't do it, Frenchy was the one Eddie was taking upstairs when he found the body, he couldn't have been the one, but Eddie couldn't say a thing or they'd have put him in prison too. *Damn* you, Ned Cullen! You're a liar and a sinner and I don't even know why I'm talking to you."

"I don't know why either," Ned said sorrowfully. "You're a good woman, Mary Elizabeth, and I never deserved your affection. Perhaps you ought to hear my confession, though I don't think some of the things I've done could ever be forgiven.

That confused her. "God forgives us all, Ned," she whispered.

"Well," he said, "perhaps there's hope for me yet. I've done some time in hell already, working for that devil Bennett. Mary Elizabeth, believe me, I never meant to leave you as I did, or to embroil poor Eddie in trouble. I was called away suddenly, unexpectedly. It was urgent *Herald* business, a matter of life and death, and I'd like to think my presence made the difference between war and peace over there."

"Over where?" asked Mary Elizabeth.

"I can't say, dear. I promised never to talk about it. I've never even told Commodore Bennett the whole story. I know that doesn't excuse what I did, but I take some consolation from the knowledge that perhaps I saved a few thousand lives over there, even if my actions did cost an innocent man his freedom back here in the city."

Her features softened. "You sound so troubled, Ned."

"I," he started, "well, I don't always sleep well at night."

"Ned," she said. She put out a hand tentatively, pressed her palm to the gauze partition behind them. "I wish I could see your face. It's been a long time. I missed you a lot after you went away. I prayed you'd come back to me, though father kept saying he'd kill you if you did. If you're telling me the truth and you really stopped a war somehow, then God forgives you, I know."

"And you?" Ned asked.

She looked down. "And me," she said, so softly he could scarcely hear her.

"Mary Elizabeth," Ned Cullen said, "I won't feel right about myself until I can set this business straight. My honor is at stake here. That's why I have to find your brother. All of the witnesses are gone, the people at the hotel, they've left their jobs or been replaced, every one of them. And this business of the lost files, well, that's a fraud for sure. Something's afoot, dear, something is definitely afoot, and your brother is going to be right in the middle of it whether he likes it or not. I must speak to him, and you're my only hope, Mary Elizabeth."

"Coney Island," she whispered.

In the darkness of the confessional, Ned grinned. "Coney Island," he repeated. "Where?"

"The Coney Island Athletic Club," she said. "He's a prize fighter now."

"Oh, great," Ned said, with a notable lack of enthusiasm. As if Eddie hadn't been sufficiently soft in the head to begin with. But he recovered quickly. "I don't know how to thank you, Mary Elizabeth," he said. She was looked right at him through the gauze. "I'm only a novice," she said. "I haven't taken my final vows yet."

"Hmmmm," said Ned. "I'll keep that in mind. But, really, Mary Elizabeth, I'm not good enough for you. Especially now that you're married to God." He smiled, though it was wasted in the darkness. "Now, for your penance, I want you to think about the things I taught you that night on the roof."

"Ned Cullen!" she said.

"Well, I'd better be going before I ruin your reputation, Sister Joseph," he said. "You've been in here so long they'll be certain you did something extraordinarily wicked. I bet you'll be the talk of the convent." Ned stood up. Another dozen nuns were lined up outside, waiting for their turn in the confessional, but Ned had assigned enough Hail Marys for one day's work, and if he tried to stick it out to the end he was afraid he'd begin snoring softly right in the middle of some elderly nun's best impure thoughts. "I can't go on with blasphemous masquerade," he said. "I'm off to see the elephant. Tell them you exposed me as an imposter and I ran off like the sacrilegious dog that I am."

Before she could reply, Ned Cullen gathered up his walking stick, gloves and pearl gray derby, opened the door, and popped out of the priest's booth. Two dozen nuns stared at him in astonishment and chagrin. "Quickly!" he shouted "It's Sister Joseph, I think she's fainted!" At least half of the sisters uttered mews of concern and began to move toward the confessional. Ned donned his hat, dodged the Mother Superior, and sprinted up the aisle.

For a man who had a fat moneybelt and a appetite for drink or women or both, there was no better place south of the Tenderloin than the Silver Dollar Saloon on Essex Street, across from the Essex Market Court. It glittered. One thousand genuine silver dollars were embedded in the floor. The giant cut-crystal chandelier sparkled from the light reflected off another five hundred polished cartwheels. On the wall behind the long mahogany bar, were a huge star and crescent, and they were made of silver dollars as well. The spittoons were bright and shiny, and the walls were hung with oil paintings in ornate frames, paintings that most of the patrons agreed were real artistic.

The glasses were crystal, and scrupulously clean, washed and rinsed after every single use. They had beer on draft, but they had bottle beer from Milwaukee too, for those who had the price of it. Iced champagne and deep red claret from France, whisky from Scotland and Ireland, cold crisp gin, all of it was available, no charge for the ice, and when you bought a drink at the Silver Dollar Saloon you knew it wouldn't be watered.

The girls were as fine as the drinks; pretty young things, most of them still in their teens and none older than thirty, gay girls with warm hands and smiles that lit up their faces, fresh young girls whose laughter sparkled like the silver dollars in the floor, got up bright as cartwheels in all the colors of the rainbow and some no rainbow had ever heard tell of, mauve and cobalt and cerise, drinking and dancing and giggling in swirling taffeta petticoats and loose velvet dresses that showed a hint of the scarlet corsets that cinched their tiny waists and swelled out the soft pink treasures of their bosom for the gentlemen to admire, and tickle if they had a mind to. The Silver Dollar had rooms upstairs too, very nicely furnished, and all the girls were free and easy and they loved champagne and wit and good times, or else they wouldn't have been there.

The crowd glittered too. Henry Munce walked in the door that blustery December night and scowled. At one table he saw a detective he knew deep in conversation with two of the city's most accomplished dips. Another table was crowded with Tammany politicians, laughing and drinking champagne, with a congressman in the middle of it, playing slap-and-giggle with the girl on his lap, a buxom dark-haired little thing in purple and yellow who was fighting a losing mock battle against the representative's hands. Another girl, a tall, slender, sweet-faced molly who looked as though she'd come in fresh from some farm in Indiana, was being led upstairs by one of the leading heavyweight contenders. Munce swept the room with his deep-set, gloomy eyes, and saw bankers and bank-sneaks, actresses and playwrights, second-story men and tenement owners, police officials and brothel-keepers, novelists and reporters, clergymen and brewers and hired thugs and restaurateurs and shipping tycoons and gamblers and stockbrokers and, on every hand, pimps and whores. At the Silver Dollar Saloon, you couldn't toss a cartwheel into the air without it falling on one or the other. The Tenth Ward was the heart of what Dr. Parkhurst called the social evil and the daily press called the maiden tribute, and the Silver Dollar Saloon was the heart of the Tenth Ward.

Henry Munce removed his battered brown derby and tucked it under his arm with the papers he was carrying. He threaded his way through the tumult and the laughter, peering into the haze of cigar smoke until he finally spied the men he wanted. He went directly to their table. "Solomon," he said loudly. "Back in your office. I want to talk." He thumped the head of his walking stick down on the table hard enough to make the glasses jump, to be sure to get their attention.

Solomon had been deep in conversation with a respectable looking gentleman in a fur-collared overcoat, while his fixer, a seedy attorney named Max Hockstim, sat by his right hand as usual. All three of them looked up. "Munce," said Solomon, with a frown of annoyance, "Can't you see that I'm busy now? Or are you blind as well as short?" Hockstim laughed at the boss's wit. "Get yourself a drink," Solomon said, "on the house. I'll be with you when I can."

Henry Munce leaned on his walking stick and looked Charles R. Solomon right in the eye. That was the advantage of keeping your feet when talking to a seated man; Munce was not unaware of such advantages. "I am not thirsty," he said. "I am impatient. Now, Solomon. Your business can wait."

"I'll be the judge of that," Solomon replied. He was a sleek well-fed man, an ample stomach pushing at the buttons of his red silk vest. He wore a silver dollar as a watch fob, and a stickpin with a silver-mounted ruby as big as a pigeon's eye. Silver Dollar Smith they called him, except for Henry Munce, who preferred to call a spade a spade and Charles Solomon Charles Solomon; but call him Smith or Solomon or Sir, he was rich and powerful and well-connected with Tammany and the gangs and Wall Street, he was the lord of the Tenth Ward and the king of the pimps and white-slavers. Munce had done business with him before.

"You want I should call the sheriff and have shorty here tossed out in the gutter?" Max Hockstim asked pleasantly, nodding toward the sheriff in question, a red-faced ex-prizefighter who was drinking shots at the bar. The weedy little lawyer had a grudge against Henry Munce. Once in court he had told a judge, "Your honor, you sure look swell in the judicial vermin," and Munce had printed the quote and made him a laughingstock.

"No need," Silver Dollar Smith said, with a thin smile. "Munce will wait until my business here is done."

"I will expedite your business," Munce said. He turned his gaze on the third man at the table and looked him over carefully. The gentleman's clothing was conservative and costly, and he was so uncomfortable that he could not meet Munce's eyes. The glass in front of him was full of beer, but he had hardly touched it. "You are on Wall Street," Henry Munce said, and nodded when the man looked up, startled. "You have never been here before, but friends have told you about the Silver Dollar Saloon. You are here for a woman. Your wife is ill, or perhaps has refused to perform her marital duties." The man in the fur-collared coat looked away from him, bored now, a slight smile flickering across his face almost too quickly for anyone but Henry Munce to notice. "No, I am wrong," Munce said. He reflected for a moment, glanced sideways at Silver Dollar Smith, and read the answer there. "You have a woman," Munce said in his deep voice. "A young friend, as they say, no doubt prettier than your wife, and gayer. I will not venture to say where you procured her. You have enjoyed her favors for some time and you have been generous with her, but now she is grown greedy, or perhaps you are simply bored. You fear she may become a threat to your position."

The respectable gentleman's eyes widened in the second before he blinked and looked away. Solomon cleared his throat. "That's enough, Munce," he said.

"I am not done," said Henry Munce. He considered further, as the gentleman squirmed beneath his fixed, gloomy stare. "A threat, yes, perhaps she threatens to blackmail you. Silver Dollar Smith is the man to see, your friends tell you. So, here you are. Solomon can always use a fresh new girl, and he has many friends and business associates in other cities, even in Europe and the Orient. You are not here for a woman, no, that was my error, you are here to arrange to have a woman carried away. Yes. Yes, most definitely!"

"No," the man blurted. He shook his head. "No, that—no, you're wrong."

"Henry Munce is not wrong," said Henry Munce.

"Damn you, Munce," Solomon said. "Get out of here!"

"Sir," said Henry Munce to the stockbroker, "permit me to introduce myself. I am Henry Munce of the *New York Morning Journal*. Our readers will be most interested in your story. *Stockbroker Sells Mistress to White Slavers* shall be the headline, I think."

The stockbroker was up as fast as if he'd heard a roundsman shout "RAID!," running for the door like a slung shot, heedless of the people in the way. He did not even pause to reclaim his hat. Henry Munce turned to Silver Dollar Smith. "I see you are done with your business," he said. "If I might beg a moment of your time, I should be most grateful."

"I should have you killed, Munce," Solomon said with a poisonous cordiality.

"You are welcome to try," Munce replied. "Henry Munce is not easy to kill."

"In my office," snapped Solomon.

"Me too?" asked Max Hockstim.

"No," said Munce.

"No," echoed Solomon. Max made a grimace.

Silver Dollar Smith kept his office in the back of the saloon. It was a comfortable room with a big oak desk, a bigger black velvet couch, and several tall wingback chairs. The oil paintings that hung against the red, flocked wallpaper were even franker and more artistic than those outside. Solomon sent for a glass of claret and, when it had come, locked the office door against the raucous laughter from outside and seated himself behind the desk. "All right, Munce," he said, "suppose you start by telling me why the hell you stepped into my goddamned business? It was none of your damn concern!"

"Christian charity," said Henry Munce, "and love of my fellow man." He set his hat and stick upon the nearest chair and hopped up nimbly to seat himself on the corner of Solomon's desk, so he loomed over the man. "Perhaps you would have sent the girl off to Shanghai, perhaps to Brussels. What does it matter? You could always bring her back, as I'm sure you would have

informed your fleet-footed friend when the opportunity arose. A little sex, a
little fear, and the man is your lap dog. Henry Munce saved him from a life of
corrupt servitude."

Silver Dollar Smith frowned. "It wouldn't have hurt him none. A few
tips, some inside market information, a casual word or two as to the travelling
plans of his rich friends, what does it cost him? I've known you too damn long
to believe you suddenly turned into some kind of goody-goody, Munce. And
get the hell off my desk. I got chairs, y'know." He opened an elaborate porcelain humidor and selected a long, elegant Havana cigar. "You want a smoke?"

"I prefer my own," said Henry Munce. Reaching into the pocket of his
jacket, he pulled out half-smoked cigar four inches long and black as tar, and
lit it with a match he struck against his boot, filling the air with blue smoke.

"God, that's vile," Solomon complained. "What the hell you want with
me, you little son of a bitch? I'm a busy man, get on with it."

Henry Munce took the file from under his arm, laid it down on Smith's
blotter, and flipped it open to display a large grainy morgue photograph. "Who
is she?" he asked.

Solomon coughed and put aside his cigar. "Jesus," he said. "You make
me sick, Munce. What happened to her?"

"Strangled, ripped open, gutted," Munce said. "Four years ago. You read
about in the newspapers. They got it wrong. She was said to be a whore known
as Old Shakespeare." He shook his head. "That was not so. Do you know
her?" He turned over the photograph to show a second shot beneath, a closer
view of the woman's face and body.

Charles Solomon made a face and pushed back in his chair, regarding
Henry Munce directly and with displeasure. "Munce, I always knew you were
an insolent little son of a bitch, but I never figured you were stupid before.
Why the hell should I know someone like this?"

"She was a whore," said Henry Munce. "Whores and politicians are your
stock in trade."

Solomon plucked up his cigar, took a puff, and scowled. "Go outside,
Munce. Look around. Look at the girls. Sixteen years old, seventeen, fourteen, maybe twenty-three, twenty-five. All *young*, you understand? And pretty.
Sweet and gay as y'please." He leaned forward and flicked ashes on the photographs. "This one is forty if she's a day. Maybe fifty. Hell, maybe sixty. If she
even tried to come into my place, the sheriff would twist her damn head off.
This kind of owl only comes out at night, when you can't see so good, and
what she's got to sell she sells to ragpickers and sailors for twenty, thirty cents,
so she's got a bed to sleep in that night."

"I know," said Henry Munce.

"Then why the hell do you come bothering me?"

"Four years have passed since the woman died. In the dives and bucket-shops and tenements, that is too long. I have made inquiries in all the low places, to no avail. Stale beer and dog's nose soften the brain, toil and degradation break the body, death forever stills the tongue. They do not know her, they do not recognize the face, they have no memories, they are not the right people. She was old, yes. Before that she was young. She was the lowest class of whore. Before that she was a seamstress, a gay girl, a wife, something other than what she ended as. She was gray and wrinkled, made gaunt by hunger and sickness and bloated by drink. Before that she may have been pretty. She died alone, for reasons unknown. But once she must have had friends, blood relations, a husband, a pimp. Henry Munce intends to find them. Perhaps this woman's identity meant nothing to the man who worked this butchery, perhaps any old whore would have done as well. But perhaps not. Until I can ascertain her name, that question must remain unanswered. I do not like unanswered questions, Solomon."

"I don't care what you like. This has nothing to do with me," Silver Dollar Smith said.

"Your interests are not confined to this saloon," Munce said. "You know as many pimps as precinct captains, and you know their whores. You are present at all the white slave auctions on Allen street. Young girls grow old. Fresh flowers wilt and lose their bloom. Gay girls grow coarse, and must be disposed of to cheaper brothels and houses of assignation." He picked up the top photograph, blew the cigar ashes off the face, and thrust it at Silver Dollar Smith. "Look closely. Who was she?"

Solomon swatted the picture away with the back of hand. "I don't know, Munce. She's a butchered cow with dirty gray hair and skin like old liver. And if I did know, why the hell do you think I'd tell you?"

"I can give you several reasons."

Solomon frowned. "Go on, let's hear 'em."

"Jack the Ripper," said Henry Munce. "Perhaps this killing is his work, perhaps not. The Ripper killed only prostitutes. His letters said he was down on whores. If the Ripper is loose in New York, it is in your interest that he be caught, before he turns his attention to your girls."

Solomon laughed, and took a sip of his claret. "Munce, you're a damn fool. I can protect my place, and even if I did lose a molly or two, there's no shortage of whores. The world is full of whores. Every damn woman in the street has a purse, you know, and what's a purse for? For coins!" He laughed again. "Let's hear your other reasons."

"Teddy Roosevelt," said Munce. "I have recently made his acquaintance. Our new police board president is a zealous man, and I suspect he would be eager to act upon certain information I am in a position to give him, particularly if he knew his action would receive sympathetic reporting in the daily press.

"I'm not frightened of that damn cowboy Roosey either," Solomon said, but he was no longer smiling. "I have friends in Tammany who'll see to it I'm protected against anything he tries to do. I have lawyers."

"Max Hockstim?" Munce said, "I have other lawyers."

Munce nodded. "So you do. Consider a third name then."

"Yes?"

"Henry Munce," said Henry Munce.

"What?" said Solomon. "You, little man?" He chuckled. "Jack the Ripper and Teddy Roosevelt don't scare me, and I'm supposed to be frightened of a dwarf?"

"Perhaps the *Journal* could not destroy you, but certain facts, if published, might prove both inconvenient and expensive for you. Should you become too well known, you might also notice some cooling in the affections of your Tammany and Wall street friends. The world is full of whores, Solomon. It is also full of brothel-keepers and saloon-owners. As to my size, perhaps some night when you are alone, you may discover that a very small man can hold very large grudges, and that a dwarf can be as strong as any normal man. The kneecap, when shattered, does not often heal well. A man with one broken knee would limp painfully until the end of his days. A man with two broken knees would live out his life in a chair, and if the blood grew poisoned, the legs might have to be removed. A dwarf can look a legless man in the eye, you know." Henry Munce paused to clear his throat and flick two inches of powdery gray ash from the end of his cigar. "Is there something wrong, Solomon?" he asked. "You do not look well. You are sweating."

"It's warm in here," Solomon said. He wiped the sweat from his forehead with a silk handkerchief plucked from his breast pocket. "I could call them in and have you killed right now. I don't give a damn how strong you are, five or six men with brass knucks could beat you into chuck, Munce."

"You locked the door," Henry Munce pointed out. "But why are we boring each other with idle threats? We are both practical men. In my profession as well as yours, one hand washes the other. Help me and Henry Munce will owe you a favor." He slid the photograph over toward Silver Dollar Smith. "Who is she?"

This time Solomon crushed out his cigar, leaned forward, and studied the photograph for a long, long time. Underneath were other photographs, large and grainy and hideously frank. He shuffled them and spread them out across the dark green blotter. "I'm not sure," he said finally.

"But?" prompted Henry Munce.

"It's too long ago," Solomon complained. "Years, Munce. How can you expect me to remember?"

Henry Munce regarded him in silence, waiting.

"The face," the saloon owner muttered, glancing back down at the police pictures. "The eyes, there's something about those eyes. Why did they take such a close picture of her eyes?"

"The pupils are said to retain the image of the last thing they see," Henry Munce said. "The police hoped that by photographing them they could record the features of the killer. It was a futile hope."

"The eyes," said Silver Dollar Smith, "are pretty. Large, attractive eyes. What color were they?"

"Violet," said Henry Munce.

Solomon nodded. "I'll tell you something, Munce. You came to the right man. Nobody in this city knows women like Silver Dollar Smith."

"A rancher must know cattle," Munce replied.

"You hear all this talk," Solomon said, "from the preachers and the folks down in the missions, all this stuff about white slavery and abduction and ruining virgins. It makes me laugh, Munce. I don't have to abduct nobody. They come to me, or they're brought." He finished his wine to lubricate his throat before expanding on his topic. "You should see them when they come in, Munce. Grimy little vagabonds in rags, faces black with dirt, with runny noses and open sores. Red-faced farm girls, fat as pigs. Factory girls who look half starved. They don't need to be to ruined, none of 'em, they been selling their damned virtue for pennies since they was seven and giving it away to bootblacks for free. Sometimes they come themselves, and sometimes it's their own mothers who bring them to me, want me to break 'em in. You should see how grateful they are when I take in their babies! They know I'm doing them a favor. Hell, it's better than lacemaking or factory work, y'know? They all know that. I can't take but a few of them of them that come, though, most of them will never be good enough for my place. The rest of them, I give 'em a silver dollar and send them to a brothel or to a pimp, wherever I think they belong."

"How generous," said Henry Munce.

"Yes," said Solomon, "The thing is, they come in, and most folks would say they all look damned awful, so how do I know which ones to take on and which ones to send off? I look at 'em, that's how! I've got a trained eye for women." He pointed to his right eye; perhaps that was one he'd trained, Munce thought. "I can tell. I look at them and I can tell. I can tell what their faces will look like after we've scrubbed them down and combed out their hair and gotten rid of the cooties. I have them take off their goddamned rags, and I look them over, some of them look like skinny boys, but I can tell which ones will have a bosom that gentlemen will pay to play with, and which ones won't, I can tell which ones will get hairy and which will be smooth and downy. You can bet on it, Munce."

"Henry Munce does not gamble," said Henry Munce.

"I can tell what their figures will look like after I've put some meat on them or laced 'em into a nice tight corset to trim those waists. I can look at 'em at ten and know how'll they look at fourteen and at twenty-two and at thirty. I know which ones can stay here till they're grandmothers and which ones are only going to be fresh for a year or two. And it works the other way too." He tapped the pictures with a plump, manicured finger. "I can look at them when they're old and dead, and I can see what they used to be like when they was only girls starting out."

"We all have our talents," said Henry Munce.

"Yes," said Solomon. He pointed at the cold dead face. "Lots of bad alcohol puffed her up around the eyes, but look at those cheekbones. It was a pretty face once. Her hair was dark before it turned gray and started falling out. Black, I think, or maybe dark brown. A good chin, you can still see that. She was pretty, Munce, I guarantee it. The body—twenty years ago, when they weren't all withered and saggy, she had a nice large bosom. I can't tell much else the way she's cut up."

"Who was she?" Munce repeated.

"I don't know," Solomon said. He raised his eyes from the pictures and looked at Munce directly. "I really don't. But there is something familiar about her. Violet eyes, you say?"

"Yes."

"That is unusual. Large, striking violet eyes, black hair, a trim waist and a large bosom." He hesitated. "There was a girl offered me, oh, four, five years ago."

"Continue," Munce said.

Silver Dollar Smith shook his head. "It can't be her," he said. "This was only a girl, fourteen, maybe fifteen. This isn't her. Your dead woman was forty, fifty, they age so fast on the streets it's hard to tell. But there is a resemblance, I'll swear to that. Twenty or thirty years ago, this dead woman must have looked a little like the girl I was offered."

"You interest me," Henry Munce said. "Who was this girl? Who offered her to you?"

"Monk Eastman," Solomon said.

"The sheriff at New Irving Hall on Broome street?" Munce said. "Short and ugly and mean?"

"That's the one," said Solomon. "An important man now. Tied in to Tammany, y'know. He gets out the votes."

"Did you take the girl from him?"

"No. I was tempted, certainly. She was lovely, no doubt of it, but there were problems. I had the girl examined, I always do, we have to check, don't want my customers taking home cupid's disease. Eastman refused to allow it at first, and when I insisted he wanted to be present, but I wouldn't permit it, I sent the girl off with an old woman I keep for that sort of thing. She was clean enough, but bleeding. A very recent abortion, my woman said, and badly done too. Well, I might have handled that, but when they were alone the girl said all kinds of crazy things, the woman told me. Things she was frightened to say with Eastman in the room, obviously, because when I tried to question her, she denied everything and wept."

"What sorts of things did she say?"

Solomon shook his head. "It's been years, I can't remember it all. It was a wild story, a rape and an abduction, and she was a society lady, her family was rich, we should save her and we'd be well rewarded. Madness, but it made me wonder. The way she spoke…she was no common molly from the tenements, obviously, she'd read, she'd had education, she was refined. The whole deal seemed queer to me. Eastman wouldn't give me a straight answer as to where he'd gotten her either. His manner made me uneasy. You know the sort of men who come to the Silver Dollar Saloon. Brokers and politicians, rich men, men from Wall Street and Fifth Avenue. I didn't fancy having one of them run into a missing daughter in one of my bedrooms some night. Eastman wasn't so important in those days, he was just one of the kind you hired if you wanted some votes changed or a leg broke or somebody killed, so I got pretty brusque with him, told him I wasn't interested, and he took her off. I never saw her face again, but I remembered those violet eyes." He looked up suddenly and snapped his fingers. "Just a second! I did see her face again, come to think on it! In a picture. Someone came looking for her. He had a small painting in a gilded frame, he was showing it around, asking if anyone had seen her.

"When did this happen?" Munce asked.

"I don't recall precisely," said Solomon. "I told you, four or five years ago, I can't be certain." He pointed to the photographs of the dead woman. "But I'm damned certain that there's a likeness there. That doesn't make a damn bit of sense, does it? A gin-sodden old cow with her guts pulled out, what could she have to do with that sweet little Fifth Avenue girl Eastman had for me, all ruffled and corsetted and perfumed up? Doesn't make a goddamned bit of sense."

"Perhaps," said Munce, "and perhaps not. This man with the painting, what did you tell him?"

"Nothing," said Silver Dollar Smith. "Nothing at all. I'm in business, Munce, I have friends to protect, and Monk Eastman is not the sort of man I wanted for an enemy. Besides, I knew the man with the picture. He was dangerous too, and when he came asking I knew it was gang business. I stay clear of gang business."

Henry Munce grimaced. "Gang business," he repeated. "Who was the man with the picture?"

"Not a man you forget," said Solomon, with a sly smile. He wanted to be prompted. Henry Munce waited in silence.

"Spanish Louie," Solomon finally said. "You know him?"

"Yes," said Henry Munce, in his deepest mortuary tone. Yes, Henry Munce knew Spanish Louie, at least by reputation. Munce nodded, reflected for a moment, and then hopped off the top of Solomon's desk, slid his photographs neatly back into their file, and gathered up his derby and walking stick. "You have been most helpful," he said to Silver Dollar Smith. "I will do you a great favor. I will keep your name out of this."

Solomon looked at him sourly. "What are you going to do now?"

"I will proceed with my inquiries," said Munce, "in all the obvious places.

"The pet store," said Solomon.

"And the graveyard," finished Munce.

"Bloody Meg's," said Kate Hawthorne.

"Bloody hell," replied the Colonel.

"I'm going there," she said with resolution, "and I'm going to find her. You're not going to take this story away from me just because I'm a woman."

The Colonel was playing with a pencil. He held it up in front of him, one thumb pressed into the point and the other into the eraser, so it was suspended above the clutter of his immense desk. "Hester Street," he said, bemused. "You're right about the address, Hawthorne." He had started calling her Hawthorne lately, which Kate took as another sign of progress; he called all the reporters by their surnames, and when he grew courteous you knew you were in for it. "I know the place. It's on Hester just off the Bowery. It's got a Bowery entrance too, that's the goddamned trouble."

"I don't understand," Kate said.

"That's because you don't have gangsters on Fifth Avenue," the Colonel said, staring at his pencil. "At least you have different kinds of gangsters."

Kate didn't know what he was talking about. "Gangsters?" she asked. "Like the Gophers?"

The Colonel looked surprised. "You've heard of the Gophers? Maybe you're not a hopeless case after all, Hawthorne. The Gophers don't have anything to do with it, though; they're a Hell's Kitchen gang."

"I happen to know they live underground all over the city, like the furtive nocturnal animal from which they take their name," Kate Hawthorne said.

The Colonel sighed a mighty put-upon sigh and looked around for help, but the city room was almost deserted. The wire editor was working on dispatches that had come in over the telegraph, a copy boy was gathering up stories for delivery to the typesetters downstairs, and two reporters were at their desks. One of them was scribbling away, the other was perusing the front page of yesterday's *Herald*, probably looking over the personals while he pretended to be checking out the competition. Neither one seemed eager to help further Kate's education.

"Never mind about the damned Gophers," the Colonel told her, "you've got enough to worry about on the East Side and the water-front. The Bowery is the border between two major gangs, Kate." His tone was patient, but the familiarity was a step backwards for her. "From the Bowery west to Broadway, that's Five Pointer territory, Paul Kelly runs it all. Prince Paul, they call him. East of the Bowery to the river, that's a goddamned mess right now, been that way ever since the Whyos disintegrated. Dozens of small gangs, young men's clubs, political associations, river pirates, whatever the hell you want to call them, it's a bad place to be, and right now it's worse than normal, because there's some Tammany goon named Eastman trying to piece it all back together and put it in his own pocket, which means more shootings, stabbings, and killings than you can swish your bustle at."

"I don't wear a bustle," Kate said stiffly. "Bustles went out when I was just a girl."

"You want to go into Bloody Meg's, you damn well better wear iron petticoats," the Colonel said. "The Bowery is the problem. It's the border between Kelly's Five Pointers and the East Side gangs, but Eastman and the others say the boundary runs down the middle of the goddamned street, and Prince Paul insists that *both* sides of the Bowery are his. Bloody Meg's has an entrance on the *east* side of the Bowery, you understand?" He pushed harder on both ends of the pencil, grimacing as the point stabbed into the fleshy part of his thumb, but finally there was a sharp crack and the pencil snapped in two. "See," the Colonel said, looking up at her. "Push from the east, push from the west, and the goddamned middle cracks wide open. Bloody Meg's is on the Bowery and Hester. That means both Kelly and Eastman claim they rule there."

Kate Hawthorne crossed her arms. "What does Bloody Meg have to say about it?"

The Colonel snorted. "From what I hear, she says any damn thing that comes into her head, and spits on both sides. She keeps the place wide open, and that means you've got dozens of thugs from rival gangs in there night and day. The only thing keeps them in line is Bloody Meg. She's supposed to be a god-damned monster. Six feet tall, and mean as they come."

"I'm sure that she's not as frightening as all that," Kate said. "These things get exaggerated."

"Thanks for telling me," said the Colonel. He snorted. "They say she's poison in a catfight, Kate. Know what she does with the women she's beaten? She bites off their ears." He leaned forward and smiled up at her broadly. "Keeps them behind the bar for trophies. In a jar full of vinegar. Pickled. What do you think of that?"

"I don't believe it for a moment," Kate said. "This is my story, and I'm going to follow it wherever it leads. If Old Shakespeare is hiding at Bloody

Meg's, that's where I'm going."

The Colonel threw up his hands. "You want to go there? Go. Get out of here, out of my city room, go get your goddamned little pink shell-like ear bitten off, maybe you'll hear better afterwards, maybe some horse sense will even be able to get in under your cute little hat. Bloody Meg will skin you and fry your liver up with green onions for the free lunch, the hell if she won't, but you want to go, go. I don't give a damn. I'll tell you this, though, I'm not sending a photographer with you. Cameras cost good money, Kate. Goddamn it, I worry about Willie Worthless coming back when I send him across the Park to City Hall, and you want to take him into Bloody Meg's?" He pointed at her with one fat finger. "And I'll tell you something else," he began, but whatever he was going to say was lost when the tall, spindly black telephone at his elbow jangled at him. The Colonel scowled; he didn't like to be interrupted once he began building up steam, Kate knew. "Goddamned stinking thing," he swore, as he scooped it up in a meaty hand. "Yes?" he bellowed into the receiver. "Yes? Oh. Ah, yes, I see. Thank you." He carefully placed the telephone back in its cradle, made a steeple of his hands, and smiled at Kate sweetly.

Kate did not like that smile one bit. "What is it?" she asked him uncomfortably. He wouldn't be looking at her like that unless the call had something to do with her.

"Your callers are on their way up," he said softly.

"Callers," she repeated warily.

"Two young gentlemen," the Colonel said. "They arrived in a cab, and they insisted on seeing you at once. One of them is distraught and carrying a horsewhip."

Two young gentleman, Kate thought suspiciously. "What did they look like?" she asked the Colonel.

The Colonel gave her a polite, innocent smile. Then he turned to his sportswriter, who was reading and drinking coffee with his feet up on a desk. "Smithfield," he called out, "pardon, but do you happen to recall my position here at the *New York World*?"

"Seated, usually," Smithfield snapped back without looking up from the *Herald*'s personals.

The Colonel's face clouded up like a thunderhead about to break. "My title, Smithfield. My *job* if you want it in a word of one syllable. What the hell is my job?"

"City editor," Smithfield said, with a chastened look.

"Ahhhh," said the Colonel. He looked to the other side of the room. "Hallis," he called out to the wire editor, "what does a city editor do?"

"Runs the paper," Hallis said. "Edits the news."

"Hires," Smithfield put in brightly.

"Fires," Hallis contributed.

The Colonel smiled at Kate. "Perhaps I'm wrong. I could be wrong, and I'm sure you'll be the first one to tell me if I am wrong, isn't that right, Hawthorne? Still, from what these fellows tell me, it seems as though I'm the city editor here." His sweet, mild voice suddenly became a typhoon roar. "That's *city editor*, and *not your goddamned social secretary*, do you understand that, Miss Katherine Fifth Avenue Hawthorne? I don't know what the hell these people look like and I don't give a good goddamned what they look like and I don't have a bloody goddamned scrufulous clue as to what the hell they are doing riding in Mister Pulitzer's elevators up to *my* city room, but I sure as hell intend to find out the minute they walk through that goddamned door, and if it turns out that these two swell gents are here just to pay their respects on you, a little social call if you will, I might even get a little upset, I might—"

Kate never had a chance to hear what else the Colonel might do, because just then the city room door banged open, and they came barging in. "Oh, bother," Kate said, so upset that she forgot to be profane.

"*Katherine!*" her brother shouted from the door. He was the one with the horsewhip. He carried it doubled-over, snapping it against the side of his long gray fur-trimmed overcoat as he strode toward her. "Katherine, get over here right now! You're coming home with me this minute, and we'll have no more nonsense about you working for the yellow press!"

Kate faced him boldly. "Your voice squeaks when you get angry, do you know that, Jeremy?" she said pleasantly. But her eyes had slipped away from him, to light on his companion, the tall, strapping, broad-shouldered blonde with the sullen expression who had entered a step behind him. "Hello, Stephen," Kate said, "how are you?"

"Quite well," Stephen Blackwood said. He had a rogue's smile, a hard arrogant curl that turned up only the right side of his thin lips. "Good to see you, Katherine." He moved into the room lazily and seated himself on the edge of a vacant desk.

"*Katherine!*" Jeremy Hawthorne screamed once again, even louder, as if he could compel her to obedience by squeezing every last bit of air out of his lungs. He made ineffectual flailing motions with the whip, like a small boy having a tantrum. The Colonel and the other denizens of the city room were staring at him with a certain amount of barely concealed amusement as he turned red.

The Hawthornes all blushed easily, Kate thought. "My apologies, Colonel," she said. "Allow me to present my brother Jeremy, he's the plump soft one with the whip, and Mister Stephen Blackwood, he's the tall rugged-looking one with the blonde hair."

"Stephen Blackwood," the Colonel mused. "Of the canal-building Blackwoods?"

"The canal-building, silver-mining, hotel-owning Blackwoods, actually," Stephen Blackwood said with a certain cool precision. He was elegantly attired in a heavy tan overcoat with a black velvet collar, and a silk top hat that he now placed casually on his knee. His thick, sandy hair was slightly mussed, as if by a wild ride in a motorcar or perhaps a woman's fingers, and he sported a lush blonde moustache that curled down at the corners of his mouth, and thick mutton-chop whiskers that framed his strong square jaw. His eyebrows were so blonde he scarcely seemed to have any, but his eyes made up for the lack. Beneath heavy lids that made him look perpetually sleepy, or perhaps just bored, they were a deep and haughty blue.

Next to Stephen Blackwood, her brother looked fat, puffy, and foolish. That was Jeremy's great tragedy, Kate reflected; since they had been boys together, Jeremy Hawthorne had wished nothing so earnestly as to be Stephen Blackwood, but try as he might, he always ended up looking fat, puffy, and foolish. As if he was bound and determined to prove the truth of Kate's thoughts, Jeremy came huffing up to her and reached out to grab her by the arm. "You're coming home right now if I have to drag you home!" he shouted.

Kate wrenched away from him angrily. It was not a difficult feat; Jeremy was four years her senior, but as far back as she could remember, Kate had always been quicker, more agile, and stronger than her brother. "Take your hands off me, Jeremy!" she snapped. "You've got no authority over me and I won't have you dictating what I may or may not do. I'm not a child any more, I'm a grown woman and a reporter, and I work here!"

"We'll see about that," her brother said. "Stephen, help me get hold of her."

Stephen Blackwood shrugged. "I never interfere in family squabbles," he said. The desk at which he had chosen to sit was piled high with recent numbers of the *World*. He hooked a copy with his silver-headed ebony walking stick, lifted it into the air, and casually let it slide down into his lap. Then he folded it over neatly and began to read.

"I'll just do it myself, then," Jeremy declared manfully.

"The hell you will," boomed the Colonel from his desk.

Kate fought to suppress a smile, and failed. She really ought to do something, she knew. She had to stand up for herself, fight her own wars, it gained a woman nothing if she allowed one male protector to replace another, although it was hard to think of the Colonel as especially male; he was more like a force of nature. Still, Jeremy was her brother and he took humiliation very badly. Kate decided that she ought to speak up decisively before something awful happened.

But there was an imp of the perverse in Kate Hawthorne too, and her resolve came to nothing as she watched her brother turn to the huge man behind the desk. Jeremy had a belligerent set to his heavy, sun-browned features. Strands of his hair, auburn like hers, were plastered to his brow with perspiration. "Are you speaking to me?" he asked the Colonel. "If so, you'd be well advised to stay out to this. It's none of your concern, sir."

"I didn't realize that," the Colonel said, sounding startled. "I was under the misapprehension that it was my concern. You come into the Pulitzer Building, come right up into the golden dome, burst into my city room screaming and swearing and brandishing a whip, try to seize one of my reporters to carry her off to God knows where, and you tell me it's none of my concern?" He turned to his sportswriter. "Smithfield," he called out, "is this my concern?"

"I'd say so," Smithfield put in, grinning.

"Hallis?" the Colonel asked.

"They're in your city room, that's a fact," the wire editor said from his desk.

The Colonel looked at Kate. "Hawthorne?" he asked.

"Oh yes, Colonel," she said, knowing it was dreadful but too weak to resist the temptation. "Definitely your concern."

"Good," he said. He opened a desk drawer, plunged his hand down among the papers, and came out holding the biggest, blackest revolver that Kate had ever seen. He pointed it at Jeremy. "Get out of my city room," he said.

Little beads of perspiration dotted Jeremy's brow. "You have no ri, ri, right," he struggled to say. "I am the head of my family, my sister..." He wet his lips. "My sister is in my charge; she owes me respect and obedience until she's wed. What sort of man are you?"

"The sort of man who has a large gun in his desk drawer," the Colonel pointed out.

Across the room, Stephen Blackwood smiled thinly. "Don't let him bluff you, Jeremy," he called out. "You're well within your rights. Stand up to him!"

Jeremy Hawthorne worked up his courage with a visible effort. "She's coming home with me!" he declared forcefully. He swept his whip dramatically across the top of the Colonel's desk, knocking over the telephone and an empty tea cup and scattering papers everywhere. It made an impressive flurry of sound.

The Colonel cocked the hammer of his revolver. It was a smaller sound and even more impressive. "Your sister is going to Bloody Meg's to look for a whore who's been dead four years," he said. "Unless you happen to live under Bloody Meg's, that means she isn't going home with you. Now get out."

"Don't do it, Jeremy," called Stephen Blackwood. "Show him the stuff you're made of!"

"The stuff he's made of," the Colonel said. "I wonder what that might be? Hallis?"

"Blood, most definitely," said Hallis.

"Smithfield?"

"Intestines, I'd say."

The Colonel made a face. "Don't show me the stuff you're made of, please. I'm dining at Delmonico's and I don't care to lose my appetite."

"Journalists," Jeremy said furiously. "You're a worthless pack of scoundrels and liars, every one of you." He pointed at the Colonel with his whip. "I want your name! Your name, do you hear me?"

"You can call me the Colonel."

"The Colonel," Jeremy sputtered. "You're no military man. Hah! The Colonel, the Commodore, do all of you take on these fraudulent titles? You're as bad as Bennett. You would never dare to shoot me, Colonel, not here in broad daylight in front of all these witnesses."

"Smithfield," said the Colonel, "you witness anything?"

Smithfield's interest in the *Herald*'s personals column suddenly grew intense and all-consuming.

"Hallis?" called the Colonel.

"Saw a wild man attack you with a bullwhip, sir," Hallis said. "Or was it a cannon? In the confusion of the moment, it was hard to be sure."

Kate Hawthorne sighed. "Go home, Jeremy," she said, before Stephen could get in another goad. "Go home before he shoots you. He'd do it in a moment. The reporters would all say it was self-defense."

"And the World would have an exclusive," the Colonel said cheerfully.

"He loves exclusives," Hallis called out.

Kate moved closer to her brother and touched his arm. "I'll come and see you in the next few days, I promise. I'm in the middle of a big story now."

Jeremy stared at her. "See that you do," he said with all the authority he could muster. Then, to the Colonel, he declared, "You'll be hearing from me again." He turned smartly on his heel and marched toward the door. "Come on, Stephen."

Blackwood rose and dusted off his trousers. "Your sister will never respect you if you let yourself get run off like this by these..." He sniffed. "...people."

"A strategic retreat," Jeremy said defensively. "He has a gun, Stephen. His lackies are probably armed as well. We'll meet again when the circumstances are more suitable."

"Whatever you say," Stephen Blackwood said, with a slight curl to his mouth. "Go on, run along. I'll meet you at the Union Club this evening. I want a few words with your sister."

"But," Jeremy said, confused again, "but Stephen, we—"

"I insist," Blackwood said. Baffled but helpless, Jeremy Hawthorne slunk back out into the marbled hall toward the elevators. Blackwood came over to the city desk. "Katherine," he said, bowing to her.

"I'm not coming with *you* either," she said.

"You still have all your spirit," he replied. "You remind me of Byron."

"The poet?" the Colonel said, baffled, the revolver still clutched in his fist.

"The horse," Kate said drily.

"Byron was the most spirited horse I ever owned," Stephen said, with that taut mocking smile of his. "And the best, once I'd broken him and trained him to the whip." He was looking right at Kate with those sullen blue eyes. Strangely enough, she was reminded of Red Mike the Gopher. Stephen must be thirty by now, she thought, but the face, the manner, and the air of command were all the same. Yet Kate found suddenly that she did not entirely care for the way he was studying her, though she was certain that at seventeen that look would have thrilled her.

It was almost as if Stephen Blackwood had caught the taste of her thoughts, for all at once he turned to the Colonel with a small smile and a charming shrug. "Please don't shoot Jeremy the next time you see him on the street," he said. "Katherine will tell you, he's harmless, more's the pity. It's tragic to say that of a man, don't you think? You really have to forgive him."

"The hell I do," the Colonel said. He put the revolver back into his desk, between a cigar box and a bottle of Irish whiskey, and slammed the drawer shut. "I'll forgive whatever goddamned son of a bitch I want to forgive."

"He had a trying time abroad," Blackwood explained. "And when he came home and found Kate had taken employment as a journalist, he was livid. I'm afraid Commodore Bennett did him a bad turn off Greece, and it's soured him on newspapers."

"Bennett?" Kate said, startled. "James Gordon Bennett? Of the *Herald?*"

Blackwood nodded. "None other."

"What was he doing with Bennett?" she asked.

"Jeremy ran into him over there. Of course, Bennett knew the Hawthornes from Newport, so he invited your brother aboard his yacht. It did not end well. You know how naive Jeremy can be." He smiled a tight, controlled smile to tell Kate and the Colonel that, of course, the three of *them* would never be so naive. "He wasn't really aware of Bennett's eccentric reputation."

"What happened?" Kate said.

"As Jeremy tells it, he made the mistake of complaining that his steward failed to wake him at the proper time, and that his bath water was the wrong temperature. Bennett assured him that the following day he would woken exactly on time, and that his bath would be brought to his cabin." Stephen gave a rueful shake of his head. "The next morning, at exactly the hour specified, a sailor under the supervision of Bennett's personal secretary poked a fire hose through the porthole of his stateroom and blasted your poor brother right out of bed. It was awfully humiliating, and when Jeremy stormed up to the bridge to complain, Bennett exploded at him and insisted he get off the yacht at once. They set him ashore in the middle of the Aegean, I'm afraid, on some dreadful little island. He was there for three days, with nothing to drink but water and goat's milk, nothing to eat but fish and charred goat, and no one for company but Greeks. The goats spoke better English."

The Colonel roared with sudden laughter, and an instant later the rest of the city rooms broke into guffaws around him.

"Oh, dear," Kate said. Despite herself, she felt sorry for her brother, who had endured more than his share of humiliation. It was only a year ago that he'd ripped out of the bottom of his own yacht off the coast of Maine. He had a stable of racehorses, but they were always running last, and she hated to think how much money he'd wagered on them and lost.

"Jeremy could never tell one newspaper from the other, any more than mother," Kate said. "She probably told him I was working for Bennett. How is he taking it?"

"He says he's going to kill them both," said Blackwood. "He won't, of course."

"Both?" Kate asked, confused.

"Bennett and his secretary, a man by the name of Ned Cullen. It was this Cullen fellow who orchestrated the firehose incident." He shrugged. "But enough of your brother. It's pleasant to see you again, Katherine. Can we talk?"

"Colonel?" Kate asked.

"Callers," the Colonel said, with a loud snort of disdain. "Get away from here." He waved them off. "Just remember I'm no goddamned chaperone, and you're due at Bloody Meg's dive, damn it. I want that story."

"You'll get it." Kate nodded to Stephen Blackwood and led him off to a vacant desk in the far corner of the room. It was not her desk precisely, since she was compelled to share it with three other reporters on space, but she did have a drawer of her own, and she had grown fond of the window. "Look," she said to Stephen, gesturing outside. "The Bridge, the Bowery, that's Broadway over there. You can see the whole city from here, and Brooklyn as well."

"Yes, I see," Blackwood said, with a bored glance through the glass. He sat himself on the corner of her desk, holding his hat and stick with a casual elegance. "I see you've grown up quite a bit these four years. You were a handsome girl, but you're turned into a striking young lady."

"What do you want, Stephen?" Kate asked him bluntly. She was not feeling especially flirtatious, she had not cared for the way he had goaded on her brother, and her mind was occupied with thoughts of Bloody Meg.

Blackwood smiled. "You're not as polite as you once were, though. I suppose that comes of working in a place like this." He looked around the city room, and chuckled. "What do I want? That comes directly to the point, doesn't it?"

"I'm a reporter," said Kate Hawthorne. "I'm supposed to come directly to the point."

"I still prefer the language of poetry," said Blackwood. "Did you keep the poems I wrote you?"

"For more than a year," Kate said, determined not to blush for once. She pressed her lips together, so any red in her cheeks would look like anger.

"Only a year?"

"I burned them when I found out you'd written the same poems to Bess Vanderkellen and Mabel Stuyvesant," she said. "I suppose there were others as well."

Stephen Blackwood looked rueful. "So you found me out! I was a fraud as a poet, I'm afraid. I had only a dozen good poems in me, but my regard for you was always sincere."

"Is that why you went to Europe? Because of your sincere regard for me?"

"Don't be insolent, Katherine, it's unbecoming in a woman. I had matters to attend to abroad, important matters. Sometimes the world makes these demands upon a man. It's not something a woman can really understand. A question of family honor was involved, and I can't tell you more than that without violating a trust. Certain things are best kept secret." He smiled. "I never meant to hurt you, believe that. My affections for you ran deep, and the truth is that I found myself thinking about you frequently during those years I spent in London."

"And Bess Vanderkellen and Mabel Stuyvesant too, I'm sure."

"No," Blackwood said. His eyes met hers frankly. "Only you, Katherine. As I said, you had more spirit than any other girl in the Four Hundred. I like spirit in women."

"And in horses," Kate said. "How could you possibly sell Byron and Shelley?"

"Not by choice," he said. "It was one of the most painful moments of my life, when I parted with them. Pray that you'll never know pain like that, Katherine." His face had a strange, strained look, his lips pressed tightly together, and Kate felt her heart go out to him. It must have been terrible to have been forced to sell those magnificent animals, she thought.

"Jeremy wants a motorcar," she said, hoping to cheer him up a bit. Jeremy's talk of motorcars seemed to bother mother almost as much as Kate's career in journalism.

"They stink, they frighten horses, and they are always breaking down," Blackwood said. "As for pure speed, I'd gladly have set Byron and Shelley against any motorcar ever built, and wager the Blackwood fortune on the outcome. Now that I'm home, I hope to find another matched pair that I can make the same boast about, and soon." He was looking at her intently. "Katherine, Byron and Shelley were not the greatest loss I suffered when duty called me abroad. I fear I also lost my place in your heart. When I left our affections were only beginning to ripen, and there was much left unsaid between us. I know that years have passed, but you are as lovely and spirited as I remember you, and I am extraordinarily fortunate to find you still unwed. It is my intention to resume my life where I was forced to leave off, in business, in politics, and with you. I've spoken to Jeremy. Your brother is not opposed."

Kate Hawthorne had been feeling almost fond of him again, until he got to the part about Jeremy. "My brother is not opposed?" she said.

"He knows me too well," Stephen said, with a self-deprecating look. "He knows I need a wife."

"Does he?" Kate said. "Well then, let him marry you himself! God knows Jeremy needs a husband." She stood up and glowered at him. "You're going to buy yourself a new team of horses, Stephen Blackwood, why not a new team of innocent young girls? I'm not a lovestruck child any more, thank you. I've learned to see clearly, and it strikes me that what I thought was your great depth of soul was really just sullenness and what seemed to me to be strength was really just cruel indifference."

Stephen smiled tolerantly, as if to say he understood.

That smile made Kate furious. "Damn you to perdition," she said. She wanted to flaunt the language she'd learned in the hope of slapping the complacency off his face. "You never made me any promises, so I certainly had no right to go about mourning and weeping like Juliet, but *you* have no right to come walking in here and expect that I'm going to twitter with joy when you tip your hat to me. I'm busy, Stephen. Right now there's a goddamned bloody whore named Old Shakespeare who was supposed to have been cut up by Jack the Ripper in 1891, but she wasn't, she's alive and hiding somewhere, and I'm one hell of a lot more interested in her story than in anything *you* might have to say to me!"

The profanity seemed to do its work. For a brief moment Stephen Blackwood looked profoundly shocked. Then his face settled back into its accustomed mask of cool self-assurance, and he stood. "I see," he said. "Well, I've never competed with a whore and a corpse before, so I suppose it will take some getting used to. I'll give you fair warning though, Katherine. I'm back in New York to stay, and I'm not the sort of man who gives up. Don't mistake me for your brother. The Blackwoods get what they want, and I want you, Katherine, with all my heart." He smiled, hooked his top hat with the tip of his stick, flipped it into the air, and caught it with a jaunty smile. "Raise your womanly walls if you must, I'll lay sweet siege to your affections, and build me a Trojan horse to steal into your dreams."

"Only if you promise to spare me your poetry," she snapped.

"Certainly," he said, laughing lightly. But his mouth twitched, just a little, as he did.

December was no time to be visiting Coney Island, Ned Cullen decided when he was halfway there, as he huddled inside the West Brighton steamer on a splintery bench by the big wood-burning stove, sandwiched between a stubble-cheeked workingman who smelled of gin and garlic and a thin old woman with a complexion like oatmeal.

Choosing the water route from Manhattan had been an unfortunate mistake, and Ned had already determined to take the nickle trolley ride back home. In summer, the sea breeze was a nymph, cool and playful, full of gentle caresses and the tangy impudence of salt. In winter, it became a positive harridan of a wind, gray and screeching as a Mother Superior, with a cold nasty bite to it that chilled him right through his heavy black overcoat. A thieving sort of wind, too; if Ned had been a trifle less quick, he would have lost his derby to the frigid, choppy waters of the bay.

He had fond memories of steamer excursions in summers past, but the voyage was decidedly more pleasant when the skies overhead were blue, the sun was beating down, and he could look forward to an evening of champagne toasts, whirligigs, and gaming in the company of some gay and likely lady. But today the only rendezvous he could anticipate was with a prize-fighter who bore him a grudge. Ned diverted himself with memories of some of the sweet girls he'd met at the Elephant in years past, and tried not to think about Eddie Fitzgerald.

The planks of the New Iron Pier were damp with salt spray when Ned wound his long cashmere scarf tightly around his neck, clamped his derby firmly down on his head, and disembarked from the steamer. He paused briefly at the end of the pier and pulled on his gloves while the other passengers scurried away like so many rodents. Beneath the blustery overcast sky, it was a gloomy scene. The long wooden benches that lined both sides of the pier were completely empty, where they ought to have been packed with families and smiling, chattering shopgirls. The huge wrought-iron planters were bare of all greenery, the slender black lamp posts looked more spidery than dainty, the clusters of gas globes were dark and unlit, and the many-storied, gabled, pinnacled amusement palace at the foot of the pier was obviously closed for the season. Ned looked east and west along the broad beach, and the only signs of life he saw were an old man contemplating the surf and a large mongrel dog digging in the sand.

A few familiar landmarks remained. To the west of the landing was Feltman's Bathing Pavilions, empty and closed now, and inland of that, on the far side of Surf Avenue, he could see the Elephant looming over all the surrounding structures, the lofty howdah on its back overtopping even the highest flagpole of the rambling, turreted Sea Beach Palace next door. Just east of the pier the Iron Tower rose three hundred feet into the air, black and skeletal against the gray December sky, reminding Ned Cullen a bit of the iron tower that Eiffel had raised in Paris, though the French structure was three times as tall and infinitely more graceful than Coney's.

But the Iron Tower was imposing enough in its own setting, dominating the beaches, hotels, casinos, freak shows, whirligigs, bazaars, restaurants, whorehouses, alleys, bathing pavilions, inclines, scenic railways, water chutes, lagoons, piers, train stations, boardwalks, race tracks, and carousels that spread out beneath it. It was the tallest structure in West Brighton, and for that matter it was taller than anything to be found in Manhattan Beach or Brighton Beach or Norton's Point either, which made it the tallest thing on Coney Island. Even the mighty Elephant Hotel—the fabled and infamous Elephant, the Colossus of Architecture, so fierce and imposing with its gray tin skin, its great tusks and long thick trunk, its legs thicker than the biggest tree, its ornate howdah and those huge glass eyes that glittered with insane fury when the proprietors turned on the lights by night—was less than half of the height of the Iron Tower.

Something was different about the Iron Tower, Ned observed as he walked down the pier. Up on top, on the observatory, where you could peer into the eye of the big telescope and see forty miles out to sea, there were people moving around, and some sort of long gangplank had been fastened to the roof, sticking out toward the water like a wooden tongue. On top of the tower, he could see the silhoutte of some sort of strange kite-like contraption. Ned wondered what was going on.

Whatever it was, though, was none of Ned Cullen's concern. His business awaited in the cavernous wooden building not far beyond the foot of the pier, near the base of the Iron Tower. A shame the way things change, Ned reflected. The last time had been to West Brighton, that building had been Paul Bauer's casino. Now it was the Coney Island Athletic Club.

The wind swirled around him and tried to snatch away his derby. Ned caught it again, gritting his teeth together, and picked up his pace. No doubt it was a lot more pleasant to contemplate the Iron Tower and remember evenings in the Elephant than it would be to confront Eddie Fitzgerald, but unless he came up with a story soon, querulous cables from Bennett would begin to arrive with monotonous frequency. He cheered himself with the thought that at this very moment elsewhere in the world, other reporters were dodging cannonballs on muddy battlefields, swatting flies the size of sparrows in unspeakable jungles, and contracting hideous diseases from ugly and disagreeable women. That put a smile back on Ned's face; there were worse things than Eddie Fitzgerald.

The high wooden walls of the Coney Island Athletic Club were covered with posters and placards, most of them faded by wind and sun and rain, advertising prize-fighting exhibitions past and present. Ned looked them over carefully as he made his way around the building to the main entrance. He finally spied what he was looking for; third billing on a date last April, Thunderbolt Tom Meegan exhibiting against Gallant Eddie the Fitz. That had to be him. Thank god, he was only a welterweight.

The door creaked as Ned Cullen pushed it open. The interior was warm and musty with the smell of mildew, liniment, and sweat. An old man in a frayed, shapeless gray coat sat smoking a pipe in the dim interior. "Yeah?" he said, in a frog croak of a voice. "Who are you? What you want?" He had a copy of the *Police Gazette* on his lap, and seemed annoyed at the interruption of his literary pursuits.

"Great piece about that housewife who did the naughty midway dance," Ned said affably. "I'm looking for an old friend of mine; perhaps you can help me."

"We ain't got no girls here," the man said. He had hair growing out of his ears, Ned noted.

"More's the pity. No, the man I want is a prizefighter. Eddie Fitzgerald."

The old man stared at him, gave a silent shake of his head, and went back to the *Police Gazette*.

"He's red-headed, about twenty-three, I'd judge, maybe twenty-four, freckled, Irish, pug nose unless Thunderbolt Tom Meegan flattened it for him. I think he fights as Gallant Eddie the Fitz."

"Oh, him," said the old man. "He trains here, yeah. He was in this morning, sparring some. You wait, I'll see if he's still here." He got up, left his newspaper on the chair, and shuffled inside in search of Gallant Eddie.

Ned picked up the *Police Gazette* and leafed through it while he waited. He saw that Minerva, the champion strong woman of America who could catch cannonballs and break horseshoes in her bare hands, was challenging the strong women of France, Germany, and Mexico once again. Ned wondered what Minerva looked like. Maybe he ought to have hired her as a bodyguard in case Gallant Eddie proved unreasonable. He had just begun reading an attractively illustrated story headlined, "White Women Fight For A Coon," when the old man returned.

"He ain't here," the man said, snatching back his *Police Gazette*. "He was in this morning, like I said, but he left. I don't think he's coming back. The Dutchman said he talked some about the Professor. I guess he probably went to see the crash. You got the time, mister?"

Ned undid the buttons of his overcoat, took out a lovely gold watch that had been given him by an equally lovely lady in Switzerland, opened the cover, and said, "Quarter past one."

"Professor's s'posed to crash at two," the old man said. "Go over by the Iron Tower 'bout them, you'll see the crowd, prob'ly find Gallant Eddie there."

"Thanks," said Ned. But his curiosity had gotten the better of him. "Ah, who's this Professor?" he asked.

"He's that fellow built the flying machine they got struck up on top of the Iron Tower. Says it's going to fly, but he don't you believe that stuff. It always crashes." The old man grinned happily. "Fun to watch, though. Sometimes it makes it past the beach, sometimes it don't. I bet me five dollars on the sand."

"A wise choice. Speaking of bets, how did Gallant Eddie do against Thunderbolt Tom Meegan?"

The old man laughed. "Lost. Thunderbolt Tom knocked his head off in the thirty-fourth round. Won me twenty dollars on that one."

"Congratulations," Ned said. "A pity about Eddie, though. He needed that head. So did I, actually. Has the lad had any other fights? I'm afraid I haven't followed his career closely."

"Career?" The old man sprayed spittle everywhere when he guffawed. "Yeah, he's fought 'em all. Lost 'em all too." Considering his age and decrepitude, Ned thought it was astonishing how little the fellow drooled; commendable, really. "He keeps coming back for more, though, either he needs the money or they punched his brains out."

"That's why they call him Gallant Eddie," Ned said, as he made his exit, feeling a trifle less apprehensive.

Outside the Athletic Club, he thrust his hands into his pocket and rocked back and forth on his heels for a moment, considering his options. He had forty-five minutes before the Professor crashed his new flying machine off the top of the Iron Tower, which certainly ought to prove diverting, and maybe good for a story too. Normally he'd take himself off to one of the casinos or dance halls along Surf Avenue, but there really wasn't time. He wished he could wander over behind the Elephant to Sea Lion Park, which the celebrated Captain Paul Boyton, the daredevil frog-man, had opened earlier that very year to vast fanfare. An artificial lagoon, a mammoth shoot-the-chutes that was the rage of West Brighton, and forty juggling sea lions too, everything presided over by Captain Boyton, whose fabulous rubber suit had made him internationally famous a few years back. Ned thought it all sounded very jolly, but of course the park had closed for the season in September; not even a juggling sea lion or a lunatic with a rubber suit was foolish enough to shoot-the-chutes in icewater. Besides, Ned knew Captain Boyton, and owed him money.

Well, there was always the Bowery. Ned smiled, tilted his derby at a rakish angle, and set off at a brisk clip to see what was new and what was old in the tawdry heart of West Brighton.

Coney's Bowery was no broad thoroughfare, like its Manhattan namesake; it was scarcely more than an alley, and only a half-mile long, but it packed a number of splendid entertainments into that crooked half-mile. A hundred ramshackle wooden buildings stood jam packed along its length, but as rickety as they might be, there was something fabulous about them as well. They were painted in garish colors, in crimson and gold and sea greens, festooned with flags and banners, cluttered with hand-painted signs and crackling electrical advertisements, bedraped with awnings, and topped with all manner of turrets and minarets and twisty little Moorish domes covered with fake gilt.

In summer, the alley was always crowded and raucous, with barkers shouting their attractions from high wooden platforms, ballyhoo going on beneath every awning, shopgirls gawking at freaks and musclemen, stern mothers pulling small children past sights unfit for their eyes, pickpockets keen for a watch to lift, young swells eyeing the hoochy-kootchy dancers and lining up before the saucier attractions, and gay girls hunting for a free-spending gent who might want to show them the elephant.

In winter, of course, it was dismal and forlorn. The cabarets were closed and padlocked, their gaily-colored awnings furled and hidden until the spring. A few dreary beer halls remained open, but they were dark, bleak little places with sawdust on the floor. The hot-corn vendors had packed it in along with the oyster bars. The bottle-toss booths and the high-strikers were boarded up. Ned passed a cellar cockfighting establishment, (closed), a rat-pit, (also closed), and a rundown merry-go-round, which looked to be closed for good, judging from the sorry conditions of its wooden nags. He paused in front of the Original Turkish Harem, wondering what Abdul the Damned would make of the place and its clapboard exterior ornamented with images of camels, scimitars, hookahs, and undulating harem girls. It was nothing to compare with Abdul's Turkish harem, Ned was fairly certain, but at least the Original Turkish Harem did not limit admission to eunuchs. A little further down the Bowery, Ned came to the Streets of Cairo, but that was closed too, which broke his heart. Paris and the *Lysistrata* were all very well and good, but thanks to Bennett he'd missed Little Egypt, who had been a sensation out at Chicago and then at Coney, all while Ned Cullen had been gone.

Even the chill winds of December could not entirely cool the Bowery's heat, however. Most of the little hotels were still open for business, and one or two shivering whores called out to Ned from their doorways as he strode past. He glanced at them and kept striding. A tattoo artist hailed him from a window above his darkened establishment. "Fix you up real swell," the man called out. Ned was tempted to ask him if he did owls, but he suppressed the impulse. At a small clam bar, he pressed up to the counter between a policeman and a sailor and paid a dime for a bowl of hot clam chowder. It was thick and red and pungent, though a trifle short on clams, and it tasted wonderful in the cold. The proprietor took one look at the cut of Ned's overcoat and asked if he was out here to see the Professor crash. Ned cheerfully admitted that he was.

A little past the clam bar were a couple of cigar shops, still open, a mirror maze, closed, and a wax museum. MONSTERS AND ATROCITIES FROZEN IN WAX! its signs proclaimed. SO REAL YOU'LL SWEAR THEY'RE BREATHING! But the sign on the entrance said CLOSED UNTIL MAY. Across the alley was a freak show, its frontage painted with larger-than-life likenesses of its star attractions: the Dog-Faced Boy, the Human Torso (NO HANDS NO LEGS HE PLAYS THE ORGAN WITH HIS NOSE), a Wild Man from Borneo, and Giselle the Fat Lady, who must have faced some very heavy competition from other West Brighton fat ladies, judging from the strident tone of her advertising. HOLY SMOKE SHE'S FAT SHE'S AWFUL FAT said the sign over her image, which was indeed enormous, so large that they had the entryway tucked between her pink columnar legs. QUEEN OF FATLAND, FATTEST LADY ON THE BOWERY, WHEN YOU SEE GISELLE YOU'LL KNOW THE OTHERS LIE, other placards screamed in vibrant scarlet. Even the letters were bulging fat.

As Ned stood reading the signs, the door between Giselle's legs popped open and a barker emerged. He wore a white shirt, blue suspenders, and no jacket, and he began shivering as soon as he stepped onto the platform. "We're open," he called down to Ned, his breath steaming in front of his face. "A dime admission, one thin dime, freaks gotta eat even when it's cold, you wouldn't believe how much Giselle can put away, queen of Fatland, fattest woman on the Bowery. Come on, come on." He slapped his hands against his arms, trying to generate a bit of heat.

"Sorry," Ned said, giving him a wistful sympathetic smile as he moved away.

Beyond the next bend was another freak show. SIMON RAJOS' HOUSE OF WONDERS read the curling blue banner painted on the frontage above the ballyhoo platform. If the pictures could be believed, within he could meet Cyclops the Giant (BIGGEST MAN IN THE WORLD HE'S HUGE HE'S FIERCE), who was at least twenty feet tall if his portrait was to scale; a bald immensity with one eye square in the center of a bulging forehead, and a mouth full of filed teeth. He was shown gorging on a screaming man, presumably one of Ulysses' crew, though Ned wondered how many of Simon Rajos' patrons would understand that classical allusion. The House Of Wonders also featured a Human Skeleton, a pair of Siamese Twins, and another Wild Man of Borneo. New York and London and Paris had so many Wild Men of Borneo that Ned wondered if there was anyone left back on Borneo. Maybe just the Wild Women. He'd have to remember to look into that some day.

A canvas banner, flapping loudly in the cold wind, announced that twice a day all summer, for only a dime, visitors could see an amazing demonstration of mesmerism by Simon Rajos Master Mesmerist. There was a picture of

Simon Rajos under the announcement. If the likeness was true, the man had a skeletal face with sunken eyes, hollow cheeks, and a swollen cranium covered with oily, slicked-down hair as black as sin. His pupils were vast purple pools filled with swirling circles of light, and they seemed to be shooting off tiny little black lightning bolts in all directions. A formidably hideous man, this Simon Rajos, Ned Cullen decided. He wondered whether Simon Rajos would be able to mesmerize the Commodore into giving him a raise. He was inclined to doubt it.

Ned was getting cold and a little tired. He unbuttoned his coat and took out his watch. Ten of two. He'd better hurry back to the Iron Tower, then. After all, he didn't want to miss seeing the Professor crash. He glanced back at the House of Wonders, at Cyclops drooling blood and Simon Rajos Master Mesmerist shooting lightning from his eyes, and set off briskly back down the Bowery.

A crowd had already gathered around the Iron Tower when Ned reached its base. About fifty people, he judged, nearly all men, wearing shabby overcoats and woolen caps. Well, he could double or triple that number if he decided to write up the Professor and his flying machine. Sizing crowds was one of the most creative parts of being a reporter. Standing back at a safe remove, Ned studied the on-lookers until he was certain he'd spotted all the dips, so he'd know who to avoid when he pushed his way through. He scanned the faces quickly, but failed to see Eddie Fitzgerald. Either Gallant Eddie wasn't here yet or Thunderbolt Tom Meegan had pounded his gallant features beyond recognition.

It was two minutes of two, and the crowd was growing as the curious drifted out of nearby buildings and craned their heads up to watch the launch. No doubt Fitzgerald would be along shortly. Ned decided to go up to the Iron Tower.

At the base of the tower, by the twin steam elevators, a short fat man stood in the way, holding a derby hat full of five dollar bills. Ned smiled at him pleasantly and tried to walk by, but the man put up a big, rough hand against the front of Ned's chest. "Five dollars to go up top," he said.

"Oh?" Ned said.

"You get a great view of the flying from up there, but you got to pay. The Professor's got costs to meet."

"Flying machines are expensive, I'm sure," Ned said. "Good idea to keep out the crowds, too. You're one of the inventor's colleagues, no doubt. What's your name?"

"Name?" the man said, confused.

Ned took out his notebook. "Certainly. For my story in the *Herald*. You read the *Herald*, don't you?"

"Yeah, sure," the man said, impressed. "I'm Malcolm Loomis. Master smith Malcolm Loomis. I helped the Professor build the aerocycle."

"Malcolm Loomis," Ned repeated carefully. He spelled it aloud while Loomis nodded and smiled and peered down at the notebook. Ned wrote the word *aerocycle* and doodled a couple of lines in his secret shorthand.

"What's that say?" the man asked.

"Malcolm Loomis, master smith and builder of the aerocycle, is a large, powerful man with an air of authority," Ned read, lying. "Tell me, Mister Loomis, what's the Professor's full name?"

"Wedge," said Malcolm Loomis. "Professor Silas Wedge."

That one Ned actually made a note of. "And is he affiliated with any university or institution hereabouts?"

"I think, um, I don't rightly know."

Ned smiled and put a light query after the word *Professor*. "How many previous, ah, *experiments* have there been, Mister Loomis?"

Loomis swallowed. "This is the fifth flight," he said.

"Flight," said Ned. He raised an eyebrow. "Nasty looking scar you've got there, Mister Loomis. Which flight was that?"

"The, um, the third flight." Loomis looked abashed.

"Well," said Ned, glancing up at the tower, "I had better get up there, don't you think? Good talking to you, though." He put away his notebook, clapped Loomis on the back, and proceeded past him to the elevators.

The elevator operator was a wizened old Negro who tried to charge him a nickel for the ride. "Really now," said Ned, "I'm the press," and that did seem to settle it. The steam elevator rattled and wheezed as it shot him three hundred feet up to the observatory atop the Iron Tower.

The platform was crowded with the people who had paid five dollars each to come up here and squabble over the telescopes. At the moment half of them were standing about sullenly with hands in pockets, watching seagulls and wondering if they'd get their money's worth. The other half were clustered around a plump and somehow ferocious looking gentleman in a checkered woolen suit, long red scarf, and tall beaver hat. Ned said, "Excuse me," parted the crowd, took off a glove, and held out his hand. "Professor Wedge, I presume." It wasn't quite Stanley finding Livingstone, but it would have to do.

"*You*," the man exclaimed loudly. He had a sleek head of white hair and whiskers like one of Captain Boyton's juggling sea lions. "You are late, sir, *late*, we are past flight time." He pointed with a hickory walking stick. "On up the ladder now, quickly, quickly."

Ned smiled. "I'm afraid you've mistaken me for someone else, Professor Wedge. I'm Ned Cullen, of the *Herald*. Mister Bennett was especially anxious that I cover this flight, sent me a cable from Turkey with special instructions in that regard. He's followed your career avidly, Professor. I'm pleased to be here today, *very* pleased. An historic occasion! Five has always been a lucky number. This *is* the aerocycle's fifth flight, am I correct?"

"Yes, that's true," Professor Wedge said. He peered through his bifocals as he shook Ned's hand with tiresome vigor. "The *Herald*, you say? The press has always ignored me in the past."

"Unfairly," said Ned. "The aerocycle is a work of genius."

"Hmpf," said the Professor. He looked suspicious, but pleased. "You are familiar with my invention, Mister, ah, pardon, your name, I did not quite—?"

"Cullen. Ned Cullen. And I'm not as familiar with the aerocycle as I'd like to be. Perhaps you'd care to show it to me, so I could explain it to the *Herald*'s readers?"

Professor Wedge looked about. "My aeronaut is late, Mister Cullen, I supposed you were he. If the flight must be delayed, perhaps I can spare you a few moments. Up to the ladder, then." The ladder in question went up through a trap to the roof of the observatory. Ned looked at it doubtfully, and cleared his throat. "It, ah, might be a bit windy up there. And there's a long way to fall."

Professor Silas Wedge looked disdainful. "Of course it's windy up there, Cullen, why do you think I put my aerocycle up there?" He made a grandiose circular motion with his hand. "The sea breeze, Cullen, the wind off the ocean, it rolls around and around. *In* at ground level, but *outward* up here, high above the earth. Out, out! His hand moved in vigorous circles. "Do you understand?"

"Certainly," Ned replied.

"Up, then!" Professor Wedge commanded. His voice boomed. "Up, up, that's where you'll find my aerocycle, can't write about it unless you *see* it, Cullen! Up!"

Resigned, Ned scrunched down his derby, took a deep breath, and hauled himself up the ladder, with Professor Wedge climbing hard on his heels. He was beginning to regret the impulse that had brought him up the Iron Tower.

When he clambered out and got unsteadily to his feet, his recriminations grew more pointed. It was *cold* up here; the wind—which was indeed blowing out toward the flat gray beach and the choppy sea—was bitter, there were no railings or guard posts to prevent one from falling off, and what was worse, the roof had a slight but definite pitch to it. Ned resolved to stay very far from the edge. He moved closer to the aerocycle, which was tied down at the center of the tower under a complex canopy of ropes.

"There she is," the Professor's booming voice announced as he appeared behind Ned, walking stick and all. "Professor Silas Wedge's aerocycle!"

Ned put a hand on top of his hat, which the cold wind was trying earnestly to remove, and squinted at the aerocycle with a certain amount of annoyance. As he had surmised, it was a bicycle with wings. Ned Cullen approved of bicycles, which had been all the rage these past few years. Anything that had such a salutary effect on women's fashion was not to be disdained, and Ned had determined that the modern sort of girl who took to cycling was likely to be a lively, open, friendly sort of girl as well. He has his doubts about aerocycles, though. What good was served by a well-turned ankle if it was flying past hundreds of feet above your head?

The heart of the aerocycle was a bicycle, a modern one with both wheels the same size, but from that simple frame blossomed the most amazingly complex and ornate contraption. The main wing was a great rigid batlike thing, mounted three feet above where the cyclist's head would be, a raked wedge a good thirty feet from tip to tip, extending well past the sides of the Iron Tower. At least the aeronaut would be shaded from sun and rain as he fell to his death, Ned thought. Fashioned of heavy, oiled canvas sailcloth, the wing stretched tightly across a framework of hollow metal tubing that spiderwebbed out from the handlebars and rear fender. Ned could hear the canvas thrumming in the wind, as if the vehicle as anxious to be off. A second set of wings, barely five feet across, were mounted aft, on the end of a tube that poked out to the rear. There was a big fan back there as well, with polished mahogany blades four feet long, and another fan, twin to the first, high up in front of the main wing. Greasy black iron chains ran everywhere. From the oversized rubber pedals to the wheels, of course, but also up to the forward fan and back to the rear, and other chains connected wingtip to wingtip and wings to cycle, and there were various pulleys and levers and handles that Ned could not begin to understand. "What's this?" he asked, reaching out for a big red switch by the high-backed leather saddle.

"Don't touch that!" the Professor shouted.

Ned flinched back. "Whatever you say, Professor."

"That is the latest Wedge innovation. It releases the wheels, Cullen!"

"Releases the wheels?"

Professor Wedge gestured. Jutting out toward the sea in front of his aerocycle was the wooden runway Ned had seen from the pier, thirty feet long and six feet wide. It was built of good stout lumber, it seemed, but the far end was completely unsupported, so it drooped and swayed beneath his own weight, and shifted at every gust of wind. Ned decided you couldn't get him out on that thing to save his mother's life. "The aeronaut must pedal to built up launch speed," the Professor said, pointing down the gangplank with his stick, "but after flight has been achieved, the wheels are only useless weight. Weight, Cullen! Weight is my bane! Therefore I have modified my aerocycle so the aeronaut may discard the wheels by simply throwing his switch. Simultaneously he will change gears, and all the power of his pedaling will be shifted to the propellers." He jabbed his stick at the fans fore and aft.

"Brilliant," said Ned. "The wings, ah, look rigid. How do they flap?"

"Flap! Flap! The aerocycle does not *flap*, Cullen. It has been proven that flight cannot be achieved by wings that flap."

"Have you told the birds?" Ned Cullen asked drily.

"The birds! Look!" Professor Wedge pointed out over the beach with his walking stick. Three forlorn seagulls were out there, wheeling in chilly circles. "Are they flapping, Cullen? Look at them and tell me."

"Well, no," Ned admitted.

"They glide, Cullen, they glide and they soar on rigid wings, and so too will my aerocycle. It is designed in accord with all of the principles set forth by the great Otto Lilienthal. You are familiar with Lilienthal, of course?"

"The German bird-man," said Ned, who was familiar with all sorts of cranks, lunatics, inventors, daredevils, and similar deranged people. Boyton the frog-man, Lilienthal the bird-man, Minerva the strong woman, they all made good copy.

"I have taken Lilienthal one step further by wedding his designs to that wonder of modern engineering, the bicycle. It is an inevitable marriage, Cullen, and one that will truly give mankind the power of flight, as soon as a few small details are worked out. You'll see, as soon as my aeronaut arrives."

"Perhaps that's him now, coming up the ladder," Ned said, nodding as a head poked up above the roof. The head was wearing a leather football helmet, and the back of it was to Ned. A thick red neck and a pair of shoulders clad in a tight blue woolen jacket followed the head onto the roof.

"You!" Professor Wedge shouted against the wind. "You are late, sir, *late!*" He hurried across the roof and pulled his aeronaut up the last foot or two.

"I'm sorry, Professor," the man said, turning and giving the aerocycle an apprehensive glance. "Some dip lifted my watch last week and I lost track of the time." He held out a hand. "Pleased to meet you, I'm Eddie Fitzgerald."

Ned Cullen, who had been sauntering closer, stopped dead in his tracks. "Oh no," he said in a small voice, but quietly as he spoke he was loud enough for Eddie Fitzgerald to hear him.

Fitzgerald looked over. For a moment his broad, round, freckled face was puzzled. Then the light of recognition flickered on, and his eyes narrowed. "You!" he said. "Ned Goddamn-You-To-Hell Cullen! Ned Trust-Me Cullen."

"Hello, Eddie," Ned said cheerfully, hoping to bluff it out. "You're looking well."

"Do you gentlemen know each other?" Professor Silas Wedge asked, glancing from Ned to his aeronaut and back again.

"We're old friends," Ned said.

"I'm going to kill you," Eddie Fitzgerald declared. He made a fist. He had enjoyed a late growth spurt, Ned noted; several inches and a good twenty pounds since they last spoke. Fitzgerald raised his hands and came forward in a stiff boxer's stance. Fortunately, he was as flat-footed as a heavyweight.

Ned backpedaled and darted under the aerocycle's wings. "Ah, Eddie, calm yourself now, there's been a little misunderstanding, that's all, no need to get upset."

"You damned, damned, damned—" Eddie couldn't seem to think of a noun strong enough for Ned. "Damned!" he repeated with fervor. "You lied to me and you made me a liar too! You ruined my sister and drove my father to a grave. Come back here, you coward." He followed Ned under the wing.

"The flight!" Professor Wedge insisted. "Stop this at once, we have history to make!"

"Listen to the Professor," Ned said earnestly, still retreating. "Eddie, I never lied to you, and I'm here to set it all right in any case. We have to talk." He smiled and slapped the side of the aerocycle. "Before you fly into history," he added. It had better be before, Ned thought; dead people gave rotten interviews.

"Face me like a man, Ned Cullen!" roared Eddie Fitzgerald.

Ned had an inspiration. "All right," he said. He stopped and put a hand up in front of him, palm open. "Hear me out a minute, though. You owe me that much."

"I don't owe you a damn thing, all the trouble you got me into," Eddie roared. His fists were cocked and ready and as he stepped up into Ned's face he didn't look nearly as incompetent as the old man had implied.

"Give me a beating, if you must," Ned said manfully. "Kill me if nothing else will appease your wounded honor. I won't resist, Eddie. But if you do, the crime will be on your head." He pointed a finger. "Yes, go on, do it, I've carried it on my conscience long enough, relieve me of the burden."

"What?" Fitzgerald said. He seemed as easily confused at twenty-three as he had been at nineteen.

Ned looked serious. "An innocent man is in prison because of us, Eddie. Frenchy, Ameer ben Ali, Mister Francis. A stranger to this land, unjustly imprisoned, and we did it."

"*You* did it!" Eddie shouted, his face going red with anger. The wind was rising all around them, and the aerocycle was thrumming vigorously.

"Stop this at once!" Professor Wedge exclaimed as he came up and tried to step between them. "This is no time for your small personal quarrels. The aerocycle awaits!" He waved his stick at the machine, in case they had failed to notice it sitting there with its gears and chains and tubes and thirty-foot canvas wings. "Flight! History! Fame and fortune!"

"I bear some blame," Ned admitted, looking down and shuffling his feet. "I won't deny it, Eddie. I did it, and only I can undo it. So if you kill me, Frenchy will spend the rest of his life in Sing-Sing for a murder he did not commit. His imprisonment will be on your soul then, once you've killed the only man who could have set him free."

Eddie squinted at him uncertainly. "I never thought of that," he said. "Ah, you're lying, Ned Cullen." But his fists came down an inch or so. "I don't know what to do."

"Get on the aerocycle!" Professor Wedge commanded.

"And think of the Professor," Ned said. "You've given him your word to be his aeronaut, haven't you? Now you could toss me right off the Iron Tower, I don't doubt it, a man like you, strong enough to last thirty-four rounds with Thunderbolt Tom Meegan, certainly you could, but then the Professor would have to tell the police and they'd come and arrest you and there wouldn't be any flight. At least not today. And it's such fine weather for it!" The wind buffeted him soundly, and he had to grab his derby. "And you've taken his money too!"

"Not yet I haven't," Eddie said. He lowered his fists a little more and looked at the Professor. "Half the money they all paid to go up the tower, that's what Mister Loomis promised me. Where is it?"

"Mister Loomis is bringing it up," the Professor said stoutly. "You'll be paid after the flight, Fitzgerald, just as Loomis said. Silas Wedge is a man of his word."

"You can't fool my friend Eddie so easily," Ned put in. "What if this aerocycle of yours crashes?"

"Yeah," Eddie said, looking from Ned to the Professor. "What if it crashes?"

"My aerocycle will not crash!"

Ned Cullen gave Eddie Fitzgerald a conspiratorial smile and raised an eyebrow.

"The others all crashed," Eddie blurted.

"Early, primitive designs," the Professor said. "Too much weight, and my aeronauts were not strong enough. We must have a strong man, a man with powerful legs to pedal hard and long and turn the propellers! That was why I ordered Loomis to engage a prize-fighter."

"And you got a good one," Ned added. "Everyone on West Brighton knows about Gallant Eddie the Fitz."

Professor Wedge sniffed at Eddie's breath. "You've been drinking!" he said accusingly.

"A few beers," Eddie said, his face sullen and confused and guilty. His hands had fallen to his sides.

Over on the far side of the aerocycle, the ladder creaked, and Malcolm Loomis' voice called out, "Hey, where is everybody? They all want to know how come there ain't been no flight."

"There's the man with the money right now," Ned said. "Eddie, if you'd like I'll hold your share for you. I could, ah, give it to Sister Joseph in the event that things don't go as planned."

Mentioning Sister Joseph was a mistake; Fitzgerald's eyes came back to Ned and remembered how angry he was. "You keep your lying hands off my money and you stay away from Mary Elizabeth too!" giving Ned a hard shove.

"My God, Eddie," Ned said, in aggrieved tones, "she's a holy sister, what kind of man do you take me for?" He shook his head sadly. "I've had enough. I won't stay here and listen to this. I'm leaving. Frenchy can rot in prison, and if you can sleep nights with that knowledge, you're not the man I thought you were, Eddie." He turned to go.

"Frenchy, Frenchy, who is this Frenchy?" shouted Professor Wedge furiously.

"Hey, are you over there?" Malcolm Loomis asked, coming around the end of the aereocycle.

"If he's in prison it's because you put him there, Ned Cullen," Eddie Fitzgerald shouted.

"I wasn't the one who lied to the police and perjured himself in court," Ned said stiffly.

"I don't care about this!" the Professor screamed. "Get on the aerocycle right this minute!"

"What's the hold-up?" asked Malcolm Loomis, stomping up to the argument.

"You told me to lie!" Fitzgerald said, red-faced. "You said you'd fix everything, that it was Jack the Ripper who did it, that you were going to catch him!"

"Jack the Ripper?" said Professor Wedge.

"You want to count the money," said Loomis, removing his hat. It was full of crisp green.

"I tried," Ned said. "Why do you think I went to Europe so suddenly? Saucy Jack's a Britisher, you know. I was hot on his trail, Eddie, I hoped to get him before he could kill again, and I didn't have time to stop and consult with you. It was a close thing. I met old Leather Apron face-to-face, and I almost had a taste of his knife, the same taste Old Shakespeare got, but at the end it was stalemate. He avoided the trap I laid for him, but I escaped with my life, barely."

"Leather Apron?" the Professor said, baffled.

"You really saw him in the flesh?" Eddie said.

"Would I lie?" Ned said.

"One hundred twenty dollars," Loomis announced.

"I know you didn't have all the facts, Eddie," Ned Cullen said, "but I still can't help feeling cross with you. I risked my life against Jack the Ripper, and you, you,"—he pointed an accusing finger at Fitzgerald— "you were too concerned about yourself to tell the truth, even when it became clear that Byrnes was going to frame an innocent man."

"I didn't know what to do," Eddie wailed. "I had to stick to my story or they would've locked me up too, for lying. Inspector Byrnes and that Clubber Williams, they scared the beejeezus out of me, Mister Cullen. You don't know what they're like. I knew Mister Francis couldn't have been the one. That trail of blood, that was the big thing in the trial, I knew it was you left that trail when you got your shoes all bloody, but I couldn't tell him, could I?"

"Trail of blood?" said Professor Wedge.

"It's my own fault," Ned said seriously. "I shouldn't be so hard on you. If you'd spoken up, Byrnes would have shifted the whole affair onto your shoulders. But it's not too late, Eddie. Help me and we can still clear it all up."

"Nope, one hundred twenty-five," said Malcolm Loomis. "I counted it wrong. When are we going to have the flight?"

"What can I do?" asked Eddie Fitzgerald, looking morose and close to tears. "I told you everything I knew back then."

"I know you did," said Ned. "I need to question the others, Eddie. But they've all vanished on me, and the police claim the files on the case are lost." He raised an eyebrow. "Byrnes' work, I'd venture."

"You must get on the aerocycle," Professor Wedge told Eddie.

"The others?" Eddie asked

"The old whore's friends, what were their names? Mary something and Lizzie the Angel?"

"Mary Healey," Eddie said. He shook his head. "Byrnes took her in along with me and Mary Miniter. I don't know Mister Cullen. They was just whores."

"Mary Miniter was no whore," Ned said. "She was the only one who definitely saw the Ripper face-to-face that night. What's become of Mary Miniter, Eddie?"

"She quit," Fitzgerald said. "The murder scared her, and afterwards she got even more scared. One day she came in and said that she just couldn't work there no more."

"Where did she go?"

"I don't know."

Ned frowned. All this effort wasted; Fitzgerald knew nothing. "What about Samuel Shine?"

Eddie Fitzgerald's brow furrowed beneath the flaps of his leather football helmet. "Samuel Shine," he repeated. "Him I heard about. Yeah, he went off to...where was it now?"

Professor Wedge made an exasperated sound, turned and plucked the thick sheaf of bills from Malcolm Loomis's hand, and thrust it in Fitzgerald's face. "Here, here!" he shouted. "The money, all of the money, it is all yours, all of it! I take nothing for myself, for all my labors, for my genius! Here, one hundred twenty dollars—"

"One hundred twenty-five," corrected the smith. Ned gave him a smile.

"One hundred twenty-five dollars, all yours, every cent, take it now." He snapped the bills against Eddie's pug nose. "But please, enough of this inane talk, enough of these delays, the people are waiting, history holds its breath. Fitzgerald, I beg you, onto the aerocycle!"

"I can't remember," Eddie said, whacking the side of his head with his fist, as if Thunderbolt Tom Meegan hadn't loosened his mind enough. He suddenly seemed to notice the money an inch in front of his face. He grabbed it. "I'll think of it later. I got to do this now," he said, wadding up the bills and stuffing them in a pocket of his trousers.

"At last!" Professor Wedge exclaimed in triumph.

"We can talk some more after it's done," Eddie Fitzgerald said, as he turned and walked a few feet and hoisted himself into the saddle of the aerocycle.

Ned Cullen sighed deeply. The wind tried to remove his hat. He caught it, and stepped back. "Good luck," he said, with all the cheer he could muster. There went his edge, he thought morosely, pedaling off to doom.

"Out of the way!" bellowed Professor Wedge. "Back, back, or you'll be knocked off the tower when we launch."

Ned backed up hastily and retreated to the rear of the aerocycle. Suddenly the windy roof of the Iron Tower observatory was a beehive of activity. Professor Wedge and Malcolm Loomis were dashing everywhere, untying ropes. Eddie Fitzgerald swallowed hard, belted himself into the saddle with three stout leather straps, placed his hands on the handlebars and his feet on the oversized pedals. The great canvas wings thrummed and vibrated in the wind. The long wooden gangplank stretched out ahead, bobbing over three hundred feet of emptiness. Ned shook his head.

The last rope was pulled in, but the aerocycle was still stationary, held in place a half-foot off the gangplank by a rigid metal stand upon a wooden block. "Remember, Fitzgerald, pedal as hard as you can, and as soon as flight has commenced pull the red lever and drop the wheels. Use the blue pull-cords to steer."

"I'm ready!" Eddie yelled. He yanked down his helmet a little tighter.

"Velocity!" Professor Wedge shouted.

Eddie Fitzgerald began to pedal. He started slowly and picked up speed. Faster and faster his legs pumped, and faster and faster the bicycle's wheels spun, until Eddie's face was red with effort and the wheels were a blur of motion.

"Launch!" proclaimed Professor Wedge. He kicked loose the block, the stand collapsed, the furiously revolving wheels hit the wood, and the aerocycle shot forward. *Shot forward like an arrow*, Ned thought, composing in his head in the off-chance the damned thing actually flew. A rather wobbly arrow, Ned reflected, but an arrow nonetheless.

All that weight, the metal tubes and the gears and the chains and thirty feet of canvas wings, it must have been hard to handle. The aerocycle hadn't even made the long gangplank before it began to veer off course to the left.

even made the long gangplank before it began to veer off course to the left. "No, no!" Professor Wedge shouted, rushing forward. "No, straight, straight, bring it back!"

The aeronaut tried manfully, wrenching the handlebars hard to the right. The aerocycle swerved unsteadily and barely avoided shooting off the side of the runway two feet from the tower, which would have snapped the wing in two and dropped Eddie the Fitz right on his Gallant head. But somehow, veering this way and then that way, wobbling back and forth as if he were about to tip over at any moment, and pedaling as if the devil or Jack the Ripper or James Gordon Bennett was hot on his tail, *somehow the intrepid aeronaut brought rolled the aerocycle all the way down the launching slip and out into the cold blue vastness of the virgin sky,* no, scratch the virgin, they'd never let that through, *the cold blue challenge of a crystal sky* and...Ned winced...and...

...and *flew!*

"I'll be damned," Ned Cullen said, edging across the roof carefully to where Professor Wedge and Malcolm Loomis stood side-by-side with bated breath. Maybe it was only the sudden ferocity of the wind, or the velocity that the Professor's contraption had picked up from Eddie's wildman pedaling, but when the aerocycle went sliding off into the air, somehow those huge batwings seemed to fill and swell and become like something alive and...and...

It lifted.

From below, a loud ragged cheer went up.

It rose. It actually *rose*, climbed higher than it started, sailed out serenely over the beach.

Professor Wedge was waving his tall beaver hat and screaming, "The wheels, the wheels," at the top of his ample lungs, but Ned was so engrossed in the story unfolding before him that he hardly noticed. The first man-powered heavier-than-air flight in history, he thought, smiling, and he was the only reporter present. Take that, Stanley! Take that, Nellie Bly and Richard Harding Davis and Jake Riis! Take that, Henry Munce! Ned felt as though a nimbus of light was forming around his head. The wind blew his derby off and sent it sailing off into the sky, but he cared not a whit.

Loomis had joined the Professor. "The wheels, the wheels," they chorused. Professor Wedge had lost his hat as well. Ned saw it flying away.

Eddie Fitzgerald must have heard them above the cheering, for suddenly the wheels were falling end over end towards the sand. The big wooden propellers began to turn, slowly at first and then faster and faster. The aerocycle was fifty feet above the top of the Iron Tower and almost to the waterline. The screams and cheers from below grew more frantic.

The wind died down suddenly.

The areocycle seemed to hesitate.

"Faster!" shouted the Professor. "Pedal faster!"

The propellers turned furiously, but it was not enough. The wind became a whisper. The aerocycle began to tilt.

The cheering gave way to groans and then silence.

Ned Cullen frowned and his nimbus went out.

Propellers busily whirring away, the aerocycle hung for a moment in the still air above the high tide mark, and then began a swift on-rushing descent.

"At least it's falling forward," Ned observed. "He'll make the water, definitely. That's a new record for you, isn't it?" He pointed. "Look," he said. "That's my hat up there, still flying. Maybe your next machine should be a big winged derby, Professor."

"Too much weight," Professor Wedge muttered sourly, as his dream fell. "We must get rid of the metal, we must use wood."

"Wood does not have the strength," Loomis said in the weary voice of a man who has made the same point a hundred times before. "The aeronaut, we must have a lighter aeronaut."

"He was only a welterweight," Ned said.

"Next time we can use a small boy," Loomis said.

"A small boy would not have the strength," Professor Wedge said. "I can't look." He turned away and shut his eyes.

Ned Cullen could look. *Gallant Eddie the Fitz ended his aeronautical career with more grace than he had ever shown in the prize ring*, he thought. And made quite a big splash too, throwing off a huge flat spurt of water like a very large stone skipping across the waves. The aerocycle's wing snapped and folded in on the rider, and then the whole thing was swallowed up beneath the salt sea.

"Knocked out again," Ned said. "He can't swim, either."

"We got a boat standing by," said Malcolm Loomis, pointing, and there it was, already setting out, three men rowing energetically.

"Just think," Ned said, "Gallant Eddie's got all the money."

They rushed down the ladder one after the other. The Iron Tower elite were crowded around the seaward telescopes, taking turns watching the rescue, so the three of them had the elevator to themselves.

When they hauled them up onto the end of the New Iron Pier, both Eddie Fitzgerald and the man who had dived down to cut him loose from his harness were waterlogged and frigid. "Good job."

Ned said, clapping the rescuer on the shoulder. "Next time, though, borrow Captain Boyton's rubber suit." The fellow had no appreciation of wit and only glared at Ned dully.

Eddie was lying flat on his back on the pier, breathing shallowly, his eyes closed. Professor Wedge and Malcolm Loomis were going through his clothing in frantic haste. "Robbing a dead hero, Professor?" Ned said. "The *Herald* frowns on that."

"Here it is," Loomis said, pulling handfuls of very damp five dollar bills out of Eddie's trousers.

"Half, take only half," Professor Wedge said, with an uncertain glance toward Ned. "He must have his fee."

Ned smiled and arched one eyebrow. "You'd better warm him up, " he said. "He's turning blue."

"This is not money," the Professor said, rising with a handful of greenbacks. "This is the next aerocycle!" He waved it in Ned's face.

"And it's wet already," Ned said. "That saves time."

Eddie Fitzgerald groaned loudly, opened his eyes, sat up, and retched out a pool of salt water onto the pier. He looked directly at Ned Cullen. "China," he croaked in a hoarse half-drowned voice, and then he couldn't breathe, and he was making a horrid sucking wheeze as he tried to get some air down his wind-pipe.

"China?" Ned said, distinctly annoyed. "Samuel Shine went to *China*?" Ned didn't know a soul in China.

They were slapping Eddie roundly on the back, great thumping blows, and all the while he was looking at Ned, trying to talk and breathe at the same time. For a man like Eddie, that wasn't easy. "China," he repeated, and that he made that sucking sound again. "China, China, China*town*."

Ned "Why didn't you just say so?"

Sam Chamberlain was late, no doubt lingering over his luncheon and fortifying himself with another glass of champagne. Henry Munce, seated in the hack in front of Sherry's, had expected no less. He had known Chamberlain a long time, and therefore had come well prepared.

He lit his cigar and took out a stack of newspapers, the morning dailies and a few late evening editions. Munce was a disciplined, systematic reader. He read every headline, glanced at each story, ripped from it its gist, committed the important facts to memory. Knowledge was more valuable than gems to Henry Munce. This morning the competition seemed to have little for him. Jacob Riis wrote of Roosevelt's latest exploits while Dana waxed waspish in the *Sun*. Godkin was boring and virtuous in the staid afternoon *Post*. Pulitzer's *World* still had not produced Old Shakespeare, Munce noted with satisfaction; its editorial crusaded against tainted milk while its lead story featured a weather prophet who had scientifically predicted the coming of a snow storm greater than the blizzard of 1888. The *Times*, minus the services of Henry Munce, ran a dry rehash of a poison plot that had been reported in the other dailies three days before. The front page of the *Herald* blithered about some ridiculous flying machine that had crashed off of the Iron Tower on Coney Island. The *Commercial Advertiser* was mostly shipping news, the *Tribune* was singing the praise of the police reforms, the *New York Mercury* had nothing but...

Something nagged at Henry Munce. He put aside the *Mercury* and picked up the discarded *Herald* to look at the story about the flying machine again. This time his eyes fell on the by-line:

BY NED CULLEN

Henry Munce scowled and put the papers away. He folded his big hands hard around the head of his iron walking stick and squeezed the owl until his veins stuck out. He puffed on his short black cigar furiously.

Munce was still sitting that way, staring into nothingness, when the coach door opened. Sam Chamberlain stood outside, dapper, monocled, and tipsy, a wilted flower in his lapel. He waved a hand to fan away some of the thick blue smoke before he climbed in.

"Cullen is back in town," Henry Munce said bluntly, without greeting or preamble.

Chamberlain seated himself and straightened with his azure blue cravat. "My successor departs," he said dryly. "All things must pass, eh, Henry? Especially the Commodore's secretaries. Cullen lasted longer than most. What has it been, four years?"

Henry Munce leaned out of his window. "Take us to Broome Street," he called out to the driver. "At once." When the coach jerked into motion, Munce settled back into the cushions and turned his gaze on his editor. "Cullen has not been discharged," he said. "He remains in the employ of the *Herald*." The newspapers lay on the seat between them; Munce tapped the headline with his stick.

Chamberlain picked up the paper, adjusted his monocle, and read the story while Munce waited in gloomy silence. "So?" he said when he was done. "What does it matter?" He coughed. "God, Henry, that cigar..."

"I do not like it," Munce said.

"Then why the hell do you smoke it?" Chamberlain demanded.

"I was referring to Cullen. Something is afoot, Sam. Just a few weeks ago, the Commodore discharged all of his most experienced and capable employees."

"I know," Chamberlain said with a lazy smile. "Willy and I have been snapping them up by the handfuls."

"When you have a moment to spare from raiding Joe Pulitzer's staff," Munce said. "That is of no moment. The point is, had Cullen given offense to the Commodore, he would not now been employed by the *Herald* in any capacity. Therefore, he has returned to New York for other reasons. Why? Perhaps because some major story required his skills. What story? That is the question I ask myself. Perhaps it is my story."

"Are you worried, Henry?" Sam said. "About—what was it you called him? A worthless n'eer-do-well, wasn't it?"

"Or words to that effect," admitted Henry Munce. He drew on his cigar, exhaled a virulent blue smoke ring, jouncing as the coach rattled over the cobbles. "Nonetheless, the man has a certain superficial charm that he uses to bilk the gullible, and his own peculiar sort of low animal cunning. He is a fraud, a drunkard, and a rake, but he is also a newspaperman, that cannot be gainsaid. Henry Munce never underestimates his opposition, however feeble and venal that opposition might be."

Sam Chamberlain peered out the window. "The Bowery," he announced in dubious tones, as the hack made its turn and immediately slowed, snarled by traffic. The curbs were deep in shadow from the elevated tracks overhead, but the center of the broad, busy street was open to the sun. Horse-drawn trolleys rode their tracks up and down the thoroughfare, and a myriad of coaches, hacks, and teamsters ratcheted over the cobblestones on iron wheels. The street was awash in gray slush and fresh horse droppings, and pedestrians swarmed the sidewalks. Shop girls rode bicycles while mobs of ill-dressed children darted from the alleys and the side streets. Toughs lounged in front of the endless succession of beer halls, distilleries, and dives, and clustered round the el's black iron pillars. Vendors sold hot chestnuts from open carts, gaudy signs cried the unique attractions of two dozen different dime museums, and here and there a wan, coarse prostitute offered her wares by the door of a cheap lodging house. The Bowery also had its theaters, its restaurants, its groceries and jewelers and clothing stores and banks, but they seemed few and lost among the saloons, pawnshops, and freak shows. Chamberlain sighed. "What a bore. Nothing important ever happens on the Bowery, Henry."

"An opinion I do not share," commented Henry Munce.

Chamberlain turned back toward Munce. "I don't know why I'm doing this," he said. "I'm the managing editor of the *New York Morning Journal*. I'm Willy's generalissimo, his good right hand, his confidant and collaborator. I am not required to go to the Bowery to talk to hoodlums. My reporters are required to go the Bowery to talk to hoodlums, but I am not. My reporters are supposed to put their lives on the line for truth, Hearst, and the *Journal*. I am supposed to edit and drink champagne at Sherry's and Delmonico's. Why am I doing this, Henry?"

"Three reasons," replied Henry Munce. "First, you are tall and polished and obviously a man of means, and such a man is necessary to my scheme. Second, you realize the magnitude of this story and you have a newspaperman's soul. Third, I took advantage of you when you were drunk. If you insist on drinking enough for six men at every opportunity, you will find yourself making foolish promises, and you must expect to be held to account for them, Sam."

Chamberlain smiled. "Oh yes. Now I recall."

The coach turned onto Broome street. They could hear the crack of a teamster's whip nearby. "There," said Munce. "We are in luck. That is the man himself coming down the sidewalk." Henry Munce rapped sharply on the ceiling of the coach with the head of his walking stick. "Driver!" he boomed. "Slow. Now." The driver reined in and the hack slowed just as they pulled abreast of the man that Munce had indicated.

He was moving down Broome street not ten feet away, walking with small flat-footed steps. Other pedestrians called out to him respectfully or moved out of his way. The hack edged ahead of him, giving them a good look. The man was squat and muscular, with a bullet-shaped head on a thick bull neck. His nose had been shattered more then once; his ears were prime cauliflower; his broad cheeks and heavy jowls were decorated with a webwork of broken veins and anceint scars. Long, dark, wild hair badly in need of a trim bristled atop his particularly shaped head like a nest of coarse wire. On top of that tangle was set a brown derby three sizes too small for him, its crown spotted with bird droppings.

But the most remarkable thing about him were the cats he carried under each arm, and the bird that rode regally upon the shoulder of his shabby, soiled black overcoat, the biggest pigeon that either Munce or Chamberlain had ever seen, a huge vain, bird whose plumage was a deep, creamy blue. The man's eyes were as black and brutal as two slugs, his scowl nothing short of ferocious. As they passed by, they could hear his pigeon cooing.

"Monk Eastman," said Henry Munce.

"My God," said Sam Chamberlain, "he's uglier than you are, Henry."

Henry Munce snorted. "I have been gathering information about him. A formidable man. For gutter scum."

Monk Eastman paused in front of a bicycle rental shop to talk to two men in long black riding coats who had been lounging outside. Both leapt to their feet when Eastman stopped. Tall men, they overtopped him by almost a foot, but from the way they stood, there was no doubt who was master. Eastman made a quick pointing motion, and one of the men snatched up a fallen bicycle, vaulted aboard, and pedaled away down Broome street. Eastman moved on. Next to the bicycle shop was a pet store; the sign said BIRDS & CATS. Monk lowered his cats to the ground, opened the door, and shooed them inside firmly with the toe of his boot. His big blue pigeon cooed and shat on his shoulder.

By then their coach was well down the street. Munce thumped on the ceiling once more, and they picked up speed again. "Pull your head in, Sam," he said.

Chamberlain nodded. "Where are we going now?" he asked

"Around the block," Munce replied, puffing on his cigar.

Chamberlain coughed. "It would be simpler if you just went in and asked your questions," he said.

"Undoubtedly," Munce admitted. "But Henry Munce is not simple. Nor is Eastman. Beneath the brutal ignorance of that face is a crude but functional mind. He is not the sort to answer questions or make admissions. Moreover, he is dangerous, and far more powerful now than is commonly realized. He will give Paul Kelly and the Five Pointers many sleepless nights. He is well connected at Tammany, rules a domain that extends from the Bowery to the East River, and has absorbed or made vassals of dozens of formerly independent gangs. By my rough estimate, a thousand armed hoodlums now swear allegiance to Monk Eastman." Henry Munce took his cigar from his mouth, squeezed it out between thumb and forefinger, and put it in a pocket. In his deepest and gloomiest tones, he added, "Monk has a cavalry."

"Cavalry?" Sam said incredulously. "You mean horses?"

"Bicycles," said Henry Munce. "Eastman owns the bicycle shop as well as the pet store. A minor gang leader known as Crazy Butch sought to win Eastman's favor by insisting that all of his underlings rent bicycles and learn to ride them. The ploy worked. Crazy Butch is Eastman's right hand. His gang is known as the Squab Wheelmen. Eastman keeps pigeons."

"Charming," said Chamberlain. "Had I known, I'd have had the stuffed squab at Sherry's."

"Bicycles, pigeons, a thousand guns, a burgeoning empire," Munce said. "But Eastman also has his weakness. Henry Munce knows it. And he has enemies. Paul Kelly is one. There is also a man known as Humpty Jackson, a hunchback who heads one of the few small, independent gangs that still dares to operate in Monk's territory. The hunchback's most feared henchman is one Spanish Louie. The details of what happened four years ago still elude me, but one thing is certain: Monk Eastman and Spanish Louie were on opposite sides of it. I plan to take advantage of that fact. Here we are." He thumped on the ceiling. "Stop."

Sam Chamberlain shook his head. "The things I do for Willy Hearst," he said, as he opened the door of the coach, stepped down, and waited for Munce to climb out. Together, they strolled into the pet store.

The establishment smelled. Dozens of bird cages lined the right-hand wall, and when the door closed behind Henry Munce, the cacophony commenced. Canaries sang wildly, pigeons cooed and burbled, a duck began to quack and squawk, and from a perch by the door a fierce red parrot started to hurl curses at them in a thick Brooklyn accent. The cages along the left-hand wall were full of cats: large cats and small cats, orange cats and striped gray tigercats, cats as sooty black as a witch's familiar, cats as white and dirty as city snow a week after its fall. Other cats roamed the store. A mother cat nursed a litter of kittens in the window. A fat orange tabby slept atop the cashbox.

Eastman was not alone. A gaunt, swarthy man was feeding the birds, while a fat man swept the floor in a desultory manner, being very careful to push the broom around the cats and not into them. Behind a frayed curtain, four other men sat in a back room, drinking and noisily playing cards. Monk himself stood at the counter, his sullen stare fixed on a stout red-faced woman. The huge blue pigeon on his shoulder stared as well. "But I have the money, sir," the woman said vigorously, holding out a hand full of coins. "If you won't sell me the kitten, then I'll take the big gray tom."

"No," Eastman said.

"Any cat," the woman said. "Any of them, then."

"I ain't selling you no kit," Eastman said. "I sold you dat other kit and it's dead. You ain't getting no more." He jerked his scarred, pock-marked, jowled head toward the door. "Outta my place," he said.

"Please," the woman said.

Eastman reached in his pocket, extracted a set of brass knuckles, and slid them onto his right hand. His pigeon clucked. The woman scrambled for the exit.

When the door closed behind her, Eastman turned to the journalists, scowling. "Yeah?" he said.

Sam Chamberlain was scratching a cat under the chin. He stood up and smiled. "Monk Eastman," he announced. "My friends down at Tammany speak very highly of you," he said in his smooth, educated, mellifluous voice.

"So who's you?" Eastman said. His scowl became a glower. He looked at Munce and pointed. "And what's he?"

"Does that matter?" Sam said. "He's a dwarf and I'm a, ah, a patron of the arts, and this is a delicate matter, names would just get in the way, don't you think? Nice bird you've got." He reached out his hand to pet Eastman's big blue pigeon.

The bird took a peck at his hand. "He don't like you guys much," Monk said. "I don't neither. Whattaya want?"

"A business matter," Henry Munce said in his deepest tone.

"I ain't selling you no kits or boids."

Munce nodded gravely. "Our business is of a different nature."

"Yes," Sam said. "My friends told me, Monk's the man to see, they said, he'll make the arrangements for you."

"What's dis?" Eastman wanted to know. "What arrangements?"

"My friend is reticent," said Henry Munce. He pointed pointedly at the fat man with the broom and the thin man feeding the birds.

Eastman nodded. "Out," he growled. The men quickly lay down broom and birdseed and made for the back room. "So whattaya need?" Eastman said when they'd gone. "A goil?"

"A beating," said Henry Munce.

Monk Eastman smiled. "Dat's easy."

"Beat him bloody," Chamberlain said cheerfully.

"We got rates," Eastman explained. "Two dollars you just want dis guy punched. Four, we black both eyes. Ten dollars we break his nose or his jaw, whatever you like. Nineteen we break a leg or an arm. You want dis guy's ear chawed off? Dat's extra."

"Sap him," said Henry Munce.

"Fifteen," said Monk Eastman. He looked at Sam Chamberlain. "Say, who's dese guys you knows at Tam'ny?"

Chamberlain smiled, and wrote two names in the dust on the countertop with a long, well-manicured finger. Eastman read them and nodded. Chamberlain wiped them out with the heel of his hand. "Discretion," he cautioned. "I wouldn't want to be linked with this man's unfortunate accident. Embarrassing."

"I got it," Eastman said. "So who is dis guy?" He looked from Chamberlain to Munce and back again.

"The man is a professional criminal," Munce said.

"Yeah?" Eastman's eyes narrowed until they were as small and beady as his pigeon's, though less bright. "Who?"

"We are told he goes by the name of Spanish Louie."

Monk frowned. "Spanish Louie?" He shook his head. "No. I ain't doing dat, I don't care whose you know at Tam'ny."

"I can pay, and pay well," said Sam Chamberlain quickly. "Forget your usual rates, Mister Eastman." He took a roll of bills out of his waistcoat and peeled off five crisp tens. "And five more when the job is done to my satisfaction," he said, placing the bills of the counter and smoothing them with the palm of his hand.

Eastman produced his brass knuckles again. "No," he said. "Out."

"Listen," said Henry Munce, thumping soundly on the floor with his thick iron stick. Eastman glanced down at him in astonishment. Munce looked back up at the flat, ugly, scarred face of the gang leader, looking him right in the eye. "You have not heard why Spanish Louie must be punished," he said.

"I don't care none," Eastman said.

"Mister Vander—that is to say, my friend here, my friend had a friend of his own," Munce said.

"Yes," Sam Chamberlain said, picking up the story, though his eyes flickered nervously from Eastman's face to his brass knuckles. "A charming young girl, sixteen, beautiful, a delight, gay and bright and most anxious to please. I set her up in her own house, bought her clothes and jewels, anything she wanted. I had, um, family duties, but I treasured my time with her. She was the joy of my life. She was mine alone."

"Spanish Louie runs girls," said Henry Munce.

"I know dat," Eastman said. "So?"

"He must have seen her the night I took her to the Silver Dollar Saloon. I should have known better."

"He accosted her on the street, carried her away, and took by force that which was mine alone," Chamberlain said.

"When he was done, he sold her in one of the Allen street whore auctions."

Monk Eastman shrugged. "Tough."

"I found her again," said Sam, "but she was coarse and cheap. She smelled of gin and had one of Cupid's diseases. He ruined her."

"I don't care about none o' dis," said Eastman.

Henry Munce said, "My friend had given her many gifts."

"I'll give you dis gift if you don't get—"

Chamberlain edged backwards. "Henry, perhaps we—"

"Jewels," Munce continued, not budging an inch, "silks and satins, gold and silver. And a kitten."

The monocle fell from Sam Chamberlain's eye. "Oh, yes," he said. "A kitten. A little white kitten with a jeweled collar. She took it everywhere. She had it with her the day that he, that he, took her."

"He smashed its head open on the gutter," said Henry Munce, "right in front of her."

"A kit?" said Monk Eastman. "A little kit?"

"He must be punished," Munce announced.

"A hundred dollars," Chamberlain offered.

Munce shook his head. "It's of no use," he said gloomily to Chamberlain. "Obviously Mister Eastman is afraid of this man Spanish Louie."

Monk Eastman snorted. "I ain't scared o' no guy, leastwise him. He's nuttin'. Any guy do that to a little kit, he deserves whatever he gets." He paused, frowning. "Only thing, he's got friends." He smiled slowly. "What kind of guys be friends with somebody like dat, though? I got friends too." He took the bills off the counter, crumbled them in his hand, and jammed them into his pocket with the brass knuckles. "Yeah, I'll help you. Personal, too. I like to beat up a guy once in a while."

"One must keep a hand in," said Henry Munce.

"Dat's right," said Eastman. "But only when the guy deserves it."

The rest was haggling and arrangements. Spanish Louie was a familiar figure around the Bowery, the docks, and the brothels of Chinatown, but he had no known address and might not be easy to find, Eastman told them. Chamberlain insisted that he wanted his vengeance soon; this week, or the deal was off. Eastman promised to have all the Squab Wheelmen looking. "Better if we took dis guy by hisself," Eastman said, "but if we can't find him, den we gotta take dem all. Dat's okay too. We know where dey meet."

Eastman and Chamberlain shook on it. Henry Munce leaned on his walking stick and did his best to ignore the large black tomcat sniffing round his trouser leg. The cat pulled back and spat at him. "We must be going," Munce reminded Chamberlain.

"At least they weren't dogs," Munce said as they rode back to the *Journal* offices on Printing House Square.

Sam Chamberlain smiled. "A gang war," he mused. "Willy will dance a little jig. We've got an inside exclusive on a gang war!" He laughed aloud. "Henry, why didn't we think of this years ago?"

"We did not think of it," Munce said. "I thought of it."

"Damned right you are, Henry!" Chamberlain said. "Oh, Willy will love this!"

When they arrived at the Tribune Building and ascended to the *Journal* city room on the second floor, Henry Munce took his leave of Sam Chamberlain and went directly to his desk by the wind. He shrugged out of his heavy overcoat, placed his battered black top hat on the blotter, lay the heavy iron walking stick next to it, climbed into the chair that Hearst had ordered custoim built for his unique physique, unlocked the desk drawer on the upper right, took out a small leather-bound journal, and paged through it with methodical deliberation until he found what he wanted. Munce took up the telephone.

"Yes?" said the voice on the other end when the call rang through. A man's voice, deep and pleasant; the tones were as rich as a good Cuban cigar, as erudite as a college professor.

"Mister Jackson, this is Henry Munce of the *New York Morning Journal.* Perhaps you are familiar with my name. I am the greatest crime reporter in the world."

There was a moment of silence, followed by a polite chuckle. "I'm sure you are. But I'm afraid my name is not Jackson, and I prefer the classics to the daily press. You've made an error."

"Henry Munce does not make errors," said Henry Munce. "Don't waste my time with these denials. You are Humpty Jackson. You are a hunchback, sir. Wear whatever alias you choose, give one false name or a hundred, and you remain a hunchback. Henry Munce has his sources. I put my intellect to the task of finding out, and it was easily done."

"Was it?" the voice said. A certain ice had crept into the tone.

"I have no intention of revealing your whereabouts or name to your enemies, Mister Jackson," said Henry Munce.

"How reassuring. What can I do for you, Munce?"

"Less than what I can do for you, Mister Jackson."

"How is that?"

"I am a crime reporter. You are a criminal. I put to you the proposition that each of us can be of help to the other in the practice of our professions. Information is my stock in trade. From time to time, I can provide you with information that you may find of great value. In return, I will require certain information from you and your cohorts."

Jackson chuckled. "Intriguing," he said, "but I seriously doubt that you know anything that I would find of use."

"Then you are wrong," said Henry Munce.

"I have my own sources, Munce. I don't need you."

"I propose to prove otherwise," said Henry Munce. "Only a fool would take my claims at face value. You are no fool. This is my suggestion: I have recently come upon some news that I think you will find to be of great and urgent interest. I will tell you part of what I have learned. Consider it a free sample. If what I tell you proves to be true, and proves to be of use to you, I will trade the rest of my information for the answers to a few questions about some events that took place four years ago."

There was a long silence on the other end of the line. "Tell me this secret of yours," Jackson finally said, in a bored voice. "If it's something I know already, I may just have you killed, Munce."

"You have a man in your employ who is known as Spanish Louie," said Henry Munce, ignoring the threat.

In the far corner of the office, a teletype began to clatter. The sound of wind humming through the wires filled the telephone earpiece, until Jackson cleared his throat. "And what if I did?"

"Tell him to stay off the streets."

"Why?"

"Monk Eastman is looking for him. He does not have Louie's best interests in mind."

This silence was the longest yet. "I can look into this," Jackson said at last.

"I have no doubt."

"Do you work for Monk?" Jackson said. "If he wants a war, I can give it to him."

"I doubt it. He has a thousand men. You have perhaps fifty. If you ignore my warning, you may find that you have forty-nine. Nor do I work for Monk Eastman, though I have indeed encountered him in pursuit of my professional duties. I work for William Randolph Hearst and the *New York Journal*, sir. When you have determined to your satisfaction that I am telling the truth, you may reach me through the *Journal* offices. At that time I will gladly trade you the rest of what I have learned for the answers to a few simple questions that I wish to ask of Spanish Louie. I would be most grateful if you could keep him alive until that time."

Humpty Jackson laughed. "You're something."

"I am Henry Munce," said Henry Munce. "Good day."

The morning air was full of the crisp smells of winter when Kate Hawthorne climbed out of the hack on Hester Street. "Here's the place, if you're sure now, m'am," the driver said, touching his cap. "But I don't think this is a good place for a lady like yourself, if you'll pardon my sayin'."

"I can take care of myself," Kate said as she paid him.

"I could wait for you," the driver offered.

"That won't be necessary," Kate said.

He shrugged, and cracked his whip smartly. Another cab was clattering down the middle of Hester Street as he pulled out; the two drivers swore at each other colorfully and at the top of their lungs. The passenger in the second hack, a husky fellow in a checked suit, stared out at Kate briefly, as if he could not imagine what she was doing here, then politely looked away. He had a pugnacious jaw and a wiry soup-strainer moustache that completely hid his mouth.

Kate turned her back on the street and stood uncertainly at the top of the short flight of stairs that led down to Bloody Meg's basement dive. She wished she was half as sure of herself as she'd led the Colonel to believe, but it had gone too far, there was nothing to be done but go through with it now. She reflected on some of the dangerous places Nellie Bly had gone into, without an instant of hesitation; that lifted her spirits considerably.

The cold wind plucked loose a strand of her auburn hair and whipped it across her face. Kate reached up and tucked it back into place, took a deep breath, and descended with resolute, firm steps. As she reached the bottom, the door banged open and a squirrelly little man with an unpleasant rummy odor exited, favored her with a moist smile, and held open the door for her, bowing in an obscene mockery of gallantry as she swept past him.

The cellar was dark and dank; dusty light fell in long shafts from narrow windows high in the bare brick walls. Sawdust underfoot muffled the sound of her footsteps. The air was warm and heavy with the smell of stale beer. At this hour, the establishment was almost deserted, as Kate had hoped it might be.

And behind the bar along the far wall, filling a pitcher, stood a short, stout matron with a round, cheery red face and thick shock of gray hair.

A vast sense of relief washed over Kate. She couldn't help but smiling as she went over to the bar.

The woman gave her a long hard look. "And what is it that's so funny now, missy?" she asked.

"Oh," said Kate lightly, "pardon me, it's just...well, you weren't what I'd been led to expect, that's all. They tell the most amazing stories about you."

"They do?" the matron said.

"Oh, yes. Ludicrous stories, really."

The woman beamed. She had a sweet smile, a kindly doting smile that reminded Kate of Grandmother Hawthorne, a smile that went more with fresh-baked bread and oatmeal than with stale beer. "And what sort of things do they say, now?" she asked.

"It makes me feel silly to repeat them, actually," Kate said. "Oh, you know, stories about how fierce you are, huge and cruel, about how you, well, beat people bloody and, well, please don't take offense now, but they actually told me that you, well, that you bite off, ah, ears."

"What a thing to be sayin', now."

Kate Hawthorne laughed lightly; it was all so silly. "They even say that you keep the ears in a jar behind the bar." She glanced past the woman, to the long, cluttered counter against the wall. It was crowded with bottles, tall bottles and squat bottles, bottles with famous labels and others with none at all.

A wash basin stacked high with dirty glasses soaking in gray water. The obligatory swipes tub. A bucket of pickled eggs. An ornate wooden clock, with a naked woman in the center, her arms pointing to the hours. And a big old pickling jar, dusty, full of a thin yellowish fluid and...there were things floating in the jar...pickles, surely, Kate thought, or eggs, or....but they didn't look like...they looked like...

"What's wrong, missy?" the stout woman said. Suddenly she no longer reminded Kate of Grandmother Hawthorne. "Want a closer look, do you?" She lifted the pickling jar and set in on the bar right front of Kate.

"Ears," Kate said. Her voice had grown small and quiet.

They were floating around and around now, agitated when the jar was moved. Some of them were old and puckered, wrinkled little things, you could hardly tell what they'd been, but one big one up near the top was definitely, indubitably, and most certainly a human ear. It was still wearing a small brass earring.

Kate Hawthorne took a small step backwards and wet her lips. "Very nice, thank you," she said in her politest voice. "I, ah, if you have some time free, I wonder if you could help me, Meg."

"I ain't Bloody Meg," the woman said.

"You're not?"

A crash and a clatter rang all the way across the room, as a set of wide double doors to the back were kicked open. The stout woman jerked her thumb in that direction. "She is."

Kate Hawthorne turned. "Oh, bother," she said, as Bloody Meg hove into view.

The Colonel had said she was six feet tall. She was at least that, and so broad across the shoulders and hips that she looked almost square. Breasts like cannonballs strained at the fabric of her sweaty man's shirt. She kept her skirt up with a pair of wide black suspenders, and a revolver was tucked into her waistband. Her hair…it couldn't possibly be real hair, Kate thought…her hair was orange, and her face was as wide and cratered as the full moon. She was carrying a keg of beer over each shoulder.

The sweet matronly barkeep was braying like a jackass, hysterical with laughter. Bloody Meg, scowling and sweating, lumbered across the room, lowered the kegs to the sawdust-covered floor with a grunt, and stood up to lean against the bar. Her bare arms were each as thick around as a leg of lamb. "What's so bloody funny, Sadie?" she demanded.

Sadie pointed.

Blushing, Kate composed herself, smiled, and extended a white-gloved hand. "Very pleased to meet you," she said, "I'm Kate Hawthorne."

Bloody Meg stared at Kate's hand. "Too bleeding good to shake me hand without a glove, is it?" she said. She cracked her knuckles. She had an overpowering odor; a smell made up in equal parts of sweat, yeast, and vinegar.

"Certainly not," Kate said. She took off her glove very quickly.

Bloody Meg took her hand and squeezed.

Kate winced, tried to squeeze back, and gave it up instantly as a foolish notion. Her hand felt like a dove caught in a vise. She pressed her lips toether and tried not to whimper. She looked Bloody Meg straight in the eye. Meg's eye was small and brown and bloodshot, squinting out at her from amid folds of fat.

"Pleased to meetcha," Bloody Meg said, releasing Kate's hand. She grinned. Her teeth were green. "I could of broken all your cuntin' fingers if I'd had a mind to," she said cheerfully.

"I have no doubt," Kate replied. She flexed the half-crushed hand, trying to get some circulation back into her fingers.

Bloody Meg looked her up and down. "Ain't you the one?" she said. "I don't see many like you down here, dear. Whattaya want? You didn't bloody well come down here for no stale beer." She guffawed.

"I'm from the *World*," Kate began.

"And what bloody world is that, dearie?" Meg said. She had a loud rubbery voice, full of boom and snap.

"The *New York World*," Kate said crisply. "Mister Pulitzer's newspaper. I'm looking for a prostitute."

Sadie brayed, and even Meg smiled. "You are, are you?"

Kate blushed again. She ignored it. "She sometimes goes by the name of Old Shakespeare. I've been given to understand that you might be able to take me to her."

"What cunt-face told you that swill?" Bloody Meg inquired pleasantly. But her eyes went to Sadie as she spoke, and the two women exchanged what had every appearance of being a meaningful glance.

"Is she here?" Kate asked. "I assure you, I mean her no harm. I just want to ask her a few questions."

"She ain't here," Bloody Meg said.

"Are you sure?"

"You calling me a liar, dearie?"

"Certainly not," Kate said.

"And even if she was here, which she bloody well ain't, she won't be having no traffic with your sort," Meg added.

"You've gone and got her into more'n enough troubles already, haven't you?" Sadie blurted. "You with your write-ups and all."

Bloody Meg turned on her. "Shut your damned hole, Sadie," she said.

"So you do know where she is," Kate said crisply. "Please, take me to her. I'll only take a few minutes of her time. She has a story to tell, one the *World* wants to know." Kate took her handbag from under her arm and opened her coin purse. "I can pay for information," she said.

Snorting, Bloody Meg knocked the purse from her hand with a massive backhanded slap that scattered coins all over the cellar and left Kate's hand stinging. "Keep your bloody money, dearie."

(and that, alas, was as far as I got...)

Introduction to Skin Trade

My first script for *The Twilight Zone* started out as an adaptation of Donald Westlake's chilling Christmas story "Nackles," and somehow ended up being a rewrite of a teleplay about an Elvis impersonator who goes back in time and meets the real Elvis. The next thing I knew, I was out in Los Angeles, part of *The Twilight Zone* writing staff—initially as a lowly Staff Writer (you know the position is lowly if the title actually includes the word "writer"), and later as a Story Editor.

The Twilight Zone was a unique show, an anthology series where the stories were the stars. Many of our best episodes were adaptations of classic SF and fantasy short stories, including four of the five teleplays I contributed. It was the perfect series for someone like me. If you had asked me back in 1986, I would have told you that my gig there was a one-time thing, that as soon as the Zone went off the air I'd be going back to novels and short stories.

I was wrong about that. No sooner had CBS pulled the plug on *The Twilight Zone* then I found myself writing a *Max Headroom* script, and not long after that I was hired for a new show called *Beauty and the Beast*. I put in three seasons with *B&B*, writing thirteen scripts for the series and rising from Executive Story Consultant (the first season) to Supervising Producer (the third). By the time *Beauty and the Beast* died its premature death, I had climbed high enough on the Hollywood ladder to dream about creating a show of my own. I spent much of the next five years pitching series ideas, writing pilots (and producing one of them, *Doorways*), and doing screenplays for feature films.

Yet despite all the writing I did for television and film, I never really thought of myself as a screenwriter. Your first love is always the truest, and books were my first love.

Though I ended up spending years in Los Angeles, I never truly moved there. While I was working, I would rent a furnished apartment in one of the sprawling Oakwood complexes, or a guest house in someone's back yard, but the moment my project wrapped I would hop into my Mazda RX-7 and head east for Santa Fe. My sweet lady Parris held the fort for me at home, for months and sometimes years. Santa Fe remained my legal residence, the place where I hung my hats and paid my taxes, the place where I kept my *books* and all the rest of my stuff. Santa Fe was home. Santa Fe was real. Santa Fe was me.

And the books, the stories... those were me too.

There is a lot of stress in any Hollywood job, and a lot of long hours. As you climb the ladder it only gets worse. The last thing any television writer needs is a second job, but that was just what I had. Just as I had to visit Santa Fe from time to time, to remind myself of who I was, I had to keep publishing books and short stories as well. If I hadn't... well, the readers had short memories even in the 80s, and they have only grown shorter.

One of the ways I kept my hand in was through *Wild Cards*, the shared world anthology series that I edited, starting in 1986. Not only did I edit the *Wild Cards* books, but I wrote for them as well, contributing much of the interstitial narrative that helped turn a collection of stories into what we called mosaic novels. *Wild Cards* began at virtually the same time as my job on *Twilight Zone*, and continued through three seasons of *Beauty and the Beast*, through my feature assignments and pilots, right up into the present day, and that steady stream of books helped to keep my name alive in the worlds of science fiction and fantasy.

But *Wild Cards* was not the end of it. I wrote other stories as well. "The Skin Trade" was the first of those, and perhaps the most important.

In 1983, Paul Mikol and Scot Stadalsky had launched Dark Harvest, a new small press publisher specializing in horror. The first book they published was a beautiful limited edition of my collected horror stories, *Songs the Dead Men Sing*. From there Dark Harvest went on to become the most important and prolific of the small specialty publishers, in large part because of *Night Visions*, their annual original anthology.

Every *Night Visions* featured three writers, each of whom would contribute 30,000 words of original fiction. There was a different guest editor for every volume as well, and Dark Harvest tabbed me to edit *Night Visions 3*, which featured work by Ramsey Campbell, Lisa Tuttle, and a new British horror writer that very few people had ever heard of, a fellow named Clive Barker. Clive's contribution to the book was a single long novella called "The Hellbound Heart," the seed from which all those Hellraiser films later sprouted. No editor ever had an easier job than I did on *Night Visions 3*.

So when Paul Mikol asked me if I would like to be a part of *Night Visions 5*, this time not as the editor, but as one of the three featured writers, I was delighted to accept... especially when he told me that I would be sharing the book with a new writer named Dan Simmons, and some other guy named Stephen King. That was some company. I couldn't say "Yes" fast enough.

It was only later that I got cold feet. What had I done? I didn't have 30,000 words of unpublished horror stories. Hell, I didn't have 30 words. Nor did I have time to write 30,000 words. I was on staff at Beauty and the Beast when Dark Harvest approached me, writing scripts and attending story meetings and pitch sessions all day, and editing Wild Cards at night and on weekends. And my god, I was going to be in a book with Stephen King and

Dan Simmons! Tens of thousands of King's readers would be picking up *Night Visions 5* and maybe sampling my work for the first time, and Simmons had blown everyone in the field away with *Song of Kali*, his bone-chilling first novel. There was no way I could hope to hang in there with those two home run hitters with anything except my very best work. I almost called Paul Mikol back and chickened out right then and there.

I couldn't, though. I had given my word, and besides, I was bound and determined to keep my hand in.

King and Simmons each contributed three stories of varied length to *Night Visions 5*, but I decided to take the same approach Clive Barker had taken so successfully for *Night Visions 3*. My third of the book would be a single 30,000 word novella. I had my setting, a fictional decaying midwestern city that was part Chicago and part Dubuque, Iowa and part my own nightmares. Several years before, I had written a vampire novel, *Fevre Dream*, but I had never given the other great movie monster its due, so this would be a werewolf story. And I had just the werewolf...

Looking back, I still don't know how I ever got "The Skin Trade" written. I wrote it in the Seward offices of *Beauty and the Beast*, working alone in an empty building after everyone else had gone home. Some nights I worked so late I had to drink whole pots of coffee to keep myself awake, and then I got so wired I *couldn't* sleep, even when I went home and tumbled into bed. Thankfully I never gave Willie's lines to Vincent or vice versa, but there were times when it was a close thing.

Stephen King delivered his third of the book, and then Dan Simmons, and still I was nowhere close. My original deadline came and went, and I had to beg Dark Harvest for more time. Douglas Winter was the editor of *Night Visions 5*, and I don't doubt that both he and Paul Mikol got more than a few grey hairs waiting for me to finish and wondering if I ever would.

But when I finally sent in the story, Paul wrote to me to say, "All right, it kills me, but it was worth the wait." *Night Visions 5* sold out in hardcover and made a record paperback sale (thanks to Stephen King, of course), and in 1989 "The Skin Trade" won the World Fantasy Award for Best Novella, and I took home one of Gahan Wilson's wonderfully gloomy busts of H. P. Lovecraft to adorn my mantle.

Maybe you can go home after all. Even if you write for television...

Skin Trade

Willie smelled the blood a block away from her apartment.

He hesitated and sniffed at the cool night air again. It was autumn, with the wind off the river and the smell of rain in the air, but the scent, *that* scent, was copper and spice and fire, unmistakable. He knew the smell of human blood.

A jogger bounced past, his orange sweats bright under the light of the full moon. Willie moved deeper into the shadows. What kind of fool ran at this hour of the night? *Asshole,* Willie thought, and the sentiment emerged in a low growl. The man looked around, startled. Willie crept back further into the foliage. After a long moment, the jogger continued up the bicycle path, moving a little faster now.

Taking a chance, Willie moved to the edge of the park, where he could stare down her street from the bushes. Two police cruisers were parked outside her building, lights flashing. What the hell had she gone and done?

When he heard the distant sirens and saw another set of lights approaching, flashing red and blue, Willie felt close to panic. The blood scent was heavy in the air, and set his skull to pounding. It was too much. He turned and ran deep into the park, for once not caring who might see him, anxious only to get away. He ran south, swift and silent, until he was panting for breath, his tongue lolling out of his mouth. He wasn't in shape for this kind of shit. He yearned for the safety of his own apartment, for his La-Z-Boy and a good shot of Primateen Mist.

Down near the riverfront, he finally came to a stop, wheezing and trembling, half-drunk with blood and fear. He crouched near a bridge abutment, staring at the headlights of passing cars and listening to the sound of traffic to soothe his ragged nerves.

Finally, when he was feeling a little stronger, he ran down a squirrel. The blood was hot and rich in his mouth, and the flesh made him feel ever so much stronger, but afterwards he got a hairball from all the goddamned fur.

"Willie," Randi Wade said suspiciously, "if this is just some crazy scheme to get into my pants, it's not going to work."

The small man studied his reflection in the antique oval mirror over her couch, tried out several faces until he found a wounded look he seemed to like, then turned back to let her see it. "You'd think that? You'd think that of *me?* I come to you, I need your help, and what do I get, cheap sexual innuendo. You ought to know me better than that, Wade, I mean, Jesus, how long have we been friends?"

"Nearly as long as you've been trying to get into my pants," Randi said. "Face it, Flambeaux, you're a horny little bastard."

Willie deftly changed the subject. "It's very amateur hour, you know, doing business out of your apartment." He sat in one of her red velvet wingback chairs. "I mean, it's a nice place, don't get me wrong, I love this Victorian stuff, can't wait to see the bedroom, but isn't a private eye supposed to have a sleazy little office in the bad part of town? You know, frosted glass on the door, a bottle in the drawer, lots of dust on the filing cabinets..."

Randi smiled. "You know what they charge for those sleazy little offices in the bad part of town? I've got a phone machine, I'm listed in the yellow pages..."

"AAA-Wade Investigations," Willie said sourly. "How do you expect people to find you? Wade, it should be under W; if God had meant everybody to be listed under A, he wouldn't have invented all those other letters." He coughed. "I'm coming down with something," he complained, as if it were her fault. "Are you going to help me, or what?"

"Not until you tell me what this is all about," Randi said, but she'd already decided to do it. She liked Willie, and she owed him. He'd given her work when she needed it, with his friendship thrown into the bargain. Even his constant, futile attempts to jump her bones were somehow endearing, although she'd never admit it to Willie. "You want to hear about my rates?"

"Rates?" Willie sounded pained. "What about friendship? What about old time's sake? What about all the times I bought you lunch?"

"You never bought me lunch," Randi said accusingly.

"Is it my fault you kept turning me down?"

"Taking a bucket of Popeye's extra spicy to an adult motel for a snack and a quickie does not constitute a lunch invitation in my book," Randi said.

Willie had a long, morose face, with broad rubbery features capable of an astonishing variety of expressions. Right now he looked as though someone had just run over his puppy. "It would not have been a quickie," he said with vast wounded dignity. He coughed, and pushed himself back in the chair, looking oddly childlike against the red velvet cushions. "Randi," he said, his voice suddenly gone scared and weary, "this is for real." She'd first met Willie Flambeaux when his collection agency had come after her for the unpaid bills left by her ex. She'd been out of work, broke, and desperate, and Willie had taken pity on her and given her work at the agency. As much as she'd hated hassling people for money, the job had been a godsend, and she'd stayed long enough to wipe out her debt. Willie's lopsided smile, endless propositions, and mordant intelligence had somehow kept her sane. They'd kept in touch, off and on, even after Randi had left the hounds of Hell, as Willie liked to call the collection agency.

All that time, Randi had never heard him sound scared, not even when discoursing on the prospect of imminent death from one of his many grisly and undiagnosed maladies. She sat down on the couch. "Then I'm listening," she said. "What's the problem?"

"You see this morning's *Courier?*" he asked. "The woman that was murdered over on Parkway?"

"I glanced at it," Randi said.

"She was a friend of mine."

"Oh, Jesus." Suddenly Randi felt guilty for giving him a hard time. "Willie, I'm so sorry."

"She was just a kid," Willie said. "Twenty-three. You would have liked her. Lots of spunk. Bright too. She'd been in a wheelchair since high school. The night of her senior prom, her date drank too much and got pissed when she wouldn't go all the way. On the way home he floored it and ran head-on into a semi. Really showed her. The boy was killed instantly. Joanie lived through it, but her spine was severed, she was paralyzed from the waist down. She never let it stop her. She went on to college and graduated with honors, had a good job."

"You knew her through all this?"

Willie shook his head. "Nah. Met her about a year ago. She'd been a little overenthusiastic with her credit cards, you know the tune. So I showed up on her doorstep one day, introduced her to Mr. Scissors, one thing led to another and we got to be friends. Like you and me, kind of." He looked up into her eyes. "The body was mutilated. Who'd do something like that? Bad enough to kill her, but…" Willie was beginning to wheeze. His asthma. He stopped, took a deep breath. "And what the fuck does it mean? *Mutilated,* Jesus, what a nasty word, but mutilated *how?* I mean, are we talking Jack the Ripper here?"

"I don't know. Does it matter?"

"It matters to me." He wet his lips. "I phoned the cops today, tried to get more details. It was a draw. I wouldn't tell them my name and they wouldn't give me any information. I tried the funeral home too. A closed casket wake, then the body is going to be cremated. Sounds to me like something getting covered up."

"Like what?" she said.

Willie sighed. "You're going to think this is real weird, but what if…" He ran his fingers through his hair. He looked very agitated. "What if Joanie was… well, savaged ripped up, maybe even… well, partially eaten… you know, like by… some kind of animal."

Willie was going on, but Randi was no longer listening.

A coldness settled over her. It was old and gray, full of fear, and suddenly she was twelve years old again, standing in the kitchen door listening to her mother make that sound, that terrible high thin wailing sound. The men were still trying to talk to her, to make her understand...*some kind of animal,* one of them said. Her mother didn't seem to hear or understand, but Randi did. She'd repeated the words aloud, and all the eyes had gone to her, and one of the cops had said, *Jesus, the kid,* and they'd all stared until her mother had finally gotten up and put her to bed. She began to weep uncontrollably as she tucked in the sheets... her mother, not Randi. Randi hadn't cried. Not then, not at the funeral, not ever in all the years since.

"Hey. *Hey!* Are you okay?" Willie was asking.

"I'm fine," she said sharply.

"Jesus, don't scare me like that, I got problems of my own, you know? You looked like... hell, I don't know what you looked like, but I wouldn't want to meet it in a dark alley."

Randi gave him a hard look. "The paper said Joan Sorenson was murdered. An animal attack isn't murder."

"Don't get legal on me, Wade. I don't know, I don't even know that an animal was involved, maybe I'm just nuts, paranoid, you name it. The paper left out the grisly details. The fucking paper left out a lot." Willie was breathing rapidly, twisting around in his chair, his fingers drumming on the arm.

"Willie, I'll do whatever I can, but the police are going to go all out on something like this, I don't know how much I'll be able to add."

"The police," he said in a morose tone. "I don't trust the police." He shook his head. "Randi, if the cops go through her things, my name will come up, you know, on her Rolodex and stuff."

"So you're afraid you might be a suspect, is that it?"

"Hell, I don't know, maybe so."

"You have an alibi?"

Willie looked very unhappy. "No. Not really. I mean, not anything you could use in court. I was supposed to... to see her that night. Shit, I mean, she might have written my name on her fucking *calendar* for all I know. I just don't want them nosing around, you know?"

"Why not?"

He made a face. "Even us turnip-squeezers have our dirty little secrets. Hell, they might find all those nude photos of you." She didn't laugh. Willie shook his head. "I mean, god, you'd think the cops would have better things to do than go around solving murders—I haven't gotten a parking ticket in over a year. Makes you wonder what the hell this town is coming to." He had begun to wheeze again. "Now I'm getting too worked up again, damn it. It's you, Wade. I'll bet you're wearing crotchless panties under those jeans, right?"

Glaring at her accusingly, Willie pulled a bottle of Primateen Mist from his coat pocket, stuck the plastic snout in his mouth, and gave himself a blast, sucking it down greedily.

"You must be feeling better," Randi said.

"When you said you'd do anything you could to help, did that include taking off all of your clothes?" Willie said hopefully.

"No," Randi said firmly. "But I'll take the case."

River Street was not exactly a prestige address, but Willie liked it just fine. The rich folks up on the bluffs had "river views" from the gables and widow's walks of their old Victorian houses, but Willie had the river itself flowing by just beneath his windows. He had the sound of it, night and day, the slap of water against the pilings, the foghorns when the mists grew thick, the shouts of pleasure-boaters on sunny afternoons. He had moonlight on the black water, and his very own rotting pier to sit on, any midnight when he had a taste for solitude. He had eleven rooms that used to be offices, a men's room (with urinal) *and* a ladies' room (with Tampax dispenser), hardwood floors, lovely old skylights, and if he ever got that loan, he was definitely going to put in a kitchen. He also had an abandoned brewery down on the ground floor, should he ever decide to make his own beer. The drafty red brick building had been built a hundred years ago, which was about how long the flats had been considered the bad part of town. These days what wasn't boarded up was industrial, so Willie didn't have many neighbors, and that was the best part of all.

Parking was no problem either. Willie had a monstrous old lime-green Cadillac, all chrome and fins, that he left by the foot of the pier, two feet from his door. It took him five minutes to undo all his locks. Willie believed in locks, especially on River Street. The brewery was dark and quiet. He locked and bolted the doors behind him and trudged upstairs to his living quarters.

He was more scared than he'd let on to Randi. He'd been upset enough last night, when he'd caught the scent of blood and figured that Joanie had done something really dumb, but when he'd gotten the morning paper and read that she'd been the victim, that she'd been tortured and killed and mutilated... *mutilated,* dear god, what the hell did that *mean,* had one of the others... no, he couldn't even think about that, it made him sick.

His living room had been the president's office back when the brewery was a going concern. It fronted on the river, and Willie thought it was nicely furnished, all things considered. None of it matched, but that was all right. He'd picked it up piece by piece over the years, the new stuff usually straight repossession deals, the antiques taken in lieu of cash on hopeless and long-overdue debts. Willie nearly always managed to get *something,* even on the accounts that everyone else had written off as a dead loss. If it was something he liked, he paid off the client out of his own pocket, ten or twenty cents on the dollar, and kept the furniture. He got some great bargains that way.

He had just started to boil some water on his hotplate when the phone began to ring.

Willie turned and stared at it, frowning. He was almost afraid to answer. It could be the police… but it could be Randi too, or some other friend, something totally innocent. Grimacing, he went over and picked it up. "Hello."

"Good evening, William." Willie felt as though someone was running a cold finger up his spine. Jonathan Harmon's voice was rich and mellow; it gave him the creeps. "We've been trying to reach you."

I'll bet you have, Willie thought, but what he said was, "Yeah, well, I been out."

"You've heard about the crippled girl, of course."

"*Joan,*" Willie said sharply. "Her name was Joan. Yeah, I heard. All I know is what I read in the paper."

"I own the paper," Jonathan reminded him. "William, some of us are getting together at Blackstone to talk. Zoe and Amy are here right now, and I'm expecting Michael any moment. Steven drove down to pick up Lawrence. He can swing by for you as well, if you're free."

"No," Willie blurted. "I may be cheap, but I'm never free." His laugh was edged with panic.

"William, your life may be at stake."

"Yeah, I'll bet, you sonofabitch. Is that a threat? Let me tell you, I wrote down everything I know, *everything,* and gave copies to a couple of friends of mine." He hadn't, but come to think of it, it sounded like a good idea. "If I wind up like Joanie, they'll make sure those letters get to the police, you hear me?"

He almost expected Jonathan to say, calmly, "I *own* the police," but there was only silence and static on the line, then a sigh. "I realize you're upset about Joan—"

"Shut the fuck up about Joanie," Willie interrupted. "You got no right to say jackshit about her, I know how you felt about her. You listen up good, Harmon, if it turns out that you or that twisted kid of yours had anything to do with what happened, I'm going to come up Blackstone one night and kill you myself, see if I don't. She was a good kid, she… she…" Suddenly, for the first time since it had happened, his mind was full of her—her face, her laugh, the smell of her when she was hot and bothered, the graceful way her muscles moved when she ran beside her, the noises she made when their bodies joined together. They all came back to him, and Willie felt tears on his face. There was a tightness in his chest as if iron bands were closing around his lungs. Jonathan was saying something, but Willie slammed down the receiver without bothering to listen, then pulled the jack. His water was boiling merrily away on the hotplate. He fumbled in his pocket and gave himself a good belt off his inhaler, then stuck his head in the steam until he could breathe again. The tears dried up, but not the pain.

Afterwards he thought about the things he'd said, the threats he made, and he got so shaky that he went back downstairs to double check all his locks.

Courier Square was far gone in decay. The big department stores had moved to suburban malls, the grandiose old movie palaces had been chopped up into multi-screens or given over to porno, once-fashionable storefronts now housed palm readers and adult bookstores. If Randi had really wanted a seedy little office in the bad part of town, she could find one on Courier Square. What little vitality the Square had left came from the newspaper.

The Courier Building was a legacy of another time, when downtown was still the heart of the city and the newspaper its soul. Old Douglas Harmon, who'd liked to tell anyone who'd listen that he was cut from the same cloth as Hearst and Pulitzer, had always viewed journalism as something akin to a religious vocation, and the "gothic deco" edifice he built to house his newspaper looked like the result of some unfortunate mating between the Chrysler Building and some especially grotesque cathedral. Five decades of smog had blackened its granite facade and acid rain had eaten away at the wolfshead gargoyles that snarled down from its walls, but you could still set your watch by the monstrous old presses in the basement and a Harmon still looked down on the city from the publisher's office high atop the Iron Spire. It gave a certain sense of continuity to the square and the city.

The black marble floors in the lobby were slick and wet when Randi came in out of the rain, wearing a Burberry raincoat a of couple sizes too big for her, a souvenir of her final fight with her ex-husband. She'd paid for it, so she was damn well going to wear it. A security guard sat behind the big horseshoe-shaped reception desk, beneath a wall of clocks that once had given the time all over the world. Most were broken now, hands frozen into a chronological cacophony. The lobby was a gloomy place on a dark afternoon like this, full of drafts as cold as the guard's face. Randi took off her hat, shook out her hair, and gave him a nice smile. "I'm here to see Barry Schumacher."

"Editorial. Third floor." The guard barely gave her a glance before he went back to the bondage magazine spread across his lap. Randi grimaced and walked past, heels clicking against the marble.

The elevator was an open grillwork of black iron; it rattled and shook and took forever to deliver her to the city room on the third floor. She found Schumacher alone at his desk, smoking and staring out his window at the rain-slick streets. "Look at that," he said when Randi came up behind him. A streetwalker in a leather miniskirt was standing under the darkened marquee of the Castle. The rain had soaked her thin white blouse and plastered it to her breasts. "She might as well be topless," Barry said. "Right in front of the Castle too. First theater in the state to show *Gone With the Wind,* you know that? All the big movies used to open there." He grimaced, swung his chair around, ground out his cigarette. "Hell of a thing," he said.

"I cried when Bambi's mother died," Randi said.

"In the Castle?"

She nodded. "My father took me, but he didn't cry. I only saw him cry once, but that was later, much later, and it wasn't a movie that did it."

"Frank was a good man," Schumacher said dutifully. He was pushing retirement age, overweight and balding, but he still dressed impeccably, and Randi remembered a young dandy of a reporter who'd been quite a rake in his day. He'd been a regular in her father's Wednesday night poker game for years. He used to pretend that she was his girlfriend, that he was waiting for her to grow up so they could get married. It always made her giggle. But that had been a different Barry Schumacher; this one looked as if he hadn't laughed since Kennedy was president. "So what can I do for you?" he asked.

"You can tell me everything that got left out the story on that Parkway murder," she said. She sat down across from him.

Barry hardly reacted. She hadn't seen him much since her father died; each time she did, he seemed grayer and more exhausted, like a man who's been bled dry of passion, laughter, anger, everything.

"What makes you think anything was left out?"

"My father was a cop, remember? I know how this city works. Sometimes the cops ask you to leave something out."

"They ask," Barry agreed. "Them asking and us doing, that's two different things. Once in a while we'll omit a key piece of evidence, to help them weed out fake confessions. You know the routine." He paused to light another cigarette.

"How about this time?"

Barry shrugged. "Hell of a thing. Ugly. But we printed it, didn't we?"

"Your story said the victim was mutilated. What does that mean, exactly?"

"We got a dictionary over by the copyeditors' desk, you want to look it up."

"I don't want to look it up," Randi said, a little too sharply. Barry was being an asshole; she hadn't expected that. "I know what the word means."

"So you saying we should have printed all the juicy details?" Barry leaned back, took a long drag on his cigarette. "You know what Jack the Ripper did to his last victim? Among other things, he cut off her breasts. Sliced them up neat as you please, like he was carving white meat off a turkey, and piled the slices on top of each other, beside the bed. He was very tidy, put the nipples on top and everything." He exhaled smoke. "Is that the sort of detail you want?

You think that kind of stuff belongs in a family newspaper? You know how many kids read the *Courier* everyday?"

"I don't care what you print in the *Courier*," Randi said. "I just want to know the truth. Am I supposed to infer that Joan Sorenson's breasts were cut off?"

"I didn't say that," Schumacher said.

"No. You didn't say much of anything. Was she killed by some kind of animal?"

That did draw a reaction. Schumacher looked up, his eyes met hers, and for a moment she saw a hint of the friend he had been in those tired eyes behind their wire-rim glasses. "An animal?" he said softly. "Is that what you think? This isn't about Joan Sorenson at all, is it? This is about your father." Barry got up and came around his desk. He put his hands on her shoulders and looked into her eyes. "Randi, honey, let go of it. I loved Frank too, but he's dead, he's been dead for.... Hell, it's almost twenty years now. The coroner said he got killed by some kind of rabid dog, and that's all there is to it."

"There was no trace of rabies, you know that as well as I do. My father emptied his gun. What kind of rabid dog takes six shots from a police .38 and keeps on coming, huh?"

"Maybe he missed," Barry said.

"He didn't miss!" Randi said sharply. She turned away from him. "We couldn't even have an open casket, too much of the body had been..." Even now, it was hard to say without gagging, but she was a big girl now and she forced it out. "... eaten," she finished softly. "No animal was ever found."

"Frank must have put some bullets in it, and after it killed him the damned thing crawled off somewhere and died," Barry said. His voice was not unkind. He turned her around to face him again. "Maybe that's how it was and maybe not. It was a hell of a thing, but it happened eighteen years ago, honey, and it's got nothing to do with Joan Sorenson."

"Then tell me what happened to her," Randi said.

"Look, I'm not supposed to..." He hesitated, and the tip of his tongue flicked nervously across his lips. "It was a knife," he said softly. "She was killed with a knife, it's all in the police report, just some psycho with a sharp knife." He sat down on the edge of his desk, and his voice took on its familiar cynicism again. "Some weirdo seen too many of those damn sick holiday movies, you know the sort, *Halloween, Friday the 13th,* they got one for every holiday"

"All right." She could tell from his tone that she wouldn't be getting any more out of him. "Thanks."

He nodded, not looking at her. "I don't know where these rumors come from. All we need, folks thinking there's some kind of wild animal running around, killing people." He patted her shoulder. "Don't be such a stranger, you hear? Come by for dinner some night. Adele is always asking about you."

"Give her my best." She paused at the door. "Barry…" He looked up, forced a smile. "When they found the body, there wasn't anything missing?"

He hesitated briefly. "No," he said.

Barry had always been the big loser at her father's poker games. He wasn't a bad player, she recalled her father saying, but his eyes gave him away when he tried to bluff… like they gave him away right now.

Barry Schumacher was lying.

The doorbell was broken, so he had to knock. No one answered, but Willie didn't buy that for a minute. "I know you're there, Mrs. Juddiker," he shouted through the window. "I could hear the TV a block off. You turned it off when you saw me coming up the walk. Gimme a break, okay?" He knocked again. "Open up, I'm not going away.

Inside, a child started to say something, and was quickly shushed. Willie sighed. He hated this; why did they always put him through it? He took out a credit card, opened the door, and stepped into a darkened living room, half-expecting a scream. Instead he got shocked silence.

They were gaping at him, the woman and two kids. The shades had been pulled down and the curtains drawn. The woman wore a white terrycloth robe, and she looked even younger than she'd sounded on the phone. "You can't just walk in here," she said.

"I just did," Willie said. When he shut the door, the room was awful dark. It made him nervous. "Mind if I put on a light?" She didn't say anything, so he did. The furniture was all ratty Salvation Army stuff, except for the gigantic big-screen projection TV in the far corner of the room. The oldest child, a little girl who looked about four, stood in front of it protectively. Willie smiled at her. She didn't smile back.

He turned back to her mother. She looked maybe twenty, maybe younger, dark, maybe ten pounds overweight but still pretty. She had a spray of brown freckles across the bridge of her nose. "Get yourself a chain for the door and use it," Willie told her. "And don't try the no-one's-home game on us hounds of hell, okay?" He sat down in a black vinyl recliner held together by electrical tape. "I'd love a drink. Coke, juice, milk, anything, it's been one of those days." No one moved, no one spoke. "Aw, come on," Willie said, "cut it out. I'm not going to make you sell the kids for medical experiments, I just want to talk about the money you owe, okay?"

"You're going to take the television," the mother said.

Willie glanced at the monstrosity and shuddered. "It's a year old and it weighs a million pounds. How'm I going to move something like that, with my bad back? I've got asthma too." He took the inhaler out of his pocket, showed it to her. "You want to kill me, making me take the damned TV would do the trick."

That seemed to help a little. "Bobby, get him a can of soda," the mother said. The boy ran off. She held the front of her robe closed as she sat down on the couch, and Willie could see that she wasn't wearing anything underneath. He wondered if she had freckles on her breasts too, sometimes they did. "I told you on the phone, we don't have any money. My husband run off. He was out of work anyway, ever since the pack shut down."

"I know," Willie said. The pack was short for meat-packing plant, which is what everyone liked to call the south side slaughterhouse that had been the city's largest employer until it shut its doors two years back. Willie took a notepad out of his pocket, flipped a few pages. "Okay, you bought the thing on time, made two payments, then moved, left no forwarding address. You still owe two-thousand-eight-hundred-sixteen dollars. And thirty-six cents. We'll forget the interest and late charges." Bobby returned and handed him a can of Diet Chocolate Ginger Beer. Willie repressed a shudder and cracked the pop top.

"Go play in the back yard," she said to the children. "Us grown-ups have to talk." She didn't sound very grown-up after they had left, however; Willie was half-afraid she was going to cry. He hated it when they cried. "It was Ed bought the set," she said, her voice trembling. "It wasn't his fault. The card came in the mail."

Willie knew that tune. A credit card comes in the mail, so the next day you run right out and buy the biggest item you can find. "Look, I can see you got plenty of troubles. You tell me where to find Ed, and I'll get the money out of him."

She laughed bitterly. "You don't know Ed. He used to lug around those big sides of beef at the pack, you ought to see the arms on him. You go bother him and he'll just rip your face off and shove it up your asshole, mister."

"What a lovely turn of phrase," Willie said. "I can't wait to make his acquaintance."

"You won't tell him it was me that told you where to find him?" she asked nervously.

"Scout's honor," Willie said. He raised his right hand in a gesture that he thought was vaguely boy-scoutish, although the can of Diet Chocolate Ginger Beer spoiled the effect a little.

"Were you a scout?" she asked.

"No," he admitted. "But there was one troop that used to beat me up regularly when I was young."

That actually got a smile out of her. "It's your funeral. He's living with some slut now, I don't know where. But weekends he tends bar down at Squeaky's."

"I know the place."

"It's not real work," she added thoughtfully. "He don't report it or nothing. That way he still gets the unemployment. You think he ever sends anything over for the kids? No way!"

"How much you figure he owes you?" Willie said.

"Plenty," she said.

Willie got up. "Look, none of my business, but it is my business, if you know what I mean. You want, after I've talked to Ed about this television, I'll see what I can collect for you. Strictly professional, I mean, I'll take a little cut off the top, give the rest to you. It may not be much, but a little bit is better than nothing, right?"

She stared at him, astonished. "You'd do that?"

"Shit, yeah. Why not?" He took out his wallet, found a twenty. "Here," he said. "An advance payment. Ed will pay me back." She looked at him incredulously, but did not refuse the bill. Willie fumbled in the pocket of his coat. "I want you to meet someone," he said. He always carried a few cheap pairs of scissors in the pocket of his coat. He found one and put it in her hand. "Here, this is Mr. Scissors. From now on, he's your best friend."

She looked at him like he'd gone insane.

"Introduce Mr. Scissors to the next credit card that comes in the mail," Willie told her, "and then you won't have to deal with assholes like me."

He was opening the door when she caught up to him. "Hey, what did you say your name was?"

"Willie," he told her.

"I'm Betsy." She leaned forward to kiss him on the cheek, and the white robe opened just enough to give him a quick peep at her small breasts. Her chest was lightly freckled, her nipples wide and brown. She closed the robe tight again as she stepped back. "You're no asshole, Willie," she said as she closed the door.

He went down the walk feeling almost human, better than he'd felt since Joanie's death. His Caddy was waiting at the curb, the ragtop up to keep out the off-again on-again rain that had been following him around the city all morning. Willie got in and started her, then glanced into the rearview mirror just as the man in the back seat sat up.

The eyes in the mirror were pale blue. Sometimes, after the spring runoff was over and the river had settled back between its banks, you could find stagnant pools along the shore, backwaters cut off from the flow, foul-smelling places, still and cold, and you wondered how deep they were and whether there was anything living down there in that darkness. Those were the kind of eyes he had, deepset in a dark, hollow-cheeked face and framed by brown hair that fell long and straight to his shoulders.

Willie swiveled around to face him. "What the hell were you doing back there, catching forty winks? Hate to point this out, Steven, but this vehicle is actually one of the few things in the city that the Harmons do not own. Guess you got confused, huh? Or did you just mistake it for a bench in the park?

Tell you what, no hard feelings, I'll drive you to the park, even buy you a newspaper to keep you warm while you finish your little nap.

"Jonathan wants to see you," Steven said, in that flat, chill tone of his. His voice, like his face, was still and dead.

"Yeah, good for him, but maybe I don't want to see Jonathan, you ever think of that?" He was dogmeat, Willie thought; he had to suppress the urge to bolt and run.

"Jonathan wants to see you," Steven repeated, as if Willie hadn't understood. He reached forward. A hand closed on Willie's shoulder. Steven had a woman's fingers, long and delicate, his skin pale and fine. But his palm was crisscrossed by burn scars that lay across the flesh like brands, and his fingertips were bloody and scabbed, the flesh red and raw. The fingers dug into Willie's shoulder with ferocious, inhuman strength. "Drive," he said, and Willie drove.

"I'm sorry," the police receptionist said. "The chief has a full calendar today. I can give you an appointment on Thursday."

"I don't want to see him on Thursday. I want to see him now." Randi hated the cophouse. It was always of full of cops. As far as she was concerned, cops came in three flavors; those who saw an attractive woman they could hit on, those who saw a private investigator and resented her, and the old ones who saw Frank Wade's little girl and felt sorry for her. Types one and two annoyed her; the third kind really pissed her off.

The receptionist pressed her lips together, disapproving. "As I've explained, that simply isn't possible."

"Just tell him I'm here," Randi said. "He'll see me."

"He's with someone at the moment, and I'm quite sure that he doesn't want to be interrupted."

Randi had about had it. The day was pretty well shot, and she'd found out next to nothing. "Why don't I just see for myself?" she said sweetly. She walked briskly around the desk, and pushed through the waist-high wooden gate.

"You can't go in there!" the receptionist squeaked in outrage, but by then Randi was opening the door. Police Chief Joseph Urguhart sat behind an old wooden desk cluttered with files, talking to the coroner. Both of them looked up when the door opened. Urguhart was a tall, powerful man in his early sixties. His hair had thinned considerably, but what remained of it was still red, though his eyebrows had gone completely gray. "What the hell—" he started.

"Sorry to barge in, but Miss Congeniality wouldn't give me the time of day," Randi said as the woman came rushing up behind her.

"Young lady, this is the police department, and I'm going to throw you out on your ass," Urquhart said gruffly as he stood up and came around the desk, "unless you come over here right now and give your Uncle Joe a big hug."

Smiling, Randi crossed the bearskin rug, wrapped her arms around him, and laid her head against his chest as the chief tried to crush her. The door closed behind them, too loudly. Randi broke the embrace. "I miss you," she said.

"Sure you do," he said, in a faintly chiding tone. "That's why we see so much of you."

Joe Urquhart had been her father's partner for years, back when they were both in uniform. They'd been tight, and the Urquharts had been like an aunt and uncle to her. His oldest daughter had babysat for her, and Randi had returned the favor for the younger girl. After her father's death, Joe had looked out for them, helped her mother through the funeral and all the legalities, made sure the pension fund got Randi through college. Still, it hadn't been the same, and the families drifted apart, even more so after her mother had finally passed away. These days Randi saw him only once or twice a year, and felt guilty about it. "I'm sorry," she said. "You know I mean to keep in touch, but—"

"There's never enough time, is there?" he said.

The coroner cleared her throat. Sylvia Cooney was a local institution, a big brusque woman of indeterminate age, built like a cement mixer, her iron gray hair tied in a tight bun at the back of her smooth, square face. She'd been coroner as long as Randi could remember. "Maybe I should excuse myself," she said.

Randi stopped her. "I need to ask you about Joan Sorenson. When will autopsy results be available?"

Cooney's eyes went quickly to the chief, then back to Randi. "Nothing I can tell you," she said. She left the office and closed the door with a soft click behind her.

"That hasn't been released to the public yet," Joe Urquhart said. He walked back behind his desk, gestured. "Sit down."

Randi settled into a seat, let her gaze wander around the office. One wall was covered by commendations, certificates, and framed photographs. She saw her father there with Joe, both of them looking so achingly young, two grinning kids in uniform standing in front of their black-and-white. A moose head was mounted above the photographs, peering down at her with its glassy eyes. More trophies hung from the other walls. "Do you still hunt?" she asked him.

"Not in years," Urquhart said. "No time. Your dad used to kid me about it all the time. Always said that if I ever killed anyone on duty, I'd want the head stuffed and mounted. Then one day it happened, and the joke wasn't so funny anymore." He frowned. "What's your interest in Joan Sorenson?"

"Professional," Randi said.

"Little out of your line, isn't it?"

Randi shrugged. "I don't pick my cases."

"You're too good to waste your life snooping round motels," Urquhart said. It was a sore point between them. "It's not too late to join the force."

"No," Randi said. She didn't try to explain; she knew from past experience that there was no way to make him understand. "I went out to the precinct house this morning to look at the report on Sorenson. It's missing from the file; no one knows where it is. I got the names of the cops who were at the scene, but none of them had time to talk to me. Now I'm told the autopsy results aren't being made public either. You mind telling me what's going on?"

Joe glanced out the windows behind him. The panes were wet with rain. "This is a sensitive case," he said. "I don't want the media blowing this thing all out of proportion.

"I'm not the media," Randi said.

Urquhart swiveled back around. "You're not a cop either. That's your choice. Randi, I don't want you involved in this, do you hear?"

"I'm involved whether you like it or not," she said. She didn't give him time to argue. "How did Joan Sorenson die? Was it an animal attack?"

"No," he said. "It was not. And that's the last question I'm going to answer." He sighed. "Randi," he said, "I know how hard you got hit by Frank's death. It was pretty rough on me too, remember? He phoned me for back-up. I didn't get there on time. You think I'll ever forget that?" He shook his head. "Put it behind you. Stop imagining things."

"I'm not imagining anything," Randi snapped. "Most of the time I don't even think about it. This is different."

"Have it your way," Joe said. There was a small stack of files on the corner of the desk near Randi. Urquhart leaned forward and picked them up, tapped them against his blotter to straighten them. "I wish I could help you." He slid open a drawer, put the file folders away. Randi caught a glimpse of the name on the top folder: *Helander.* "I'm sorry," Joe was saying. He started to rise. "Now, if you'll excuse—"

"Are you just rereading the Helander file for old time's sake, or is there some connection to Sorenson?" Randi asked.

Urguhart sat back down. "Shit," he said.

"Or maybe I just imagined that was the name on the file."

Joe looked pained. "We have reason to think the Helander boy might be back in the city."

"Hardly a boy any more," Randi said. "Roy Helander was three years older than me. You're looking at him for Sorenson?"

"We have to, with his history. The state released him two months ago, it turns out. The shrinks said he was cured." Urquhart made a face. "Maybe,

maybe not. Anyway, he's just a name. We're looking at a hundred names."

"Where is he?"

"I wouldn't tell you if I knew. He's a bad piece of business, like the rest of his family. I don't like you getting mixed up with his sort, Randi. Your father wouldn't either."

Randi stood up. "My father's dead," she said, "and I'm a big girl now."

Willie parked the car where 13th Street dead-ended, at the foot of the bluffs. Blackstone sat high above the river, surrounded by a ten-foot high wrought iron fence with a row of forbidding spikes along its top. You could drive to the gatehouse easily enough, but you had to go all the way down Central, past downtown, then around on Grandview and Harmon Drive, up and down the hills and all along the bluffs where aging steamboat gothic mansions stood like so many dowagers staring out over the flats and river beyond, remembering better days. It was a long, tiresome drive.

Back before the automobile, it had been even longer and more tiresome. Faced with having to travel to Courier Square on a daily basis, Douglas Harmon made things easy for himself. He built a private cable car; a two-car funicular railway that crept up the gray stone face of the bluffs from the foot of 13th below to Blackstone above.

Internal combustion, limousines, chaffeurs, and paved roads had all conspired to wean the Harmons away from Douglas' folly, making the cable car something of a back door in more recent years, but that suited Willie well enough. Jonathan Harmon always made him feel like to ought to come in by the servant's entrance anyway.

Willie climbed out of the Caddy and stuck his hands in the sagging pockets of his raincoat. He looked up. The incline was precipitous, the rock wet and dark. Steven took his elbow roughly and propelled him forward. The car was wooden, badly in need of a whitewash, with bench space for six. Steven pulled the bell cord; the car jerked as they began to ascend. The second car came down to meet them, and they crossed halfway up the bluff. The car shook and Willie spotted rust on the rails. Even here at the gate of Blackstone, things were falling apart.

Near the top of the bluff, they passed through a gap in the wrought iron fence, and the New House came into view, gabled and turreted and covered with Victorian gingerbread. The Harmons had lived there for almost a century, but it was still the New House, and always would be. Behind the house the estate was densely forested, the narrow driveway winding through thick stands of old growth. Where the other founding families had long ago sold off or parceled out their lands to developers, the Harmons had held tight, and Blackstone remained intact, a piece of the forest primeval in the middle of the city.

Against the western sky, Willie glimpsed the broken silhouette of the tower, part of the Old House whose soot-dark stone walls gave Blackstone its name. The house was set well back among the trees, its lawns and courts overgrown, but even when you couldn't see it you knew it was there somehow. The tower was a jagged black presence outlined against the red-stained gray of the western horizon, crooked and forbidding. It had been Douglas Harmon, the journalist and builder of funicular railways, who had erected the New House and closed the Old, immense and gloomy even by Victorian standards, but neither Douglas, his son Thomas, or his grandson Jonathan had ever found the will to tear it down. Local legend said the Old House was haunted. Willie could just about believe it. Blackstone, like its owner, gave him the creeps.

The cable car shuddered to a stop, and they climbed out onto a wooden deck, its paint weathered and peeling. A pair of wide French doors led into the New House. Jonathan Harmon was waiting for them, leaning on a walking stick, his gaunt figure outlined by the light that spilled through the door. "Hello, William," he said. Harmon was barely past sixty, Willie knew, but long snow-white hair and a body wracked by arthritis made him look much older. "I'm so glad that you could join us," he said.

"Yeah, well, I was in the neighborhood, just thought I'd drop by," Willie said. "Only thing is, I just remembered, I left the windows open in the brewery. I better run home and close them, or my dust bunnies are going to get soaked."

"No," said Jonathan Harmon. "I don't think so."

Willie felt the bands constricting across his chest. He wheezed, found his inhaler, and took two long hits. He figured he'd need it. "Okay, you talked me into it, I'll stay," he told Harmon, "but I damn well better get a drink out of it. My mouth still tastes like Diet Chocolate Ginger Beer."

"Steven, be a good boy and get our friend William a snifter of Remy Martin, if you'd be so kind. I'll join him. The chill is on my bones. Steven, silent as ever, went inside to do as he was told. Willie made to follow, but Jonathan touched his arm lightly. "A moment," he said. He gestured. "Look."

Willie turned and looked. He wasn't quite so frightened anymore. If Jonathan wanted him dead, he figured Steven would've tried already, and maybe succeeded. Steven was a dreadful mistake by his father's standards, but there was a freakish strength in those scarred hands. No, this was some other kind of deal.

They looked east over the city and the river. Dusk had begun to settle, and the streetlights were coming on down below, strings of luminescent pearls that spread out in all directions as far as the eye could see and leapt across the river on three great bridges. The clouds were gone to the east, and the horizon was a deep cobalt blue. The moon had begun to rise.

"There were no lights out there when the foundations of the Old House were dug," Jonathan Harmon said. "This was all wilderness. A wild river coursing through the forest primeval, and if you stood on high at dusk, it must have seemed as though the blackness went on forever. The water was pure, the air was clean, and the woods were thick with game...deer, beaver, bear...but no people, or at least no white men. John Harmon and his son James both wrote of seeing Indian campfires from the tower from time to time, but the tribes avoided this place, especially after John had begun to build the Old House.

"Maybe the Indians weren't so dumb after all," Willie said.

Jonathan glanced at Willie, and his mouth twitched. "We built this city out of nothing," he said. "Blood and iron built this city, blood and iron nurtured it and fed its people. The old families knew the power of blood and iron; they knew how to make this city great. The Rochmonts hammered and shaped the metal in smithies and foundries and steel mills, the Anders family moved it on their flatboats and steamers and railroads, and your own people found it and pried it from the earth. You come from iron stock, William Flambeaux, but we Harmons were always blood. We had the stockyards and the slaughterhouse, but long before that, before this city or this nation existed, the Old House was a center of the skin trade. Trappers and hunters would come here every season with furs and skins and beaver pelts to sell the Harmons, and from here the skins would move down river. On rafts, at first, and then on flatboats. Steam came later, much later."

"Is there going to be a pop quiz on this?" Willie asked.

"We've fallen a long way," he said, looking pointedly at Willie. "We need to remember how we started. Black iron and red, red blood. You need to remember. Your grandfather had the Flambeaux blood, the old pure strain."

Willie knew when he was being insulted. "And my mother was a Pankowski," he said, "which makes me half-frog, half-polack, and all mongrel. Not that I give a shit. I mean, it's terrific that my great-grandfather owned half the state, but the mines gave out around the turn of the century, the depression took the rest, my father was a drunk, and I'm in collections, if that's okay with you." He was feeling pissed off and rash by then. "Did you have any particular reason for sending Steven to kidnap me, or was it just a yen to discuss the French and Indian War?"

Jonathan said, "Come. We'll be more comfortable inside; the wind is cold." The words were polite enough, but his tone had lost all faint trace of warmth. He led Willie inside, walking slowly, leaning heavily on the cane. "You must forgive me," he said. "It's the damp. It aggravates the arthritis, inflames my old war wounds." He looked back at Willie. "You were unconscionably rude to hang up on me. Granted, we have our differences, but simple respect for my position—"

"I've been having a lot of trouble with my phone lately," Willie said. "Ever since they deregulated, service has turned to shit."

Jonathan led him into a small sitting room. There was a fire burning in the hearth; the heat felt good after a long day tromping through the cold and the rain. The furnishings were antique, or maybe just old, Willie wasn't too clear on the difference.

Steven proceeded them Two brandy snifters, half-full of amber liquid, sat on a low table. Steven squatted by the fire, his tall lean body folded up like a jackknife. He looked up as they entered and stared at Willie a moment too long, as if he'd suddenly forgotten who he was or what he was doing there. Then his flat blue eyes went back to the fire, and he took no more notice of them or their conversation.

Willie looked around for the most comfortable chair and sat in it. The style reminded him of Randi Wade, but that just made him feel guilty. He picked up his cognac. Willie was couth enough to know that he was supposed to sip but cold and tired and pissed-off enough so that he didn't care. He emptied it in one long swallow, put it down on the floor beside the chair, and relaxed back into the chair as the heat spread through his chest.

Jonathan, obviously in some pain, lowered himself carefully onto the edge of the couch, his hands closed round the head of his walking stick. Willie found himself staring. Jonathan noticed. "A wolf's head," he said. He moved his hands aside to give Willie a clear view. The firelight reflected off the rich yellow metal. The beast was snarling, snapping.

Its eyes were red. "Garnets?" Willie guessed. Jonathan smiled the way you might smile at a particularly doltish child. "Rubies," he said, "set in 18 karat gold." His hands, large and heavily-veined, twisted by arthritis, closed round the stick again, hiding the wolf from sight.

"Stupid," Willie said. "There's guys in this city would kill you as soon as look at you for a stick like that."

Jonathan's smile was humorless. "I will not die on account of gold, William." He glanced at the window. The moon was well above the horizon. "A good hunter's moon," he said. He looked back at Willie. "Last night you all but accused me of complicity in the death of the crippled girl." His voice was dangerously soft. "Why would you say such a thing?"

"I can't imagine," Willie said. He felt light-headed. The brandy had rushed right to his mouth. "Maybe the fact that you can't remember her name had something to do with it. Or maybe it was because you always hated Joanie, right from the moment you heard about her. My pathetic little mongrel bitch, I believe that was what you called her, isn't it funny the way the little turns of phrase stick in the mind? I don't know, maybe it was just me, but somehow I got this impression that you didn't exactly wish her well. I haven't even mentioned Steven yet."

"Please don't," Jonathan said icily. "You've said quite enough. Look at me, William. Tell me what you see."

"You," said Willie. He wasn't in the mood for asshole games, but Jonathan Harmon did things at his own pace.

"An old man," Jonathan corrected. "Perhaps not so old in years alone, but old nonetheless. The arthritis grows worse every year, and there are days when the pain is so bad I can scarcely move. My family is all gone but for Steven, and Steven, let us be frank, is not all that I might have hoped for in a son." He spoke in firm, crisp tones, but Steven did not even look up from the flames. "I'm tired, William. It's true, I did not approve of your crippled girl, or even particularly of you. We live in a time of corruption and degeneracy, when the old truths of blood and iron have been forgotten. Nonetheless, however much I may have loathed your Joan Sorenson and what she represented, I had no taste of her blood. All I want is to live out my last years in peace."

Willie stood up. "Do me a favor and spare me the old sick man act. Yeah, I know all about your arthritis and your war wounds. I also know who you are and what you're capable of. Okay, you didn't kill Joanie. So who did? Him?" He jerked a thumb toward Steven.

"Steven was here with me."

"Maybe he was and maybe he wasn't," Willie said.

"Don't flatter yourself, Flambeaux, you're not important enough for me to lie to you. Even if your suspicion was correct, my son is not capable of such an act. Must I remind you that Steven is crippled as well, in his own way?"

Willie gave Steven a quick glance. "I remember once when I was just a kid, my father had to come see you, and he brought me along. I used to love to ride your little cable car. Him and you went inside to talk, but it was a nice day, so you let me play outside. I found Steven in the woods, playing with some poor sick mutt that had gotten past your fence. He was holding it down with his foot, and pulling off its legs, one by one, just ripping them out with his bare hands like a normal kid might pull petals off a flower. When I walked up behind him, he had two off and was working on the third. There was blood all over his face. He couldn't have been more than eight."

Jonathan Harmon sighed. "My son is…disturbed. We both know that, so there is no sense in my denying it. He is also dysfunctional, as you know full well. And whatever residual strength remains is controlled by his medication. He has not had a truly violent episode for years. Have you, Steven?"

Steven Harmon looked back at them. The silence went on too long as he stared, unblinking, at Willie. "No," he finally said.

Jonathan nodded with satisfaction, as if something had been settled. "So you see, William, you do us a great injustice. What you took for a threat was only an offer of protection. I was going to suggest that you move to one of our guests rooms for a time. I've made the same suggestion to Zoe and Amy."

Willie laughed. "I'll bet. Do I have to fuck Steven too, or is that just for the girls?"

Jonathan flushed, but kept his temper. His futile efforts to marry off Steven to one of the Anders sisters was a sore spot. "I regret to say they declined my offer. I hope you will not be so unwise. Blackstone has certain…protections…but I cannot vouch for your safety beyond these walls."

"Safety?" Willie said. "From what?"

"I do not know, but I can tell you this—in the dark of night, there are things that hunt the hunters."

"Things that hunt the hunters," Willie repeated. "That's good, has a ice beat, but can you dance to it?" He'd had enough. He started for the door. "Thanks but no thanks. I'll take my chances behind my own walls." Steven made no move to stop him. Jonathan Harmon leaned more heavily on his cane. "I can tell you how she was really killed," he said quietly.

Willie stopped and stared into the old man's eyes. Then he sat back down.

It was on the south side in a neighborhood that made the flats look classy, on an elbow of land between the river and that old canal that ran past the park. Algae and raw sewage choked the canal and gave off a smell that drifted for blocks. The houses were single-story clapboard affairs, hardly more than shacks. Randi hadn't been down here since the pack had closed its doors. Every third house had a sign on the lawn, flapping forlornly in the wind, advertising a property for sale or for rent, and at least half of those were dark. Weeds grew waist-high around the weathered rural mailboxes, and they passed at least two burned-out lots.

Years had passed, and Randi didn't remember the number, but it was the last house on the left, she knew, next to a Sinclair station on the corner. The cabbie cruised until they found it. The gas station was boarded up, even the pumps gone, but the house stood there much as she recalled. It had a For Rent sign on the lawn, but she saw a light moving around inside. A flashlight, maybe? It was gone before she could be sure.

The cabbie offered to wait. "No," she said. "I don't know how long I'll be." After he was gone, she stood on the barren lawn for a long time, staring at the front door, before she finally went up the walk.

She'd decided not to knock, but the door opened as she was reaching for the knob. "Can I help you, miss?"

He loomed over her, a big man, thick-bodied but muscular. His face was unfamiliar, but he was no Helander. They'd been a short, wiry family, all with same limp, dirty blonde hair. This one had hair black as wrought iron, and shaggier than the department usually liked. Five o'clock shadow gave his jaw a distinct blue-black cast. His hands were large, with short blunt fingers. Everything about him said cop.

"I was looking for the people who used to live here."

"The family moved away when the pack closed," he told her. "Why don't you come inside?" He opened the door wider. Randi saw bare floors, dust, and his partner, a beer-bellied black man standing by the door to the kitchen.

"I don't think so," she said.

"I insist," he replied. He showed her a gold badge pinned to the inside of his cheap grey suit.

"Does that mean I'm under arrest?"

He looked taken back. "No. Of course not. We'd just like to ask you a few questions." He tried to sound friendlier. "I'm Rogoff."

"Homicide," she said.

His eyes narrowed. "How—?"

"You're in charge of the Sorenson investigation," she said. She'd been given his name at the cophouse that morning. "You must not have much of a case if you've got nothing better to do than hang around here waiting for Roy Helander to show."

"We were just leaving. Thought maybe he'd get nostalgic, hole up at the old house, but there's no sign of it." He looked at her hard and frowned. "Mind telling me your name?"

"Why?" she asked. "Is this a bust or a come-on?"

He smiled. "I haven't decided yet."

"I'm Randi Wade." She showed him her license.

"Private detective," he said, his tone carefully neutral. He handed the license back to her. "You working?"

She nodded.

"Interesting. I don't suppose you'd care to tell me the name of your client."

"No."

"I could haul you into court, make you tell the judge. You can get that license lifted, you know. Obstructing an on going police investigation, withholding evidence."

"Professional privilege," she said.

Rogoff shook his head. "PIs don't have privilege. Not in this state."

"This one does," Randi said. "Attorney-client relationship. I've got a law degree too." She smiled at him sweetly. "Leave my client out of it. I know a few interesting things about Roy Helander I might be willing to share."

Rogoff digested that. "I'm listening."

Randi shook her head. "Not here. You know the automat on Courier Square?" He nodded. "Eight o'clock," she told him. "Come alone. Bring a copy of the coroner's report on Sorenson."

"Most girls want candy or flowers," he said.

"The coroner's report," she repeated firmly. "They still keep the old case records downtown?"

"Yeah," he said. "Basement of the courthouse."

"Good. You can stop by and do a little remedial reading on the way. It was eighteen years ago. Some kids had been turning up missing. One of them was Roy's little sister. There were others—Stanski, Jones, I forget all the names. A cop named Frank Wade was in charge of the investigation. A gold badge, like you. He died."

"You saying there's a connection?"

"You're the cop. You decide." She left him standing in the doorway and walked briskly down the block.

Steven didn't bother to see him down to the foot of the bluffs. Willie rode the little funicular railway alone, morose and lost in thought. His joints ached like nobody's business and his nose was running. Every time he got upset his body fell to pieces, and Jonathan Harmon had certainly upset him. That was probably better than killing him, which he'd half expected when he found Steven in his car, but still...

He was driving home along 13th Street when he saw the bar's neon sign on his right. Without thinking, he pulled over and parked. Maybe Harmon was right and maybe Harmon had his ass screwed on backwards, but in any case Willie still had to make a living. He locked up the Caddy and went inside.

It was a slow Tuesday night, and Squeaky's was empty. It was a workingman's tavern. Two pool tables, a shuffleboard machine in back, booths along one wall. Willie took a bar stool. The bartender was an old guy, hard and dry as a stick of wood. He looked mean. Willie considered ordering a banana daiquiri, just the see what the guy would say, but one look at that sour, twisted old face cured the impulse, and he asked for a boilermaker instead. "Ed working tonight?" he asked when the bartender brought the drinks.

"Only works weekends," the man said, "but he comes in most nights, plays a little pool."

"I'll wait," Willie said. The shot made his eyes water. He chased it down with a gulp of beer. He saw a pay phone back by the men's room. When the bartender gave him his change, he walked back, put in a quarter, and dialed Randi. She wasn't home; he got her damned machine. Willie hated phone machines. They'd made life a hell of a lot more difficult for collection agents, that was for sure. He waited for the tone, left Randi an obscene message, and hung up.

The men's room had a condom dispenser mounted over the urinals. Willie read the instructions as he took a leak. The condoms were intended for prevention of disease only, of course, even though the one dispensed by the left-hand slot was a French tickler. Maybe he ought to install one of these at home, he thought. He zipped up, flushed, washed his hands.

When he walked back out into the taproom, two new customers stood over the pool table, chalking up cues. Willie looked at the bartender, who nodded. "One of you Ed Juddiker?" Willie asked. Ed wasn't the biggest—his buddy was as large and pale as Moby Dick—but he was big enough, with a real stupid-mean look on his face. "Yeah?"

"We need to talk about some money you owe." Willie offered him one of his cards.

Ed looked at the hand, but made no effort to take the card. He laughed. "Get lost," he said. He turned back to the pool table. Moby Dick racked up the balls and Ed broke.

That was all right, if that was the way he wanted to play it. Willie sat back on the bar stool and ordered another beer. He'd get his money one way or the other. Sooner or later Ed would have to leave, and then it would be his turn.

Willie still wasn't answering his phone. Randi hung up the pay phone and frowned. He didn't have an answering machine either, not Willie Flambeaux, that would be too sensible. She knew she shouldn't worry. The hounds of hell don't punch time-clocks, as he'd told her more than once. He was probably out running down some deadbeat. She'd try again when she got home. If he still didn't answer, then she'd start to worry.

The automat was almost empty. Her heels made hollow clicks on the old linoleum as she walked back to her booth and sat down. Her coffee had gone cold. She looked idly out the window. The digital clock on the State National Bank said 8:13. Randi decided to give him ten more minutes.

The red vinyl of the booth was old and cracking, but she felt strangely comfortable here, sipping her cold coffee and staring off at the Iron Spire across the square. The automat had been her favorite restaurant when she was a little girl. Every year on her birthday she would demand a movie at the Castle and dinner at the automat, and every year her father would laugh and oblige. She loved to put the nickels in the coin slots and make the windows pop open, and fill her father's cup out of the old brass coffee machine with all its knobs and levers.

Sometimes you could see disembodied hands through the glass, sticking a sandwich or a piece of pie into one of the slots, like something from an old horror movie. You never saw any people working at the automat, just hands; the hands of people who hadn't paid their bills, her father once told her, teasing. That gave her the shivers, but somehow made her annual visits even more delicious, in a creepy kind of way. The truth, when she learned it, was much less interesting. Of course, that was true of most everything in life.

These days, the automat was always empty, which made Randi wonder how the floor could possibly stay so filthy, and you had to put quarters into the coin slots beside the little windows instead of nickels. But the banana cream pie was still the best she'd ever had, and the coffee that came out of those worn brass spigots was better than anything she'd ever brewed at home.

She was thinking of getting a fresh cup when the door opened and Rogoff finally came in out of the rain. He wore a heavy wool coat. His hair was wet. Randi looked out at the clock as he approached the booth. It said 8:17. "You're late," she said.

"I'm a slow reader," he said. He excused himself and went to get some food. Randi watched him as he fed dollar bills into the change machine. He wasn't bad-looking if you liked the type, she decided, but the type was definitely cop.

Rogoff returned with a cup of coffee, the hot beef sandwich with mashed potatoes, gravy, and overcooked carrots, and a big slice of apple pie.

"The banana cream is better," Randi told him as he slid in opposite her.

"I like apple," he said, shaking out a paper napkin.

"Did you bring the coroner's report?"

"In my pocket." He started cutting up the sandwich. He was very methodical, slicing the whole thing into small bite-sized portions before he took his first taste. "I'm sorry about your father."

"So was I. It was a long time ago. Can I see the report?"

"Maybe. Tell me something I don't already know about Roy Helander."

Randi sat back. "We were kids together. He was older, but he'd been left back a couple of times, till he wound up in my class. He was a bad kid from the wrong side of the tracks and I was a cop's daughter, so we didn't have much in common…until his little sister disappeared."

"He was with her," Rogoff said.

"Yes he was. No one disputed that, least of all Roy. He was fifteen, she was eight. They were walking the tracks. They went off together, and Roy came back alone. He had blood on his dungarees and all over his hands. His sister's blood."

"Three kids had already vanished. Jessie Helender made four. The way most people looked at it, Roy was always a little strange. He was solitary, inarticulate, used to hook school and run off to some secret hideout he had in the woods. He liked to play with the younger kids instead of boys his own age. A degenerate from a bad family, a child molester who had actually raped and killed his own sister, that was they said. They gave him all kinds of tests, decided he was deeply disturbed, and sent him away to some kiddie snakepit. He was still a juvenile, after all. Case closed, and the city breathed easier."

"If you don't have any more than that, the coroner's report stays in my pocket," Rogoff said.

"Roy said he didn't do it. He cried and screamed a lot, and his story wasn't coherent, but he stuck to it. He said he was walking along ten feet or so behind his sister, balancing on the rails and listening for a train, when a monster came out of a drainage culvert and attacked her."

"A monster," Rogoff said.

"Some kind of big shaggy dog, that was what Roy said. He was describing a wolf. Everybody knew it."

"There hasn't been a wolf in this part of the country for over a century."

"He described how Jessie screamed as the thing began to rip her apart. He said he grabbed her leg, tried to pull her out of its jaws, which would explain why he had her blood all over him. The wolf turned and looked at him and growled. It had red eyes, burning red eyes, Roy said, and he was real scared, so he let go. By then Jessie was almost certainly dead. It gave him one last snarl and ran off, carrying the body in its jaws." Randi paused, took a sip of coffee. "That was his story. He told it over and over, to his mother, the police, the psychologists, the judge, everyone. No one ever believed him."

"Not even you?"

"Not even me. We all whispered about Roy in school, about what he'd done to his sisters and those other kids. We couldn't quite imagine it, but we knew it had to be horrible. The only thing was, my father never quite bought it."

"Why not?"

She shrugged. "Instincts, maybe. He was always talking about how a cop had to go with his instincts. It was his case, he'd spent more time with Roy than anyone else, and something about the way the boy told the story had affected him. But it was nothing that could be proved. The evidence was overwhelming. So Roy was locked up." She watched his eyes as she told him. "A month later, Eileen Stanski vanished. She was six."

Rogoff paused with a forkful of the mashed potatoes, and studied her thoughtfully. "Inconvenient," he said.

"Dad wanted Roy released, but no one supported him. The official line was that the Stanski girl was unconnected to the others. Roy had done four, and some other child molester had done the fifth.

"It's possible."

"It's bullshit," Randi said. "Dad knew it and he said it. That didn't make him any friends in the department, but he didn't care. He could be a very stubborn man. You read the file on his death?"

Rogoff nodded. He looked uncomfortable.

"My father was savaged by an animal. A dog, the coroner said. If you want to believe that, go ahead." This was the hard part. She'd picked at it like an old scab for years, and then she'd tried to forget it, but nothing ever made it easier. "He got a phone call in the middle of the night, some kind of lead about the missing kids. Before he left he phoned Joe Urquhart to ask for back-up."

"Chief Urquhart?"

Randi nodded. "He wasn't chief then. Joe had been his partner when he was still in uniform. He said Dad told him he had a hot tip, but not the details, not even the name of the caller."

"Maybe he didn't know the name."

"He knew. My father wasn't the kind of a cop who goes off alone in the middle of the night on an anonymous tip. He drove down to the stockyards by himself. It was waiting for him there. Whatever it was took six rounds and kept coming. It tore out his throat and after he was dead it ate him. What was left by the time Urquhart got there…Joe testified that when he first found the body he wasn't even sure it was human."

She told the story in a cool, steady voice, but her stomach was churning. When she finished Rogoff was staring at her. He set down his fork and pushed his plate away. "Suddenly I'm not very hungry anymore."

Randi's smile was humorless. "I love our local press. There was a case a few years ago when a woman was kidnapped by a gang, held for two weeks. She was beaten, tortured, sodomized, raped hundreds of times. When the story broke, the paper said she'd been quote *assaulted* unquote. It said my father's body had been mutilated. It said the same thing about Joan Sorenson. I've been told her body was intact." She leaned forward, looked hard into his dark brown eyes. "That's a lie."

"Yes," he admitted. He took a sheet of paper from his breast pocket, unfolded it, passed it across to her. "But it's not the way you think."

Randi snatched the coroner's report from his hand, and scanned quickly down the page. The words blurred, refused to register. It wasn't adding up the way it was supposed to.

Cause of death: exsanguination.

Somewhere far away, Rogoff was talking. "It's a security building, her apartment's on the fourteenth floor. No balconies, no fire escapes, and the doorman didn't see a thing. The door was locked. It was a cheap spring lock, easy to jimmy, but there was no sign of forced entry."

The instrument of death was a blade at least twelve inches long, extremely sharp, slender and flexible, perhaps a surgical instrument.

"Her clothing was all over the apartment, just ripped to hell, in tatters. In her condition, you wouldn't think she'd put up much of a struggle, but it looks like she did. None of the neighbors heard anything, of course. The killer chained her to her bed, naked, and went to work. He worked fast, knew what he was doing, but it still must have taken her a long time to die. The bed was soaked with her blood, through the sheets and mattress, right down to the box spring."

Randi looked back up at him, and the coroner's report slid from her fingers onto the porcelain table. Rogoff reached over and took her hand.

"Joan Sorenson wasn't devoured by any animal, Miss Wade. She was flayed alive, and left to bleed to death. And the part of her that's missing is her skin."

It was a quarter past midnight when Willie got home. He parked the Caddy by the pier. Ed Juddiker's wallet was on the seat beside him. Willie opened it, took out the money, counted. Seventy-nine bucks. Not much, but it was a start. He'd give half to Betsy this first time, credit the rest to Ed's account. Willie pocketed the money and locked the empty wallet in the glovebox. Ed might need the driver's license. He'd bring it by Squeaky's over the weekend, when Ed was on, and talk to him about a payment schedule.

Willie locked up the car and trudged wearily across the rain-slick cobbles to his front door. The sky above the river was dark and starless. The moon was up by now, he knew, hidden somewhere behind those black cotton clouds. He fumbled for his keys, buried down under his inhaler, his pillbox, a half-dozen pairs of scissors, a handkerchief, and the miscellaneous other junk that made his coat pocket sag. After a long minute, he tried his pants pocket, found them, and started in on his locks. He slid the first key into his double deadbolt.

The door opened slowly, silently.

The pale yellow light from a street lamp filtered through the brewery's high, dusty windows, patterning the floor with faint squares and twisted lines. The hulks of rusting machines crouched in the dimness like great dark beasts. Willie stood in the doorway, keys in hand, his heart pounding like a triphammer. He put the keys in his pocket, found his Primateen, took a hit. The hiss of the inhaler seemed obscenely loud in the stillness.

He thought of Joanie, of what had happened to her.

He could run, he thought. The Cadillac was only a few feet behind him, just a few steps, whatever was waiting in there couldn't possibly be fast enough to get him before he reached the car. Yeah, hit the road, drive all night, he had enough gas to make Chicago, it wouldn't follow him there. Willie took the first step back, then stopped, and giggled nervously. He had a sudden picture of himself sitting behind the wheel of his big lime-green chrome boat, grinding the ignition, grinding and grinding and flooding the engine as something dark and terrible emerged from inside the brewery and crossed the cobblestones behind him. That was silly, it was only in bad horror movies that the ignition didn't turn over, wasn't it? Wasn't it?

Maybe he had just forgotten to lock up when he'd left for work that morning. He'd had a lot on his mind, a full day's work ahead of him and a night of bad dreams behind, maybe he'd just closed the fucking door behind him and forgotten about his locks.

He never forgot about his locks.

But maybe he had, just this once.

Willie thought about changing. Then he remembered Joanie, and put the thought aside. He stood on one leg, pulled off his shoe. Then the other. Water soaked through his socks. He edged forward, took a deep breath, moved into the darkened brewery as silently as he could, pulling the door shut behind him. Nothing moved. Willie reached down into his pocket, pulled out Mr. Scissors. It wasn't much, but it was better than bare hands. Hugging the thick shadows along the wall, he crossed the room and began to creep upstairs on stockinged feet.

The streetlight shone through the window at the end of the hall. Willie paused on the steps when his head came up to the level of the second-story landing. He could look up and down the hallway. All the office doors were shut. No light leaking underneath or through the frosted-glass transoms. Whatever waited for him waited in darkness.

He could feel his chest constricting again. In another moment he'd need his inhaler. Suddenly he just wanted to get it over with. He climbed the final steps and crossed the hall in two long strides, threw open the door to his living room, and slammed on the lights.

Randi Wade was sitting in his beanbag chair. She looked up blinking as he hit the lights. "You startled me," she said.

"I startled you!" Willie crossed the room and collapsed into his La-Z-Boy. The scissors fell from his sweaty palm and bounced on the hardwood floor. "Jesus H. Christ on a crutch, you almost made lose control of my personal hygiene. What the hell are you doing here? Did I forget to lock the door?"

Randi smiled. "You locked the door and you locked the door and then you locked the door some more. You're world class when it comes to locking doors, Flambeaux. It took me twenty minutes to get in."

Willie massaged his throbbing temples. "Yeah, well, with all the women who want this body, I got to have some protection, don't I?" He noticed his wet socks, pulled one off, grimaced. "Look at this," he said. "My shoes are out in the street getting rained on, and my feet are soaking. If I get pneumonia, you get the doctor bills, Wade. You could have waited."

"It was raining," she pointed out. "You wouldn't have wanted me to wait in the rain, Willie. It would have pissed me off, and I'm in a foul mood already."

Something in her voice made Willie stop rubbing his toes to look up at her. The rain had plastered loose strands of light brown hair across her forehead, and her eyes were grim. "You look like a mess," he admitted.

"I tried to make myself presentable, but the mirror in your ladies' room is missing.

"It broke. There's one in the men's room."

"I'm not that kind of a girl," Randi said grimly. Her voice was hard and flat. "Willie, your friend Joan wasn't killed by an animal. She was flayed. The killer took her skin."

"I know," Willie said, without thinking.

Her eyes narrowed. They were gray-green, large and pretty, but right now they looked as cold as marbles. "You *know?*" she echoed. Her voice had gone very soft, almost to a whisper, and Willie knew he was in trouble. "You give me some bullshit story and send me running all around town, and you *know?* Do you know what happened to my father too, is that it? It was just your clever little way of getting my attention?"

Willie gaped at her. His second sock was in his hand. He let it drop to the floor. "Hey, Randi, gimme a break, okay? It wasn't like that at all. I just found out a few hours ago, honest. How could I know? I wasn't there, it wasn't in the paper." He was feeling confused and guilty. "What the hell am I supposed to know about your father? I don't know jackshit about your father. All the time you worked for me, you mentioned your family maybe twice."

Her eyes searched his face for signs of deception. Willie tried to give her his warmest, most trustworthy smile. Randi grimaced. "Stop it," she said, wearily. "You look like a used car salesman. All right, you didn't know about my father. I'm sorry. I'm a little wrought up right now, and I thought..." She paused thoughtfully. "Who told you about Sorenson?"

Willie hesitated. "I can't tell you," he said. "I wish I could, I really do. I can't. You wouldn't believe me anyway." Randi looked very unhappy. Willie kept talking. "Did you find out whether I'm a suspect? The police haven't called."

"They've probably been calling all day. By now they may have an APB out on you. If you won't get a machine, you ought to try coming home occasionally." She frowned. "I talked to Rogoff from Homicide." Willie's heart stopped, but she saw the look on his face and held up a hand. "No, your name wasn't mentioned. By either of us. They'll be calling everyone who knew her, probably, but it's just routine questioning. I don't think they'll be singling you out."

"Good," Willie said. "Well, look, I owe you one, but there's no reason for you to go on with this. I know it's not paying the rent, so—"

"So what?" Randi was looking at him suspiciously. "Are you trying to get rid of me now? After you got me involved in the first place?" She frowned. "Are you holding out on me?"

"I think you've got that reversed," Willie said lightly. Maybe he could joke his way out of it. "You're the one who gets bent out of shape whenever I offer to help you shop for lingerie."

"Cut the shit," Randi said sharply. She was not amused in the least, he could see that. "We're talking about the torture and murder of a girl who was supposed to be a friend of yours. Or has that slipped your mind somehow?"

"No," he said, abashed. Willie was very uncomfortable. He got up and crossed the room, plugged in the hotplate. "Hey, listen, you want a cup of tea? I got Earl Grey, Red Zinger, Morning Thunder—"

"The police think they have a suspect," Randi said.

Willie turned to look at her. "Who?"

"Roy Helander," Randi said.

"Oh, boy," Willie said. He'd been a PFC in Hamburg when the Helander thing went down, but he'd had a subscription to the *Courier* to keep up on the old hometown, and the headlines had made him ill. "Are they sure?"

"No," she said. "They're just rounding up the usual suspects. Roy was a great scapegoat last time, why not use him again? First they have to find him, though. No one's really sure that he's still in the state, let alone the city."

Willie turned away, busied himself with hotplate and kettle. All of a sudden he found it difficult to look Randi in the eye. "You don't think Helander was the one who grabbed those kids."

"Including his own sister? Hell no. Jessie was the last person he'd ever have hurt; she actually *liked* him. Not to mention that he was safely locked away when number five disappeared. I knew Roy Helander. He had bad teeth and he didn't bathe often enough, but that doesn't make him a child molester. He hung out with younger kids because the older ones made fun of him. I don't think he had any friends. He had some kind of secret place in the woods where he'd go to hide when things got too rough, he—"

She stopped suddenly, and Willie turned toward her, a teabag dangling from his fingers. "You thinking what I'm thinking?" The kettle began to scream.

Randi tossed and turned for over an hour after she got home, but there was no way she could sleep. Every time she closed her eyes she would see her father's face, or imagine poor Joan Sorenson, tied to that bed as the killer came closer, knife in hand. She kept coming back to Roy Helander, to Roy Helander and his secret refuge. In her mind, Roy was still the gawky adolescent she remembered, his blonde hair lank and unwashed, his eyes frightened and confused as they made him tell the story over and over again. She wondered what had become of that secret place of his during all the years he'd been locked up and drugged in the state mental home, and she wondered if maybe sometimes he hadn't dreamt of it as he lay there in his cell. She thought maybe he had. If Roy Helander had indeed come home, Randi figured she knew just where he was.

Knowing about it and finding it were too different things, however. She and Willie had kicked it around without narrowing it down any. Randi tried to remember but it had been so long ago, a whispered conversation in the schoolyard. A secret place in the woods, he'd said, a place where no one ever came that was his and his alone, hidden and full of magic. That could be anything, a cave by the river, a treehouse, even something as a simple as a cardboard lean-to. But where were these woods? Outside the city were suburbs and industrial parks and farms, the nearest state forest was forty miles north along the river road. If this secret place was in one of the city parks, you'd think someone would have stumbled on it years ago. Without more to go on, Randi didn't have a prayer of finding it. But her mind worried it like a pit bull with a small child.

Finally her digital alarm clock read 2:13, and Randi gave up on sleep altogether. She got out of bed, turned on the light, and went back to the kitchen. The refrigerator was pretty dismal, but she found a couple of bottles of Pabst. Maybe a beer would help put her to sleep. She opened a bottle and carried it back to bed.

Her bedroom furnishings were a hodge-podge. The carpet was a remnant, the blonde chest-of-drawers was boring and functional, and the four-poster queen-sized bed was a replica, but she did own a few genuine antique—the massive oak wardrobe, the full-length clawfoot dressing mirror in its ornate wooden frame, and the cedar chest at the foot of the bed. Her mother always used to call it a hope chest. Did little girls still keep hope chests? She didn't think so, at least not around here. Maybe there were still places where hope didn't seem so terribly unrealistic, but this city wasn't one of them.

Randi sat on the floor, put the beer on the carpet, and opened the chest.

Hope chests were where you kept your future, all the little things that were part of the dreams they taught you to dream when you were a child. She hadn't been a child since she was twelve, since the night her mother woke her with that terrible inhuman sound. Her chest was full of memories now.

She took them out, one by one. Yearbooks from high school and college, bundles of love letters from old boyfriends and even that asshole she'd married, her school ring and her wedding ring, her diplomas, the letters she'd won in track and girls' softball, a framed picture of her and her date at the senior prom.

Way, way down at the bottom, buried under all the other layers of her life, was a police .38. Her father's gun, the gun he emptied the night he died. Randi took it out and carefully put it aside. Beneath it was the book, an old three-ring binder with a blue cloth cover. She opened it across her lap.

The yellowed *Courier* story on her father's death was scotch-taped to the first sheet of paper, and Randi stared at that familiar photograph for a long time before she flipped the page. There were other clippings; stories about the missing children that she'd torn futively from *Courier* back issues in the public library, magazine articles about animal attacks, serial killers, and monsters, all sandwiched between the lined pages she'd filled with her meticulous twelve-year-old's script. The handwriting grew broader and sloppier as she turned the pages; she'd kept up the book for years, until she'd gone away to college and tried to forget. She'd thought she'd done a pretty good job of that, but now, turning the pages, she knew that was a lie. You never forget. She only had to glance at the headlines, and it all came back to her in a sickening rush.

Eileen Stanski, Jessie Helander, Diane Jones, Gregory Corio, Erwin Weiss. None of them had ever been found, not so much as a bone or a piece of clothing. The police said her father's death was accidental, unrelated to the case he was working on. They'd all accepted that, the chief, the mayor, the newspaper, even her mother, who only wanted to get it all behind them and go on with their lives. Barry Schumacher and Joe Urquhart were the last to buy in, but in the end even they came around, and Randi was the only one left. Mere mention of the subject upset her mother so much that she finally stopped talking about it, but she didn't forget. She just asked her questions quietly, kept up her binder, and hid it every night at the bottom of the hope chest.

For all the good it had done.

The last twenty odd pages in the back of the binder were still blank, the blue lines on the paper faint with age. The pages were stiff as she turned them. When she reached the final page, she hesitated. Maybe it wouldn't be there, she thought. Maybe she had just imagined it. It made no sense anyway. He would have known about her father, yes, but their mail was censored, wasn't it? They'd never let him send such a thing.

Randi turned the last page. It was there, just as she'd known it would be.

She'd been a junior in college when it arrived. She'd put it all behind her. Her father had been dead for seven years, and she hadn't even looked at her binder for three. She was busy with her classes and her sorority and her boyfriends, and sometimes she had bad dreams but mostly it was okay, she'd grown up, she'd gotten real. If she thought about it at all, she thought that maybe the adults had been right all along, it had just been some kind of an animal.

...some kind of animal...

Then one day the letter had come. She'd opened it on the way to class, read it with her friends chattering beside her, laughed and made a joke and stuck it away, all very grown-up. But that night, when her roommate had gone to sleep, she took it out and turned on her tensor to read it again, and felt sick. She was going to throw it away, she remembered. It was just trash, a twisted product of a sick mind.

Instead she'd put it in the binder.

The scotch tape had turned yellow and brittle, but the envelope was still white, with the name of the institution printed neatly in the left-hand corner. Someone had probably smuggled it out for him. The letter itself was scrawled on a sheet of cheap typing paper in block letters. It wasn't signed, but she'd known who it was from.

Randi slid the letter out of the envelope, hesitated for a moment, and opened it.

IT WAS A WEREWOLF

She looked at it and looked at it and looked at it, and suddenly she didn't feel very grown up any more. When the phone rang she nearly jumped a foot.

Her heart was pounding in her chest. She folded up the letter and stared at the phone, feeling strangely guilty, as if she'd been caught doing something shameful. It was 2:53 in the morning. Who the hell would be calling now? If it was Roy Helander, she thought she might just scream. She let the phone ring.

On the fourth ring, her machine cut in. "This is AAA-Wade Investigations, Randi Wade speaking. I can't talk right now, but you can leave a message at the tone, and I'll get back to you."

The tone sounded. "Uh, hello," said a deep male voice that was definitely not Roy Helander.

Randi put down the binder, snatched up the receiver. "Rogoff? Is that you?"

"Yeah," he said. "Sorry if I woke you. Listen, this isn't by the book and I can't figure out a good excuse for why I'm calling you, except that I thought you ought to know."

Cold fingers crept down Randi's spine. "Know what?"

"We've got another one," he said.

Willie woke in a cold sweat.

What was that?

A noise, he thought. Somewhere down the hall.

Or maybe just a dream? Willie sat up in bed and tried to get a grip on himself. The night was full of noises. It could have been a towboat on the river, a car passing by underneath his windows, anything. He still felt sheepish about the way he'd let his fear take over when he found his door open. He was just lucky he hadn't stabbed Randi with those scissors. He couldn't let his imagination eat him alive. He slid back down under the covers, rolled over on his stomach, closed his eyes.

Down the hall, a door opened and closed.

His eyes opened wide. He lay very still, listening. He'd locked all the locks, he told himself, he'd walked Randi to the door and locked all his locks, the springlock, the chain, the double deadbolt, he'd even lowered the police bar. No one could get in once the bar was in place, it could only be lifted from inside, the door was solid steel. And the back door might as well be welded shut, it was so corroded and unmovable. If they broke a window he would have heard the noise, there was no way, no way. He was just dreaming.

The knob on his bedroom door turned slowly, clicked. There was a small metallic rattle as someone pushed at the door. The lock held. The second push was slightly harder, the noise louder.

By then Willie was out of bed. It was a cold night, his jockey shorts and undershirt small protection against the chill, but Willie had other things on his mind. He could see the key still sticking out of the keyhole. An antique key for a hundred-year-old lock. The office keyholes were big enough to peek through. Willie kept the keys inside them, just to plug up the drafts, but he never turned them...except tonight. Tonight for some reason he'd turned that key before he went to bed and somehow felt a little more secure when he heard the tumblers click. And now that was all that stood between him and whatever was out there.

He backed up against the window, glanced out at the cobbled alley behind the brewery. The shadows lay thick and black beneath him. He seemed to recall a big green-metal dumpster down below, directly under the window, but it was too dark to make it out.

Something hammered at the door. The room shook.

Willie couldn't breathe. His inhaler was on the dresser across the room, over by the door. He was caught in a giant's fist and it was squeezing all the breath right out of him. He sucked at the air.

The thing outside hit the door again. The wood began to splinter. Solid wood, a hundred years old, but it split like one of your cheap-ass hollow-core modern doors.

Willie was starting to get dizzy. It was going to be real pissed off, he thought giddily, when it finally got in here and found that his asthma had already killed him. Willie peeled off his undershirt, dropped it to the floor, hooked a thumb in the elastic of his shorts.

The door shook and shattered, falling half away from its hinges. The next blow snapped it in two. His head swam from lack of oxygen. Willie forgot all about his shorts and gave himself over to the change.

Bones and flesh and muscles shrieked in the agony of transformation, but the oxygen rushed into his lungs, sweet and cold, and he could breathe again. Relief shuddered through him and he threw back his head and gave it voice. It was a sound to chill the blood, but the dark shape picking its way through the splinters of his door did not hesitate, and neither did Willie. He gathered his feet up under him, and leapt. Glass shattered all around him as he threw himself through the window, and the shards spun outward into the darkness. Willie missed the dumpster, landed on all fours, lost his footing, and slid three feet across the cobbles.

When he looked up, he could see the shape above him, filling his window. Its hands moved, and he caught the terrible glint of silver, and that was all it took. Willie was on his feet again, running down the street faster than he had ever run before.

The cab let her off two houses down. Police barricades had gone up all around the house, a dignified old Victorian manor badly in need of fresh paint. Curious neighbors, heavy coats thrown on over pajamas and bathrobes, lined Grandview, whispering to each other and glancing back at the house. The flashers on the police cars lent a morbid avidity to their faces.

Randi walked past them briskly. A patrolman she didn't know stopped her at the police barrier. "I'm Randi Wade," she told him. "Rogoff asked me to come down."

"Oh," he said. He jerked a thumb back at the house. "He's inside, talking to the sister."

Randi found them in the living room. Rogoff saw her, nodded, waved her off, and went back to his questioning. The other cops looked at her curiously, but no one said anything. The sister was a young-looking forty, slender and dark, with pale skin and a wild mane of black hair that fell half down her back. She sat on the edge of a sectional in a white silk teddy that left little to the imagination, seemingly just as indifferent to the cold air coming through the open door as she was to the lingering glances of the policemen.

One of the cops was taking some fingerprints off a shiny black grand piano in the corner of the room. Randi wandered over as he finished. The top of the piano was covered with framed photographs. One was a summer scene, taken somewhere along the river, two pretty girls in matching bikinis standing on either side of an intense young man. The girls were dappled with moisture, laughing for the photographer, long black hair hanging wetly down across wide smiles. The man, or boy, or whatever he was, was in a swimsuit, but you could tell he was bone dry. He was gaunt and sallow, and his blue eyes stared into the lens with a vacancy that was oddly disturbing. The girls could have been as young as eighteen or as old as twenty. One of them was the woman Rogoff was questioning, but Randi could not have told you which one. Twins. She glanced at the other photos, half-afraid she'd find a picture of Willie. Most of the faces she didn't recognize, but she was still looking them over when Rogoff came up behind her.

"Coroner's upstairs with the body," he said. "You can come up if you've got the stomach."

Randi turned away from the piano and nodded. "You learn anything from the sister?"

"She had a nightmare," he said. He started up the narrow staircase, Randi close behind him. "She says that as far back as she can remember, whenever she had bad dreams, she'd just cross the hall and crawl in bed with Zoe." They reached the landing. Rogoff put his hand on a glass doorknob, then paused. "What she found when she crossed the hall this time is going to keep her in nightmares for years to come."

He opened the door. Randi followed him inside.

The only light was a small bedside lamp, but the police photographer was moving around the room, snapping pictures of the red twisted thing on the bed. The light of his flash made the shadows leap and writhe, and Randi's stomach writhed with them. The smell of blood was overwhelming. She remembered summers long ago, hot July days when the wind blew from the south and the stink of the slaughterhouse settled over the city. But this was a thousand times worse.

The photographer was moving, flashing, moving, flashing. The world went from gray to red, then back to gray again. The coroner was bent over the corpse, her motions turned jerky and unreal by the strobing of the big flash gun. The white light blazed off the ceiling, and Randi looked up and saw the mirrors there. The dead woman's mouth gaped open, round and wide in a silent scream. He'd cut off her lips with her skin, and the inside of her mouth was no redder than the outside. Her face was gone, nothing left but the glistening wet ropes of muscle and here and there the pale glint of bone, but he'd left her eyes. Large dark eyes, pretty eyes, sensuous, like her sister's downstairs. They were wide open, staring up in terror at the mirror on the ceiling. She'd been able to see every detail of what was being done to her. What had she found in the eyes of her reflection? Pain, terror, despair? A twin all her life, perhaps she'd found some strange comfort in her mirror image, even as her face and her flesh and her humanity had been cut away from her.

The flash went off again, and Randi caught the glint of metal at wrist and ankle. She closed her eyes for a second, steadied her breathing, and moved to the foot of the bed, where Rogoff was talking to the coroner.

"Same kind of chains?" he asked.

"You got it. And look at this." Coroner Cooney took the unlit cigar out of her mouth and pointed.

The chain looped tightly around the victim's ankle. When the flash went off again, Rand saw the other circles, dark, black lines, scored across the raw flesh and exposed nerves. It made her hurt just to look.

"She struggled," Rogoff suggested. "The chain chafed against her flesh."

"Chafing leaves you raw and bloody," Cooney replied. "What was done to her, you'd never notice chafing. That's a burn, Rogoff, a third-degree burn. Both wrists, both ankles, wherever the metal touched her. Sorenson had the same burn marks. Like the killer heated the chains until they were white hot. Only the metal is cold now. Go on, touch it."

"No thanks," Rogoff said. "I'll take your word for it."

"Wait a minute," Randi said.

The coroner seemed to notice her for the first time. "What's she doing here?" she asked.

"It's a long story," Rogoff replied. "Randi, this is official police business, you'd better keep—"

Randi ignored him. "Joan Sorenson had the same kind of burn marks?" she asked Cooney. "At wrist and ankle, where the chains touched her skin?"

"That's right," Cooney said. "So what?"

"What are you trying to say?" Rogoff asked her.

She looked at him. "Joan Sorenson was a cripple. She had no use of her legs, no sensation at all below the waist. So why bother to chain her ankles?"

Rogoff stared at her for a long moment, then shook his head. He looked over to Cooney. The coroner shrugged. "Yeah. So. An interesting point, but what does it mean?"

She had no answer for them. She looked away, back at the bed, at the skinned, twisted, mutilated thing that had once been a pretty woman.

The photographer moved to a different angle, pressed his shutter. The flash went off again. The chain glittered in the light. Lightly, Randi brushed a fingertip across the metal. She felt no heat. Only the cold, pale touch of silver.

The night was full of sounds and smells.

Willie had run wildly, blindly, a gray shadow streaking down black rain-slick streets, pushing himself harder and faster than he had ever pushed before, paying no attention to where he went, anywhere, nowhere, everywhere, just so it was far away from his apartment and the thing that waited there with death shining bright in its hand. He darted along grimy alleys, under loading docks, bounded over low chain-link fences. There was a cinder-block wall somewhere that almost stopped him, three leaps and he failed to clear it, but on the fourth try he got his front paws over the top, and his back legs kicked and scrabbled and pushed him over. He fell onto damp grass, rolled in the dirt, and then he was up and running again. The streets were almost empty of traffic, but as he streaked across one wide boulevard, a pick-up truck appeared out of nowhere, speeding, and caught him in its lights. The sudden glare startled him; he froze for a long instant in the center of the street, and saw shock and terror on the driver's face. A horn blared as the pick-up began to brake, went into a skid, and fishtailed across the divider.

By then Willie was gone.

He was moving through a residential section now, down quiet streets lined by neat two-story houses. Parked cars filled the narrow driveways, realtor's signs flapped in the wind, but the only lights were the street lamps... and sometimes, when the clouds parted for a second, the pale circle of the moon. He caught the scent of dogs from some of the back yards, and from time to time heard a wild, frenzied barking, and knew that they had smelled him too. Sometimes the barking woke owners and neighbors, and then lights would come on in the silent houses, and doors would open in the backyards, but by then Willie would be blocks away, still running.

Finally, when his legs were aching and his heart was thundering and his tongue lolled redly from his mouth, Willie crossed the railroad tracks, climbed a steep embankment, and came hard up against a ten-foot chain-link fence with barbed wire strung along the top. Beyond the fence was a wide, empty yard and a low brick building, windowless and vast, dark beneath the light of the moon. The smell of old blood was faint but unmistakable, and abruptly Willie knew where he was.

The old slaughterhouse. The pack, they'd called it, bankrupt and abandoned now for almost two years. He'd run a long way. At last he let himself stop and catch his breath. He was panting, and as he dropped to the ground by the fence, he began to shiver, cold despite his ragged coat of fur.

He was still wearing jockey shorts, Willie noticed after he'd rested a moment. He would have laughed, if he'd had the throat for it. He thought of the man in the pick-up and wondered what he'd thought when Willie appeared in his headlights, a gaunt gray spectre in a pair of white briefs, with glowing eyes as red as the pits of hell.

Willie twisted himself around and caught the elastic in his jaws. He tore at them, growling low in his throat, and after a brief struggle managed to rip them away. He slung them aside and lowered himself to the damp ground, his legs resting on his paws, his mouth half-open, his eyes wary, watchful. He let himself rest. He could hear distant traffic, a dog barking wildly a half-mile away, could smell rust and mold, the stench of diesel fumes, the cold scent of metal. Under it all was the slaughterhouse smell, faded but not gone, lingering, whispering to him of blood and death. It woke things inside him that were better left sleeping, and Willie could feel the hunger churning in his gut.

He could not ignore it, not wholly, but tonight he had other concerns, fears that were more important than his hunger. Dawn was only a few hours away, and he had nowhere to go. He could not go home, not until he knew it was safe again, until he had taken steps to protect himself. Without keys and clothes and money, the agency was closed to him too. He had to go somewhere, trust someone.

He thought of Blackstone, thought of Jonathan Harmon sitting by his fire, of Steven's dead blue eyes and scarred hands, of the old tower jutting up like a rotten black stake. Jonathan might be able to protect him, Jonathan with his strong walls and his spiked fence and all his talk of blood and iron.

But when he saw Jonathan in his mind's eye, the long white hair, the gold wolf's head cane, the veined arthritic hands twisting and grasping, then the growl rose unbidden in Willie's throat, and he knew Blackstone was not the answer.

Joanie was dead, and he did not know the others well enough, hardly knew all their names, didn't want to know them better.

So. in the end, like it or not, there was only Randi.

Willie got to his feet, weary now, unsteady. The wind shifted, sweeping across the yards and the runs, whispering to him of blood until his nostrils quivered. Willie threw back his head and howled, a long shuddering lonely call that rose and fell and went out through the cold night air until the dogs began to bark for blocks around. Then, once again, he began to run.

Rogoff gave her a lift home. Dawn was just starting to break when he pulled his old black Ford up to the front of her six-flat. As she opened the door, he shifted into neutral and looked over at her. "I'm not going to insist right now," he said, "but it might be that I need to know the name of your client. Sleep on it. Maybe you'll decide to tell me."

"Maybe I can't," Randi said. "Attorney-client privilege, remember?"

Rogoff gave her a tired smile. "When you sent me to the courthouse, I had a look at your file too. You never went to law school."

"No?" She smiled back. "Well, I meant to. Doesn't that count for something?" She shrugged. "I'll sleep on it, we can talk tomorrow." He got out, closed the door, moved away from the car. Rogoff shifted into drive, but Randi turned back before he could pull away. "Hey, Rogoff, you have a first name?"

"Mike," he said.

"See you tomorrow, Mike."

He nodded and pulled away just as the streetlamps began to go out. Randi walked up the stoop, fumbling for her key.

"*Randi!*"

She stopped, looked around. "Who's there?"

"Willie." The voice was louder this time. "Down here by the garbage cans."

Randi leaned over the stoop and saw him. He was crouched down low, surrounded by trash-bins, shivering in the morning chill. "You're naked," she said.

"Somebody tried to kill me last night. I made it out. My clothes didn't. I've been here an hour, not that I'm complaining mind you, but I think I have pneumonia and my balls are frozen solid. I'll never be able to have children now. Where the fuck have you been?"

"There was another murder. Same m.o.," Willie shook so violently that the garbage cans rattled together. "Jesus," he said, his voice gone weak. "Who?"

"Her name was Zoe Anders."

Willie flinched. "Fuck fuck fuck," he said. He looked back up at Randi. She could see the fear in his eyes, but he asked anyway. "What about Amy?"

"Her sister?" Randi said. He nodded. "In shock, but fine. She had a nightmare." She paused a moment. "So you knew Zoe too. Like Sorenson?"

"No. Not like Joanie." He looked at her wearily. "Can we go in?"

She nodded and opened the door. Willie looked so grateful she thought he was about to lick her hand.

The underwear was her ex-husband's, and it was too big. The pink bathrobe was Randi's, and it was too small. But the coffee was just right, and it was warm in here, and Willie felt bone-tired and nervous but glad to be alive, especially when Randi put the plate down in front of him. She'd scrambled the eggs up with cheddar cheese and onion and done up a rasher of bacon on the side, and it smelled like nirvana. He fell to eagerly.

"I think I've figured out something," she said. She sat down across from him.

"Good," he said. "The eggs, I mean. That is, whatever you figured out, that's good too, but Jesus, I *needed* these eggs. You wouldn't believe how hungry you get—" He stopped suddenly, stared down at the scrambled eggs, and reflected on what an idiot he was, but Randi hadn't noticed. Willie reached for a slice of bacon, bit off the end. "Crisp," he said. "Good."

"I'm going to tell you," Randi said, as if he hadn't spoken at all. "I've got to tell somebody, and you've known me long enough so I don't think you'll have me committed. You may laugh." She scowled at him. "If you laugh, you're back out in the street, minus the boxer shorts and the bathrobe."

"I won't laugh," Willie said. He didn't think he'd have much difficulty not laughing. He felt rather apprehensive. He stopped eating.

Randi took a deep breath and looked him in the eye. She had very lovely eyes, Willie thought. "I think my father was killed by a werewolf," she said seriously, without blinking.

"Oh, Jesus," Willie said. He didn't laugh. A very large invisible anaconda wrapped itself around his chest and began to squeeze. "I," he said, "I, I, I." Nothing was coming in or out. He pushed back from the table, knocking over the chair, and ran for the bathroom. He locked himself in and turned on the shower full-blast, twisting the hot tap all the way around. The bathroom began to fill up with steam. It wasn't nearly as good as a blast from his inhaler, but it did beat suffocating. By the time the steam was really going good, Willie was on his knees, gasping like a man trying to suck an elephant through a straw. Finally he began to breathe again.

He stayed on his knees for a long time, until the spray from the shower had soaked through his robe and his underwear and his face was flushed and red. Then he crawled across the tiled floor, turned off the shower, and got unsteadily to his feet. The mirror above the sink was all fogged up. Willie wiped it off with a towel and peered in at himself. He looked like shit. Wet shit. Hot wet shit. He felt worse. He tried to dry himself off, but the steam and the shower spray had gone everywhere and the towels were as damp as he was. He heard Randi moving around outside, opening and closing drawers. He wanted to go out and face her, but not like this. A man has to have some pride. For a moment he just wanted to be home in bed with his Primateen on the end table, until he remembered that his bedroom had been occupied the last time he'd been there.

"Are you ever coming out?" Randi asked.

"Yeah," Willie said, but it was so weak that he doubted she heard him. He straightened and adjusted the frilly pink robe. Underneath the undershirt looked as though he'd been competing in a wet tee-shirt contest. He sighed, unlocked the door, and exited. The cold air gave him goosepimples.

Randi was seated at the table again. Willie went back to his place. "Sorry," he said. "Asthma attack."

"I noticed," Randi replied. "Stress related, aren't they?"

"Sometimes."

"Finish your eggs," she urged. "They're getting cold."

"Yeah," Willie said, figuring he might as well, since it would give him something to do while he figured out what to tell her. He picked up his fork.

It was like the time he'd grabbed a dirty pot that had been sitting on top of his hotplate since the night before and realized too late that he'd never turned the hotplate off. Willie shrieked and the fork clattered to the table and bounced, once, twice, three times. It landed in front of Randi. He sucked on his fingers. They were already starting to turn red. Randi looked at him very calmly and picked up the fork. She held it, stroked it with her thumb, touched its prongs thoughtfully to her lip. "I brought out the good silver while you were in the bathroom," she said. "Solid sterling. It's been in the family for generations."

His fingers hurt like hell. "Oh, Jesus. You got any butter? Oleo, lard, I don't care, anything will..." He stopped when her hand went under the table and came out again holding a gun. From where Willie sat, it looked like a very big gun.

"Pay attention, Willie. Your fingers are the least of your worries. I realize you're in pain, so I'll give you a minute or two to collect your thoughts and try to tell me why I shouldn't blow off your fucking head right here and now." She cocked the hammer with her thumb.

Willie just stared at her. He looked pathetic, like a half-drowned puppy. For one terrible moment Randi thought he was going to have another asthma attack. She felt curiously calm, not angry or afraid or even nervous, but she didn't think she had it in her to shoot a man in the back as he ran for the bathroom, even if he was a werewolf.

Thankfully, Willie spared her that decision. "You don't want to shoot me," he said, with remarkable aplomb under the circumstances. "It's bad manners to shoot your friends. You'll make a hole in the bathrobe."

"I never liked that bathrobe anyway. I hate pink."

"If you're really so hot to kill me, you'd stand a better chance with the fork," Willie said.

"So you admit that you're a werewolf?"

"A lycanthrope," Willie corrected. He sucked at his burnt fingers again and looked at her sideways. "So sue me. It's a medical condition. I got allergies, I got asthma, I got a bad back, and I got lycanthropy, is it my fault? I didn't kill your father. I never killed anyone. I ate half a pit bull once, but can you blame me?" His voice turned querulous. "If you want to shoot me, go ahead and try. Since when do you carry a gun anyway? I thought all that shit about private eyes stuffing heat was strictly television?"

"The phrase is *packing* heat, and it is. I only bring mine out for special occasions. My father was carrying it when he died."

"Didn't do him much good, did it?" Willie said softly.

Randi considered that for a moment. "What would happen if I pulled the trigger?" The gun was getting heavy, but her hand was steady.

"I'd try to change. I don't think I'd make it, but I'd have to try. A couple bullets in the head at this range, while I'm still human, yeah, that'd probably do the job. But you don't want to miss and you *really* don't want to wound me. Once I'm changed, it's a whole different ballgame."

"My father emptied his gun on the night he was killed," Randi said thoughtfully.

Willie studied his hand and winced. "Oh fuck," he said. "I'm getting a blister."

Randi put the gun on the table and went to the kitchen to get him a stick of butter. He accepted it from her gratefully. She glanced toward the window as he treated his burns. "The sun's up," she said, "I thought werewolves only changed at night, during the full moon?"

"Lycanthropes," Willie said. He flexed his fingers, sighed. "That full moon shit was all invented by some screenwriter for Universal, go look at your literature, we change at will, day, night, full moon, new moon, makes no difference. Sometimes I *feel* more like changing during the full moon, some kind of hormonal thing, but more like getting horny than going on the rag, if you know what I mean." He grabbed his coffee. It was cold by now, but that didn't stop Willie from emptying the cup. "I shouldn't be telling you all this, fuck, Randi, I like you, you're a friend, I care about you, you should only forget this whole morning, believe me, it's healthier."

"Why?" she said bluntly. She wasn't about to forget anything. "What's going to happen to me if I don't? Are you going to rip my throat out? Should I forget Joanie Sorenson and Zoe Anders too? How about Roy Helander and all those missing kids? *Am I supposed to forget what happened to my father?*" She stopped for a moment, lowered her voice. "You came to me for help, Willie, and pardon me, but you sure as hell look as though you still need it."

Willie looked at her across the table with a morose, hangdog expression on his long face. "I don't know whether I want to kiss you or slap you," he finally admitted. "Shit, you're right, you know too much already." He stood up. "I got to get into my own clothes, this wet underwear is giving me pneumonia. Call a cab, we'll go check out my place, talk. You got a coat?"

"Take the Burberry," Randi said. "It's in the closet."

The coat was even bigger on him than it had been on Randi, but it beat the pink bathrobe. He looked almost human as he emerged from the closet, fussing with the belt. Randi was rummaging in the silver drawer. She found a large carving knife, the one her grandfather used to use on Thanksgiving, and slid it through the belt of her jeans. Willie looked at it nervously. "Good idea," he finally said, "but take the gun too."

The cab-driver was the quiet type. The drive crosstown passed in awkward silence. Randi paid him while Willie climbed out to check the doors. It was a blustery overcast day, and the river looked gray and choppy as it slapped against the pier.

Willie kicked his front door in a fit of pique, and vanished down the alley. Randi waited by the pier and watched the cab drive off. A few minutes later Willie was back, looking disgusted. "This is ridiculous," he said. "The back door hasn't been opened in years, you'd need a hammer and chisel just to knock through the rust. The loading docks are bolted down and chained with the mother of all padlocks on the chains. And the front door... there's a spare set of keys in my car, but even if we got those, the police bar can only be lifted from inside. So how the hell did it get in, I ask you?"

Randi looked at the brewery's weathered brick walls appraisingly. They looked pretty solid to her, and the second floor windows were a good twenty feet off street level. She walked around the side to take a look down the alley. "There's a window broken," she said.

"That was me getting out," Willie said, "not my nocturnal caller getting in."

Randi had already figured out that much from the broken glass all over the cobblestones. "Right now I'm more concerned about how *we're* going to get in." She pointed. "If we move that dumpster a few feet to the left and climb on top, and you climb on my shoulders, I think you might be able to hoist yourself in."

Willie considered that. "What if it's still in there?"

"What?" Randi said.

"Whatever was after me last night. If I hadn't jumped through that window, it'd be me without a skin this morning, and believe me, I'm cold enough as is." He looked at the window, at the dumpster, and back at the window. "Fuck," he said, "we can't stand here all day. But I've got a better idea. Help me roll the dumpster away from the wall a little."

Randi didn't understand, but she did as Willie suggested. They left the dumpster in the center of the alley, directly opposite the broken window. Willie nodded and began unbelting the coat she'd lent him. "Turn around," he told her. "I don't want you freaking out. I've got to get naked and your carnal appetites might get the best of you."

Randi turned around. The temptation to glance over her shoulder was irresistible. She heard the coat fall to the ground. Then she heard something else...soft padding steps, like a dog. She turned. He'd circled all the way down to the end of the alley. Her ex-husband's old underwear lay puddled across the cobblestones atop the Burberry coat. Willie came streaking back toward the brewery, building speed. He was, Randi noticed, not a very prepossessing wolf. His fur was a dirty gray-brown color, kind of mangy, his rear looked too large and his legs too thin, and there was something ungainly about the way he ran. He put on a final burst of speed, leapt on top of dumpster, bounded off the metal lid, and flew through the shattered window, breaking more glass as he went. Randi heard a loud *thump* from inside the bedroom.

She went around to the front. A few moments later, the locks began to unlock, one by one, and Willie opened the heavy steel door. He was wearing his own bathrobe, a red tartan flannel, and his hand was full of keys. "Come on," he said. "No sign of night visitors. I put on some water for tea."

"The fucker must have crawled out of the toilet," Willie said. "I don't see any other way he could have gotten in."

Randi stood in front of what remained of his bedroom door. She studied the shattered wood, ran her finger lightly across one long, jagged splinter, then knelt to look at the floor. "Whatever it was, it was strong. Look at these gouges in the wood, look at how sharp and clean they are. You don't do that with a fist. Claws, maybe. More likely some kind of knife. And take a look at this." She gestured toward the brass doorknob, which lay on the floor amidst a bunch of kindling.

Willie bent to pick it up.

"Don't touch," she said, grabbing his arm. "Just look."

He got down on one knee. At first he didn't notice anything. But when he leaned close, he saw how the brass was scored and scraped.

"Something sharp," Randi said, "and hard." She stood up. "When you first heard the sounds, what direction were they coming from?"

Willie thought for a moment. "It was hard to tell," he said. "Toward the back, I think."

Randi walked back. All along the hall, the doors were closed. She studied the banister at the top of the stairs, then moved on, and began opening and closing doors. "Come here," she said, at the fourth door.

Willie trotted down the hall. Randi had the door ajar. The knob on the hall side was fine; the knob on the inside displayed the same kind of scoring they'd seen on his bedroom door. Willie was aghast. "But this is the *men's room*," he said. "You mean it did come out of the toilet? I'll never shit again."

"It came out of this room," Randi said. "I don't know about the toilet." She went in and looked around. There wasn't much to look at. Two toilet stalls, two urinals, two sinks with a long mirror above them and antique brass soap dispensers beside the water taps, a paper towel dispenser, Willie's towels and toiletries. No window. Not even a small frosted-glass window. No window at all.

Down the hall the tea kettle began to whistle. Randi looked thoughtful as they walked back to the living room. "Joan Sorenson died behind a locked door, and the killer got to Zoe Anders without waking her sister right across the hall."

"The fucking thing can come and go as it pleases," Willie said. The idea gave him the creeps. He glanced around nervously as he got out the teabags, but there was nobody there but him and Randi.

"Except it can't," Randi said. "With Sorenson and Anders, there was no damage, no sign of a break-in, nothing but a corpse. But with you, the killer was stopped by something as simple as a locked door."

"Not stopped," Willie said, "just slowed down a little." He repressed a shudder and brought the tea over to his coffee table.

"Did he get the right Anders sister?" she asked.

Willie stood there stupidly for a moment holding the kettle poised over the cups. "What do you mean?"

"You've got identical twins sharing the same house. Let's presume it's a house the killer's never visited before. Somehow he gains entry, and he chains, murders, and flays only *one* of them, without even waking the other." Randi smiled up at him sweetly. "You can't tell them apart by sight, he probably didn't know which room was which, so the question is, did he get the werewolf?"

Willie poured the tea. This time he wasn't flustered. It was nice to know that she wasn't infallible. "Yes," he said, "and no. They were twins, Randi. Both lycanthropes." She looked honestly surprised. "How did you know?" he asked her.

"Oh, the chains," she said negligently. Her mind was far away, gnawing at the puzzle. "Silver chains. She was burned wherever they'd touched her flesh. And Joan Sorenson was a werewolf too, of course. She was crippled, yes… but only as a human, not after her transformation. That's why her legs were chained, to hold her if she changed." She looked at Willie with a baffled expression on her face. "It doesn't make sense, to kill one and leave the other untouched. Are you sure that Amy Anders is a werewolf too?"

"A lycanthrope," he said. "Yes. Definitely. They were even harder to tell apart as wolves. At least when they were human they dressed differently. Amy liked white lace, frills, that kind of stuff, and Zoe was into leather." There was a cut-glass ashtray in the center of the coffee table filled with Willie's private party mix :aspirin, Allerest, and Tums. He took a handful of pills and swallowed them dry.

"Look, before we go on with this, I want one card on the table," Randi said.

For once he was ahead of her. "If I knew who killed your father, I'd tell you, but I don't, I was in the service, overseas.I vaguely remember something in the *Courier*, but to tell the truth I'd forgotten all about it until you threw it at me last night. What can I tell you?" He shrugged.

"Don't bullshit me, Willie. My father was killed by a werewolf. You're a werewolf. You must know something."

"Hey, try substituting *Jew* or *diabetic* or *bald man* for werewolf in that statement, and see how much sense it makes. I'm not saying you're wrong about your father because you're not, it fits, it all fits, everything from the condition of the body to the empty gun, but even if you buy that much, then you got to ask *which* werewolf."

"How many of you *are* there?" Randi asked incredulously.

"Damned if I know," Willie said. "What do you think, we get together for a lodge meeting every time the moon is full? The purebloods, hell, not many, the pack's been getting pretty thin these last few generations. But there's lots of mongrels like me, halfbreeds, quarterbreeds, what have you, the old families had their share of bastards. Some can work the change, some can't. I've heard of a few who change one day and never do manage to change back. And that's just from the old bloodlines, never mind the ones like Joanie."

"You mean Joanie was different?"

Willie gave her a reluctant nod. "You've seen the movies. You get bitten by a werewolf, you turn into a werewolf, that is assuming there's enough of you left to turn into anything except a cadaver." She nodded, and he went on, "Well, that part's true, or partly true, it doesn't happen as often as it once did. Guy gets bit nowadays, he runs to a doctor, gets the wound cleaned and treated with antiseptic, gets his rabies shots and his tetanus shots and his penicillin and fuck-all knows what else, and he's fine. The wonders of modern medicine."

Willie hesitated briefly, looking in her eyes, those lovely eyes, wondering if she'd understand, and finally he plunged ahead. "Joanie was such a good kid, it broke my heart to see her in that chair. One night she told me that the hardest thing of all was realizing that she'd never know what it felt like to make love. She'd been a virgin when they hit that truck. We'd had a few drinks, she was crying, and…well, I couldn't take it. I told her what I was and what I could do for her, she didn't believe a word of it, so I had to show her. I bit her leg, she couldn't feel a damn thing down there anyway, I bit her and I held the bite for a long time, worried it around good. Afterwards I nursed her myself. No doctors, no antiseptic, no rabies vaccine. We're talking major league infection here, there was a day or two when her fever was running so high I thought maybe I'd killed her, her leg had turned nearly black, you could see the stuff going up her veins. I got to admit it was pretty gross, I'm in no hurry to try it again, but it worked. The fever broke and Joanie changed."

"You weren't just friends," Randi said with certainty. "You were lovers."

"Yeah," he said. "As wolves. I guess I look sexier in fur. I couldn't even begin to keep up with her, though. Joanie was a pretty active wolf. We're talking almost every night here."

"As a human, she was still crippled," Randi said.

Willie nodded, held up his hand. "See." The burns were still there, and a blood blister had formed on his index finger. "Once or twice the change has saved my life, when my asthma got so bad I thought I was going to suffocate. That kind of thing doesn't cross over, but it's sure as hell waiting for you when you cross back. Sometimes you even get nasty surprises. Catch a bullet as a wolf and it's nothing, a sting and a slap, heals up right away, but you can pay for it when you change into human form, especially if you change too soon and the damn thing gets infected. And silver will burn the shit out of you no matter what form you're in. LBJ was my favorite president, just *loved* them cupro-nickle-sandwich quarters."

Randi stood up. "This is all a little overwhelming. Do you *like* being a werewolf?"

"A lycanthrope." Willie shrugged. "I don't know, do you like being a woman? It's what I am."

Randi crossed the room and stared out his window at the river. "I'm very confused," she said. "I look at you and you're my friend Willie. I've known you for years. Only you're a werewolf too. I've been telling myself that werewolves don't exist since I was twelve, and now I find out the city is full of them. Only someone or something is killing them, flaying them. Should I care? Why should I care?" She ran a hand through her tangled hair. "We both know that Roy Helander didn't kill those kids. My father knew it too. He kept pressing, and one night he was lured to the stockyards and some kind of animal tore out his throat. Every time I think of that I think maybe I ought to find this werewolf killer and sign up to help him. Then I look at you again." She turned and looked at him. "And damn it, you're *still* my friend."

She looked as though she was going to cry. Willie had never seen her cry and he didn't want to. He hated it when they cried. "Remember when I first offered you a job, and you wouldn't take it, because you thought all collection agents were pricks?"

She nodded.

"Lycanthropes are skinchangers. We turn into wolves. Yeah, we're carnivores, you got it, you don't meet many vegetarians in the pack, but there's meat and there's meat. You won't find nearly as many rats around here as you will in other cities this size. What I'm sayin is the skin may change, but what you do is still up to the person inside. So stop thinking about werewolves and werewolf-killers and start thinking about murderers, cause that's what we're talking about."

Randi crossed the room and sat back down. "I hate to admit it, but you're making sense."

"I'm good in bed too," Willie said with a grin.

The ghost of a smile crossed her face. "Fuck you."

"Exactly my suggestion. What kind of underwear are you wearing?"

"Never mind my underwear," she said. "Do you have any ideas about these murderers? Past or present?"

Sometimes Randi had a one track mind, Willie thought; unfortunately, it never seemed to be the track that led under the sheets. "Jonathan told me about an old legend," he said.

"Jonathan?" she said.

"Jonathan Harmon, yeah, that one, old blood and iron, the *Courier*, Blackstone, the pack, the founding family, all of it."

"Wait a minute. He's a wer—a lycanthrope?"

Willie nodded. "Yeah, leader of the pack, he—"

Randi leapt ahead of him. "And it's hereditary?"

He saw where she was going. "Yes, but—"

"Steven Harmon is mentally disturbed," Randi interrupted. "His family keeps it out of the papers, but they can't stop the whispering. Violent episodes, strange doctors coming and going from Blackstone, shock treatments. He's some kind of pain freak, isn't he?"

Willie sighed. "Yeah. Ever see his hands? The palms and fingers are covered with silver burns. Once I saw him close his hand around a silver cartwheel and hold it there until smoke started to come out between his fingers. It burned a big round hole right in the center of his palm." He shuddered. "Yeah, Steven's a freak all right, and he's strong enough to rip your arm out of your socket and beat you to death with it, but he didn't kill your father, he couldn't have."

"Says you," she said.

"He didn't kill Joanie or Zoe either. They weren't just murdered, Randi. They were skinned. That's where the legend comes in. The word was *skinchangers*, remember? What if the power was *in* the skin? So you catch a werewolf, flay it, slip into the bloody skin…and change."

Randi was staring at him with a sick look on her face. "Does it really work that way?"

"Someone thinks so."

"Who?"

"Someone who's been thinking about werewolves for a long time. Someone's who gone way past obsession into full-fledged psychopathy. Someone who thinks he saw a werewolf once, who thinks werewolves done him wrong, who hates them, wants to hurt them, wants revenge...but maybe also, down deep, someone who wants to know what's it like."

"Roy Helander," she said.

"Maybe if we could find this damned secret hideout in the woods, we'd know for sure."

Randi stood up. "I racked my brain for hours. We could poke around a few of the city parks some, but I'm not sanguine on our prospects. No. I want to know more about these legends, and I want to look at Steven with my own eyes. Get your car, Willie. We're going to pay a visit to Blackstone."

He'd been afraid she was going to say something like that. He reached out and grabbed another handful of his party mix. "Oh, Jesus," he said, crunching down on a mouthful of pills. "This isn't the Addams Family, you know. Jonathan is for real."

"So am I," said Randi, and Willie knew the cause was lost.

It was raining again by the time they reached Courier Square. Willie waited in the car while Randi went inside the gunsmith's. Twenty minutes later, when she came back out, she found him snoring behind the wheel. At least he'd had the sense to lock the doors of his mammoth old Cadillac. She tapped on the glass, and he sat right up and stared at her for a moment without recognition. Then he woke up, leaned over, and unlocked the door on the passenger side. Randi slid in beside him.

"How'd it go?"

"They don't get much call for silver bullets, but they know someone upstate who does custom work for collectors," Randi said in a disgusted tone of voice.

"You don't sound too happy about it."

"I'm not. You wouldn't believe what they're going to charge me for a box of silver bullets, never mind that it's going to take two weeks. It was going to take a month, but I raised the ante." She looked glumly out the rain-streaked window. A torrent of gray water rushed down the gutter, carrying its flotilla of cigarette butts and scraps of yesterday's newspaper.

"Two weeks?" Willie turned the ignition and put the barge in gear. "Hell, we'll both probably be dead in two weeks. Just as well; the whole idea of silver bullets makes me nervous."

They crossed the square, past the Castle marquee and the Courier Building, and headed up Central, the windshield wipers clicking back and forth rhymthically. Willie hung a left on 13th and headed toward the bluff while Randi took out her father's revolver, opened the cylinder, and checked to see that it was fully loaded. Willie watched her out of the corner of his eye as he drove. "Waste of time," he said. "Guns don't kill werewolves, werewolves kill werewolves."

"Lycanthropes," Randi reminded him.

He grinned and for a moment looked almost like the man she'd shared an office with, a long time ago.

Both of them grew visibly more tense as they drove down 13th, the Caddy's big wheels splashing through the puddles. They were still a block away when she saw the little car crawling down the bluff, white against the dark stone. A moment later, she saw the lights, flashing red-and-blue.

Willie saw them too. He slammed on the brakes, lost traction, and had to steer wildly to avoid slamming into a parked car as he fishtailed. His forehead was beading with sweat when he finally brought the car to a stop, and Randi didn't think it was from the near-collision. "Oh, Jesus," he said, "oh, Jesus, notH arm on too, I don't *believe* it." He began to wheeze, and fumbled in his pocket for an inhaler.

"Wait here, I'll check it out," Randi told him. She got up, turned up the collar of her coat, and walked the rest of the way, to where 13th dead-ended flush against the bluff. The coroner's wagon was parked amidst three police cruisers. Randi arrived at the same time as the cable car. Rogoff was the first one out. Behind him she saw Cooney, the police photographer, and two uniforms carrying a bodybag. It must have gotten pretty crowded on the way down.

"You." Rogoff seemed surprised to see her. Strands of black hair were plastered to his forehead by the rain.

"Me," Randi agreed. The plastic of the bodybag was slick and wet, and the uniforms were having trouble with it. One of them lost his footing as he stepped down, and Randi thought she saw something shift inside the bag. "It doesn't fit the pattern," she said to Rogoff. "The other killings have all been at night."

Rogoff took her by the arm and drew her away, gently but firmly. "You don't want to look at this one, Randi."

There was something in his tone that made her look at him hard. "Why not? It can't be any worse than Zoe Anders, can it? Who's in the bag, Rogoff? The father or the son?"

"Neither one," he said. He glanced back behind them, up toward the top of the bluff, and Randi found herself following his gaze. Nothing was visible of Blackstone but the high wrought-iron fence that surrounded the estate. "This time his luck ran out on him. The dogs got to him first. Cooney says the scent of blood off of... of what he was wearing... well, it must have driven them wild. They tore him to pieces, Randi." He put his hand on her shoulder, as if to comfort her.

"No," Randi said. She felt numb, dazed.

"Yes," he insisted. "It's over. And believe me, it's not something you want to see."

She backed away from him. They were loading the body in the rear of the coroner's wagon while Sylvia Cooney supervised the operation, smoking her cigar in the rain. Rogoff tried to touch her again, but she whirled away from him, and ran to the wagon. "Hey!" Cooney said.

The body was on the tailgate, half-in and half-out of the wagon. Randi reached for the zipper on the body bag. One of the cops grabbed her arm. She shoved him aside and unzipped the bag. His face was half gone. His right cheek and ear and part of his jaw had been torn away, devoured right down the bone. What features he had left were obscured by blood.

Someone tried to pull her away from the tailgate. She spun and kicked him in the balls, then turned back to the body and grabbed it under the arms and pulled. The inside of the bodybag was slick with blood. The corpse slid loose of the plastic sheath like a banana squirting out of its skin and fell into the street. Rain washed down over it, and the runoff in the gutter turned pink, then red. A hand, or part of a hand, fell out of the bag almost like an afterthought. Most of the arm was gone, and Randi could see bones peeking through, and places where huge hunks of flesh had been torn out of his thigh, shoulder, and torso. He was naked, but between his legs was nothing but a raw red wound where his genitalia had been.

Something was fastened around his neck, and knotted beneath his chin. Randi leaned forward to touch it, and drew back when she saw his face. The rain had it washed it clean. He had one eye left, a green eye, open and staring. The rain pooled in his socket and ran down his cheek. Roy had grown gaunt to the point of emaciation, with a week's growth of beard, but his long hair was still the same color, the color he'd shared with all his brothers and sisters, that muddy Helander blond.

Something was knotted under his chin, a long twisted cloak of some kind, it had gotten all tangled when he fell. Randi was trying to straighten it when they caught her by both arms and dragged her away bodily. "No," she said wildly. "What was he wearing? What was he *wearing, damn you! I have to see!*" No one answered. Rogoff had her right arm imprisoned in a grip that felt like steel. She fought him wildly, kicking and shouting, but he held her until the hysteria had passed, and then held her some more as she leaned against his chest, sobbing.

She didn't quite know when Willie had come up, but suddenly there he was. He took her away from Rogoff and led her back to his Cadillac, and they sat inside, silent, as first the coroner's wagon and then the police cruisers drove off one by one. She was covered with blood. Willie gave her some aspirin from a bottle he kept in his glove compartment. She tried to swallow it, but her throat was raw, and she wound up gagging it back up. "It's all right," he told her, over and over. "It wasn't your father, Randi. Listen to me, please, it *wasn't your father!*"

"It was Roy Helander," Randi said to him at last. "And he was wearing Joanie's skin."

Willie drove her home; she was in no shape to confront Jonathan Harmon or anybody. She'd calmed down, but the hysteria was still there, just under the surface, he could see it in the eyes, hear it in her voice. If that wasn't enough, she kept telling him the same thing, over and over. "It was Roy Helander," she'd say, like he didn't know, "and he was wearing Joanie's skin."

Willie found her keys and helped her upstairs to her apartment. Inside, he made her take a couple of sleeping pills from the all-purpose pharmaceutical in his glove box, then turned down the bed and undressed her. He figured if anything would snap her back to herself, it would be his fingers on the buttons of her blouse, but she just smiled at him, vacant and dreamy, and told him that it was Roy Helander and he was wearing Joanie's skin. The big silver knife jammed through her belt loops gave him pause. He finally unzipped her fly, undid her buckle, and yanked off the jeans, knife and all. She didn't wear panties. He'd always suspected as much.

When Randi was finally in bed asleep, Willie went back to her bathroom and threw up.

Afterwards he made himself a gin-and-tonic to wash the taste of vomit out of his mouth, and went and sat alone in her living room in one of her red velvet chairs. He'd had even less sleep than Randi these past few nights, and he felt as though he might drift off at any moment, but he knew somehow that it was important not to. It was Roy Helander and he was wearing Joanie's skin. So it was over, he was safe.

He remembered the way his door shook last night, a solid wood door, and it split like so much cheap paneling. Behind it was something dark and powerful, something that left scars on brass doorknobs and showed up in places it had no right to be. Willie didn't know what had been on the other side of his door, but somehow he didn't think that the gaunt, wasted, half-eaten travesty of a man he'd seen on 13th street quite fit the bill. He'd believe that his nocturnal visitor had been Roy Helander, with or without Joanie's skin, about the same time he'd believe that the man had been eaten by dogs. *Dogs!* How long did Jonathan expect to get away with that shit? Still, he couldn't blame him, not with Zoe and Joanie dead, and Helander trying to sneak into Blackstone dressed in a human skin.

...there are things that hunt the hunters.

Willie picked up the phone and dialed Blackstone.

"Hello." The voice was flat, affectless, the voice of someone who cared about nothing and no one, not even himself.

"Hello, Steven," Willie said, quietly. He was about to ask for Jonathan when a strange sort of madness took hold of him, and he heard himself say, "Did you watch? Did you see what Jonathan did to him, Steven? Did it get you off?"

The silence on the other end of the line went on for ages. Sometimes Steven Harmon simply forgot how to talk. But not this time. "Jonathan didn't do him. I did. It was easy. I could smell him coming through the woods. He never even saw me. I came around behind him and pinned him down and bit off his ear. He wasn't very strong at all. After a while he changed into a man, and then he was all slippery, but it didn't matter, I—"

Someone took the phone away. "Hello, who is this?" Jonathan's voice said from the receiver.

Willie hung up. He could always call back later. Let Jonathan sweat awhile, wondering who it had been on the other end of the line. "After a while he changed into a man," Willie repeated aloud. Steven did it himself. Steven couldn't do it himself. Could he? "Oh Jesus," Willie said.

Somewhere far away, a phone was ringing.

Randi rolled over in her bed. "Joanie's skin," she muttered groggily in low, half-intelligible syllables. She was naked, with the blankets tangled around her. The room was pitch dark. The phone rang again. She sat up, a sheet curled around her neck. The room was cold, and her head pounded. She ripped loose the sheet, threw it aside. Why was she naked? What the hell was going on? The phone rang again and her machine cut in. "This is AAA-Wade Investigations, Randi Wade speaking. I can't talk right now, but you can leave a message at the tone, and I'll get back to you."

Randi reached out and speared the phone just in time for the beep to sound in her ear. She winced. "It's me," she said. "I'm here. What time is it? Who's this?"

"Randi, are you all right? It's Uncle Joe." Joe Urquhart's gruff voice was a welcome relief. "Rogoff told me what happened, and I was very concerned about you. I've been trying to reach you for hours."

"Hours?" She looked at the clock. It was past midnight. "I've been asleep. I think." The last she remembered, it had been daylight and she and Willie had been driving down 13th on their way to Blackstone to..."

It was Roy Helander and he was wearing Joanie's skin.

"Randi, what's wrong? You sure you're okay? You sound wretched. Damn it, *say* something."

"I'm here," she said. She pushed hair back out of her eyes. Someone had opened her window, and the air was frigid on her bare skin. "I'm fine," she said. "I just... I was asleep. It shook me up, that's all. I'll be fine."

"If you say so." Urquhart sounded dubious.

Willie must have brought her home and put her to bed, she thought. So where was he? She couldn't imagine that he'd just dump her and then take off, that wasn't like Willie.

"Pay attention," Urquhart said gruffly. "Have you heard a word I've said?"

She hadn't. "I'm sorry. I'm just... disoriented, that's all. It's been a strange day."

"I need to see you," Urquhart said. His voice had taken on a sudden urgency. "Right away. I've been going over the reports on Roy Helander and his victims. There's something out of place, something disturbing. And the more I look at these case files and Cooney's autopsy report, the more I keep thinking about Frank, about what happened that night." He hesitated. "I don't know how to say this. All these years... I only wanted the best for you, but I wasn't... wasn't completely honest with you."

"Tell me," she said. Suddenly she was a lot more awake.

"Not over the phone. I need to see you face to face, to show it to you. I'll swing by and get you. Can you be ready in fifteen minutes?"

"Ten," Randi said.

She hung up, hopped out of bed and opened the bedroom door. "Willie?" she called out. There was no answer. "Willie!" she repeated more loudly. Nothing. She turned on the lights, padded barefoot down the hall, expecting to find him snoring away on her sofa. But the living room was empty.

Her hands were sandpaper dry, and when she looked down she saw that they were covered with old blood. Her stomach heaved. She found the clothes she'd been wearing in a heap on the bedroom floor. They were brown and crusty with dried blood as well. Randi started the shower, and stood under the water for a good five minutes, running it so hot that it burned the way that silver fork must have burned in Willie's hand. The blood washed off, the water turning faintly pink as it whirled away and down. She toweled off thoroughly, and found a warm flannel shirt and a fresh pair of jeans. She didn't bother with her hair; the rain would wet it down again soon enough. But she made a point of finding her father's gun and sliding the long silver carving knife through the belt loop of her jeans.

As she bent to pick up the knife, Randi saw the square of white paper on the floor by her end table. She must have knocked it off when she'd reached for the phone.

She picked it up, opened it. It was covered with Willie's familiar scrawl, a page of hurried, dense scribbling. *I got to go, you're in no condition*, it began. *Don't go anywhere or talk to anyone. Roy Helander wasn't sneaking in to kill Harmon, I finally figured it out. The damned Harmon family secret that's no se-cret at all, I should have twigged, Steven—*

That was as far as she'd gotten when the doorbell rang.

Willie hugged the ground two-thirds of the way up the bluff, the rain coming down around him and his heart pounding in his chest as he clung to the tracks. Somehow the grade didn't seem nearly as steep when you were riding the cable car as it did now. He glanced behind him, and saw 13th street far below. It made him dizzy. He wouldn't even have gotten this far if it hadn't been for the tracks. Where the slope grew almost vertical, he'd been able to scrabble up from tie to tie, using them like rungs on a ladder. His hands were full of splinters, but it beat trying to crawl up the wet rock, clinging to ferns for bare life.

Of course, he could have changed, and bounded up the tracks in no time at all. But somehow he didn't think that would have been such a good idea. *I could smell him coming*, Steven had said. The human scent was fainter, in a city full of people. He had to hope that Steven and Jonathan were inside the New House, locked up for the night. But if they were out prowling around, at least this way Willie thought he had a ghost of a chance.

He'd rested long enough. He craned his head back, looking up at the high black iron fence that ran along the top of the bluff, trying to measure how much further he had to go. Then he took a good long shot off his inhaler, gritted his teeth, and scrambled for the next tie up.

The windshield wipers swept back and forth almost silently as the long dark car nosed through the night. The windows were tinted a gray so dark it was almost black. Urquhart was in civvies, a red-and-black lumberjack shirt, dark woolen slacks, and a bulky down jacket. His police cap was his only concession to uniform. He stared straight out into the darkness as he drove. "You look terrible," she told him.

"I feel worse." They swept under an overpass and around a long ramp onto the river road. "I feel old, Randi. Like this city. This whole damn city is old and rotten."

"Where are we going?" she asked him. At this hour of night, there was no other traffic on the road. The river was a black emptiness off to their left. Streetlamps swam in haloes of rain to the right as they sailed past block after cold, empty block stretching away toward the bluffs.

"To the pack," Urquhart said. "To where it happened."

The car's heater was pouring out a steady blast of warm air, but suddenly Randi felt deathly cold. Her hand went inside her coat, and closed around the hilt of the knife. The silver felt comfortable and comforting. "All right," she said. She slid the knife out of her belt and put it on the seat between them.

Urquhart glanced over. She watched him carefully. "What's that?" he said.

"Silver," Randi said. "Pick it up."

He looked at her. "What?"

"You heard me," she said. "Pick it up."

He looked at the road, at her face, back out at the road. He made no move to touch the knife.

"I'm not kidding," Randi said. She slid away from him, to the far side of the seat, and braced her back against the door. When Urguhart looked over again, she had the gun out aimed right between his eyes. "Pick it up," she said very clearly.

The color left his face. He started to say something, but Randi shook her head curtly. Urquhart licked his lips, took his hand off the wheel, and picked up the knife. "There," he said, holding it up awkwardly while he drove with one hand. "I picked it up. Now what am I supposed to do with it?"

Randi slumped back against the seat. "Put it down," she said with relief. Joe looked at her.

He rested for a long time in the shrubs on top of the bluff, listening to the rain fall around him and dreading what other sounds he might hear. He kept imagining soft footfalls stealing up behind him, and once he thought he heard a low growl somewhere off to his right. He could feel his hackles rise, and until that moment he hadn't even known he *had* hackles, but it was nothing, just his nerves working on him, Willie had always had bad nerves. The night was cold and black and empty.

When he finally had his breath back, Willie began to edge past the New House, keeping to the bushes as much as he could, well away from the windows. There were a few lights on, but no other sign of life. Maybe they'd all gone to bed. He hoped so.

He moved slowly and carefully, trying to be as quiet as possible. He watched where his feet came down, and every few steps he'd stop, look around, listen. He could change in an instant if he heard anyone… or any*thing* …coming toward him. He didn't know how much good that would do, but maybe, just maybe, it would give him a chance.

His raincoat dragged at him, a water-logged second skin as heavy as lead. His shoes had soaked through, and the leather squished when he moved. Willie pushed away from the house, further back into the trees, until a bend in the road hid the lights from view. Only then, after a careful glance in both directions to make sure nothing was coming, did he dare risk a dash across the road.

Once across he plunged deeper into the woods, moving faster now, a little more heedless. He wondered where Roy Helander had been when Steven had caught him. Somewhere around here, Willie thought, somewhere in this dark primal forest, surrounded by old growth, with centuries of leaves and moss and dead things rotting in the earth beneath his feet.

As he moved away from the bluff and the city, the forest grew denser, until finally the trees pressed so close together that he lost sight of the sky, and the raindrops stopped pounding against his head. It was almost dry here. Overhead, the rain drummed relentlessly against a canopy of leaves. Willie's skin felt clammy, and for a moment he was lost, as if he'd wandered into some terrible cavern far below the earth; a dismal, cold place where no light ever shone.

Then he stumbled between two huge, twisted old oaks, and felt air and rain against his face again, and raised his head, and there it was ahead of him, broken windows gaping down like so many blind eyes from walls carved from rock that shone like midnight and drank all light and hope. The tower loomed up to his right, some monstrous erection against the stormclouds, leaning crazily.

Willie stopped breathing, groped for his inhaler, found it, dropped it, picked it up. The mouthpiece was slimy with humus. He cleaned it on his sleeve, shoved it in his mouth, took a hit, two, three, and finally his throat opened up again.

He glanced around, heard only the rain, saw nothing. He stepped forward toward the tower. Toward Roy Helander's secret refuge.

The big double gate in the high chain-link fence had been padlocked for two years, but it was open tonight, and Urquhart drove straight through. Randi wondered if the gate had been opened for her father as well. She thought maybe it had.

Joe pulled up near one of the loading docks, in the shadow of the old brick slaughterhouse. The building gave them some shelter from the rain, but Randi still trembled in the cold as she climbed out. "Here?" she asked. "This where you found him?"

Urquhart was staring off into the stockyard. It was a huge area, subdivided into a dozen pens along the railroad siding. There was a maze of chest-high fencing they called the "runs" between the slaughterhouse and the pens, to force the cows into a single line and herd them along inside, where a man in a blood-spattered apron waited with a hammer in his hand. "Here," Joe said, without looking back at her.

There was a long silence. Somewhere far off, Randi thought she heard a faint, wild howl, but maybe that was just the wind and the rain. "Do you believe in ghosts?" she asked Joe.

"Ghosts?" The chief sounded distracted.

She shivered. "It's like… I can feel him, Joe. Like he's still here, after all this time, still watching over me."

Joe Urquhart turned toward her. His face was wet with rain, or maybe tears. "I watched over you," he said. "He asked me to watch over you, and I did, I did my best."

Randi heard a sound somewhere off in the night. She turned her head, frowning, listening. Tires crunched across gravel and she saw headlights outside the fence. Another car coming.

"You and your father, you're a lot alike," Joe said wearily. "Stubborn. Won't listen to nobody. I took good care of you, didn't I take good care of you? I got my own kids, you know, but you never wanted for nothing, did you? So why the hell didn't you listen to me?"

By then Randi knew. She wasn't surprised. Somehow she felt as though she'd known for a long time. "There was only one phone call that night," she said. "You were the one who phoned for back-up, not dad."

Urguhart nodded. He was caught for a moment in the headlights of the on-coming car, and Randi saw the way his jaw trembled as he worked to get out the words. "Look in the glove box," he said.

Randi opened the car door, sat on the edge of the seat, and did as he said. The glove compartment was unlocked. Inside was a bottle of aspirin, a tire pressure gauge, some maps, and a box of cartridges. Randi opened the box and poured some bullets out into her palm. They glimmered pale and cold in the car's faint dome light. She left the box on the seat, climbed out, kicked the door shut. "My silver bullets," she said. "I hadn't expected them quite so soon."

"Those are the ones Frank ordered made up, eighteen years ago," Joe said. "After he was buried, I went by the gunsmith and picked them up. Like I said, you and him, you were a lot alike."

The second car pulled to a stop, pinning her in its high beams. Randi threw a hand across her eyes against the glare. She heard a car door opening and closing.

Urquhart's voice was anguished. "I told you to stay away from this thing, damn it. I *told* you! Don't you understand? They *own* this city!"

"He's right. You should have listened," Rogoff said, as he stepped into the light.

Willie groped his way down the long dark hall with one hand on the wall, placing each foot carefully in front of the last. The stone was so thick that even the sound of the rain did not reach him. There was only the echo of his careful footsteps, and the rush of blood inside his ears. The silence within the Old House was profound and unnerving, and there was something about the walls that bothered him as well. It was cold, but the stones under his fingers were moist and curiously warm to the touch, and Willie was glad for the darkness.

Finally he reached the base of the tower, where shafts of dim light fell across crabbed, narrow stone steps that spiraled up and up and up. Willie began to climb. He counted the steps at first, but somewhere around two hundred he lost the count, and the rest was a grim ordeal that he endured in silence. More than once he thought of changing. He resisted the impulse.

His legs ached from the effort when he reached the top. He sat down on the steps for a moment, his back to a slick stone wall. He was breathing hard, but when he groped for his inhaler, it was gone. He'd probably lost it in the woods. He could feel his lungs constricting in panic, but there was no help for it.

Willie got up.

The room smelled of blood and urine and something else, a scent he did not place, but somehow it made him tremble. There was no roof. Willie realized that the rain had stopped while he'd been inside. He looked up as the clouds parted, and a pale white moon stared down.

And all around other moons shimmered into life, reflected in the tall empty mirrors that lined the chamber. They reflected the sky above and each other, moon after moon after moon, until the room swam in silvered moonlight and reflections of reflections of reflections.

Willie turned around in a slow circle and a dozen other Willies turned with him. The moon-struck mirrors were streaked with dried blood, and above them a ring of cruel iron hooks curved up from the stone walls. A human skin hung from one of them, twisting slowly in some wind he could not feel, and as the moonlight hit it seemed to writhe and change, from woman to wolf to woman, both and neither.

That was when Willie heard the footsteps on the stairs.

"The silver bullets were a bad idea," Rogoff said. "We have a local ordinance here. The police get immediate notice any time someone places an order for custom ammunition. Your father made the same mistake. The pack takes a dim view of silver bullets."

Randi felt strangely relieved. For a moment she'd been afraid that Willie had betrayed her, that he'd been one of them after all, and that thought had been like poison in her soul. Her fingers were still curled tight around a dozen of the bullets. She glanced down at them, so close and yet so far.

"Even if they're still good, you'll never get them loaded in time," Rogoff said.

"You don't need the bullets," Urquhart told her. "He just wants to talk. They promised me, honey, no one needs to get hurt."

Randi opened her hand. The bullets fell to the ground. She turned to Joe Urquhart. "You were my father's best friend. He said you had more guts than any man he ever knew."

"They don't give you any choice," Urquhart said. "I had kids of my own. They said if Roy Helander took the fall, no more kids would vanish, they promised they'd take care of it, but if we kept pressing, one of my kids would be the next to go. That's how it works in this town. Everything would have been all right, but Frank just wouldn't let it alone."

"We only kill in self-defense," Rogoff said. "There's a sweetness to human flesh, yes, a power that's undeniable, but it's not worth the risk."

"What about the children?" Randi said. "Did you kill them in self-defense too?"

"That was a long time ago," Rogoff said.

Joe stood with his head downcast. He was beaten, Randi saw, and she realized that he'd been beaten for a long time. All those trophies on his walls, but somehow she knew that he had given up hunting forever on the night her father died. "It was his son," Joe muttered quietly, in a voice full of shame. "Steven's never been right in the head, everyone knows that, he was the one killed the kids, *ate* them. It was horrible, Harmon told me so himself, but he still wasn't going to let us have Steven. He said he'd... he'd control Steven's...appetites...if we closed the case. He was good as his word too, he put Steven on medication, and it stopped, the murders stopped."

She ought to hate Joe Urquhart, she realized, but instead she pitied him. After all this time, he still didn't understand. "Joe, he lied. It was never Steven."

"It was Steven," Joe insisted, "it had to be, he's insane. The rest of them...you can do business with them, Randi, listen to me now, you can talk to them."

"Like you did," she said. "Like Barry Schumacher."

Urquhart nodded. "That's right. They are just like us, they got some crazies, but not all of them are bad. You can't blame them for taking care of their own, we do the same thing. Look at Mike here, he's a good cop."

"A good cop who's going to change into a wolf in a minute or two and tear out my throat," Randi said.

"Randi, honey, listen to me," Urquhart said. "It doesn't have to be like that. You can walk out of here, just say the word. I'll get you onto the force, you can work with us, help us to... to keep the peace. Your father's dead, you won't bring him back, and the Helander boy, he deserved what he got, he was *killing* them, skinning them alive, it was self-defense. Steven is sick, he's always been sick—"

Rogoff was watching her from beneath his tangle of black hair. "He still doesn't get it," she said. She turned back at Joe. "Steven is sicker than you think. Something is missing. Too inbred, maybe. Think about it. Anders and Rochmonts, Flambeauxes and Harmons, the four great founding families, all werewolves, marrying each other generation after generation to keep the lines pure, for how many centuries? They kept the lines pure all right. They bred themselves Steven. He didn't kill those children. Roy Helander saw a *wolf* carry off his sister, and Steven can't change into a wolf. He got the bloodlust, he got inhuman strength, he burns at the touch of silver, but that's all. The last of the purebloods *can't work the change!*"

"She's right," Rogoff said quietly.

"Why do you think you never found any remains?" Randi put in. "Steven didn't kill those kids. His father carried them off, up to Blackstone."

"The old man had some crazy idea that if Steven ate enough human flesh, it might fix him, make him whole," Rogoff said.

"It didn't work," Randi said. She took Willie's note out of her pocket, let the pages flutter to the ground. It was all there. She finished reading it before she'd gone down to meet Joe. Frank Wade's little girl was nobody's fool.

"It didn't work," Rogoff echoed, "but by then Jonathan had got the taste. Once you get started, it's hard to stop." He looked at Randi for a long time, as if he were weighing something. Then he began…

…to change. Sweet cold air filled his lungs, and his muscles and bones ran with fire as the transformation took hold. He'd shrugged out of pants and coat, and he heard the rest of his clothing ripping apart as his body writhed, his flesh ran like hot wax, and he reformed, born anew.

Now he could see and hear and smell. The tower room shimmered with moonlight, every detail clear and sharp as noon, and the night was alive with sound, the wind and the rain and the rustle of bats in the forest around them, and traffic sounds and sirens from the city beyond. He was alive and full of power, and something was coming up the steps. It climbed slowly, untiring, and its smells filled the air. The scent of blood hung all around it, and beneath he sensed an aftershave that masked an unwashed body, sweat and dried semen on its skin, a heavy tang of wood smoke in its hair, and under it all the scent of sickness, sweetly rotten as a grave.

Willie backed all the way across the room, staring at the arched door, the growl rising in his throat. He bared long yellowed teeth, and slaver ran between them.

Steven stopped in the doorway and looked at him. He was naked. The wolf's hot red eyes met his cold blue ones, and it was hard to tell which were more inhuman. For a moment Willie thought that Steven didn't quite comprehend. Until he smiled, and reached for the skin that twisted above him, on an iron hook.

Willie leapt.

He took Steven high in the back and bore him down, with his hand still clutched around Zoe's skin. For a second Willie had a clear shot at his throat, but he hesitated and the moment passed. Steven caught Willie's foreleg in a pale scarred fist, and snapped it in half like a normal man might break a stick. The pain was excruciating. Then Steven was lifting him, flinging him away. He smashed up hard against one of the mirrors, and felt it shatter at the impact. Jagged shards of glass flew like knives, and one of them lanced through his side.

Willie rolled away, the glass spear broke under him, and he whimpered. Across the room, Steven was getting to his feet. He put out a hand to steady himself.

Willie scrambled up. His broken leg was knitting already, though it hurt when he put his weight on it. Glass fragments clawed inside him with every step. He could barely move. Some fucking werewolf he turned to be.

Steven was adjusting his ghastly cloak, pulling flaps of skin down over his own face. The skin trade, Willie thought giddily, yeah, that was it, and in a moment Steven would use that damn flayed skin to do what he could never manage on his own, he would *change*, and then Willie would be meat.

Willie came at him, jaws gaping, but too slow. Steven's foot pistoned down, caught him hard enough to take his breath away, pinned him to the floor. Willie tried to squirm free, but Steven was too strong. He was bearing down, crushing him. All of a sudden Willie remembered that dog, so many years ago.

Willie bent himself almost double and took a bite out of the back of Steven's calf.

The blood filled his mouth, exploding inside him. Steven reeled back. Willie jumped up, darted forward, bit him again. This time he sank his teeth in good and held, worrying at the flesh. The pounding in his head was thunderous. He was full of power, he could feel it swelling within him. Suddenly he knew that he could tear Steven apart, he could taste the fine sweet flesh close to the bone, could hear the music of his screams, could imagine the way it would feel when he held him in his jaws and shook him like a rag doll and felt the life go out of him in a sudden giddy rush. It swept over him, and Willie bit and bit and bit again, ripping away chunks of meat, drunk on blood.

And then, dimly, he heard Steven screaming, screaming in a high shrill thin voice, a little boy's voice. "No, daddy," he was whining, over and over again. "No, please, don't bite me, daddy, don't bite me any more."

Willie let him go and backed away.

Steven sat on the floor, sobbing. He was bleeding like a sonofabitch. Pieces were missing from thigh, calf, shoulder, and foot. His legs were drenched in blood. Three fingers were gone off his right hand. His cheeks were slimy with gore.

Suddenly Willie was scared.

For a moment he didn't understand. Steven was beaten, he could see that, he could rip out his throat or let him live, it didn't matter, it was over. But something was wrong, something was terribly, sickeningly wrong. It felt as though the temperature had dropped a hundred degrees, and every hair on his body was prickling and standing on end. What the hell was going on? He growled low in his throat and backed away, toward the door, keeping a careful eye on Steven.

Steven giggled. "You'll get it now," he said. "You called it. You got blood on the mirrors. You called it back again. The room seemed to spin. Moonlight ran from mirror to mirror to mirror, dizzyingly. Or maybe it wasn't moonlight.

Willie looked into the mirrors.

The reflections were gone. Willie, Steven, the moon, all gone. There was blood on the mirrors and they were full of fog, a silvery pale fog that shimmered as it moved.

Something was moving through the fog, sliding from mirror to mirror to mirror, around and around. Something hungry that wanted to get out.

He saw it, lost it, saw it again. It was in front of him, behind him, off to the side. It was a hound, gaunt and terrible; it was a snake, scaled and foul; it was a man, with eyes like pits and knives for its fingers. It wouldn't hold still, every time he looked its shape seemed to change, and each shape was worse than the last, more twisted and obscene. Everything about it was lean and cruel. Its fingers were sharp, so sharp, and he looked at them and felt their caress sliding beneath his skin, tingling along the nerves, pain and blood and fire trailing behind them. It was black, blacker than black, a black that drank all light forever, and it was all shining silver too. It was a nightmare that lived in a funhouse mirror, the thing that hunts the hunters.

He could feel the evil throbbing through the glass. "Skinner," Steven called.

The surface of the mirrors seemed to ripple and bulge, like a wave cresting on some quicksilver sea. The fog was thinning, Willie realized with sudden terror; he could see it clearer now, and he knew it could see him. And suddenly Willie Flambeaux knew what was happening, knew that when the fog cleared the mirrors wouldn't be mirrors anymore, they'd be doors, *doors,* and the skinner would come…

…sliding forward, through the ruins of his clothing, slitted eyes glowing like embers from a muzzle black as coal. He was half again as large as Willie had been, his fur thick and black and shaggy, and when he opened his mouth, his teeth gleamed like ivory daggers.

Randi edged backward, along the side of the car. The knife was in her hand, moonlight running off the silver blade, but somehow it didn't seem like very much. The huge black wolf advanced on her, his tongue lolling between his teeth, and she put her back up against the car door and braced herself for his leap.

Joe Urquhart stepped between them.

"No," he said. "Not her too, you owe me, talk to her, give her a chance, I'll make her see how it is."

The wolf growled a warning.

Urquhart stood his ground, and all of a sudden he had his revolver out, and he was holding it in two shaky hands, drawing a bead. "Stop. I mean it. She didn't have time to load the goddamned silver bullets, but I've had eighteen fucking years. I'm the fucking police chief in this fucking city, and you're under arrest."

Randi put her hand on the door handle, eased it open. For a moment the wolf stood frozen, baleful red eyes fixed on Joe, and she thought it was actually going to work. She remembered her father's old Wednesday night poker games; he'd always said Joe ran one hell of a bluff.

Then the wolf threw back his head and howled, and all the blood went out of her. She knew that sound. She'd heard it in her dreams a thousand times. It was in her blood, that sound, an echo from far off and long ago, when the world had been a forest and humans had run naked in fear before the hunting pack. It echoed off the side of the old slaughterhouse and trembled out over the city, and they must have heard it all over the flats, heard it and glanced outside nervously and checked their locks before they turned up the volumes on their TVs.

Randi opened the door wider and slid one leg inside the car as the wolf leapt.

She heard Urquhart fire, and fire again, and then the wolf slammed into his chest and smashed him back against the car door. Randi was half into the car, but the door swung shut hard, crunching down on her left foot with awful force before she could get it inside. She heard a bone break under the impact, and shrieked at the sudden flare of pain. Outside Urquhart fired again, and then he was screaming. There were ripping sounds and more screams and something wet spattered against her ankle.

Her foot was trapped, and the struggle outside slammed her open door against it again and again and again. Each impact was a small explosion as the shattered bones grated together and ripped against raw nerves. Joe was screaming and droplets of blood covered the tinted window like rain. Her head swam, and for a moment Randi thought she'd faint from the pain, but she threw all her weight against the door and moved it just enough and drew her foot inside and when the next impact came it slapped the door shut hard and Randi pressed the lock.

She leaned against the wheel and almost threw up. Joe had stopped screaming, but she could hear the wolf tearing at him, ripping off chunks of flesh. *Once you get started it's hard to stop,* she thought hysterically. She got out the .38, cracked the cylinder with shaking hands, flicked out the shells. Then she was fumbling around on the front seat. She found the box, tipped it over, snatched up a handful of silver.

It was silent outside. Randi stopped, looked up.

He was on the hood of the car.

Willie *changed.*

He was running on instinct now; he didn't know why he did it, he just did. The pain was there waiting for him along with his humanity, as he'd known it would be. It shrieked through him like a gale wind, and sent him whimpering to the floor. He could feel the glass shard under his ribs, dangerously close to a lung, and his left arm bent sickening downward at a place it was never meant to bend, and when he tried to move it, he screamed and bit his tongue and felt his mouth fill with blood.

The fog was a pale thin haze now, and the mirror closest to him bulged outward, throbbing like something alive.

Steven sat against the wall, his blue eyes bright and avid, sucking his own blood from the stumps of his fingers. "Changing won't help," he said in that weird flat tone of his. "Skinner don't care. It knows what you are. Once it's called, it's got to have a skin." Willie's vision was blurry with tears, but he saw it again then, in the mirror behind Steven, pushing at the fading fog, pushing, pushing, trying to get through.

He staggered to his feet. Pain roared through his head. He cradled his broken arm against his body, took a step toward the stairs, and felt broken glass grind against his bare feet. He looked down. Pieces of the shattered mirror were everywhere.

Willie's head snapped up. He looked around wildly, dizzy, counting. Six, seven, eight, nine...the tenth was broken. Nine then. He threw himself forward, slammed all his body weight into the nearest mirror. It shattered under the impact, disintegrated into a thousand pieces. Willie crunched the biggest shards underfoot, stamped on them until his heels ran wet with blood. He was moving without thought. He caromed around the room, using his own body as a weapon, hearing the sweet tinkling music of breaking glass. The world turned into a red fog of pain, and a thousand little knives sliced at him everywhere, and he wondered, if the skinner came through and got him, whether he'd even be able to tell the difference.

Then he was staggering away from another mirror, and white hot needles were stabbing through his feet with every step, turning into fire as they lanced up his calves. He stumbled and fell, hard. Flying glass had cut his face to ribbons, and the blood ran down into his eyes.

Willie blinked, and wiped the blood away with his good hand. His old raincoat was underneath him, bloodsoaked and covered with ground glass and shards of mirror. Steven stood over him, staring down. Behind him was a mirror. Or was it a door?

"You missed one," Steven said flatly.

Something hard was digging into his gut, Willie realized. His hand fumbled around beneath him, slid into the pocket of his raincoat, closed on cold metal.

"Skinner's coming for you now," Steven said.

Willie couldn't see. The blood had filled his eyes again. But he could still feel. He got his fingers through the loops and rolled and brought his hand up fast and hard, with all the strength he had left, and put Mr. Scissors right through the meat of Steven's groin.

The last thing he heard was a scream, and the sound of breaking glass.

Calm, Randi thought, *calm,* but the dread that filled her was more than simple fear. Blood matted his jaws, and his eyes stared at her through the windshield, glowing that hideous baleful red. She looked away quickly, tried to chamber a bullet. Her hands shook, and it slid out of her grip, onto the floor on the car. She ignored it, tried again.

The wolf howled, turned, fled. For a moment she lost sight of him. Randi craned her head around, peering nervously out through the darkness. She glanced into the rearview mirror, but it was fogged up, useless. She shivered, as much from cold as from fear. *Where is he?* she thought wildly.

Then she saw him, running toward the car.

Randi looked down, chambered a bullet, and had a second in her fingers when he came flying over the hood and smashed against the glass. Cracks spiderwebbed out from the center of the windshield. The wolf snarled at her. Slaver and blood smeared the glass. Then he hit the glass again. Again. Again. Randi jumped with every impact. The windshield cracked and cracked again, then a big section in the center went milky and opaque.

She had the second bullet in the cylinder. She slid in a third. Her hands were shaking as much from cold as from fear. It was freezing inside the car. She looked out into the darkness through a haze of cracks and blood smears, loaded a fourth bullet, and was closing the cylinder when he hit the windshield again and it all caved in on her.

One moment she had the gun and the next it was gone. The weight was on her chest and the safety glass, broken into a million milky pieces but still clinging together, fell across her face like a shroud. Then it ripped away, and the blood-soaked jaws and hot red eyes were right there in front of her.

The wolf opened his mouth and she was feeling the furnace heat of his breath, smelling the awful carnivore stench.

"You fucker!" she screamed, and almost laughed, because it wasn't much as last words go.

Something sharp and silvery bright came sliding down through the back of his throat.

It went so quickly Randi didn't understand what was happening, no more than he did. Suddenly the bloodlust went out of the dark red eyes, and they were full of pain and shock and finally fear, and she saw more silver knives sliding through his throat before his mouth filled with blood. And then the great black-furred body shuddered, and struggled, as something pulled it back off her, front paws beating a tattoo against the seat. There was a smell like burning hair in the air. When the wolf began to scream, it sounded almost human.

Randi choked back her own pain, slammed her shoulder against the door, and knocked what was left of Joe Urquhart aside. Halfway out the door, she glanced back.

The hand was twisted and cruel, and its fingers were long bright silver razors, pale and cold and sharp as sin. Like five long jointed knives the fingers had sunk through the back of the wolf's neck, and grabbed hold, and pulled, and the blood was coming out between his teeth in great gouts now and his legs were kicking feebly. It yanked at him then, and she heard a sickening wet *crunching* as the thing began to *pull* the wolf through the rearview mirror with inexorable, unimaginable force, to whatever was on the other side. The great black-furred body seemed to waver and shift for a second, and the wolf's face took on an almost human cast.

When his eyes met hers, the red light had gone out of them; there was nothing there but pain and pleading.

His first name was Mike, she remembered. Randi looked down. Her gun was on the floor.

She picked it up, checked the cylinder, closed it, jammed the barrel up against his head, and fired four times.

When she got out of the car and put her weight on her ankle, the pain washed over her in great waves. Randi collapsed to her hands and knees. She was throwing up when she heard the sirens.

"...some kind of animal," she said.

The detective gave her a long, sour look, and closed his notebook. "That's all you can tell me?" he said. "That Chief Urguhart was killed by some kind of animal?"

Randi wanted to say something sharp, but she was all fucked up on painkillers. They'd had to put two pins in her ankle and it still hurt like hell, and the doctors said she'd have to stay another week. "What do you want me to tell you?" she said weakly. "That's what I saw, some kind of animal. A wolf."

The detective shook his head. "Fine. So the chief was killed by some kind of animal, probably a wolf. So where's Rogoff? His car was there, his blood was all over the inside of the chief's car, so tell me...*where the fuck is Rogoff?*"

Randi closed her eyes, and pretended it was the pain. "I don't know," she said.

"I'll be back," the detective said when he left.

She lay with her eyes closed for a moment, thinking maybe she could drift back to sleep, until she heard the door open and close. "He won't be," a soft voice told her. "We'll see to it."

Randi opened her eyes. At the foot of the bed was an old man with long white hair leaning on a gold wolf's head cane. He wore a black suit, a mourning suit, and his hair fell to his shoulders. "My name is Jonathan Harmon," he said.

"I've seen your picture. I know who you are. And what you are." Her voice was hoarse. "A lycanthrope."

"Please," he said. "A werewolf."

"Willie... what happened to Willie?"

"Steven is dead," Jonathan Harmon said.

"Good," Randi spat. "Steven and Roy, they were doing it together, Willie said. For the skins. Steven hated the others, because they could work the change and he couldn't. But once your son had his skin, he didn't need Helander anymore, did he?"

"I can't say I will mourn greatly. To be frank, Steven was never the sort of heir I might have wished for." He went to the window, opened the curtains, and looked out. "This was once a great city, you know, a city of blood and iron. Now it's all turned to rust."

"Fuck your city," Randi said. "What about Willie?"

"It was a pity about Zoe, but once the skinner has been summoned, it keeps hunting until it takes a skin, from mirror to mirror to mirror. It knows our scent, but it doesn't like to wander far from its gates. I don't know how your mongrel friend managed to evade it twice, but he did... to Zoe's misfortune, and Michael's." He turned and looked at her. "You will not be so lucky. Don't congratulate yourself too vigorously, child. The pack takes care of its own. The doctor who writes your next prescription, the pharmacist who fills it, the boy who delivers it... any of them could be one of us. We don't forget our enemies, Miss Wade. Your family would do well to remember that."

"You were the one," she said with a certainty. "In the stockyards, the night my father..."

Jonathan nodded curtly. "He was a crack shot, I'll grant him that. He put six bullets in me. My war wounds, I call them. They still show up on x-rays, but my doctors have learned not to be curious."

"I'll kill you," Randi said.

"I think not." He leaned over the bed. "Perhaps I'll come for you myself some night. You ought to see me, Miss Wade. My fur is white now, pale as snow, but the stature, the majesty, the power, those have not left me. Michael was a halfbreed, and your Willie, he was hardly more than a dog. The pureblood is rather more. We are the dire wolves, the nightmares who haunt your racial memories, the dark shapes circling endlessly beyond the light of your fires."

He smiled down at her, then turned and walked away. At the door he paused. "Sleep well," he said.

Randi did not sleep at all, not even when night fell and the nurse came in and turned out the lights, despite all her pleading. She lay there in the dark staring up at the ceiling, feeling more alone than she'd ever been. He was dead, she thought. Willie was dead and she'd better start getting used to the idea. Very softly, alone in the darkness of the private room, she began to cry.

She cried for a long time, for Willie and Joan Sorenson and Joe Urguhart and finally, after all this time, for Frank Wade. She ran out of tears and kept crying, her body shaking with dry sobs. She was still shaking when the door opened softly, and a thin knife of light from the hall cut across the room.

"Who's there?" she said hoarsely. "Answer, or I'll scream."

The door closed quietly. "Ssssh. Quiet, or they'll hear." It was a woman's voice, young, a little scared. "The nurse said I couldn't come in, that it was after visiting hours, but he told me to get to you right away." She moved close to the bed.

Randi turned on her reading light. Her visitor looked nervously toward the door. She was dark, pretty, no more than twenty, with a spray of freckles across her nose. "I'm Betsy Juddiker," she whispered. "Willie said I was to give you a message, but it's all crazy stuff…"

Randi's heart skipped a beat. "Willie… tell me! I don't care how crazy it sounds, just tell me."

"He said that he couldn't phone you hisself because the pack might be listening in, that he got hurt bad but he's okay, that he's up north, and he's found this vet who's taking care of him good. I know, it sounds funny, but that's what he said, a vet."

"Go on."

Betsy nodded. "He sounded hurt on the phone, and he said he couldn't… couldn't *change* right now, except for a few minutes to call, because he was hurt and the pain was always waiting for him, but to say that the vet had gotten most of glass out and set his leg and he was going to be fine. And then he said that on the night he'd gone, he'd come by *my* house and left something for you, and I was to find it and bring it here." She opened her purse and rummaged around. "It was in the bushes by the mailbox, my little boy found it." She gave it over.

It was a piece of some broken mirror, Randi saw, a shard as long and slender as her finger. She held it in her hand for a moment, confused and uncertain. The glass was cold to the touch, and it seemed to grow colder as she held it.

"Careful, it's real sharp," Betsy said. "There was one more thing, I don't understand it all, but Willie said it was important. He said to tell you that there were no mirrors where he was, not a one, but last he'd seen, there were plenty up in Blackstone."

Randi nodded, not quite grasping it, not yet. She ran a finger thoughtfully along the shiny sliver of glass.

"Oh, look," Betsy said. "I told you. Now you've gone and cut yourself."

Introduction to Star Port

In the summer of 1993, I was working for Columbia Pictures Television. I had what Hollywood calls a "development deal," which meant that I spent most of my days coming up with ideas for new television series. I would kick the better notions around with the development executives at Columbia, and when we came up with one we liked, they would set up pitch meetings at the networks.

On August 6, 1993, we had one such meeting at the Fox network, to pitch a light-hearted supernatural horror show called *Night's Masters,* based on a short story by Roger Zelazny. The meeting seemed to go well, but a week later Fox called to say that they weren't interested in *Night's Masters.* They *were* interested in having me create a show for them, they said, only what they *really* wanted was a science fiction cop show.

SF cop shows had been done before, of course. In fact, Fox had only recently cancelled one: *Alien Nation,* based on the film by Rockne S. O'Bannon. Rock and I had worked together on *The Twilight Zone,* and I saw no sense in redoing what he'd already done. His film had focused on one human cop and his alien partner, so I decided that I would make mine an ensemble show, after the fashion of *Hill Street Blues.* And where Rock had brought one alien race to Earth, I'd bring hundreds, half a galaxy's worth of aliens. Rock's aliens, the Newcomers, had been refugees. Mine would be traders, with technologies far more advanced than ours, which would invert the power relationship and create all sorts of interesting problems, complications and culture shock for the series to explore.

I called the show *Starport.* On September 24, 1993, I was back at the Fox network, pitching once again. Within the week we had a script deal for a two-hour movie for television that would double as the pilot for the series.

I spent the rest of 1993 fleshing out my large cast of colorful aliens and all-too-human cops, outlining the pilot, and then revising the outline after conferences with both Columbia and Fox, and finally writing the teleplay. I did three drafts of *Starport.* The earliest, the Genesis Draft as I dubbed it, was delivered to Columbia on January 9, 1994. Studios and screenwriters gauge the length of scripts using the rough but time-honored measure of a minute a page, but on television an hour does *not* equal sixty minutes, since you need to allow time for the commercials. At 133 pages, the Genesis Draft of *Starport* was too long... but that was no surprise. My scripts were *always* too long, to start with. Maybe that was the novelist in me, fighting to get out.

I have always found it easier to trim and tighten a long script than to pad a short one, and I think it gives a stronger shooting script as well.

Columbia was enthusiastic about the Genesis Draft, but they felt the last two acts were weak. I had introduced the alien character I called the "spiderhound" in this draft, but had done very little with him, and the biggest action sequence was in the first half of the script. While I generally prefer reactions like, "My god, this is brilliant, don't change a word," the Columbia guys were pretty sharp, and I couldn't disagree with anything they said. So I went back to Santa Fe and started the rewrite.

My next pass was completed on January 17, 1994, the date of the great Northridge, California earthquake, so I called it the Earthquake Draft. I tightened, trimmed, and polished my dialogue and description throughout and did some minor reshuffling of scenes, but more importantly I loosed the spiderhound to give us the big climax missing in the Genesis Draft. This new ending was much more exciting, everyone agreed (also much more expensive to film, what with the climactic fight on top of the Sears Tower, but we won't talk about that). But the new scenes had made it even longer than its precursor—all of 139 pages, way *way* too long for a two-hour TV movie. I would have to make cuts. Deep cuts.

I knew from past experience that I could lose five or six pages with a page-by-page, line-by-line trim, cutting a word here, a phrase there, targeting widows in dialogue (the extra word that makes a speech a line longer) and description in the body copy. But five or six pages wouldn't help much here. To get the pilot down to size, I was going to have to lose scenes, characters, subplots.

I do not recall who first proposed dropping the Staako Nihi character. I do remember that I resisted. Staako's contribution to the main storyline of the pilot was minor, it was true, but I intended him to be an important character in the series to follow. Besides, he was one of my favorite characters. *Starport* was intended to be a blend of drama and action/adventure, but even the most serious stories benefit from a certain amount of humor. I did not think the pilot would be as strong if we lost Staako Nihi.

All the same, the script had to be shortened, the Fox network was waiting, and I had no good alternatives to offer. My friends at Columbia soothed my misgivings by pointing out that Staako could still be a part of the series, once we got our production order. We could introduce him in the first episode, build a whole show around his arrival. But first we had to get the pilot script down to an acceptable length. They were right again. So I gnashed my teeth, booted up WordStar once again, and performed a Nihiectomy.

The operation was successful, but the patient died.

Columbia delivered my official First Draft of *Starport* to Fox on January 24, 1994. Sans Staako Nihi, this version weighed in at 118 pages. That was still long, and we all knew that further cuts would be necessary when we went to film, but that was a normal part of the process. The studio was optimistic about our chances. Fox had asked for an SF cop show, and we had given them a damned good one. We loved our cast of characters, aliens and humans alike, and the franchise was so rich that I could have come up with a whole season's worth of episodes in an afternoon, without breaking a sweat. All we needed was our production order from Fox.

It never came.

From the network there was only silence... and then, finally, a pass. I got the bad news secondhand from Columbia. As near as I could gather, Fox had not wanted quite so much SF in their SF cop show. They found the multiplicity of alien races "confusing," and suggested maybe that there should only be one alien race.

"But that's *Alien Nation*," I said when they told me that. "They just cancelled *Alien Nation*."

Well, no one ever said networks had to make sense.

Starport was my last TV pilot. I had written four of them, supervised the writing of the fifth. Only one had been filmed. That was *Doorways*, and that's another story...

I worked ten years in Hollywood, roughly. The first five were spent writing for *The Twilight Zone* and *Beauty and the Beast*, where every script I wrote was filmed and aired shortly thereafter. But after the cancellation of *Beauty and the Beast*, I moved up to creating my own shows and to writing feature films. I was making more money than ever, and no doubt could have continued to do so for another ten or twenty years. But *Starport* and *Doorways* and *The Survivors* and *Wild Cards* and *Fadeout* had all taught me a valuable lesson about myself. I wanted... I *needed*... an audience.

No matter how big the checks are, there is no joy in telling stories that no one ever gets to hear. It is the child's first cry that makes all the pain of labor worth enduring, but my children were being smothered at birth, and I could not stand it.

It has always been in the back of my mind that one day I might turn my *Starport* script into a novel, but that day may be a long time coming. So I welcomed this chance to publish the screenplay, and at long last introduce the world to these characters I had loved so much. There was no question about which version I would use. The First Draft is slightly more polished in places, since it had the benefit of one more pass through my computer... but the Earthquake Draft is stronger overall, bigger, funnier, richer. Readers don't need to worry about production budgets or running times, thankfully. Just about the story.

ACT I

FADE IN

EXT. - CHARLIE'S APARTMENT - DAWN

An old building across the street from ivy-covered WRIGLEY FIELD. On the ground floor is a neighborhood tavern; above, apartments.

INT. - CHARLIE'S BEDROOM - DAWN - TIGHT ON CHARLIE

CHARLIE BAKER—tall, dark, twenty-eight—is knotting his tie in front of a mirror as his RADIO ALARM comes on.

>   NEWSCAST
> ...estimated at 7.3 on the Richter
> scale. As the death toll continues to
> mount, President Clinton declared
> Memphis a national disaster area and
> promised immediate federal aid.

The ends of the tie come out wildly uneven.

>   STACY (O.S.)
> Charlie? What time is it?

Charlie rips apart the knot, and starts again.

WIDEN

to reveal the bedroom behind him. BOOKSHELVES jammed with paperbacks, a STARCHART on the wall, clothing scattered on the floor. In the bed, STACY, a attractive blonde wearing a sheet, rubs sleep from her eyes.

>   NEWSCAST
> In Chicago, protests continue as
> National Motors prepares to finalize
> its controversial powercell deal with
> the Skrit—

Stacy TURNS OFF the radio, sees the time, YAWNS.

                    STACY
          Come back to bed.

The ends of the tie come out wrong again.

                    CHARLIE
          Damn it.

                    STACY
          Here, let me. You're hopeless with
          ties.

Stacy presses herself against his back, her hands go around him, and she knots
the tie deftly. Perfect. Charlie's impressed.

                    CHARLIE
          You're good.

                    STACY
          Thought you learned that last night.
          Want me to make coffee?

Without waiting for an answer, Stacy shrugs into his bathrobe, a red flannel
job that's much too big for her.

                    CHARLIE
          There's a pot on the stove, help
          yourself.

He dons a sports jacket, checks out the mirror.

                    CHARLIE
          You think this color's okay?

                    STACY
          Fine.

                    CHARLIE
          Seven years in uniform, all you know is blue.

He crosses the room, scoops a REVOLVER off his dresser, checks the cylinder, and slides it into a holster in the small of his back. Then he grabs his ID folder... something is missing.

> CHARLIE
> Where's my badge?

He looks around. On the dresser, the floor, the bed.

> STACY
> (mock interview)
> Detective Baker, are you telling me
> that you lost your gold shield within
> twenty-four hours of getting it?

Now Charlie is looking in and among the bedclothes.

> CHARLIE
> You're not funny, Stacy. It has to be
> here someplace, we didn't go
> anywhere last night.

Charlie is growing frantic. Taking pity on him, Stacy scoops up her discarded bra, dangles it by the strap. His gold detective shield is pinned to one cup. Charlie looks at it, sheepish.

> STACY
> Here. You deputized me, remember?
> It was just after—

> CHARLIE
> Never mind what it was after.

Charlie unhooks the badge and hands Stacy back her brassiere. He stands there awkwardly for a moment.

> CHARLIE
> Well... I better get going.... make
> sure you lock up when you...

She steps close and kisses him.

STACY
Don't forget my phone number, okay?
And if you bump into Gort, tell him
klaatu barada nicto for me.

CUT TO:

EXT. - EL - DAY - ESTABLISHING

The venerable Howard Street elevated train clanks along.

INT. - EL - DAY

The train is crowded with businessmen in three-piece suits, blue-collar
workers, secretaries reading fat paperback novels or tabloids. UNIONS TO
NATMO: 'NO POWERCELLS' reads one headline; CUBS DROP 5TH
STRAIGHT says another. Charlie watches the passing scenery, the familiar
sights of urban Chicago.

ANGLE PAST CHARLIE

The el is rattling along at its top speed when outside the window a   SKIM-
MER—a flying car, sleek and futuristic, matte black with mirrored silver windows zooms up alongside.
The skimmer matches velocity with the elevated train, effortlessly keeping
pace. One by one, the passengers look up. Most go right back to their books
and papers; this is no big deal.

COMMUTER
Boy, that's the way to commute, huh?
Wouldn't you love to own one of those
babies?

BUSINESSMAN
They don't sell them to *us*.

COMMUTER
Sure they do, if you got a couple
million spare change. The Saudis
bought a dozen.

SECRETARY
I read that Jay Leno's got one.

The skimmer BANKS and ACCELERATES, veering away from the train and
flying down a cross street, finally vanishing.

BUSINESSMAN
They shouldn't be allowed to fly them
in the city. If one of them crashes—

CHARLIE
They don't crash.

BUSINESSMAN
Who says? The munchkins? I mean,
what the hell you expect them to say?

CHARLIE
They're designed not to crash. Even
if you try to smash into something,
the skimmer won't let you.
(he stands)
Excuse me, this is my stop.

The doors fold open; outside, the station sign reads LAWRENCE And below
that, in smaller letters, STARPORT CHICAGO. The businessman smiles
pointedly as Charlie EXITS here.

BUSINESSMAN
Figures.

CUT TO:

EXT. - LAWRENCE EL STATION - DAY

Uptown: one of Chicago's toughest neighborhoods, a lakeside melting pot of a
dozen ethnic groups, well leavened with poverty and urban decay. The station is
surrounded by retail merchants: a bakery, a shoe-shine stand, a pizza place. And a
tiny FRUIT-AND-VEGETABLE STAND under the tracks.
A dozen young punks are trashing the stand. The attackers are whites in their
teens and twenties, male and female, dressed in combat boots and paramili-

tary cammies. On their jackets, *EARTHBLOOD* is written over a SWASTIKA with a GLOBE at its center.

The sidewalk displays have been shoved over. A SKINHEAD with a SWAS-TIKA TATTOO over his ear is smashing windows with a BASEBALL BAT. His friends are inside, dumping cartons of fruit on the floor. The owner of the shop—whom we cannot see—is down on the sidewalk, SCREAMING shrilly, while several Earthblood girls KICK him. The younger   members of the gang are THROWING fruit at passers-by, other stores, the el, etc.

The scene is noise, chaos, violence... and there's something odd about the fruits and vegetables. They don't look much like our familiar fruits and veggies, and the signs say like FRESH PUFFBALLS and BLOODBELLYS $5/DOZ and TREE EYES RIPE NOW.

ANGLE ON CHARLIE

as he steps from the el station into the riot. A thrown fruit—a "bloodbelly"—hits a wall and EXPLODES just over his head, showering him with viscous red pulp.

> CHARLIE
> (surprised, reacting)
> Son of a... *hey!*

Charlie whips out his ID wallet to flash his badge with one hand while he gropes for his gun with the other.

> CHARLIE
> (shouted)
> *Freeze, police!*

A wiry Earthblood with dyed GREEN HAIR whirls toward Charlie and SMASHES him across the face with a tray of fruit. The wood splinters, fruits scatter, and Charlie goes down.

TIGHT ON CHARLIE'S ID

The ID wallet FLIES from his hand as he falls, skitters across the sidewalk, and slides right down a sewer grate.

RESUME

Greenhair jumps on top of Charlie, grabbing for the gun. People are SCREAM-ING and FIGHTING all around. We hear the sound of POLICE SIRENS, growing steadily closer.

Greenhair gets both hands around Charlie's wrist and smashes his hand against the sidewalk, trying to loosen the gun. Charlie grabs a swollen green fruit with his free hand, and SMASHES it into Greenhair's face. Greenhair lets go of Charlie's wrist.

The sirens are louder now. Some of the punks start to SCATTER. Others are too caught up. Three POLICE CARS brake to a   screeching halt, spilling out uniformed cops. Some of the punks RUN; others choose to stand and fight. Cops take off after the runners.

Officer ERNIE B. MANNING—black, thirties, a jock who joined the force when an injury ended his baseball career—is out of his unit fast. The skinhead with the bat comes at him swinging.   Manning ducks the blow, GRABS the skinhead by the throat, and SLAMS him against a wall. The bat drops to the sidewalk.

Manning's partner, Officer LISA RUTLEDGE, is right behind him, gun drawn. Rutledge is a rookie, early twenties, short, pretty. The first thing she spots is Charlie, gun in hand.

> RUTLEDGE
> *Drop the gun!*

> CHARLIE
> You don't—

> RUTLEDGE
> (shouted)
> I said *drop it! NOW!*

She's aimed, one hand on the gun, the other bracing her wrist. Charlie lets his pistol fall to the sidewalk.

> RUTLEDGE
> Okay. Against the wall. Spread 'em.

Behind her, Manning has cuffed the skinhead and is marching him toward his unit. Other cops are dragging back captured punks. Charlie faces the wall, spreading his hands. Rutledge moves in behind him, scoops up his gun, KICKS his legs further apart.

> RUTLEDGE
> You're under arrest. You have the

right—

>   CHARLIE
> I'm a cop, for chrissake.

Rutledge gives him a look. Charlie's a sight; hair wild, jacket torn, shirt red with the "blood" of the fruit.

>   RUTLEDGE
> Uh huh, sure you are.

She yanks down his hands behind his back, CUFFS him.

>   CHARLIE
> I swear—

>   RUTLEDGE
>   (spinning him around)
> Let's see a badge, then.

Charlie looks around. The sidewalk looks like a war zone; busted crates, shattered glass, and smears of fruit everywhere you look. No sign of his ID anywhere.

>   CHARLIE
> I... lost it...

>   RUTLEDGE
> Right, sure. Happens to me all the
> time. Get moving.

>   CHARLIE
> It's got to be around here someplace—

Rutledge marches him toward her squad car while Manning and another cop (WEBER) help the fruitseller up. The fruitseller isn't human. He's a CHESEEN, four feet tall and alien. On the streets, he's called a "munchkin."

>   RUTLEDGE   WEBER
> You have the right to remain   You all right?
> silent. You have the right to

an attorney. If you can't
afford one, one will be
appointed for you.

FRUITSELLER

Aysach leesay noaha.
somu wailaanis
(angry)
Chai! Sleeva *chai!*

CHARLIE

Listen to me, dammit…

WEBER

What did he say?

RUTLEDGE

Anything you say can be
used against you in court,
especially crap about being
a cop. In.

MANNING

I don't speak munchkin.
How the hell do I know?

Rutledge pushes Charlie into the back of her unit.

INT. - SQUAD CAR - CONTINUOUS

Rutledge SLAMS the door, and Charlie finds himself locked in next to the
young skinhead that Manning arrested.

CHARLIE

I don't believe this.

SKINHEAD

Life's a bitch, man. Then you die.

CUT TO:

EXT. - THE ZOO - DAY

Once, the cops called Uptown precinct by another name, but since Starport
opened it's been "the Zoo."

INT. - THE ZOO - MAIN ENTRANCE

The hall is crowded with COPS coming and going as Charlie, the skinhead,
and the other Earthbloods are herded past.

                    SKINHEAD
        I want a shyster, man! I got my
        rights. Get your hands off!

                    CHARLIE
                  (to Manning)
        Listen, if you'd just let me speak to
        the captain...

                    RUTLEDGE
        Shut up and keep moving.

INT. - ZOO SQUADROOM - DAY

An elderly Italian woman, MRS. MASSACOLA sits giving a statement to
uniformed officer JOHN PARK, 28, handsome, Korean-American, polite.
Park types on an ancient Remington.

                    PARK
        How do you spell that, ma'am?

                    MRS. MASSACOLA
        Massacola. Just like it sounds,
        officer.
                  (upset)
        It's not just the money. All my
        credit cards were in there. And my
        pictures, all the pictures of my
        grandkids...

                    PARK
        We'll do our best to get them back
        for you, Mrs. Massacola. Can you
        describe the purse?

                    MRS. MASSACOLA
        Brown. It was brown.
                  (hesitating)
        Or did I take the black one today?

INT. - ZOO SQUADROOM - SIMULTANEOUS

A few feet away, SGT. RICHARD MONDRAGON—Hispanic, forty, a tough in-your-face kind of cop—chews out Park's partner, officer LOUIS MO-RELLO, overweight, late thirties, and voluble.

> MONDRAGON
> You were there, you had him, and you
> let him get away, that's all I know.

> MORELLO
> Gimme a break, sarge, the guy took
> off, what the hell were we supposed
> to do?

> MONDRAGON
> You run him down. That's the way we
> did it when I was on the streets.
> Maybe if you spent more time in the
> gym and less in the donut shop—

> MORELLO
> Hey, no offense, sarge, but when you
> were on the streets the bad guys
> didn't have wings.

> MONDRAGON
> (taken aback)
> Excuse me?

> MORELLO
> Nobody told us the little dirtbag
> could fly.

CUT TO:

INT. - BOBBI'S OFFICE - DAY

A cubicle in the rear of the squadroom, its walls covered with citations, awards, and photographs. The door is open. Behind a cluttered desk, LT. BOBBI KELLEHER is on the phone. She's 33, a slender, striking redhead in shirtsleeves and shoulder-holster.

>   BOBBI
>   (arguing into phone)
>   We've already assigned a half-dozen
>   men to the hotel. Look, I can't give
>   every visiting dignitary—yes, but
>   that was the *Pope*—

Detective EMILE STAMM appears at her door; 45, a veteran cop, heavy-set, with hard eyes. A guy who has seen it all. Bobbi spots him and waves him inside the office.

>   BOBBI
>   (into phone)
>   Then tell the Topman to call the
>   mayor and get us approved for more
>   overtime. No, I don't need to talk
>   to the Topman myself. No—

Stamm takes a stubby black cigar out of a pocket.

>   BOBBI
>   (to Stamm)
>   Stamm, if you light that thing, I'm
>   going to shove it up your—
>   (quickly, into phone)
>   Chay'ash Seyseyeen. This is
>   Lieutenant Kelleher. Profit to
>   your house too.

Stamm LIGHTS his cigar. He looks over a photo of a young Bobbi in uniform, on the day she graduated the Academy. Beside it is a picture of her with her Irish cop family, a father, and three older brothers, all in uniform. One brother wears a different uniform than the others. Stamm BLOWS SMOKE at the photograph.

>   BOBBI
>   We do understand the importance of
>   these talks. Topman, we'll do
>   everything in our power to protect
>   the trade envoy, but you must
>   understand—
>   (beat, harder)

Fine. You speak to the mayor. Speak
to the governor. Hell, you might as
well speak to President Clinton,
maybe *she'll* be able to help you.

She hangs up the receiver abruptly, pissed.

>   BOBBI
> Stamm, I warned you about that cigar.

>   STAMM
> Sorry, lieutenant. I must not have
> heard. Didn't want to eavesdrop.

Both know perfectly well that he heard every word. Stamm LICKS his thumb
and forefinger and snuffs out the cigar, pocketing it again.

>   STAMM
> Word is you're going to stick me with
> a new partner.

>   BOBBI
> Detective Charles C. Baker. Transfer
> from the four-four. Seven years on
> the force, just got his gold shield.

>   STAMM
> C'mon, lieutenant, gimme a break. I
> don't do virgins.

>   BOBBI
> No, Stamm, what you do is go through
> partners like a hypochondriac goes
> through Kleenex. Baker's supposed to
> be a good cop.

>   STAMM
> Yeah, well, so where the hell is this
> paragon?

>   BOBBI
> He should be here any...

(glances at watch)
He's late.

> STAMM
> A detective who can't find the
> precinct house. Just what we need.
> He'll fit right in.

CUT TO:

INT. - CELL - TIGHT ON CHARLIE

He has a "Why, me?" look on his face. The punks are SHOUTING through the bars.

> SKINHEAD
> Hey, man, why don't you lock up the
> freakin' *aliens?*

Outside the cells, LIVINGSTONE—an older black cop with an ample gut —sits at a steel desk with a chessboard in front of him.

> FAT EARTHBLOOD
> We don't want their stinkin' fruit.
> Stuff's poison!

> SKINHEAD
> You ought to arrest *them* for selling
> that crap.

Livingstone looks up from his chessmen.

> LIVINGSTONE
> You boys look good behind bars.

The punks HOOT and CURSE at him. Charlie gets up.

> CHARLIE
> Excuse me, officer, there's been a
> mistake. I'm a cop.

SKINHEAD
(shouted, grinning)
Me too! Hell, yes.

FAT EARTHBLOOD
Screw you, I'm with the FBI.

As Livingstone gives a silent shake of his head, Mondragon ENTERS and looks over the prisoners.

MONDRAGON
All right, gentlemen, we're going to
take you up and book you, one at a
time. You get one phone call apiece.

CHARLIE
Listen, if I could just see the
Captain Swoboda for a minute...

Mondragon ignores him and points to the skinhead.

MONDRAGON
You first, pretty boy.

Livingstone unlocks the cell and the skinhead swaggers out. Charlie sits down shaking his head.

CUT TO:

INT. - ZOO INTERROGATION ROOM - DAY

Bobbi and Assistant State's Attorney SAM WINEGLASS are waiting as Mondragon escorts the skinhead into the room.

MONDRAGON
Here he is, lieutenant.
(closing door)
Word is, he tried to use Ernie's head
for batting practice.

> SKINHEAD AARON
> What is he kvetching about? I
> whiffed, didn't I?
>   (pinches his cheek)
> Tell him almost only counts in horse
> shoes and grenades, sarge.

Mondragon shakes his head, EXITS. The skinhead—undercover officer
AARON STEIN, late twenties, bright and quick and funny, with a thousand
voices and a boyish grin—leans back in his chair. Without the shaved head,
the tattoos, and the swastika over his ear, he's strikingly handsome in a dark,
intense sort of way.

> BOBBI
> Aaron, this is Sam Wineglass from the
> State's Attorney's office. Sam,
> Detective Aaron Stein.

Wineglass is staring at the undercover officer in horror.

> WINEGLASS
> That isn't a real tattoo.
>   (more weakly)
> Is it?

> AARON
> Only my hairdresser will ever know
> for sure.

> BOBBI
> What the hell did you think you were
> doing at the el?

> AARON
> Getting arrested. Hollander watches
> me day and night, it was the only way
> to report in.

> WINEGLASS
> We got eight of them off the streets,
> anyway.

                    AARON
Well, put them back *on* the streets.
They'll walk anyway. Entrapment.
This morning's little prank was all
my idea.

                    WINEGLASS
Little *prank?* Felony assault,
battery, malicious destruction
of property…

                    AARON
          (breaks in, singing)
…and a partridge in a pear tree.
          (beat, harder)
Dime store crap, counselor. The big
prize is still behind door number
three. I had to sell Hollander on my
devotion to the cause.
          (looks at Bobbi)
Earthblood's going to try and whack
the Skrit trade envoy.

This is absolutely the *last* thing that Bobbi wanted to hear.

                    BOBBI
Damn it! You're sure?

                    AARON
Oh yeah. I can't tell you when and
where… yet… but believe me,
lieutenant, it's going down.

                    BOBBI
          (to Wineglass)
Can we bring them in?

                    WINEGLASS
Conspiracy charges are hard to prove
if they haven't actually done
anything.

> AARON
> How does arms smuggling strike your
> fancy?
> (off their reaction)
> Hollander's ugly but he's not stupid.
> He's not going to try and snuff one
> of Our Friends From The Stars with a
> Saturday night special. Word is,
> he's got it fixed to get his hands on
> some heavy-duty firepower.

> WINEGLASS
> Are we talking Uzis here? Hand
> grenades, bazookas, what?

> AARON
> Nah. We're talking...
> (beat, leans forward)
> ...*ray guns.*

A long beat. Bobbi looks *very* unhappy. Shaking her head, she glances at Sam
Wineglass.

> WINEGLASS
> I think we better tell Captain
> Swoboda about this situation. He's
> not going to be happy.

> BOBBI
> He's not going to be happy? Wait
> till we tell *Topman!*

CUT TO:

EXT. - FLEA MARKET - DAY

We hear the WAIL of SIRENS as a police car pulls up to a flea market on a
vacant lot in the heart of Uptown. A tense CROWD has gathered, watching.
Something is wrong.

ANGLE ON RUTLEDGE AND MANNING

as they force their way through the crowd.

ANXIOUS WOMAN	VENDOR
The police are here!	What the hell took you so long?

TEENAGER	
Careful, she's got a	RUTLEDGE
swordstick...	What's the problem?

The spectators move aside, and Rutledge and Manning step right in the middle of a tense, explosive confrontation. Two TOURISTS—husband and wife—have been backed up against an overturned table of bric-a-brac. An expensive CAMERA hangs around the man's neck.

Around them, in a loose semicircle that permits no escape, are six NHAR. Although aliens, these are no munchkins; the Nhar are the most human-looking of all the species in the Harmony...but few humans have ever looked so good. Tall, lean, muscular, they move with the feral grace of panthers. There is a deadly beauty about this species; their street name is "angels."

The angels have sharp features, high cheekbones, pale skins. Males and females alike dress in high boots, flowing cloaks, armor and silk; the accents and honor badges of these six are MAROON, signifying their cadre.

Nocturnal, they wear HOODS to shield their faces when they go out in the light of Earth's bright sun.

Most Nhar have silver- or gold-colored hair, worn long, but the leader of this group, a tall fierce woman named DAHRYS NHAR-KQL, has a mane of *jet black* hair. In her hands is a *SWORDSTICK*, a kind of quarterstaff with a grip in its center and razor-sharp blades at both ends. Dahrys is glaring at the tourists with murder in her eyes. The cops know they've got trouble.

> RUTLEDGE
> (low, to Manning)
> Oh oh. Angels.

> MANNING
> Worse. Maroon cadre.

> IOWA HUSBAND
> The police... thank god...

Dahrys looks toward the cops. It is clear that she and the other angels are not afraid of the police.

DAHRYS
Do you champion these thieves?

IOWA WIFE
Listen to her. She's crazy. *She's*
the thief, she pulled that knife on
my husband... tried to take our camera...

DAHRYS
Still your tongue, human... or die
beside your mate.

IOWA WIFE
(hysterical, to cops)
You heard her, you heard her! Arrest
them!

The spectators MUTTER encouragement, and there are angry SHOUTS
directed at the aliens. The angels ignore it.

RUTLEDGE
Will everybody just shut up and calm
down for a moment?

Manning SEES the problem. He looks at the tourists.

MANNING
Can I see the camera?

The tourist is confused, frightened. He lifts the strap over his head, hands
Manning the camera.

MANNING
Very nice. Where you folks from?

IOWA HUSBAND
I... I... Iowa, we... we're on
vacation...

MANNING
How many pictures you take of them?
(indicating angels)

                    IOWA HUSBAND
          I don't... three or four... they
          were so colorful... we never saw...
                    MANNING
          ...aliens before. No.

Manning takes the camera by its strap, swings it over his head in a high arc,
and SMASHES it against the ground. The camera SHATTERS. The tourist
GAPES, stunned.

                    IOWA WIFE
          What are you *doing?* Our camera...

Manning pulls the tangle of film from the broken camera, holds it up in front
of Dahrys.

                    MANNING
          Is honor satisfied?

                    DAHRYS
          No. The theft is undone, yet the
          insult stands.

                    RUTLEDGE
              (to tourists)
          Tell her you're sorry.
              (off their looks)
          These are Nhar. Angels. When you
          took their picture, you stole their
          images.

                    IOWA HUSBAND
          I didn't... I didn't know, I didn't
          mean to...

                    MANNING
          You hear him. He didn't mean to take
          anything of yours. He's sorry. And
          he's not even armed. Look at him.

A tense moment. Dahrys glances from the tourists to the cops.

> DAHRYS
> This apology is a poor thing, yet I
> will hear it.
>   (hard, to tourists)
> Should it happen again...

And with that, she MOVES...

ANGLE ON AN OLD TOASTER

On the ground at the feet of the tourists, where it fell from the overturned table. Dahrys' blade lashes out and SPEARS the metal toaster like a fish. She flings it HIGH in the air. As it falls, her swordstick FLASHES, a BLUR of motion; Dahrys spins it as deftly as a cheerleader with a baton.
When the toaster lands, it has been carved neatly into FOUR PIECES, the metal gleaming raw and bright where the alien blade sliced through it like butter.

RESUME

Dahrys stops the swordstick with both hands, TWISTS; the blades telescope back into the grip, and she hangs it from her belt.

> DANRYS
> Treasure this lesson as a gift from
> Dahrys Nhar-Kql, *aryanne* of the
> maroon cadre of the children of the
> endless night.
>   (to another angel)
> Pay the human for his toasting
> machine.

The angel TOSSES a handful of bills at the foot of the vendor as Dahrys and the maroons walk off. The spectators make way, silent, shaken. When they are gone, the tourist looks to Manning.

> IOWA HUSBAND
> But... but... who's going to pay for
> my camera?
> MANNING
> Send the bill to Topman, care of Starport Chicago.

FADE OUT

ACT II

EXT. - ZOO - MAIN ENTRANCE - DAY

THREE Starport skimmers, decorated with the blazon of the Harmony of Worlds, land in front of the Zoo. Two are small, fast; the center one is as large as a stretch limo and as sleek as tomorrow.

INT. - SWOBODA'S OFFICE - DAY

CAPTAIN JOSEPH SWOBODA is a heavy-set, jowly Polish cop pushing retirement age. On the wall behind him is a framed picture of Mayor Richard J. Daley. On his desk are a tiny American flag and a bottle of Maalox. He's measuring out a spoonful as Bobbi listens.

> SWOBODA
> I spent my whole life on the force,
> Bobbi. Until Starport opened, I
> figured I'd seen just about
> everything...
> (gulps Maalox)
> He looks like a cockroach.

> BOBBI
> Who?

> SWOBODA
> The Skrit trade envoy. The mayor's
> office told me, he looks like a
> cockroach, he's five feet three
> inches tall only he's a cockroach.

> BOBBI
> Three hundred fourteen species in the
> Harmony... figures that some might be
> insects...

> SWOBODA
> The mayor is going to give him a key
> to the city. He'll probably shake
> hands with him. Do cockroaches shake

hands? Do cockroaches *have* hands?

Swoboda glances up at Daley's picture.

>   SWOBODA
>   Mayor Daley would *never* have given a
>   cockroach the key to the city.

>   BOBBI
>   Well… if it was a Democrat…

They look up, distracted, at the sound of a COMMOTION beyond the glass walls of Swoboda's office.

>   CUT TO:

INT. - ZOO - MAIN ENTRANCE - SIMULTANEOUS

as the alien called TOPMAN comes striding through the doors, surrounded by his curious entourage.
The Topman is a 'munchkin,' like the fruitseller…but a far more formidable one. He is four feet tall, portly, with a large head, an expressive mouth, mottled skin. Loose flaps of bright orange-red skin—his *dewlaps*—dangle beneath his jaw. He is richly dressed in Cheseen robes and wears a MEDALLION OF OFFICE. His dewlap marches in front of him as he strides toward the office, a swollen RED BALLOON that quivers with fury.
Beside him, matching her strides diplomatically to his shorter ones, walks MELANTHA MOORE, Starport's UN liaison, a sophisticated black woman in horn-rim glasses and tailored suit.
They are protected, front and rear, by four ANGELS of the silver cadre, commanded by LYHANNE NHAR-LYS: tall, gorgeous, with long silver-gold hair and sharp cheekbones. SILVER accents on boots, belt, cloak, and trim highlight the splendor of his clothing and mark his cadre.

INT. - SWOBODA'S OFFICE - DAY

Swoboda RISES as an angel opens the door to Swoboda's office, uninvited. Topman, Melantha, and Lyhanne ENTER, with one angel guard. The other three assume positions outside in the squadroom.

SWOBODA
Gentleman. Ah, this is a... I
didn't... ah, profit to your house...

Standing around Swoboda's office, the humans all tower over the Topman.
This just makes him madder.

TOPMAN
This is *not* a day of profit.
(beat, generally)
Lift me up!

Lyhanne and the other angel lift the Topman by either arm, and put him on
top of Swoboda's desk, waving his arms in anger.

TOPMAN
The Harmony of Worlds brings to
humans affection of three hundred
fourteen sibling species, brings
wisdom, wealth, trade, technology—

MELANTHA
Chay'ash, please...

TOPMAN
(ignoring her)
Harmony opens road to the stars, and
humans repay with ingrateful violent
thuggery and assassinations.

Melantha speaks up in a lilting WEST INDIAN ACCENT.

MELANTHA
Chay'ash Seyseyseen is very upset
about this threat to the life of the
Skrit trade envoy. As United Nations
liaison to Starport Chicago, I must
tell you that we share his concerns.

BOBBI
We *all* share the Topman's concerns,
Melantha.

                    LYHANNE
So you say. Yet what *action* do you
mean to take?

                    SWOBODA
We're not at liberty to reveal the
details of our investigation.

                    LYHANNE
Nothing. As I thought.

                    BOBBI
Before you start telling us how to do
our job, maybe you should get your
own house in order. We have
information that Earthblood is being
provided with energy weapons from
inside Starport.

Topman's dewlaps SWELL with outrage until he looks as though his chin
might explode. He WAVES his arms again.

                    TOPMAN
Impossible! Unthinkable!
Inconceivable! Starport Security
would never allow this.

INT. - ZOO SQUADROOM - SIMULTANEOUS

Through the glass partition, the cops can see the Topman on the desk,   waving
his arms. Stamm, eyeing Topman, gets one of those looks on his face, lowers
his voice and begins to SING.

                    STAMM
              (sung, low, pompous)
          As the mayor of the munchkin city/ In
          the county of the land of Oz...

He begins to WADDLE around, repeating the same refrain. The other cops
look at him with astonishment; then Morello JOINS IN. Park is choking on
his laughter.

RESUME SWOBODA'S OFFICE

Where no one has yet noticed the singing in the squadroom.

> LYHANNE
> The silver Nhar have guarded Starport
> Chicago since Earth was opened. We
> are honor-sworn to keep all forbidden
> weapons from human hands.

The Topman has calmed down; as his anger fades, his dewlaps DEFLATE, sagging into loose folds of flesh under his broad chin.

> BOBBI
> (hard, ironic)
> I guess we have nothing to worry
> about then.
> (notices singing)
> Excuse me a moment.
> (opens door)
> All right, *cut the crap.*

Bobbi SLAMS the door. The singing stops.

> SWOBODA
> Look, ray guns or no ray guns, it's
> our recommendation that the trade
> talks be postponed.

> LYHANNE
> Such a change would be a stain upon
> the *palann* of Starport and the
> Harmony of Worlds. If your blue
> cadre cannot keep the envoy safe, my
> silvers will. Show me where these
> assassins hide, and this night they
> will drown in their own life's blood.

> BOBBI
> Like hell. We have *laws* on Earth,
> Lyhanne. We don't just go out and
> slaughter our criminals.

                    LYHANNE
And that is your folly, lieutenant.

                    BOBBI
Topman, the *last* thing this city
needs is a bunch of angels playing
vigilante on the streets. You had no
right—

                    TOPMAN
Do *not* presume to instruct me in my
duty! As Chay'ash of Starport, my
responsibility—

                    BOBBI
—*ends* at your perimeter. The last
time I looked, the city of Chicago
was still part of the planet Earth.

                    TOPMAN
Our sovereign rights have been
guaranteed by treaties with every
human nation. Even the silly little
ones.

                    MELANTHA
            (polite but firm)
Yes, Chay'ash, but only within the
boundaries of Starport Chicago,
Starport Singapore, and Starport
Copenhagen.

                    LYHANNE
Honor does not end at a line on a
map.

The Topman's dewlaps are SWELLING again as he works himself up.

                    TOPMAN
And human violence knows no rules!
Another incident this morning, I am
briefed! Peaceful fruit-nut-and-

vegetable-selling species three
Cheseen merchant, smashed and kicked
and brutalized. It is not to be
tolerated!

> BOBBI
> There are a couple million people in
> this city. Some of them don't like
> aliens very much. Hell, some of them
> don't like each other very much.

> SWOBODA
> Topman, we're doing all that's
> humanly possible to—

> TOPMAN
> All that is *humanly* possible is *not*
> sufficient!

And with that, he JUMPS off the desk.

> TOPMAN
> Come. My ears are full with ample
> excuses.

He goes striding out of the office angrily. Melantha gives the police a sympathetic shrug, and follows. Lyhanne is the last to depart. Bobbi Keller points an angry finger at him.

> BOBBI
> Lyhanne, I warn you… if we turn up
> even *one* dead nazi…

Lyhanne's only reply is a formal BOW.

> LYHANNE
> Honor.

Then he too is gone. Captain Swoboda COLLAPSES heavily into his chair, shaking his head. He pulls out his bottle of Maalox.

SWOBODA
I was three years six months two days
from my pension when that first
starship landed. Remember how they
said they'd been watching us, waiting
until we were ready for contact?
Nearly fifty years... You'd think
they could have waited four more.

CUT TO:

EXT. - UPTOWN STREETS - DAY

A squad car passes down the street.

INT. - SQUAD CAR - DAY

Park and Morello. Park drives, Morello kvetches.

MORELLO
What did he expect me to do, flap my
arms and think about Christmas? You
ask me, Mondragon's had a bug up his
tush ever since he made sergeant.
He's like me. A man of action can't
get happy behind a desk.

PARK
(amused)
A man of action?

MORELLO
Don't give me that look. Yeah, okay,
I'm not into your kung-fu chop-socky
stuff, so what? I'm still who I am,
you know?

PARK
A man of action.

MORELLO
Damn straight.

Suddenly Park spots something, hits the gas.

PARK
There he is.

As Morello looks around wildly, the car ACCELERATES.

CUT TO:

EXT. - UPTOWN STREET - SIMULTANEOUS

A tug-of-war is in progress between a FAT WOMAN and a hunched little alien purse SNATCHER who looks like a cross between a monkey and a bat. They yank her purse back and forth.

FAT WOMAN
Help! Thief! Leggo!

The Snatcher HISSES at her, showing a mouth full of sharp yellow teeth. Startled, the fat woman releases the purse and falls on her ass. The squad car pulls up with a SQUEAL of brakes. Morello spills out. Park, a beat behind, has to come around the car.

MORELLO
Hold it, you little—

Morello GRABS for the Snatcher; the Snatcher spreads bat-like wings, flapping. Morello misses his feet by inches, and goes flat on his gut on the sidewalk.

ANGLE ON THE SNATCHER

Flapping his wings, and holding the purse, he HOVERS ten feet above, LAUGHING. His laughter is a raucous alien cackle.

PARK

takes a running start, and VAULTS into the air in a flying somersault. The
Snatcher's so busy laughing that he doesn't react until Park RIPS the purse
out of his grip. The Snatcher HISSES in rage as Park lands lightly on his feet,
purse in hand.

MORELLO

rolls over and gets unsteadily to his feet, fumbling with his holster and
SHOUTING.

> MORELLO
> Get down here, I'm warning you, I
> swear…

Morello gets his pistol out and swings it right up into camera. There's a loud
SPLAT; Morello's pistol, hand, and hat are covered with a thick, viscous, dripping purplish-red OOZE.

RESUME SCENE

Gagging, Morello drops his gun. The Snatcher FLAPS away into the distance,
LAUGHING loudly. Park helps the fat woman to her feet.

> PARK
> Are you all right, ma'am?

She NODS. Park hands back her purse. Morello is scraping off purple ooze;
he's pissed and nauseated in equal parts.

> MORELLO
> (choked with fury)
> He… it… it… it…

> PARK
> I saw.

Park picks up Morello's gun with two fingers, fastitious, careful not to touch
the ooze.

> MORELLO
> That's it. I swear, that's *it*. No
> more Mister Nice Guy.

(takes gun)
Next time, I shoot off his wings.

CUT TO:

INT. - ZOO HOLDING TANKS - ON STAMM

as he stands outside the bars, looking over the prisoners.

        STAMM
Which one of you douchebags killed
Detective Baker and stole his gun?

        CHARLIE
Here. Me. I mean, I'm Baker. I
didn't kill anyone.

Stamm notes the red stains all over Charlie's clothes.

        STAMM
So how come you're covered with
blood?

        CHARLIE
It's fruit juice.

        STAMM
That's what they all say.
        (studies Charlie)
They ran a make on your gun. Imagine
the red faces when it turned out to
be one of ours.
        (beat)
Yo, Livingstone, better unlock
my partner here, we need to get him a
bib.

Livingstone gets up, with a final reluctant glance at his chessboard, and approaches with the keys.

CUT TO:

INT. - ZOO MEN'S ROOM - DAY - ON AARON STEIN

Inspecting himself in the cracked men's room mirror. He runs a hand across his shaved head, brushes his teeth with a finger, adjusts his leathers. Mondragon ENTERS behind him, frowning. Aaron sees him in the mirror.

> AARON
> So how do I look?

> MONDRAGON
> Like something I'd like to flush down
> the toilet.
> (beat, serious)
> I can't believe the Red Witch is
> sending you back in.

> AARON
> I haven't learned all the words to
> "Earthland Über Alles" yet.

> MONDRAGON
> I want you to wear a wire.

> AARON
> Love to. Darling idea. So kind of
> you to suggest it.
> (conspiratorially)
> The thing is, just between you and
> me, there's this little nazi nancy
> with a serious case of hot pants.
> Can't keep her hands off me. So
> imagine, there we are, petting in the
> bunker, and she slides her hand under
> my shirt to adjust my love buttons,
> and *surprise,* it's a *wire!* Talk
> about your *faux pas!*

Aaron gives a smile and a helpless shrug and sidles toward the exit. Mondragon scowls at him.

MONDRAGON
Only you would have this kind of
problem, Aaron.

AARON
Hey, I knew the job was dangerous
when I took it.

CUT TO:

INT. - ZOO SQUADROOM

Morello—stripped to his undershirt—is connecting up a VCR to a television
on his desk. Or trying to. Park watches. Charlie ENTERS the squadroom
with Stamm.

STAMM
Hey, nice look, Morello. You
undercover as a couch potato, or you
just forget your shirt?

PARK
(discreetly)
An alien threw up on him.

STAMM
I had that urge myself from time to
time.

MORELLO
Eat it, Stamm.

STAMM
That's "Eat it, *Detective* Stamm,"
buttface.

Stamm points Charlie at an empty desk.

STAMM
That's yours there.
(Charlie sits)

My last partner died in that chair.
Massive cerebral hemorrhage, went
just like that. (snaps his fingers)

                    CHARLIE
How many partners have you had,
anyway?

                    STAMM
You can't count that high.

Morello is still sweating over the VCR connection.

                    MORELLO
You know, Park, you could help me
with this. You people made this damn
thing.
                    PARK
My people are Korean. That's a
Japanese VCR.

                    CHARLIE
Here, let me.
            (changes wires)
That should do it.

There's a videotape on the desk. Stamm picks it up.

                    STAMM
            (reading)
Our Friends From The Stars, a
layman's guide to the Harmony of
Worlds. Whassamatter, Morello, they
were out of *Debbie Does Starport?*

He TOSSES the tape at Morello, who grabs it from the air.

                    MORELLO
I'm doing some research.

                    CHARLIE
Maybe I can help. I'm kind of an

amateur xenologist.
            (off Morello's blank
            look)
I've read everything I can get my
hands on about the aliens.

                PARK
We're trying to get a make on a purse
snatcher. Alien, but he's not
Cheseen or Nhar.

                CHARLIE
Can you describe him?

                MORELLO
Oh, yeah. Short, smaller than a
munchkin even, but hairy, with
these wings, sort of a monkey-bat look.

Charlie ponders that; he looks puzzled.

                CHARLIE
Really? That's weird. I don't...
none of the winged species I know
fit your description.

                MORELLO
So whattaya saying, it was Stamm who
puked on me?

Morello pushes in in the videotape, which begins to play. An image of a
STARFIELD comes up on screen.

                ANNOUNCER
Space. The last unknown. For
thousands of years, men have gazed up
into the starry night, wondering what
was out there. Until now... until
the answer came to us...

On that, the music swells as a great Harmony starship comes WHOOSHING
through the starfield.

STAMM   ANNOUNCER
Who'd of thought, all   The Harmony of Worlds.
those years, the answer   Fleets of great faster-than-light
was "munchkins"?   starships linking nine thousand
                                         inhabited planets, moons, and
                                         colonies. A trading web that
                                         unites an entire galactic arm.
CHARLIE   The ancient wisdoms and
(to Morello)   accumulated science of three
I tell you, there's no   hundred fourteen sentient species.
species like that.   The Harmony of Worlds.
                                         Our Friends From The Stars.

On the TV, the image of space DISSOLVES into a shot of a huge, crowded
FOOTBALL STADIUM at night.

                    ANNOUNCER
            They came to us during the Super
            Bowl…

                                                              CUT TO:

EXT. - STARPORT - DAY - ESTABLISHING

Starport Chicago rises from the waters of Lake Michigan, an artificial island
three miles across. The skyline of Chicago is visible to the west. In the center
of the island cluster warehouses, offices, dwellings for a dozen different species, each stranger than the one before, products of no earthly   architecture.
The rest is a vast LANDING FIELD, splashed with distinctive blazon of the
Harmony. ALIEN STARSHIPS sit on the field; built by different species, they
look no more alike than a Chinese junk looks like the *Queen Mary*. As we
watch, a pot-bellied FREIGHTER sinks slowly into the ground on a huge
ELEVATOR.
Three skimmers come WHOOSHING by camera, and swoop down on the
Tower, an alien minaret fifty stories high…they vanishes into a hangar about
forty floors up, and we

                                                              CUT TO:

TNT. - TOPMAN'S OFFICE - DAY

Lyhanne and Melantha join Topman in his office, a round donut-shaped room that fills the entire top floor of the tower, its floor-to-ceiling windows looking out over Starport and the lake. A high-speed pneumatic elevator occupies the "hole" of the donut.

Most of the furnishings are SMALL, munchkin scale, although there are a few oversized chairs for visitors; in this environment, humans would seem out of proportion, alien. The Topman sits behind his desk; the office is so designed that, despite his height, he looks down on everyone.

Out on the field, the freighter vanishes under the field, and huge DOORS close over the subterranean landing bay.

TIGHT ON TOPMAN'S HAND

as he passes it across a small featureless globe on his vast asymmetrical desk. The globe FLASHES.

RESUME

As the windows DARKEN; in a moment they have transformed into a solid opaque wall of brushed metal. Simultaneously, a cut crystal DECANTER and three GLASSES rise from his desk. Topman is calm; his dewlaps dangle, loose and sagging.

> TOPMAN
> Human drink. Orange chocolate
> liqueur. Great profit in all things
> chocolate. Taste.
> (pours)
> Profit to your house!

Topman TOSSES back a glass as if it were a shot, pours another, as his guests sip theirs more delicately.

> TOPMAN
> Very refreshing!
> (he smiles)
> So, Lyhanne, my good right hand, I
> trust in you to keep the Skrit safe.
> Immense profit in powercell contract,
> it must be protected.

                    LYHANNE
          On my honor, Chay'ash, no harm will
          come to the his excellency.

We hear the pneumatic WHOOSH of the elevator arriving. Lyhanne
turns…and tenses as Dahrys Nhar-Kql of the rival maroon cadre steps out.
The two angels regard each other stiffly, with hostility. The only one to BOW
is Melantha.

                    MELANTHA
          Honor.

Dahrys does not bow in reply. Her look is insolent.

                    DAHRYS
          And what would you know of honor,
          human?
                    (to Topman)
          Chay'ash, the maroon cadre of the
          children of the endless night cries
          protest. Again, our contracts are
          being set aside by meddling humans.

                    TOPMAN
          Again, you break human trading laws.
          Warnings you have had.

                    DAHRYS
          If we wish to buy and humans wish to
          sell, by what right does this
          'lawyer' cadre dare interfere?

                    MELANTHA
          By treaty right, Mercantile-Captain.
          The silver and white cadres operate
          within UNITO codes. If the maroons
          wish to trade on Earth, they must—

Dahrys' hand goes to the swordstick on her belt.

                    DAHRYS
          Be careful before you tell an *aryanne*

of the maroon Nhar what she must and
must not do.

> LYHANNE
> (soft but chilling)
> You speak strongly to unarmed humans,
> maroon.

> DANRYS
> This is no quarrel of yours, silver.
> Unless you have gone human yourself?

In a flash, Lyhanne's BLADE is in his hand. Topman SLAMS both hands
down hard on the top of his desk.

> TOPMAN
> That is *sufficient!* Does my office
> resemble some Nhar honor pit? No!
> Put up steel *now!*

Reluctantly, the rival Nhar put away their weapons.

> TOPMAN
> Better. Dahrys Nhar-Kql, your
> protest is noted… but remember,
> this is human planet Earth. Now go.

Stiffly, Dahrys gives the Topman a BOW, and EXITS. As the elevator
WHOOSHES her away, Topman pours another little glass of chocolate.

> TOPMAN
> Lyhanne, good friend, no insult is
> meant, but sometimes I am thinking
> you Nhar are too much like these
> humans. The Quell'ash Eyohi thinks
> you even look alike. I cannot see
> this, myself.
> (drinks, thinking)
> You species three fifteen humans are
> perverse and frustrating peoples, yet
> a world that gives chocolate to the
> Harmony cannot be all bad, nai?

            MELANTHA
We have our virtues, Chay'ash.

The Topman considers that, reflective.

            TOPMAN
Yes. You are speaking true. I think
I must help humans. That is why we
have come, yes, to help, to trade, to
share knowledge and wisdom. And I know
just the way!

                             FADE OUT

END OF ACT II

ACT III

INT. - ZOO SQUADROOM - DAY

Charlie is filling out paperwork at his desk. Stamm smokes his cigar, filling the air with a haze of blue smoke. Charlie COUGHS.

>   CHARLIE
>   Do you have too smoke that thing in here?
>   STAMM
>   Let me share something with you,
>   Skip. A partner is only a partner,
>   but a good cigar is a smoke.

Kelleher EXITS Swoboda's office, spots Charlie, walks over. She COUGHS, glares at Stamm.

>   BOBBI
>   There are worlds in the Harmony where
>   they breathe poison gas, I hear.
>   Ever thought of emigrating, Stamm?
>   (waves at the air)
>   You Baker? What happened to you,
>   you're a mess...

Stamm STUBS OUT his cigar and answers for Charlie.

>   STAMM
>   Man went *mano-a-mano* with a tomato
>   from space. Lost his shield, too.

>   BOBBI
>   Shut up, Stamm.
>   (to Charlie)
>   Detective Baker, your partner's the
>   biggest jerk in the department. I
>   owe you an apology, but I've got to
>   partner him with *somebody*.

>   CHARLIE
>   We'll get along fine, lieutenant.

                    BOBBI
No you won't, but never mind. The
Skrit trade envoy arrives tomorrow.
I want you two to check out security
at his hotel. Don't screw up.
          (Charlie NODS)
One more thing. The Topman has
decided to protect the envoy with a
squad of angels.

                    CHARLIE
Silver cadre?

Bobbi's surprised—and pleased—that he knows the difference.

                    BOBBI
Yes, thank god. Makes it a little
easier. They've been here longest,
they're not as volatile as the
others. So long as they stick to
guard duty, don't provoke them. I'm
talking to you, Stamm.
          (beat)
Anyway, welcome to the Zoo, Baker.

She EXITS. Charlie watches her walk off appreciatively. Stamm watches Charlie
watching Bobbi and offers his advice.

                    STAMM
Don't even think it, Skippie. She's
not a woman, she's just a cop.
Daddy's girl, Irish cop family,
married to the force. Hell, she
wouldn't even give *me* a tumble.

                                                        CUT TO:

EXT. - FIRE-DAMAGED TENEMENT - DAY

The top floor is burned out, the lower stories boarded shut. Greenhair lifts a
board for Aaron Stein.

                    GREENHAIR
            Safe house. Like the wops use for
            their gang wars. Inside.

Aaron slips in through a broken window.

INT. - EARTHBLOOD CRIB - DAY

A dozen gang members lounge on trashed furniture in the abandoned   apartment. Over the windows hangs a homemade *EARTHBLOOD* flag. Greenhair slips in behind Aaron.

                    GREENHAIR
            Hey, look what I found…

One of the girls—KIM, nineteen, a freckle-faced strawberry blonde who looks like a nazi cheerleader—rushes to embrace him. Aaron lifts her in the air and SPINS her around.

                    KIM
                (breathless)
            How'd you get out?

                    AARON
            The fruit freak didn't press charges.
            He's so scared he wet his little
            munchkin pants.

Kim KISSES him. She puts a lot of passion into it. Then a HAND falls on Aaron's shoulder, and SPINS him back, out of Kim's arms.

REVERSE ANGLE

Aaron finds himself face-to-face with "Major" HOLLANDER, the leader of Earthblood, tall and hard, mid-thirties, with long blonde hair and close-set blue eyes. He wears cammies, Army Surplus chic.

                    HOLLANDER
            Then where are the others? How come
            nobody walks but you?

                    AARON
        I was the first guy processed. Get
        off my back, Hollander, I'm sick of
        this stuff.

                    HOLLANDER
        Shut your mouth and remember who
        you're talking to. I *am* Earthblood,
        and you're a punk.

                    GREENHAIR
        Chill out, major. Loverboy's okay.
        He took a swing at this nigger cop
        this morning, I thought the nigger's
        head was out of there.

Hollander gives Aaron a long, hard, suspicious stare.

                    HOLLANDER
        Maybe he's all right.

Hollander starts to turn away. Aaron calls after.

                    AARON
        Any time you want a piece of me, man,
        you know where the alley is.

Kim takes his hand and pulls him away. With a final defiant glance at Hollander, Aaron lets the girl lead him off to another room.

                                                    CUT TO:

INT. - CRIB BEDROOM - DAY

A back bedroom in the abandoned apartment. Aaron and Kim share a bare mattress on the floor.

                    AARON
        What's Hollander's problem?

                    KIM
        He's just careful, that's all.

                    AARON
He's full of crap, that's what he is.
Man keeps talking about these energy
guns, but all I see is his mouth
flapping.
                (she giggles)
What is it? I say something funny?
Come on, tell me.

                    KIM
        (nervous whisper)
Tonight.

                    AARON
Tonight? What's tonight?

He nibbles her ear. She GIGGLES again.

                    KIM
We get the guns tonight. Hollander's
got a source out at Starport.

                    AARON
If I'm a good boy, you think he'll
let me play with one?

                    KIM
Wouldn't you rather play with *me?*

She kisses him hungrily, and we

                                        CUT TO:

INT. - SWOBODA'S OFFICE - DAY

Swoboda has his Maalox out again.

                    BOBBI
        (incredulous)
The Topman has invited us out to
Starport for *drinks?*

                    SWOBODA
Excellent chocolate drinks, he says.
Both of us. Tonight. He's sending
a skimmer.
          (gulps Maalox)
If god had meant cars to fly, he
wouldn't have given them tires.

                    BOBBI
          (suspicious)
Why is he being so nice?

                    SWOBODA
He says he has a delightful surprise.
That was how he put it. A delightful
surprise.

                    BOBBI
I can hardly wait.

                                        CUT TO:

EXT. - LAKEFRONT HOTEL - DAY

Chanting PICKETS surround a modern luxury hotel, kept at bay by a line of
police. A NEWS CREW is out front filming. The reporter, Stacy, was last
seen in Charlie's bedroom. She holds up a *POWERCELL,* the size of the watch
battery, GLOWING with energy.

                    STACY
This is a Skrit powercell, the small
heart of a big controversy that has
brought hundreds of protestors to
this hotel on the windy shores of
Lake Michigan. National Motors says
its new electric cars will run for
three years on the power from a
single cell. That's progress, they
claim… but the protestors have a
different view…

INT. - UNMARKED CAR - DAY

Charlie drives slowly through the pickets as Stamm smokes.

>   STAMM
>   Looks like Heinz 57 varieties are out
>   this morning.

The protestors give way reluctantly, waving their placards. The slogans are a mishmash; printed signs reading EARTH POWER and GAS NOT GIZMOS and NO POWERCELLS and BOYCOTT NATMO mingle with crude hand-lettered ones that shout ALIENS GO HOME and JESUS WAS A *HUMAN*. One man, standing apart from all the others, has a sign that reads BEAM ME UP, SCOTTY.

>   STAMM
>   The union guys are scared for their
>   jobs, but these other buttheads...

>   CHARLIE
>   Change brings out the best and the
>   worst in a society.

>   STAMM
>   I guess the best are sleeping in
>   today.

EXT. - HOTEL - DAY

As Stamm and Charlie climb from their car, a stout black female sergeant named HOPPER meets them.

>   STAMM
>   How's it going, sergeant? Natives
>   getting restless?

>   SGT. HOPPER
>   (very sarcastic)
>   Oh, they're a regular herd of lambs.

CHARLIE
Flock… It's a flock of lambs.

STAMM
My new partner, Skip.

SGT. HOPPER
(looks him over)
Two months.

STAMM
The Red Witch wants to detach a
couple uniforms from picket detail to
seal off the penthouse. One man on
the door, one inside…

CUT TO:

INT. - PRESIDENTIAL SUITE - DAY - ANGLE ON THE DOOR

We hear the WHIRR-CLICK of a high-tech lock; Stamm and Baker   EN-
TER, escorted by a short, officious HOTEL MANAGER.

HOTEL MANAGER
…without the keycard, the elevator
won't go to this floor, so there's no
way for anyone to… to…

His voice trails off as he looks up and sees…

REVERSE ANGLE - ON THE ANGELS

Lyhanne and four other Nhar stand facing them; two men, two women; feral,
gorgeous, with silver-gold hair and silver markings.

STAMM
So these must be the maids.

LYHANNE
Who are you, and what is your purpose
here?

> STAMM
> We'll ask the questions.
> (flashes his badge)
> Detective Emile Stamm. Skip'd show
> you his badge too, only he lost it.
> We're thinking of having a shield
> tattooed on his butt. Mind telling
> me how you got in here, Gabriel?

The other angels BRISTLE at the insult. One woman speaks.

> JHENNAR
> Human, you have the pride of
> addressing Lyhanne Nhar-Lys, an
> *aryanne* of the silver Nhar. If your
> tongue can learn no better respect,
> perhaps I should remove it.

Long CLAWS snap out of her glove, as Charlie BOWS.

> CHARLIE
> Honor.
> (they bow back)
> My blademate meant no insult.

> JHENNAR
> Yet insult was given.

> STAMM
> Hey, lady, kiss my rosy—

> CHARLIE
> (loudly interrupting)
> My blademate lacks the words to
> convey his deep sense of shame.

> LYHANNE
> Sheath your steel, Jhennar. I take
> no insult from such as him, he knows
> no better.
> (to Charlie)
> I would beg the honor of your name and rank.

                        CHARLIE
            Detective Charles Claudius Baker, of
            the Uptown Precinct.

                        STAMM
            When you two are done bowing and
            scraping, let me know. I'd like some
            answers here.

Lyhanne indicates a pair a sliding glass doors that open on a penthouse   terrace.

                        LYHANNE
            The garden beyond is large enough for
            a skimmer to land. Those doors
            provided our entry.

                        STAMM
            Skip, check the other rooms.

                        LYHANNE
            It has been done. There is no threat
            here. The room is secure.

                        STAMM
            Well, pardon me, Moroni, but I think
            we'll check that out for ourselves.

                                        DISSOLVE TO:

INT. - STARPORT - SUBTERRANEAN LOADING BAR - SUNSET

Lohb are unloading an alien freighter with floating FORKLIFTS.
Topman stands before the gaping hold of the ship, confronting six Lohb—
all in Starport coveralls, looking much alike—and a Cheseen SHIP'S
CAPTAIN. Topman is furious.

                        TOPMAN
            How could this happen? *How?* You,
            Wa'sheen, your ship it was, your
            cargo—

SHIP'S CAPTAIN
Chay'ash, kohassa delaerys nai banash
bo wallehion...

TOPMAN
No, I am not hearing excuses. And
talk human tongue English, this is
Earth, we must think like species
three fifteen.

SHIP'S CAPTAIN
My ship and my cargo, yes, but
reliance was made on Starport
security. *Your* security.

TOPMAN
The Nhar will hear of this, I am
promising, and there will be much
yelling with stern voices. I have
humans coming tonight to drink
chocolate!
        (to the Lohb)
The Lohb saw nothing?

SIX LOHE answer in perfect harmony, simultaneously.

LOHB WORKERS
Nothing, Chay'ash Topman.

The Topman's dewlaps are starting to PUFF UP.

TOPMAN
Hundreds of Lohb eyes everywhere,
seeing nothing. The silver cadre of
the Nhar, knowing nothing. Star
captains of my own species three
Cheseen, doing nothing.
        (loudly, frustrated)
What mad dream is this!

CUT TO:

EXT. - ZOO - NIGHT

A sleek Starport skimmer, decorated with the blazon of the Harmony of Worlds, lands in front of the precinct house. Swoboda and Kelleher walk down the steps as the doors silently OPEN.

> SWOBODA
> If there's no driver in there, I'm
> not getting in.

CUT TO:

TIGHT ON SWOBODA'S HAND

His knuckles WHITE as he grips an armrest for dear life.

INT. - SKIMMER - NIGHT

Swoboda stares straight ahead as the streets rush by outside in a blur. The pilot is a LOHB, a humanoid, hairless alien in Starport coveralls, antennae sprouting from his face.

> LOHB PILOT
> Would you enjoy to hear listen to
> music tune melody?

> SWOBODA
> No. No, we're fine.

The skimmer is zipping along at a bat out of hell now. The Lohb SWIVELS around to SMILE encouragingly at his passengers.

> LOHB PILOT
> Possibly prefer talk converse gossip
> share-views?

Swoboda makes a CHOKING sound.

> SWOBODA
> No thank you. Shouldn't you watch
> where you're flying?

>   LOHB PILOT
> Not necessary vital important.

>   BOBBI
> Just humor us, okay?

Swoboda MOPS his brow with a handkerchief, but the Lohb misinterprets "humor us" to mean "tell us a joke."

>   LOHB
> Humor funny ha-ha, hokay.
>   (beat, thinking)
> Species twenty-six, ninety-one and
> two hundred fourteen walk into
> tavern saloon bar. Saloon tender proprietor
> speaks remarks, saying…

OFF the look that passes between Swoboda and Kelleher, we

>   CUT TO:

EXT. - MORELLO'S HOUSE - NIGHT - ESTABLISHING

An older single-family house, working class neighborhood.

INT. - MORELLO'S HOUSE - NIGHT

Morello ENTERS, hangs up his coat. The furnishings are modest, well-used. Here and there we glimpse TOYS. A TV blares in the living room, a man and a woman arguing on a newstalk program.

>   MORELLO   MAN ON TV
> I'm home…   We could run the el for a year
>   with fifty Skrit powercells. A
> Two small girls, aged five   single cell the size of a
> and seven, go running past   watch battery will power a
> full-bore, headed upstairs.   car for *three years!*

>   FIVE YEAR OLD   WOMAN ON TV
> Hello, daddy.   Only no one will have
>   the money to buy a

SEVEN YEAR OLD
Hello, daddy.

MORELLO
Hey, *hey,* what I
tell you about running
in the house? Hey,
where's my hug?

Too late; they're gone.
Neither heard a word. A
teenaged boy, 13, is
watching the television.

MORELLO
Hey, Joey. What's on?

JOEY
Television. I got to
do a report.

car. We're talking
about destroying the entire
petroleum industry.

MAN ON TV
The fossil fuels were going to
run out anyway. The sooner
we end our national
dependence on Arab oil—

WOMAN ON TV
—the sooner we become
dependent on the Skrit for
these powercells.

MAN ON TV
Powercells that will provide
us with all the energy we
could possibly need and help
clean up our environment. I
ask you,what's wrong
with that?

A woman's voice CALLS out through the cellar door.

ALLY (O.S.)
Louie, is that you?

INT. - MORELLO BASEMENT - NIGHT

The Morello basement is filled with dozens of BIRD CAGES, and what seems
like hundreds of PARAKEETS. The cages are open, and the birds are flying
everywhere, fluttering, flapping, hopping from cage to cage. ALLISON MO-
RELLO, a slender dark-haired woman of forty, moves calmly through the chaos,
filling water bottles, replacing cuttlebones, doling out seed.
The parakeets buzz Morello as he comes clumping down the steps. He ducks
and weaves between them. His wife talks to him without glancing up from
her tasks.

ALLY
Did you have a good day? Princess Di
gave us another egg this morning. I
can't think what I'll name this one.

                    MORELLO
You'll think of something.

A bird lands on her hand. It hops from finger to finger.

                    ALLY
Well, Cher is feeling perky.

Several birds land on Morello's head and shoulders as he comes up behind his
wife. She still doesn't look at him.

                    MORELLO
Lieutenant's sending us out to
Starport tomorrow.

Ally TURNS sharply, alarmed. Her birds scatter.

                    ALLY
Oh dear. You be careful out there,
Louie. Those aliens can't be
trusted. It was in the paper.

                    MORELLO
                (suspicious)
What paper? What are you talking
about?

                    ALLY
                (looking in cages)
It's around her someplace...Here.
I knew it. Read that.

She slides out a tray, and produces the front page of a tabloid she'd been using
to line the bottom of the cage. Triumphant, she hands it to Morello.
The paper is the NATIONAL SCOOP. The headline reads, "ELVIS
SIGHTED AT STARPORT." It's illustrated with a picture of Old Fat Elvis
surrounded by munchkins, all in white sequined suits. "*Munchkins Took Him
To Space,*" says the subhead.

                    MORELLO
Ally, how many times I told you not
to read this garbage?

          ALLY
Now don't you take that tone with me,
Mister Grumpy. If it could happen to
Elvis, it could happen to you.

                                        CUT TO:

EXT. - STARPORT - NIGHT

The port is dark for the night, but the lights are on in the Topman's office
high in the tower.

INT. - TOPMAN'S OFFICE - NIGHT

Lyhanne stands facing the Topman and Melantha, disturbed.

          LYHANNE
Fireclaws. This changes all.
          (beat, thinking)
This should not have been. This
could not have been.

          TOPMAN
Yet this *is*. Weapons are gone,
taken… and with a fireclaw, even a
human can burn skimmers out of sky.

          LYHANNE
The tunnel will be safer. We will
move the envoy with human ground
transport.

          MELANTHA
The Chay'ash and I have already made
the arrangements. National Motors
will send a limousine. The police
will provide an escort.

          TOPMAN
Yet if no skimmer is seen, the
Earthbloods may look elsewhere.

> LYHANNE
> I will fly the skimmer myself. A
> fireclaw is a coward's weapon.

> TOPMAN
> Yet a man killed by a coward and a
> man killed by a hero are both dead,
> nai?

The WHOOSH of the elevator heralds the arrival of Kelleher and Swoboda. Topman turns with a forced smile.

> TOPMAN
> My good human friends! Appreciation
> for your presence. Your flight was
> swift and excellent?

> SWOBODA
> Well... swift...

Lyhanne BOWS to the two humans.

> LYHANNE
> Pardons. I must go. Duty.

Bobbi and Swoboda NOD politely. Lyhanne DEPARTS. Melantha Moore is already pouring chocolate liqueur.

> BOBBI
> Topman, what's this all about?

> TOPMAN
> Excellent clever question,
> lieutenant. I invited you here for
> two reasons. As you species three
> fifteen humans say, is good news and
> bad news.

> SWOBODA
> Yes...

>   TOPMAN
> Bad news is, three fireclaws are
> missing from a cargo marked for trans-
> shipment to Endymion.

Swoboda and Kelleher exchange a look.

>   SWOBODA
> What's a fireclaw?

>   LYHANNE
> Energy weapon, for spitting bursts of
> shaped plasma, very hot.

>   BOBBI
> Nice of you to mention it this
> morning.

>   MELANTHA
> He did not know. After you raised
> the possibility, the Chay'ash
> commanded an immediate inventory.

>   TOPMAN
> I am damp with humiliation, yet
> confident nonetheless. Silver Nhar
> and blue humans together will keep
> the Skrit safe, nai?

No one says a word until Swoboda fills the silence.

>   SWOBODA
> What's the good news?

>   TOPMAN
> Good news is named Staako Nihi, great
> Earth scholar, species two thirty two
> Nihinni. Harmony is giving you *help!*

                                        CUT TO:

EXT. - UPTOWN BAR & GRILL - NIGHT

A cop bar. Steaks and burgers, beer and boilermakers. A hole-in-the-wall beneath the shadow of the elevated tracks. Beer signs in the windows, cop cars by the curb.

INT. - UPTOWN BAR & GRILL - NIGHT

Dark and smoky. Half the customers are cops. Rutledge and Manning sit at the bar with uniforms BUSCO and WEBER.

> RUTLEDGE
> Why are you beating yourself up? You
> played it just right.

> MANNING
> It makes me sick. Smashing the
> camera, hell, I should have taken
> that swordstick off her and stuck it
> up her—

> RUTLEDGE
> That would have gotten somebody
> killed, and you know it.

> MANNING
> What the hell were they doing in a
> flea market anyway?

> BUSCO
> (laughing)
> Maybe angels got to buy fleas the
> same way real people do.

> RUTLEDGE
> They were tourists. Out seeing the
> sights.

> MANNING
> And *we're* the sights. Come to Earth
> and see the natives and their
> colorful bazaars. And now they got
> us protecting this space cockroach.
> Well, screw that. Where I grew up,

you see a cockroach, you step on it.

They all LAUGH; Manning grows angry.

> MANNING
> Go on, laugh. Won't be so funny when
> the munchkins and the cockroaches put
> *you* out of work.

Emile Stamm ENTERS behind them, with Charlie (he's cleaned up a little)
in tow. Stamm puts two fingers in his mouth, and WHISTLES loudly for
attention.

> STAMM
> Yo, boys and girls. This is my new
> partner, Skip.

The other cops look Charlie up and down, appraisingly.

> RUTLEDGE
> I say six months.

Busco takes out a five, slaps it down on the bar.

> BUSCO
> With Stamm, you kidding? Three
> weeks, if he's smart.

> WEBER
> If he's smart, he'll be begging the
> Red Witch for mercy first thing
> tomorrow morning.

Stamm points to the other cops, rattling off names and insults. Charlie shakes
hands with each in turn.

> STAMM   CHARLIE
> Salvatore Busco, Mike   It's not Skip. Just
> Webber, we call him the   Charlie, Chaz, Chuck,
> Nose, can't think why.   whatever. It's not Skip.

He pinches Weber on the nose, moves on to Manning.

STAMM
Ernie Banks Manning.

MANNING
My father was a Cubs fan.

STAMM
Whole family are losers.

MANNING
Your partner's the north end of a
southbound horse, Skip.

CHARLIE
I've noticed. It's Charlie.

Stamm reaches up to pinch Lisa Rutledge on the cheek. Lisa threatens him
with a fist. Stamm backs off.

STAMM
The pretty one here is Lisa Rutledge.
Watch out you don't sexually harass
her now, Skip, Rut's the academy
pistol champ.

RUTLEDGE   CHARLIE
It's not Rut.   It's not Skip.

RUTLEDGE
You look familiar. Have we met?

CHARLIE
Only when you cuffed me.

CUT TO:

CLOSE ON A CROWBAR

as it is shoved in the crack of an alien "crate," a black plastic OVOID emblazoned with Harmony logo. The plastic CRACKS.
INT. - EARTHBLOOD CRIB - NIGHT - ON HOLLANDER

as he pulls an artifact from the crate. It is a weapon; matte black and shining silver, a glove-and-gauntlet affair.

                    KIM
          What is it, a glove?

                    HOLLANDER
          Shut up and watch.

He slides the device over his hand, FLEXES his fingers, then makes a fist. ENERGY crackles around his hand.

                    GREENHAIR
          Hot damn... hey, watch where you
          point that thing.

Hollander turns and aims his fist right in Aaron's face.

                    HOLLANDER
          Open your mouth, why don't you?

                    KIM
          Cut it out, that's not funny!

Aaron doesn't flinch, but neither does he move a muscle. Energy SURGES ominously around Hollander's hand. Then—finally—he WHIRLS toward an beat-up COUCH across the room, CLENCHING HIS FINGERS.

ANGLE ON THE COUCH

as a BOLT of superheated PLASMA flies from Hollander's fist, hits the couch, and BLOWS IT APART.

RESUME

The pieces of the couch are SMOKING. Greenhair and the others pull out two more gauntlets. They talk excitedly: "Did you *see* that?" and "Righteous!" and "There's two more" and "Hey, gimme one." Hollander LAUGHS, as Aaron watches with growing anxiety.

                                                  CUT TO:

INT. - BOBBI'S LOFT - NIGHT

A renovated loft in the warehouse district. Streetlight pours in through the tall windows. The interior is one huge open space, with kitchen and living area and bed room flowing into each other. We HEAR the sound of a freight elevator ascending. Then an accordion gate RATTLES back noisily and Bobbi Kelleher steps into the loft, bone-weary after the long hard day.

She drops her coat on a chair. The loft is messy, lived-in, cluttered... empty. Bobbi opens the fridge, takes a slug of milk from a carton. Then she hears a soft FOOTFALL. Tenses. She puts down the milk, slides out her police revolver.

>   BOBBI
>   Who's there?

REVERSE ANGLE

As a floor lamp TURNS ON suddenly, to reveal Lyhanne standing beside an open window, long silver-gold hair moving in the wind.

>   LYHANNE
>   Do you truly believe that a primitive
>   firearm can protect you against an
>   *aryanne* of the silver Nhar?

He takes a step toward her, graceful as a panther.

>   BOBBI
>   You're flesh and blood. A bullet
>   would kill you as dead as any human.

>   LYHANNE
>   Only if it struck me.

Lyhanne gently pushes her gun out of the way, pulls her to him, and KISSES her. Bobbi SHUDDERS, and the gun falls from her fingers. She wraps her arms around Lyhanne and kisses him back. They hold each other as if they never wished to let go.

>   BOBBI
>   Oh, god...

Lyhanne strokes Bobbi's long red hair, a wonder to him; the Nhar are silver- and golden-haired, and sometimes black, but never red.

                    LYHANNE
Hair-like-fire...
          (kisses her)
I wanted you today... I wanted to
touch you... to take you there
before your captain and the Chay'ash
and all the Harmony of Worlds.

                    BOBBI
We can't...
          (kissing)
this isn't...
          (kissing, breathless)
...*damn you*...

                    LYHANNE
          (softly)
You have...

Releasing her, Lyhanne WHIRLS, moving faster than seems possible. A long
metal blade appears from nowhere, FLASHING silver, slicing through the
metal pole of the floor lamp as if it were a straw. SPARKS fly; the room is
plunged into darkness.

SILHOUETTE LYHANNE AND BOBBI

Streetlight runs down the long blade as Lyhanne drops it, forgotten, to the
floor. Silhouetted against the windows, Lyhanne lifts Bobbi in his arms, and
carries her to bed.

                                        FADE OUT

END OF ACT III

ACT IV

INT. - EARTHBLOOD CRIB - BACK BEDROOM - ECU AARON'S EYES

Closed. He seems to be asleep. Then, suddenly, they SNAP OPEN.

WIDEN

Aaron is stretched across the mattress, with Kim curled up in his arms, asleep. He turns his head, LISTENING. Nothing. Slowly, silently, Aaron eases his arm out from under Kim's head. He gets up. Tries the window. No good; it's painted shut. Aaron looks around, but there's only one exit.

WITH AARON

as he steps into the front room of the apartment, keeping to the wall, hidden by darkness and shadows. The pride of Earthblood is draped over the furniture and sprawled on the floor, passed out or asleep. Hollander himself is stretched out in the wreck of a RECLINER, like a king on his throne, the gauntlet on his arm.
The front door is nailed shut. Very carefully, Aaron moves to the broken window. The board CREAKS as he lifts it. Hollander MUTTERS in his sleep. Aaron freezes. Hollander subsides. Silently, Aaron slips through the window.

EXT. - CRIB - ON AARON

He's halfway out when we hear the challenge.

> SNAKE
> Turn it around, loverboy.

SNAKE is Hollander's right hand, a gaunt man with a snake tattooed on his arm, and a shiny PUMP SHOTGUN cradled beneath it.

> AARON
> I need some fresh air.

> SNAKE
> Then suck it up right here.

> AARON
> That's crap.

                    SNAKE
          That's orders.

Snake PUMPS his shotgun for emphasis, and there's nothing Aaron can do
but crawl sullenly back into the crib.

                                                      CUT TO:

EXT. - STARPORT BAR - MIDNIGHT

The dead of night. Most of Starport is dark now, even the tower, but lights
still glimmer atop a vaulted DOME that looks like a cross between a ribbed
mushroom and a flying saucer.
We ZOOM IN on the windows, glimpses ALIEN GLYPHS crawled across
the roof of the dome like neon lights, and hear the UPSWELL of WILD
ALIEN MUSIC. This is the other side of Starport Chicago; a twenty-four-
hour entertainment and relaxation facility.

INT. - STARPORT BAR - MIDNIGHT

The *Star Wars* cabaret meets Studio 54. The wild music FILLS the crowded
dome. We glimpse Cheseen drinking at low tables; Lohb serving and bussing
drinks; human tourists taking in the exotic sights of Starport; and other,
stranger races, distant travelers eating tree eyes and bloodbellies.
But at this hour it is the nocturnal Nhar who dominate. It is Nhar music
playing, and in the center of the room, two angels—a male of the WHITE
cadre and Dahrys of the maroon—"dance."
Their dance is a martial art, a kind of sparring. Each holds a gleaming metal
quarterstaff. They move to the music, circling, spinning, flying at each other,
their staffs RINGING together. Both are blindingly fast. The sounds of their
staffs clashing together is somehow part of the music.

ANGLE ON JOHN PARK

He stands by the bar, beside a pair of silver Nhar, engrossed in the drama of
the Nhar dance.

                    PARK
          They're so fast...

LOHB BARTENDER
Fast swift quick. They are Nhar.

PARK
It's beautiful, but is it a… a
dance… a martial art… what?

SILVER NHAR
To query a Lohb about *gaharre* is to
query a fish about the stars, human.

Out on the floor, the music hits a crescendo. Dahrys picks up her tempo, and
suddenly the male's staff is sent FLYING from his hands. He BOWS, drops
to one knee.

PARK
What's happening now? Is there some
meaning?

SILVER NHAR
The maroon has won the dance. It is
all meaning in the *gaharre*.

Dahrys lifts her shimmering metal quarterstaff over her head. She is
FLUSHED, exhilarated, wild. She CALLS OUT.

DAHRYS
And who now will face Dahrys Nhar-Kql
in *gaharre*?
(silence)
Is there no pride among the children
of the endless night? Are there no
males beneath this dome?

Park takes a step toward the dance floor, The Nhar GRABS him.

SILVER NHAR
No.

PARK
I'm good with a staff. My own people
have a martial arts tradition too.

I want to give it a try...

>   SILVER NHAR
> You do not 'try' *gaharre*. You do it,
> and you do it correctly. To perform
> badly is mortal insult.
>   (off Park's reaction)
> The maroon has beaten three males
> this night. Before the dawn, she
> will taste them all. It is a mating
> dance, human.

He takes up a crystal of wine and walks off.

>   PARK
> Oh.

Dahrys still has no more takers. She sweeps the room with her eyes, contemptuously. Then she drops her staff.

>   DAHRYS
> The cadres of Chicago are soft and
> sterile as humans.

Softer MUSIC begins. Dahrys strides directly over to the bar, where she snaps out a command to the Lohb.

>   DAHRYS
> *Shevanne.* Ice it until it bleeds.
>   (turning, to Park)
> The silvers have gone soft on this
> world. I saw him stop you, human.
> One more step and... yours would have
> been a rare death. I would have
> shattered your hands first, then
> elbows, then knees. Perhaps I would
> have killed you on the floor.
>   (sips her drink)
> Or perhaps I would have saved you for... later.

She gives him a taunting, cold-as-ice SMILE and goes walking off.

CUT TO:

INT. - BOBBI'S LOFT - NIGHT

Bobbi and opens her eyes to find herself alone in bed. Lyhanne is dressing, donning his steel.

> BOBBI
> You're going…

> LYHANNE
> I must. Dawn is but hours away, and
> there is much to be done this night.

> BOBBI
> I keep forgetting you're nocturnal.

She slips out of bed, nude, and into a robe.

> BOBBI
> You shouldn't have come.

> LYHANNE
> I could not stay away.

> BOBBI
> There's no future in this, Lyhanne.

> LYHANNE
> My future is the next night in your
> arms, my hair-like-fire.

> BOBBI
> My family almost disowned me for
> going to my senior prom with a
> Methodist. I don't think they'd
> approve of me dating outside the species.

> LYHANNE
> Speak the word, and I will teach them
> to honor your choices.

> BOBBI
>(wry, incredulous)
>Sometimes when we're together, I
>forget that you're not human. Then
>you say something like that…

She moves to the kitchen area, puts on water for coffee.

> LYHANNE
>The Chay'ash is right, you are a
>perverse and contradictory species.

A beat; then Lyhanne switches gears, the lover becoming once more the warrior, an *aryanne* of the silver Nhar.

> LYHANNE
>The Skrit will land at halfday. Our
>cadres share a common purpose. I
>would not have us at blades.

> BOBBI
>Then keep your nose clean…

Lyhanne stares at her, lost. He touches his nose.

> BOBBI
>It means, don't break any laws.

> LYHANNE
>That I cannot promise, my hair-like-
>fire. Honor.

He BOWS, and is gone in a swirl of cloth and steel, sliding through the open window onto her fire escape. OFF all the emotions   warring in Bobbi's eyes, we

DISSOLVE TO:

A MAP OF CHICAGO

Scotch-taped to a wall. Hollander POINTS.

> HOLLANDER
> The freak is supposed to stay at the
> Starview Marriott, here. They'll
> bring him over in a skimmer.

INT. - EARTHBLOOD CRIB - DAWN

Aaron stands among the gang members, one arm draped around Kim,   listening to Hollander lay out the plan.

> HOLLANDER
> Buckner and Jax by the lake. Ice,
> Gunner, you two here. I'll be on the
> roof across from the hotel, with a
> clean shot at his windows.

> GREENHAIR
> What if we burn the wrong skimmer?

> HOLLANDER
> Then some other freak buys himself a
> space farm. So?
> (beat)
> The rest of you stay here. We're not
> taking chances on some weak sister
> dropping a dime. Snake, anybody
> tries to walk, waste 'em.

OFF Aaron's look, desperate as a trapped animal, we

CUT TO:

INT. - SWOBODA'S OFFICE - MORNING

Swoboda is on the phone with the mayor. Bobbi listens.

> SWOBODA
> Yes, your honor. That would be very
> valuable. I understand. No, I don't
> know *exactly* how much money Starport
> brings into the city but I'm sure...
> An office, yes, definitely. Thank

you, your honor.

He hangs up the phone, looking shell-shocked.

> SWOBODA
> We have to find the liaison an
> office. They're going to base him
> right here in the precinct.
>   (off her look)
> What was I supposed to say?

> BOBBI
> You could have tried 'No.'

> SWOBODA
> I'm two years from my pension. I
> don't say no to the mayor.

He waves pink telephone slips at her.

> SWOBODA
> The State's Attorney, the chief of
> police, the United Nations, they all
> this liaison is a great idea.
>   (beat)
> Maybe it won't be so bad. I don't
> know, maybe he'll actually be a help.

> BOBBI
> And who said we *needed* help?

CUT TO:

INT. - THE ZOO - SNACK ROOM - MORNING

Formica tables and folding chairs. Snack machines stand along the walls like
suspects in a lineup; candy dispensers, coffee and hot drinks, sandwich machines, a microwave from another era. Most of the day watch is on hand,
feeding quarters to the machines and gulping down morning coffee as
Mondragon issues assignments.

>   MONDRAGON
> ...the skimmer will only be a decoy.
> We'll move the envoy on the ground.
> Natmo's providing an armored limo, a
> driver, and two vice-presidents.
> We're providing the escort. Atkins
> and Grabowski, Park and Morello.
>   (checks clipboard)
> Next item. Aaron Stein. He should
> have checked in by now. I want all
> units to keep an eye peeled for known
> members of Earthblood. If you make
> contact, call it in and await orders.
> And be wary, they may be armed with
> weapons from Starport...

                                                CUT TO:

EXT. - STARPORT - DAY

A STARSHIP is landing, its lines like nothing we have ever seen before, ornate and organic and somehow suggesting the insectile. Eight multi-jointed
LANDING LEGS unfold as it descends, and it touches down on the field
like a metal spider.

EXT. - SKRIT STARSHIP - A FEW MOMENTS LATER

A long black LIMOUSINE pulls up at the foot of the spider-ship, flanked by
two squad cars. Morello and Park get out of one unit.

>   MORELLO
> It's going to be a cockroach, I just
> know it. Look at that ship. Ernie
> was right.

Park stifles a YAWN with the back of his hand.

>   PARK
> Ernie's a xenophobe.
>   MORELLO
> I don't care what religion he is, he

>   was right about this Skrit guy. I
>   got nothing against munchkins, but
>   Jesus, Mary, and Joseph, there are limits.

Now Park does YAWN.

>   MORELLO
>   What, is this boring you?

>   PARK
>   I was out late last night.

>   MORELLO
>   Hot date?

>   PARK
>   More of a... martial arts exhibition.

Morello's mind returns to the Skrit.

>   MORELLO
>   So what are we going to do if he *is*
>   a cockroach?

>   PARK
>   Take him to his hotel.

ANOTHER ANGLE - ON THE LOHB

LOHB workers swarm around the ship. One operates a hand-held device that lowers a landing ramp; a second drives a fork-lift; a third and a fourth carry unroll a RED CARPET.

Lyhanne and four other angels of the silver cadre take up positions on either side of the red carpet. Two Natmo vice-presidents in power ties and Armani suits emerge from the limo. We hear a WHINE as the airlock cycles, and down the ramp comes the SKRIT TRADE ENVOY, closely attended by a female MUNCHKIN TRANSLATOR.

The trade envoy isn't *quite* a cockroach, but it certainly is insectile; five feet tall, maggot white and chitinous, with huge multi-faceted eyes and mandibles. It is dressed in lace and velvet, like a Regency dandy. Its "hands" are nests of moving white worms. We hear Morello's voice, muttered, OVER.

> MORELLO (O.S.)
> Oh boy. Oh boy oh boy.

When the Skrit trade envoy reaches the base of the ramp, Lyhanne bends in a formal HALF-BOW.

> LYHANNE
> Your excellency. Honor.

The vice-presidents hurry forward, smiling broadly.

> KLINE
> Welcome to Earth.

> WACHTEL
> On behalf of National Motors and the
> city of Chicago—

The Skrit INTERRUPTS, twittering in a series of CLICKS and WHISTLES and soft SQUELCHY SOUNDS.

> TRANSLATOR
> His excellency wishes to ask if he is
> improperly dressed. His excellency
> was advised that this clothing was
> proper human dress for all formal
> occasions.

Kline and Wachtel exchange a look; his excellency is a few centuries too late. Fortunately, the Skrit does not wait for an answer. He twitters something else.

> TRANSLATOR
> His excellency is glad to see that
> you have Lohb here. They are
> superior workers.

The Skrit wanders over to where the cops are standing. Morello looks green. The Skrit touches his badge.

> TRANSLATOR
> His excellency admires your metal
> ornament.

                    KLINE
                 (to Morello)
          Give him your badge.

Morello's hand closes over the badge protectively.

                 MORELLO
        No way.

                 WACHTEL
        Are you trying to cause an incident?
        Give him the damn badge, it's only a
        piece of tin.

                 LYHANNE
        You ask too much.
                 (to the Skrit)
        Excellency, this man is a warrior of
        the human blue cadre. The metal is his
        honor token. He would die before
        he would give it up.

The translator SQUEAKS and TWITTERS; the Skrit TWEAKS and
SQUITTERS back.

                 TRANSLATOR
        His excellency says such tokens
        belong to the warriors who have won
        them. He compliments this human on
        his great prowess.
        (Morello BEAMS)
        His excellency would go to his nest
        now, the voyage has been fatiguing.

                 WACHTEL
        Certainly, your excellency.

The trade envoy walks toward Park and Morello's police unit.
                 KLINE
        Ah, no, please, this way, the
        limo…

The translator and the trade envoy exchange another round of twittering, the envoy's suddenly HARSH and ANGRY.

> TRANSLATOR
> Black is the color for criminals and
> steriles. His excellency says that
> he will not be insulted. He will
> return to his ship.

> WACHTEL   KLINE
> No, he can't,   No one told us,
> please...   we only...

> LYHANNE
> Assure his excellency that no insult
> was intended. The humans are
> ignorant of the ways of the Skrit.
> I offer a solution...

                                                        CUT TO:

INT. - ZOO SUB-BASEMENT - DAY

Livingstone rattles a ring of KEYS as he leads Mondragon down the basement steps. Mondragon is complaining.

> MONDRAGON
> Find him an office, she says. Where
> am I supposed to find him an office?
> Why is it my job? I was cited for
> distinguished service, I made more
> busts than anyone in this precinct,
> my job is not finding offices.

They reach the base of the stairs. It's dark and gloomy down here, well below street level. Livingstone turns on the light; a bare bulb swinging on a frayed cord. Everything is dusty, cobwebbed.

> MONDRAGON
> You don't see her offering *her*
> office, do you? I asked her, could

we use part of Records, and she tells
me we don't have enough room for the
files. The union won't let me touch
the lounge.

Livingstone pushes open an old WOODEN DOOR and clicks on another
bare bulb to reveal:

INT. - STORAGE ROOM - DAY
A dank, windowless pit with cinderblock walls, a sagging ceiling, and rotting
furniture and cardboard boxes stacked everywhere.

                    LIVINGSTONE
    This used to be a coal cellar.

                    MONDRAGON
    It's cold, damp, and filthy.
              (sniffs)
    And it smells like something died in
    here.

                    LIVINGSTONE
    Most likely rats.

Mondragon gives the room a long, careful look-over; it remains thoroughly
dismal and disgusting. He NODS.

                    MONDRAGON
    Perfect.

                                              CUT TO:

INT. - EARTHBLOOD CRIB - DAY - TIGHT ON AARON

as he necks with Kim. His lips are all over her, his hand wandering under her
tee-shirt...but we see one EYE open cautiously while he caresses her, checking out the room.

RACK FOCUS
to reveal Snake watching them, cold-eyed, his snake tattoo on his arm and his
shotgun cradled underneath it.

SNAKE
You two are disgusting. Take it in
the back.

AARON
Always listen to the man with the
shotgun.

Aaron draws Kim to her feet. Hot and bothered, she follows him.

CUT TO:

INT. - EARTHBLOOD CRIB - BACK BEDROOM - WITH AARON AND
KIM

Aaron sits on the bare mattress, draws Kim down to him, kisses her. As she
wraps herself around him, he takes out a pair of HANDCUFFS.

KIM
What's that? What are you doing?

He kisses her, snaps a cuff around her hand, kisses her, handcuffs her to the
radiator.

AARON
I don't want you trying to run off.

KIM
(coy, playful)
Why? What are you going to do to me?

He pulls off her shoe. Her eyes are bright, excited.

KIM
Kinky. Hurry up.

Aaron hurries all right. He pulls off her sock, rolls it up, and stuffs it in her
mouth. Her eyes go WIDE. She begins to object, but the sock MUFFLES her
words. Aaron goes to the window, tries to open it. No go; the damn thing is
painted shut. Kim is making more noise now, THUMPING against the bed,
SHOUTING through the gag.

He tries the window again, really puts his back into it. Nothing. Kim starts RATTLING the handcuff against the radiator, loudly. From outside, we hear FOOTSTEPS. Desperate, Aaron draws back, takes a running start, and LEAPS through the window.

EXT. - ALLEY - DAY

Aaron flies out the window in an explosion of shattered glass, hits the pavement hard, rolls. A moment later, Snake appears behind him in the window. Snake brings up the shotgun, FIRES as Aaron RUNS. The blast takes him in the rear—his butt and upper thighs—and blows him off his feet, into a dumpster. Biting back pain, Aaron pulls himself up and staggers off.

CUT TO:

EXT. - STARPORT - DAY

A sleek silver SKIMMER sits on the field, its cockpit open as Lyhanne climbs inside. His angels attend. He takes off a SILVER METAL, hands it to one of his men.

> LYHANNE
> Should I perish, give this honor
> token to the human Bobbi Kelleher of
> the blue cadre.

The other angel BOWS, obedient, and closes the top of the cockpit. He steps back, and the skimmer LIFTS from the ground.

CUT TO:

INT. - STARPORT TUNNEL - DAY

Deep under the lake, a huge cavernous SHAFT has been driven from Starport to Chicago. Twisting LIGHTS and alien GLYPHS play across the walls, while sleek MAGLEV TRAINS slide past silently and big SEMIS and alien TRUCKS roll along a subterranean freeway...along with two POLICE CARS and a long black limo...

CUT TO:

INT. - SQUAD CAR - TUNNEL

Park drives, the Skrit envoy beside him. In back, Morello shares a seat with the munchkin translator.

                      TRANSLATOR
            I assure you, Officer Morello, my
            species knows nothing of this
            'Elvis'.

                                          CUT TO:

EXT. - UPTOWN INTERSECTION - DAY

A big luxury sedan has stopped for a light. Suddenly Aaron Stein WRENCHES OPEN the driver's side door.

                      DRIVER
            Get away, leave me alone, I'll call
            the police...

                      AARON
            I am the police. Give me your
            phone... *now*...

The driver hastily hands Aaron his cellular phone.

                      DRIVER
              (sees the blood)
            My god... you're bleeding.

                      AARON
            Happens every time I get shot.
            (punches 911)
            This is police officer Aaron Stein,
            I have an emergency...

                                            CUT TO:

EXT. - THE ZOO - MOMENTS LATER

as squad cars PEEL out of the lot, sirens SCREAMING and lights   FLASH-
ING. OVER, we hear MONDRAGON'S voice...

> MONDRAGON (O.S.)
> All units, calling all units...

CUT TO:

INT. - SKIMMER (AERIAL) - DAY

Lyhanne's skimmer sails across the choppy waters of Lake Michigan, approaching the lakeshore of Chicago, and

EXT. - LINCOLN PARK - DAY

A pair of Earthblood assassins, BUCKNER and JAX, have taken up   posi-
tion near the lakefront. Buckner wears the fireclaw; Jax carries an Uzi. When
Lyhanne's SKIMMER appears in the distance, Jax POINTS...but before
Buckner can lift his arm, two police cars come SCREECHING up,   dis-
gorging cops with guns.
The skimmer FLASHES BY OVERHEAD as the cops are stripping the
Earthblood men of their weapons.

EXT. - SEEDY HOTEL ROOM - DAY

Greenhair sits by the window, wearing a fireclaw. His partner prowls the room
with a handgun. Greenhair scans the skies.

> GREENHAIR
> Here he comes.

Outside, Lyhanne's skimmer is flying this way. Greenhair lifts his arm; his
partner crosses to the window to watch... and the door BURSTS inward,
kicked off its hinges by Stamm.

> STAMM
> Police! Get 'em up! *Now,*
> buttface...

Greenhair raises his hands over his head; his partner drops the gun. Charlie moves towards them.

> GREENHAIR
> You again…

> CHARLIE
> Me again.

Greenhair makes a fist; ENERGY crackles around his hand.

> CHARLIE
> Don't even think about it.
> (re: Stamm)
> He loves to shoot Nazis.

Greenhair takes a look at Stamm, and opens his fingers.

CUT TO:

INT. - HOTEL CORRIDOR - DAY

The elevator OPENS. Morello and Park step out first. Park checks the corridor. Sgt. Hopper and the angel Jhennar flank the door to the suite. Park NODS to Morello.

> MORELLO
> All clear. Right this way, your
> excellency.

The Skrit trade envoy and his munchkin translator exit the elevator, flanked by Kline and Wachtel.

INT. - PRESIDENTIAL SUITE - DAY

Jhennar opens the door from the inside. Bows low.

> JHENNAR
> Honor.

The Skrit enters with his translator and the Natmo men. Park and Morello stop just inside the door. A truly IMMENSE FLORAL BOUQUET sits on the table. A banner across the flowers shouts *Welcome to Chicago*. Angels stand at guard.

> WACHTEL
> Here we are.

A well-tailored young woman steps forward, smiling.

> TIMBERMAN
> Your excellency, I'm Ms. Timberman,
> from the mayor's office. On behalf
> of the people of Chicago, the mayor
> would like to welcome you to our
> planet and our city.

The Skrit STARES at her outstretched hand; the translator SQUEAKS; the envoy grasps her hand, pale white tendrils writhing wormlike between her fingers. Timberman's smile assumes a frozen rigidity.

> TRANSLATOR
> His excellency hopes that your eggs
> may delight in many joyful
> fertilizations.

No one knows quite what to say to that. As the humans exchange glances, the Skrit releases Timberman's hand and wanders to the sliding glass doors, past the angels and the huge floral display.

> CUT TO:

EXT. - HOTEL PENTHOUSE - HOLLANDER'S POV

as the Skrit moves INTO PLAIN VIEW.

EXT. - ROOFTOP - ON HOLLANDER

Hollander KNEELS behind the parapet, on the roof of a tall building di-rectly across from the hotel. He has a good, unobstructed view down at the penthouse. When he sees the Skrit, he raises his arm, closes his fingers in a fist. ENERGY seethes around his hand.

EXT. - ROOFTOP - ON THE DOOR

Across the roof, the fire door suddenly BANGS OPEN. Rutledge and Manning step out, guns drawn. Manning gives a tilt of his head: you go that way. Rutledge NODS. They split, one going right and one left around the elevator housing.

WITH RUTLEDGE

as she swings around the corner and crosses the roof, sure-footed, quiet, wary. And there he is—Hollander, squatting behind the parapet, intent on the target below, power coiling around his arm. Rutledge snaps down her gun, uses her other hand to brace her wrist. She has him, dead to rights. She SINGS OUT.

> RUTLEDGE
> Police. Don't move!

SLOW-MOTION

as Hollander REACTS, turning his head, eyes narrowing as he sees her. He starts to SWING his arm in her direction, turning the power of the fireclaw her way.

INTERCUT SLOW-MOTION

ECU RUTLEDGE. Surprised by Hollander's move. Frozen.

ECU RUTLEDGE'S GUN. Her finger is poised on the trigger, but it does not move.

CU FIRECLAW. Swinging toward her, alive with energy, coming up in her face.

ECU POLICE REVOLVER. As it FIRES.

RESUME NORMAL SPEED

As the bullet SLAMS Hollander around in the same instant as the fireclaw lets loose with a sizzling PULSE OF ENERGY. The blast GOES WILD.

Hollander stumbles over the parapet and FALLS.

EXT. - TALL BUILDING - DAY

Hollander SCREAMS as he plunges to his death.

ECU POLICE REVOLVER

Barrel SMOKING. We WIDEN and find that it is

MANNING

holding the smoking gun. He holsters it and moves toward his partner. Rutledge is still standing there, locked in a firing position, gun aimed and hand on wrist.

She looks at Manning, her eyes lost and confused.

>   RUTLEDGE
>   I… I… I couldn't…

Her hand begins to TREMBLE. Manning takes the gun gently from her fingers, his voice soothing, gentle.

>   MANNING
>   It's okay. It's over now. It's all
>   over..

She's still SHAKY as he puts a comforting arm around her.

                                                            CUT TO:

INT. - PRESIDENTIAL SUITE - DAY

The trade envoy is standing near the flowers.

>   KLINE
>   If there is anything else his
>   excellency requires…

In b.g., through the sliding glass doors, we glimpse a SKIMMER gliding in silently to touch down in the garden.

WACHTEL
...anything that would makes his
stay on Earth more comfortable...

Lyhanne strides across the roof, opens the doors. The other angels BOW deeply.
Lyhanne returns a half-bow.

LYHANNE
Honor.

The Skrit replies with TWITTERINGS and SQUEAKS.

TRANSLATOR
His excellency praises the bold...
his excellency wishes to... his...

The Skrit lifts both hands in the air, his tendrils whipping from side to side.
The insectiod head snaps from side to side, mandibles working frantically.

TIMBERMAN
What is it? What's wrong?

The Skrit takes an unsteady step, his whole body SHAKING violently. He
falls. Hands and feet beat a frantic tattoo on the floor. Lyhanne reaches the
envoy first, as the Skrit goes STILL.

LYHANNE
He's not breathing.

Then Morello is there, pushing the angel out of the way.

MORELLO
Out of the way. *Move* it.

Morello begins CPR, ripping open the Skrit's velvet jacket and lace shirt,
slamming fists against his chest, breathing into his mandibles. The munchkin
translator does not understand.

TRANSLATOR
What is he doing? Stop him! He's
hurting his excellency.

Lyhanne has been on Earth long enough to understand.

> LYHANNE
> He is trying to save his life.
> (to Morello)
> No. The hearts are lower. In the
> thorax. Crack the chitin. Here.

Lyhanne reaches down into the Skrit's abdomen. We hear a CRACK; he pulls up two hard plates of pale chitin, exposing soft tissue beneath. The translator begins to SHRIEK unintelligibly in Cheseen. Morello redoubles his efforts, pushing, blowing, pushing…but finally he looks at Lyhanne and SHAKES HIS HEAD.

> KLINE
> Why is he stopping?

> WAGHTEL
> He can't stop. Don't let him stop!
> His excellency—

Lyhanne RISES, his face grim.

> LYHANNE
> His excellency is dead.

FADE OUT

END OF ACT IV

ACT V

INT. - ZOO INTERROGATION ROOM - NIGHT

Swoboda and Bobbi Kelleher confront Sgt. Hopper across the table. Lyhanne
PACES, restless and full of fury.

> BOBBI
> I want a list of everyone who's been
> in and out of that room in the past
> twenty-four hours. Maids, delivery
> people, the Natmo suits, angels,
> cops, *everyone,* understand?

Hopper NODS, but Lyhanne whirls, angry.

> LYHANNE
> You *dare* suggest that one of my
> silvers would dishonor his cadre and
> betray his sworn trust?

Bobbi gives it right back to him.

> BOBBI
> Oh, stuff it, Lyhanne. I've got more
> to worry about right now than angel
> honor.

> SWOBODA
> Calm down, both of you. All we want
> to do is make sure nothing is being
> overlooked. Until we have the
> results of the autopsy, we can't even
> be certain a murder was committed.

> LYHANNE
> Then let me assure you, the envoy did
> *not* die of old age.

He whirls and EXITS, cloaks swirling. Bobbi turns to Hopper.

               BOBBI
You can go, sergeant. Have that list
on my desk a.s.a.p.

               SGT. HOPPER
Right, lieutenant.

She EXITS. Swoboda looks at Bobbi gloomily.

               SWOBODA
I'm too old for this. Have you seen
all the reporters out there? They're
hiding in the toilet stalls, I swear.

He takes his Maalox bottle out of a pocket, fumbles out a spoon, measures
out a dose.

               SWOBODA
I'm going to lose my pension. I feel
it in my gut. Less than two years to
go, and no pension. The television
was saying that powercell thing may
have died with the envoy. So now the
pollution is my fault. And the
energy crisis too.
          (swallows Maalox)
A whole world to chose from, and they
had to build Starport next to my
precinct. What do I know from
aliens? I never went to those kinds
of movie. I liked westerns. John
Ford, the Duke, Hopalong Cassidy.
Nobody remembers Hopalong Cassidy any
more.

               BOBBI
I want to put Baker on this.

               SWOBODA
          (surprised)
Baker? The transfer? Isn't he a
little... raw? I thought, someone

more experienced…

> BOBBI
> Baker's a regular Beam-Me-Up-Scotty,
> he knows more about the Harmony than
> the rest of the department combined.

> SWOBODA
> (horrified)
> He's partnered with *Stamm!*

CUT TO:

EXT. - ZOO - NIGHT

Stamm is smoking his cigar on the steps outside the precinct house, as a storm of activity rages all around him. An unruly crowd of REPORTERS and NEWS CREWS is milling around the front doors. Charlie comes rushing up, taking the steps two at a time.

> CHARLIE
> I just heard. My god, what *happened?*
> That room was clean…

> STAMM
> Tell it to Bucky Bug.

The reporters give Charlie a look, but he's a nobody, no one they recognize. Most of them ignore him… but Stacy comes pushing through the others when she spots him.

> STACY
> Charlie, are you on this case?
> What's going on? Was it murder?

> STAMM
> Suicide. We found him with a can of
> Raid clutched in his hand.

> CHARLIE
> Stace, I can't help you on this one,
> you'll have to talk to the lieutenant.

A Mercedes pulls up to the precinct house. From the passenger side emerges
DR. VINCENT BONFLEUR, an Orson Welles of a man, dignified and precise. He wears a white dinner jacket tailored to his vast dimensions, a ruffled
shirt, a paisley cummerbund.

> STAMM
> Hey look, Moby Doc.
> (to Stacy)
> Must be be your lucky night, honey.
> Normally we keep the Mole Man in the
> basement so he won't scare the
> hardened criminals, but we trot him
> out whenever we need somebody to
> grandstand for the press.

Stacy GESTURES to her camera crew. They close in.

> STACY
> Dr. Bonfleur! Are you here to
> perform an autopsy?

The other reporters follow in a feeding frenzy, SHOUTING.

> BLACK REPORTER
> Do the police think it
> was murder?

> TV NEWSMAN
> Will this impact on the
> powercell deal?

> STACY
> Was Earthblood involved
> in the assassination?

> TABLOID REPORTER
> Is there evidence of a
> conspiracy?

Bonfleur raises his hands for quiet.

> BONFLEUR
> Please, gentleman. I cannot possibly
> answer these questions until I've had
> a chance to examine the corpse.

A young woman in a low-cut evening gown gets out of the driver's side of the
Mercedes. Her name is JANE SANDERS. She's in her early twenties, tall and
leggy, with long dark hair, a perfect complexion, and the face of a model.
Together, she and Bonfleur push past the press to the doors.

BONFLEUR
Officers. Is the body inside?

STAMM
On your slab.

BONFLEUR
They tell me the deceased was the
first of his species to visit Earth.

STAMM
Probably the last, too.

Bonfleur has slipped out of his dinner jacket. Wordlessly, he hands Jane the
jacket, takes off his cuff links, begins rolling up the sleeves of his ruffled shirt.

BONFLEUR
Can either of you gentlemen tell me
anything about him?

CHARLIE
The Skrit are insectile, egg layers,
highly technological. Hive
societies, each world ruled by a
single godqueen. The envoys are male
drones. They're one of the oldest
races in the Harmony, species ten.

STAMM
Plus they're real ugly.

BONFLEUR
That shouldn't bother me, I've worked
with you for years.
        (to Charlie)
When you have a spare moment, drop
down to my laboratory. I'd love to
tell you about the autopsies I
performed on Mr. Stamm's last two
partners.
        (beat)
Jane, come.

Bonfleur marches up the stairs, Jane close behind him. Charlie can't resist an admiring glance as she passes.

>   CHARLIE
> Why does the girl look so familiar?

>   STAMM
> *Sports Illustrated* swimsuit issue.
> What she's doing with a known maggot
> like him I'll never figure.
>   (beat; studies Charlie)
> Egg-layers, species ten... what is it
> with you? How do you know all this
> crap?

>   CHARLIE
> Books, tapes... it's been, I don't
> know, sort of a hobby. When I was a
> kid, I used to mainline science
> fiction. Burroughs, Heinlein, Andre
> Norton, all that stuff. So when the
> real thing came along, it was like...
> god, I don't know, how can you
> describe it? It was like Christmas
> morning and the whole universe was
> gift-wrapped under my tree.
>   (beat, musing)
> What were you doing when the Cheseen
> landed?

>   STAMM
> I was watching the damn Super Bowl
> like everybody else, what the hell
> you think? Had five hundred bucks on
> the Panthers, they're up two
> touchdowns, and the stinkin'
> munchkins land on the fifty yard line
> and screw up the game.

He STUBS out his cigar with visible disgust, and we

                                        CUT TO:

INT. - ZOO - WOMEN'S LOCKER ROOM - NIGHT

A small, dingy room with a half-dozen lockers. Manning opens the door a crack, sticks his head in tentatively.

> MANNING
> Lisa? You still in there?
> (no answer)
> It's Ernie...

Still nothing. Concerned, he steps into the room.

ANOTHER ANGLE - ON RUTLEDGE

sitting on the bench in front of her open locker. Lost in some world of her own, she does not even look up. She's half dressed, uniform pants and bra, her uniform shirt balled up in her hands, as if she started to change and couldn't go on.

> MANNING
> You okay?

She doesn't answer, doesn't look at him. Manning sits beside her.

> MANNING
> You been in here an hour. Time to go
> home. What do you say?
> (off her silence)
> Talk to me, partner.

Rutledge bites her lip, shakes her hand. Her hands keep twisting the shirt. She's fighting back tears.

> RUTLEDGE
> I almost got you killed.

> MANNING
> Somebody told me yesterday that
> almost only counts in horseshoes and grenades.

Gently, he touches her, turns her face to his.

             MANNING
Better. You want to talk about it?
You're allowed to cry if you want.
Nobody here but us...

             RUTLEDGE
Cops don't cry.

             MANNING
That's crap. Man, every Christmas,
that *Wonderful Life* movie comes on,
I'm like a damn faucet, can't turn me
off. It's humiliating.

Despite herself, she SMILES.

             MANNING
What happened today... that was
between us. As far as the rest of
them are concerned, we took down a
bad guy, that's all.

             RUTLEDGE
Too bad we know the truth. I froze.
I had him, he was there, all I had to
do was squeeze the trigger, only...

             MANNING
...only you found out that shooting
a man's a little different from
punching holes in those paper
outlines. Think you're the first
rookie ever made that discovery?

             RUTLEDGE
How do you know that next time...

             MANNING
I know.
                (standing up)
Come on, let's get you dressed.

He takes her civilian blouse from her locker. Lisa rises and Manning helps her into it, buttoning the front.

                    RUTLEDGE
          Ernie…thanks.

                    MANNING
          Damn, the last thing I need is you
          quitting on me. I lose you, they
          might partner me with Stamm…

                                                    CUT TO:

INT. - HOSPITAL ROOM - NIGHT

Aaron is on his stomach, an IV feed in his arm, bandages on his rear and upper thighs. He's flirting with his nurse.

                    AARON
          So when do I get to give *you* a sponge
          bath? Patients should get equal
          rights around here—
                    (spots Bobbi, goes to
                    Tweetybird voice)
          Ooh, I twot I twaw a lootwenant.

                    BOBBI
          Hello, Aaron.

                    AARON
                    (Tweetybird voice)
          I did, I *did* twee a lootwenant,
          oooohhh.

                    BOBBI
                    (looking at Aaron)
          You look like hell.

                    AARON
          You ought to see the other guy.

NURSE
I'll leave you two alone.

The Nurse EXITS. Aaron calls out after her.

AARON
Remember what I said...
(to Bobbi)
Nice girl. Gives great sponge.
(beat, serious)
So... you pick up Snake and the rest
of the Fourth Reich?

Bobbi shakes her head. She's not happy about it.

BOBBI
By the time we hit the crib, they
were long gone. All except your
little girlfriend. Her we found
still cuffed to the radiator.
(beat, hard)
Aaron, what the *hell* did you think
you were doing? Damn it, she's
nineteen years old.

AARON
Last time I looked, nineteen was
legal. Little Kim was my ticket into
Earthblood. I gave her what she wanted,
she gave me what I wanted.

BOBBI
So it was all in the line of duty,
right? You must have hated every
minute of it.

AARON
So who says a guy can't enjoy his
work? And no offense, lieutenant,
but you got more serious problems
than my fringe benefits. Snake's
crazier than Hollander.

              BOBBI
We've pulled his teeth. We got all
three of the fireclaws.

              AARON
Odds are, there's plenty more where
they came from.

              BOBBI
Starport...

              AARON
       (Groucho voice)
The girl just said the secret word.
Now the duck will come down and give
her a hundred dollars.
       (beat)
You nailed the source yet?

              BOBBI
The four we've got in custody don't
know jack, and Hollander's very
sincerely dead.

Aaron rolls over, BUZZES for the nurse.

              AARON
Get my clothes, will you, lieutenant?
They're in the closet.

The nurse looks in. Aaron gives her a blinding smile.

              AARON
Be a sweetie and unhook me, would
you? I have a rendezvous with
destiny.

              BOBBI
Are you out of your mind?

              AARON
       (pompous minister voice)

And yeah verily, my child, if they
shooteth you in the butt, the good
book sayeth thou must turneth the
other cheek.

                    BOBBI
Aaron, they *know who you are.*

                    AARON
Well... some of them... let's just
look at that as one of life's little
challenges, shall we?

                                                    CUT TO:

INT. - SNACK ROOM - NIGHT

Stamm and Charlie are drinking vending-machine coffee from cardboard cups
in the snack room.

                    STAMM
Five'll getcha ten it was a woman
offed him. Ever know a skirt didn't
hate roaches?

Jane Sanders enters the room, searching in her purse for quarters, and catches
Stamm's final line.

                    JANE
I'm sure you'll find someone one of
these days, Emile.
                    (beat)
How's the coffee?

                    CHARLIE
Swell, if you like brown water.
She goes to the machine and puts in some change anyway.

                    STAMM
Vinny still up to his elbows in bug
bits?

       JANE
He's still doing the autopsy, yes.

       STAMM
So how'd you ever wind up with the
Mole Man anyway? Guy's got to have
twenty years and two hundred pounds
on you, easy.

       JANE
I was looking for a man whose
favorite tenor wasn't Elmer Fudd.

She gets her coffee and EXITS. Stamin looks at Charlie and SHRUGS.

       STAMM
Leaves me out.

                  CUT TO:

INT. - INTERROGATION ROOM - NIGHT

Vincent Bonfleur is fastening the cuffs of his ruffled dress shirt as he briefs
Swoboda, Baker, and Stamm on his findings.

       SWOBODA
       (incredulous)
Pollen?

       BONFLEUR
Just so. The envoy died of acute
respiratory arrest, brought on by
what one might call an extreme
allergic reaction. I understand
there was quite a formidable floral
bouquet in his suite. There's your
killer. Offhand, I couldn't say if
it was one particular flower or all
of them in combination, but if you
bring me a live Skrit I might be able
to nail it down.

                    STAMM
You telling us the murder weapon was
a bunch of poisoned posies?

                    BONFLEUR
I don't believe poison was involved,
although we might want to test for
pesticide residue. No, it was the
flowers themselves.

                    CHARLIE
Certain species in the Harmony eat
arsenic and mercury as an essential
part of their diet, in quantities
that would kill a human being.

                    BONFLEUR
Precisely. It would seem that our
roses and daffodils were arsenic to
the Skrit.

                    STAMM
So what are we supposed to do now,
book the florist?

Bonfleur glances at his hands with distaste; he has green and yellow goop under
his fingernails.

                    BONFLEIJR
You need to restock my surgical
gloves, the ichor inside his...
well, it was some sort of organ, I'm
sure... in any case, it ate right
through my last pair.
                    (sniffs at nails)
Odd scent. I'd say Stilton cheese,
if I didn't know better.
                    (beat, briskly)
It's entirely possible that this was
just one of those unfortunate

misunderstandings that arise between
two lifeforms largely ignorant of
each other. Perhaps the flowers were
sent in all innocence.
            (beat, shrug)
Or perhaps not.

CUT TO:

EXT. - STARPORT - NIGHT

A light burns high in the tower.

INT. - TOPMAN'S OFFICE - NIGHT

The Topman sits at his desk, hands locked together, dewlaps quivering. Across the desk, Lyhanne faces Dahrys and another angel, a tall male with honor markings that show him *aryanne* of the white cadre. The Skrit's munchkin translator is also present.

                    DAHRYS
        The silver cadre has savored its
        pride of place among the Nhar since
        Earth was opened. Too long, I say.
        Now their softness has brought death
        to the Skrit, disgrace to the
        Harmony, dishonor to all the children
        of the endless night.

                    WHITE ARYANNE
        The white cadre agrees. It is time
        for the silvers to defend their
        contracts in the honor pit.

                    DAHRYS
        They are unworthy of the honor pit.
        Let them leave this world and hide
        their shame beneath stranger stars.

Lyhanne holds his fury back with steely control.

                    LYHANNE
As the *aryanne* of the silver cadre,
the fault is mine alone.

                    DAHRYS
On that, silver and maroon speak with
a single voice.

                    LYHANNE
The silver cadre has no choice but to
yield all security functions until a
new *aryanne* has restored our honor.

                    WHITE ARYANNE
Chay'ash, the white cadre would be
pleased to assume this trust.

                    DAHRYS
The whites are as soft as the
silvers. I claim the security
contract for maroon cadre.

The Topman's dewlaps swell with rage. He SLAMS his palms down.

                    TOPMAN
Hush it! Sufficient I have heard
from all of you. Silver, white,
maroon, you squabble like humans!
You humiliate whole Harmony of
Worlds. Out, *out,* go.

                    WHITE ARRYANNE
Then who is to have security?

                    DANRYS
Do you mean to leave Starport naked
before its enemies?

                    TOPMAN
I *mean* to hear no more Nhar honor
talk tonight. What part of *OUT* do

you not grasp?

Stiffly, anger barely in check, the three angel cadre leaders BOW, turn, walk to the elevator, and EXIT. Topman is left alone with the munchkin translator.

> TOPMAN
> (wearily)
> Here I sit on wild frontier world,
> surrounded by Lohb, Nhar, and
> incompetents. Never yet should
> Harmony come here. Too soon, humans
> were not ready, *are* not ready. Yet
> decision was made, and we are here.
> As humans say, the genie cannot be
> put back in bottle after letting out.

> TRANSLATOR
> What now is this genie?

> TOPMAN
> Gaseous magical species who grant
> wishes and live in lamps.

> TRANSLATOR
> If it comes from lamp, then proper
> amount pressure would restore it to
> original container.

The Topman gives a DEEP SIGH; his dewlaps slowly DEFLATE.

> TOPMAN
> Yes, proper amount pressure.
> (he rises)
> Come. It is time for putting own
> house in order. For letting genie
> out of bottle.

CUT TO:

INT. - MORELLO'S BEDROOM - NIGHT

Very late. The bedroom is dark as Morello comes in, a little unsteady. His wife is asleep. He undresses in the dark, but as he pulls off one shoe, it falls with a THUNK. Ally STIRS.

          ALLY
Louie? What time is it?

          MORELLO
Late.

He takes off the other shoe, sits on the bed.

          ALLY
Are you all right?
    (sniffs)
You've been drinking.

          MORELLO
I stopped for a few after my shift.
    (beat, troubled)
We lost the envoy.
          ALLY
Oh, Louie…

She moves behind him, kneads his shoulders.

          MORELLO
He wasn't really a cockroach. He
looked sorta like Jeff Goldblum. You
know, *The Fly?* Only he wasn't a bad
guy. He said I had great prowess or
something. I gave him CPR… I gave
CPR to a bug…

          ALLY
If you like, I'll light a candle for
him tomorrow…
          MORELLO
A candle… I dunno…
    (turns to her)
Do bug men have souls?

She has no answer for him. As they embrace, and Morello buried his face
between her breasts, we

                                  CUT TO:

INT. - BOBBI'S LOFT - NIGHT

Bobbi Kelleher cradles Lyhanne's head against her, and strokes his long silver-gold hair.

> LYHANNE
> The trust was given to me. The
> dishonor is mine.

> BOBBI
> Lyhanne, there is no dishonor. We
> have a saying here on Earth. You win
> some, you lose some, and some get
> rained out.

Lyhanne breaks free of her comforting arms, angry.

> LYHANNE
> And when it is only a cockroach man
> Who gets "rained out" that does not
> matter so much, nai?

> BOBBI
> What are you so angry about?

> LYHANNE
> You. I am angered by you, by your
> ignorance. You give me your body,
> you take pleasure from me, yet
> otherwise you are no different from
> the rest of your species. I come to
> you in dishonor, I bring you my grief
> and you say it is nothing.
> BOBBI
> I only was only trying to—

> LYHANNE
> —make me one of you.
> (beat, hard)
> Hear and understand this: *I am not
> human.* Nor do I live by human codes.
> I was an *aryanne* of the silver Nhar,

and my shame is real.

Bobbi picks up on an ominous turn of phrase.

> BOBBI
> You... *were*... an *aryanne?*

> LYHANNE
> You truly do not comprehend what has
> happened, do you?
>   (softer, sadly)
> I am done, my hair-like-fire.
> Shamed, tainted, disgraced...your
> English words are not strong enough.
> I am... *broken.*
> (touches her hair)
> I did not come here this night for
> advice or comfort. I came to say
> farewell...

Bobbi is startled, upset.

> BOBBI
> Lyhanne, what do you mean? Where are
> you going? Are you telling me you're
> leaving Earth?

> LYHANNE
> That is... one way to say it.

The words hang there for a moment, as Bobbi slowly realizes that Lyhanne is
talking about death, not emigration.

> BOBBI
> No. *No!* You're not going to... you
> can't... goddamnit, if you think I'm
> going to let you sign up for some
> stupid angel version of hari-kari
> because of something you had no way
> to prevent, you don't... Lyhanne, I
> love you!

> LYHANNE
> I know. Yet it changes nothing. A
> Nhar who has lost his honor is
> already dead.

Lyhanne turns away, climbs up on the open window.

> LYHANNE
> When you think of me, know that
> Lyhanne Nhar-Lys of the silver cadre
> loved you as well, Bobbi Kelleher,
> with a love that passed all wisdom
> and made the stars tremble in the
> sky.

His CLOAKS swirl around him as he departs.

> BOBBI
> Lyhanne, *noooooo!*

But her shout ECHOES empty through the night; he's gone.

CUT TO:

INT. - STARPORT VAULT - NIGHT

A windowless subterranean chamber far below the surface of
Starport. The vault seems carved from smooth, seamless, shining
BLACK METAL. It is *completely empty.*
Then, in the center of the floor, a RIPPLING begins, spreads. Slowly, an ovoid
shape begins to RISE: black, of the same seamless metal as the room, gleaming, an oversized alien COFFIN. When the rippling stops, it fills the center
of the vault where nothing stood before. FOOTSTEPS ring on metal. Topman comes striding across the chamber, followed by the translator, and FOUR
LOHB WORKERS.

> FIRST LOHB
> Chay'ash, this course necessary vital
> important crucial?

> SECOND LOHB
> Species seven-nine dangerful nervous-

making scary.

                    TOPMAN
          I am Chay'ash here. When I wish
          counsel from the Lohb, I will make
          inquiry. Open it.

The coffin is a single piece, seamless. The Lohb move to the four corners.
They touch the metal in certain places with deft fingers. The entire coffin
briefly GLOWS GREEN from within. We hear a CRACK; a line appears.
The Lohb lift the lid and move it aside.

ANGLE INTO THE COFFIN

The coffin is *filled to the brim* with dark liquid, like OIL or BLACK MER-
CURY, rippling, moving.

                    FIRST LOHB
          Last final chance for rethink put-
          back change-mind.

                    TRANSLATOR
          The Lohb speaks truth. Once wakened,
          species seventy-nine will not sleep again.

                    TOPMAN
          Starport must be protected.

The Topman PUTS HIS HAND on the box in a certain place. The coffin
and its liquid contents GLOW RED.

                    SECOND LOHB
          Oh oh.

                    THIRD LOHB
          Too late.

                    FOURTH LOHB
          Done now.

The liquid inside the coffin seems to RIPPLE and FLOW, and now a SHAPE
rises, dripping, from within, *taking shape* from the 'oil' drawing the liquid

around its gleaming metallic skull to clothe itself in a strange organic "flesh." Slowly, it SITS UP in the coffin; shining metal and liquid flesh, all sharp angles and spikes and razored edges, its body shifting and morphing into new—and disturbing—shapes as it moves.

It STANDS, and we glimpse a long whiplike tail, a multiplicity of legs. Its head moves from side to side, searching, as LIGHTS dim and shift behind the visor of its eyes. The creature is huge, at least EIGHT FEET TALL. Call it a *SPIDERHOUND*. It is the scariest thing we have ever seen. It opens its mouth in a feral HISS.

ANGLE ON TOPMAN

He takes a nervous step backward, away from the thing he has woken up. He is beginning to have second thoughts.

> TOPMAN
> What is it saying?

> TRANSLATOR
> It asks who you are, and why you have
> woken it.

> TOPMAN
> Tell it that I am Aysheen Lenaerhi
> Seyseyeen of the Cinnamon Rain Cartel
> of Myessa Nine, the Chay'ash of
> Starport Chicago of planet Earth, and
> that I have woken it to be my
> new security chief and bring dismay to
> enemies of Starport.

The Spiderhound throws back its inhuman head, and HISSES again, a long chilling half shriek and half whistle.

> TRANSLATOR
> It understands you. It is *very*
> pleased.

OFF the Topman's uncertain face, we

FADE OUT

END OF ACT V

ACT VI

CLOSE ON A TARGET

The black silhouette of a human form. A tightly-grouped bunch of holes have been punched through the heart. As we watch, SHOTS rip through the paper, one two three. Then the firing stops. The target comes RUSHING FORWARD INTO CAMERA and we WIDEN to reveal

INT. - SHOOTING RANGE - DAWN

Rutledge is shooting alone, dressed in civilian clothes and EAR PROTECTORS, her gun smoking in her hand. Her face is grim, intent. Several other handguns are in front of her, ready.
The target comes sailing up. Lisa pulls it down and inspects it. The "heart" is a hole you could put your fist through, obliterated by shot after shot, tightly bunched. But one shot went wide, and punched through the silhouette's armpit. Rutledge fingers that hole with obvious distaste as an INTERCOM sounds.

> INTERCOM VOICE
> Nice grouping, Lisa.

> RUTLEDGE
> (fingering hole)
> Not nice enough. Again.

She hangs up a fresh paper target. As the line carries it away from her, she picks up a new pistol. We PUSH IN on her face tightly as she begins to FIRE.

CUT TO:

EXT. - ZOO - DAWN

A SKIMMER settles down in front of the precinct house. This is a flying truck with a bulging, ovoid rear, like a metal scarab.

INT. - ZOO SQUADROOM - DAWN

Park is on the phone, reassuring his purse snatching victim.

PARK
No, I'm sorry, Mrs. Massacola, we
haven't recovered your purse yet.
Yes, I do understand about the
pictures of your grandchildren.
We've been kind of busy lately.

A long line of Lohb workers march through the squadroom, carrying various tools and parts. Sheets of BLACK GLASS large as picture windows, sensor pacs, boxes of unrecognizable tools and unfamiliar parts, instrumental staffs eight feet tall, FLOATING globes.
The cops watch the procession pass by. The Lohb wear Starport coveralls, and they all look alike. One talks to Mondragon.

FIRST LOHB
Seeking office work-space of liaison
commissioner Staako Nihi. Would you
guide direct show?

MONDRAGON
Downstairs... the basement...
actually, the sub-basement...
(beat)
You're not... you wouldn't be... it's
not... you. Is it?

SECOND LOHB
Not me I us. We are the Lohb.

The Lohb head off to the basement.

MORELLO
What did he say, sarge?

MONDRAGON
He's not the guy. He's a larb. The
liaison's a Nihinni.

MORELLO
The liaison's a *ninny?*

                              RUTLEDGE
                    So what the hell's a larb?

                              WEBER
                    Something you don't want to order in
                    a Thai restuarant.

Ernie Manning gets up angrily.

                              MANNING
                    No. Something I don't want working
                    in my precinct.

                                                          CUT TO:

INT. - STARPORT LOADING DOCK - DAWN

Beneath the field, the Cheseen freighter is loaded and preparing for   de-
parture as the Ship's Captain strides down the gangway to confront   Topman
and the late envoy's translator.

                              SHIP'S CAPTAIN
                    What is meaning of this? Why is my
                    ship being detained, for what
                    purpose? I demand—

His voice trails off suddenly as the Spiderhound emerges from subterranean
shadows. It SPEAKS; its voice is ice and metal, whispers and shrieks, a shifting play of light.

                              TRANSLATOR
                    Sir wishes to inspect the cargo
                    shipment. Perhaps the thieves have
                    left some evidence.

Terrified, the Ship's Captain cannot take his eyes off the Spiderhound as he
hastens to consent.

                              SHIP'S CAPTAIN
                    Yes… it is good… I am consenting,
                    yes… whatever it wants, please…

ship is open, go, look, see…

The Spiderhound stares down at the munchkin as if thinking of ripping him in two… then moves up into the freighter, VANISHING in the darkness of the hold. Shaking, the captain turns to Topman.

> SHIP'S CAPTAIN
> (wary, whispering)
> This is madness. Allashais motala
> naha catai lomor Querrion.

> TOPMAN
> Querrion was a thousand years ago,
> Wa'sheen. Much we have learned since
> of species seventy-nine. They live
> now but to serve the Harmony.

> SHIP'S CAPTAIN
> So said species seventy-one, as their
> worlds died screaming.
> (shudders)
> I must be cleared for taking off now-
> this-instant. As soon as inspection
> is finish, I wish to be placing many
> lightyears between me and this
> servant of Harmony.

Turning sharply, the captain strides back aboard his ship.

> TOPMAN
> A foolish frightened man.

> TRANSLATOR
> As you say, Chay'ash.
> (beat)
> My duties are done. I am thinking
> now, best to take passage offworld.

And she hurries up the gangplank after the captain, leaving the Topman standing alone and disquieted.

CUT TO:

INT. - BOBBI'S OFFICE - MORNING

Bobbi is at her desk, red-eyed, on the phone to Starport. Her face is bleak and drawn as she yells at Topman.

> BOBBI
> You *can't* do anything? Or *won't?*
> To hell with his cultural rights, we're
> talking about a man's *life.*
> (listens, angry, hard)
> All right. I hear you. I get the
> message. You don't care.

INTERCUT:

INT. - TOPMAN'S OFFICE - SIMULTANEOUS

The Spiderhound is an ominous presence. From time to time, Topman's eyes flick nervously to his security chief.

> TOPMAN
> That is untrue. Lieutenant, you must
> understand. Respect for the laws,
> customs, religions, and traditions of
> each member species is the
> cornerstone of Harmony precepts. I
> *will* speak to him, yes, I promise you
> that, we will have words, yet I
> cannot interfere.

> BOBBI
> Thanks for nothing.

Topman is nervous enough to miss the bitterness there.

> TOPMAN
> You are welcome.
> (beat)
> Another matter. You have arrested
> four Earthbloods, nai? We have need
> of one.

RESUME BOBBI'S OFFICE

We hear only her side of the conversation again. She is in no mood to make any concessions to Starport.

> BOBBI
> (long beat, listens)
> No. No, I'm not turning any
> prisoners over to Starport Security.
> No, we can't spare just one. That's
> not how it works. They have rights.
> Of course they're guilty, but our law
> says they're innocent until—
> (beat, very angry)
> You're going to sit on your fat
> little butt and let Lyhanne kill
> himself and you have the nerve to
> tell me that *our* cultural parameters
> are stupid?

She SLAMS down the phone.

TNT. - TOPMAN'S OFFICE - DAY

The aftermath of the phone call. Topman folds his hands together. He looks troubled. The Spiderhound moves closer, looms across the desk, HISSES. Topman recoils.

> TOPMAN
> Apologies. Humans will not
> cooperate. So it goes, nai?

Topman forces a weak SMILE, gives a tiny nonchalant SHRUG. The Spiderhound throws back its head and SHRIEKS in sudden rage. Topman falls back out of his chair.

ANGLE ON THE SPIDERHOUND

as it MORPHS, its flesh running, shifting before our eyes, its legs fusing together into a broad thick tail, its arms turning into WINGS. It takes to the air like some terrifying aerial manta-ray.

> TOPMAN
> No! No! I forbid it! You must not!

I am Chay'ash, I speak for Harmony,
you must obey...

The Spiderhound hits window-wall full speed, on the wing, and melts right
through the transparent steel, soaring away over Starport, headed for the distant skyline of Chicago.

> TOPMAN
> (weakly, on the floor)
> No... you live to serve...

                                                        CUT TO:

INT. - ZOO SQUADROOM - DAY

Mondragon is trying to type a report, but the noise from the basement is deaf-
ening: HAMMERING, the WHINE of power saws, the CRACKLE of lightning, and now and again an awful SHRIEK.

> MONDRAGON
> Jesus, Mary, and Joseph! How do they
> expect us to work? What are they
> doing down there?

> PARK
> Maybe the liaison needs special life-
> support. Not everybody likes oxygen.
> Maybe he's a methane breather.

> MORELLO
> Or a fish... I read in the Snoop
> they got some species that are, like,
> these real smart fish... Hey, we
> could ask Buddy.

> MONDRAGON
> Which one is Buddy? I went down
> there a half hour ago. They all look
> the same.

                    WEBER
Captain said the ninny's some kind of
a professor type. Old and wise.
Maybe he's like Yoda…

                    MORELLO
A Yoda fish. Could be.

                    BUSCO
Hey, you better hope he's not a
parakeet, Morello, or your wife will
want to adopt him.

Morello shoots Busco a poisonous look, and we

                                                    CUT TO:

ANOTHER ANGLE - ZOO SQUADROOM - ON STAMM

Working a phone at his desk, trying to ignore the banter all around him and
the CONSTRUCTION NOISES from below. Charlie is doing the same thing
in b.g.

                    STAMM
Yeah. Yeah, okay. Okay. How the
hell do you spell that?

Stamm copies down a long name as Charlie hangs up his own call.

                    STAMM
Uh-huh. Uh-huh. C-A- what? Right.
No, I can't promise you won't be
sued. Hell, sure, get a lawyer. Get
two, what do I care?
          (hangs up)
Buttbrain.

Stamm briefs Charlie on his call as Morello and Park pass, heading out on
patrol.

                    STAMM
          Mr. Greenjeans says some woman
          ordered the flowers over the phone,
          paid with plastic. Told him exactly
          what she wanted. So now we get to go
          have a chat with Missus Massa...
          Massa...

Park HEARS the name and STOPS DEAD.

                    PARK
          Massacola?

                                              CUT TO:

TNT. - BOBBI'S OFFICE - DAY

Bobbi sits alone at her desk, her face in her hands. The sounds of construction still ring from the cellar. Stamm ENTERS with Charlie. She looks up.

                    BOBBI
          Stamm, I'm really not in the mood for
          any of your crap today, you got that?
          What do you want?

The cold, weary anger in her voice shuts Stamm up.

                    CHARLIE
          Lieutenant, I think we may have
          something...

                                              CUT TO:

EXT. - STARPORT BAR - DAY

Lyhanne stands alone in the Starport bar. The Lohb bartender sets a drink
before him; a glowing blue liquour in a slender drink. Lyhanne TOSSES it
down, his face grim. When the glass is empty, he flings it away to shatter. The
Lohb looks on curiously.

Lyhanne holds his blade with both hands, staring at it for a moment. The steel is his honor. His hands tighten around it, and he SNAPS the blade in two. The pieces fall to the floor.

> DAHRYS (O.S.)
> Boldly done, silver.

Lyhanne turns. Dahrys is watching him from across the floor, a taunting smile on her face.

> DAHRYS
> You have some small shards of honor
> left to you, I see. That is good.
> (bowing)
> Shall I stand your second?

> LYHANNE
> I would sooner ask the Lohb.

An insult; her eyes flash with anger.

> DAHRYS
> As you wish. May your death be slow
> and lingering.

Suddenly Topman bursts into the bar, panting, frantic.

> TOPMAN
> Lyhanne! Yes, I am thanking all ten
> thousand gods of Harmony, you are not
> dead. I forbid this palagar, do you
> hear, I am Chay'ash, and I say no,
> you must go on living.

That is a gross insult. In a flash, Lyhanne has grasped the Topman by his medallion and yanked him bodily off the ground. He pulls Topman close, face to face, and his voice is cold with rage.

> LYHANNE
> No man can force Lyhanne Nhar-Lys to
> live without honor.

TOPMAN
Sufficient with the honor! I have
need for you.
        (sees Dahrys)
For both of you, all of you, silver,
white, maroon, all cadres must unite!
Here, now, this instant, I give
Starport Security back to the
children of the endless night. You
have a duty to Starport, to Harmony
of Worlds, to me! Let me down!

Lyhanne drops him. Topman goes sprawling. Dahrys steps close.

DAHRYS
What is it? What are you gibbering
about?

TOPMAN
(reluctantly)
I think... I am fearful...it is
somewhat distinctly possible that
perhaps I have made...
        (long beat)
...a small mistake...

EXT. - STARPORT FIELD - DAY

Even out on the landing field, Lohb and Cheseen turn at the sound of Lyhanne's
voice ROARING from the bar.

LYHANNE (O.S.)
You did what???

                                                    CUT TO:

INT. - ZOO SNACK ROOM - DAY

Half the day shift is gathered around a street map as Stamm and Charlie co-
ordinate plans to catch the Snatcher.

> STAMM
> All right, Captain Flappy has been
> working from Lawrence to Argyll. We
> got a couple of traffic choppers to
> do flyovers, and we think we've
> spotted the batcave. Now all we have
> to do is stake it out and catch the
> little hairball.

The cops are armed for the quest. Several have NETS; Weber is twirling a
LARIAT around his head; Busco has a huge canvas MAIL SACK; Morello
has the world's largest BUTTERFLY NET.

> BUSCO
> So do we shoot him, or not?

> CHARLIE
> Not. He's our only lead to whoever
> ordered the flowers.

> STAMM
> Anyhow we don't usually kill them for
> purse snatching in this precinct.

The conversation stops suddenly when one of the LOHB walks in, looks
around. Everyone stares at him.

> STAMM
> You mind? We're working here.

> LOHB
> Sorry apologies regrets.

The alien starts to back out... but then Morello gets up.

> MORELLO
> Hey. Wait a minute.

The Lohb stops. Morello sticks out his hand.

> MORELLO
> I'm Louie Morello.

The Lohb looks at Morello's outstretched mitt.

> LOHB
> Handshaking bonding friend-making?

Morello NODS. The Lohb takes his hand. They SHAKE.

> MORELLO
> Good. Good. So, you have a name?

> LOHB
> No. I am a bud of the Lohb.

> MORELLO
> Yeah. Glad to meetcha, Buddy.

Charlie crosses the room, his own hand extended. And the ice is broken; other cops nod, offer their hands, slap his back.

> CHARLIE
> Charlie Baker. Not Skip.

> WEBER
> Weber. They call me Nose.

> BUSCO
> Salvatore Busco. How ya doing?

Buddy the Lohb looks pleased but bewildered as hands are thrust at him one after the other. Stamm throws up his hands in disgust.

> STAMM
> Yeah, and I'm freaking Mother
> Theresa. Let me know when Space
> Brothers Week is over here, maybe we
> can go catch some bad guys.

                                                    CUT TO:

EXT. - UPTOWN ROOFTOP - DAY - AERIAL

The Snatcher FLAPS from one roof to another, clutching a PURSE with his feet. He keeps low, close to the buildings, out of sight until he LANDS atop a tenement. High parapets screen it from all sides. Discarded PURSES are scattered across the roof, TORN apart.

The Snatcher RIPS apart his latest find with sharp CLAWS, yanking out wallet, jewelry, and other goodies.

RACK FOCUS

to reveal Morello, behind him, climbing stealthily over the parapet on a ladder, butterfly net in hand.

The Snatcher, oblivious, pulls out a pocket calculator, SNIFFS at it, throws it over his shoulder. It HITS Morello. The noise makes the Snatcher WHIRL. Morello JUMPS, swinging the net, CATCHING him.

> MORELLO
> Gotcha, you flying piece a—

The Snatcher SHRIEKS, and tries to take to the air. Morello is yanked off his feet and DRAGGED across the roof, but he hangs on. The Snatcher RIPS apart the thin butterfly net with his claws.

> MORELLO
> He's getting away! Get him, get him!

Park VAULTS over a parapet, Charlie comes rushing up the ladder, Busco and Weber burst up through a trap, a POLICE CHOPPER comes up out of the alley with Stamm riding shotgun, etc.

It's a disaster. Weber throws his lariat and lassoes Charlie. Charlie's net gets BLOWN back over Morello by the wind from the chopper. PURSES are flying everywhere.

Park LEAPS just as the Snatcher gets airborne. He GRABS a foot, DRAGS the Snatcher down. The Snatcher SLASHES at Park's face with its claws; Park, cat-quick, BLOCKS the blow. The Snatcher BUFFETS Park furiously with both wings, whapwhapwhapwhapwhap.

Busco JUMPS IN and YANKS DOWN his mail sack... just as Park and the Snatcher are twisting around in their struggle. He bags Park instead of the alien. The Snatcher goes FLAPPING AWAY once more. We HEAR the sound of raucous laughter.

ANGLE ON MORELLO

as he pulls himself to his feet, glum and battered.

> MORELLO
> I told you he was smart.

> CHARLIE
> There's no such species. I swear,
> there's no such species.

> STAMM
> (from the chopper)
> Hey, great job down there. Now let
> Park outta the bag.

Morello shoots him the finger.

DISSOLVE TO:

TNT. - BOBBI'S OFFICE - DAY

Bobbi is trying to work, and failing, as Manning ENTERS her office and hands her a piece of paper. She scans it quickly, frowning.

> BOBBI
> Request for a transfer.
> (beat)
> Okay, I'll bite. Why?

> MANNING
> Go look in the basement. They're
> forcing some munchkin cop down our
> throats—

> BOBBI
> He's not a munchkin, he's some
> species I've never heard of, and he's
> not a cop, he's a consultant. Any
> other half-assed rumors I can clear
> up for you?

                    MANNING
    If he's coming, I'm going. That's no
    rumor, that's fact. Yesterday I
    killed a man to save some kind of bug
    from space. That's not why I became
    a cop. Protect and serve, they told
    me when they gave me the gun. I
    figured they meant people. Real
    people. Human beings.

Bobbi has grown noticeably cooler as she listens to him.

                    BOBBI
    Fine. Here.

She SIGNS the transfer, slaps it down in her OUT basket.

                    BOBBI
    Until the transfer comes through,
    stay out of my sight. I don't like
    bigots.

The word hits Manning like a slap. He says nothing, but his eyes burn as he
turns and EXITS.

                                                    CUT TO:

EXT. - ZOO - DAY

The Lohb are filing out, carrying their tools, as Charlie returns with Stamm
and the others, bedraggled and defeated. Mondragon stands on the steps of
the precinct house, staring at the Lohb—so similar to each other.

                    MONDRAGON
    You did not get him.

                    CHARLIE
    Let's not talk about it, okay?

Mondragon sees Morello, whispers a question about the Lohb.

                    MONDRAGON
          Which one is this 'Buddy'?

Morello looks at the alien faces. He's not certain either.

                    MORELLO
          It's him... or maybe... yeah, that
          one, he's... no... oh, hell...
                    (gives up, WHISTLES)
          Hey, Buddy.

ALL of the Lohb turn around, smiling, and answer.

                    VARIOUS LOHB
          Goodbye farewell, Louie Morello.

They resume their exit. Charlie comes up and puts a friendly arm around
Morello's shoulder.

                    CHARLIE
          They're all Buddy.
                    (off their stares)
          There's only one Lohb on Earth.
          These are all buds... bodies that
          it's grown. They all share a single
          consciousness.

We can tell that Morello thinks that's pretty weird, but he takes it in stride.
He SHRUGS.

                    MORELLO
          Must make things interesting for Mrs.
          Lohb.

                                        DISSOLVE TO:

INT. - ZOO MEN'S ROOM - DAY

Manning turns the faucet, splashes water on his face, stares at his face in the
mirror. The door opens behind him. Rutledge ENTERS.

MANNING
Can't you read? This is the men's
room.

RUTLEDGE
Since when are you so modest? Who
was that in women's locker room with
me yesterday?

MANNING
(facing her)
What do you want, Lisa?

RUTLEDGE
I want to help.

MANNING
You can't.

RUTLEDGE
I'm your partner. I'm on your side.

MANNING
Are you?
(beat)
I'm out of here, Rutledge. I put in
for a transfer.

Rutledge is surprised, SHOCKED, but she recovers quickly.

RUTLEDGE
Okay. Fine. Then I'm out of here
too. If you transfer, I transfer.

MANNING
Why? You like it here. You don't
even know why I'm doing this.

Before she can reply, Swoboda ENTERS, already unzipping his fly. He is considerably confused to find Rutledge there.

                    SWOBODA
Uh... sorry.... am I in the wrong...
          (sees Manning)
No... then... what's going on?
                    RUTLEDGE
          (with mock innocence)
We're partners. We do everything
together, captain.

                                                    CUT TO:

EXT. - THE ZOO - AFTERNOON

Swoboda, Mondragon, and a ragtag welcome wagon of the idle and curious
cops. Swoboda glances at his watch. A low-flying SKIMMER appears in the
distance.

                    PARK
Here he comes.

Swoboda takes a GULP of Maalox, slips the bottle back into his pocket,
straightens his tie.

                    SWOBODA
          All right, men. Remember, the
          liaison is a visitor from a distant
          world light-years away, our ways will
          be strange to him.

The skimmer slows and settles to the street. There's a CLICK, a WHIRRING.
The skimmer's door lifts.

ANGLE ON THE PAVEMENT

as a pair of size-twenty CLOVEN HOOVES step out on the street. The calves
above them are covered with dense, thick hair.

          MORELLO (O.S.)
That's a biiiiig ninny.

Slowly we PAN UP... and UP... and UP... revealing a huge, imposing, seemingly-ferocious alien. He stands seven feet tall, with shoulders like an NFL linebacker. Hands large and strong enough to crush coconuts as if they were walnuts, topped with shiny black CLAWS. A chest like a barrel, dark thick hair, a great square jaw, and on his massive head, an imposing set of HORNS. He wears Nihinni garb, and on his chest is a complex alien computer.

RESUME

as the liaison's eyes sweep back and forth across the cops, his jaw tight. Swoboda steps forward, nervous.

> SWOBODA
> Ah. Honor... or, profit to your
> house... whatever. Welcome to the
> Uptown precinct.

And suddenly Staako Nihi's fearsome countenance splits ear-to-ear into the most GIGANTIC GRIN we have ever seen. He spreads those long arms wide, and BELLOWS in DELIGHT.

> STAAKO
> WHO LOVES THE INFANTS?

DISSOLVE TO:

TNT. - ZOO INTERROGATION ROOM - AFTERNOON

Kelleher and Wineglass face Greenhair and his PUBLIC DEFENDER.

> BOBBI
> Let me spell this out in words of one
> syllable. We want Snake and the rest
> of the Earthblood Merry Men. Tell us
> where we can find them, and we'll
> talk about leniency.

> PUBLIC DEFENDER
> My client wants full immunity.

> BOBBI
> When I was eight, I wanted a pony.

                    WINEGLASS
          Can you say, No chance in hell? Now,
          if we're talking a lesser charge…
          if this information's solid…

                    GREENHAIR
          No lesser charge. I walk. Then I
          talk.

Greenhair SMILES; he thinks he holds all the cards. Bobbi looks at him coldly
for a beat.

                    BOBBI
          Boy did you just make a mistake.
          (opens the door)
          Rutledge, Manning.
          (they appear)
          Take this piece of garbage downtown
          to lockup. I'm sick of looking at
          that hair.

                                                        CUT TO:

TNT. - ZOO SUB-BASEMENT - AFTERNOON

Livingstone leads Staako Nihi down the steps to his office. Staako has to
HUNCH, and even then his horns bump into the swinging light bulb.
Swoboda and Mondragon follow. Then come Morello, Park, Baker, Stamm,
and other curious members of the zoo crew.

                    SWOBODA
          (low, to Mondragon)
          I didn't know we had a sub-basement.
          Where did you put him, in the boiler
          room?

Mondragon just CLEARS HIS THROAT and looks awkward.

                    STAAKO
          (loud, happy)
          Earth air! Chicago air! Sweet as…

what is the word you have? Some
sweet thing! Ah, good it is to
breathe petrochemical tang, yes!
Staako SLAPS Livingstone on the back heartily.

          STAAKO
I am excited! I am fulfilled! So
long I study Earth. Stuffing head
with knowledge, that is me! One
hundred six grocheks I study Earth.
Forty-two Earth years! I study Earth
with both my brains, yes! I know
Earth people, Earth culture, all
important things, politics, religion,
history, philosophies, show tunes.
I dream Earth, I eat Earth, I drink
Earth, I defecate Earth, Earth,
Earth. Staako Nihi is Earth Nerd, is
how you say, right?

The tumbledown wooden door has been replaced by smooth metal.
Laser etched under the Harmony blazon, the legend SPECIAL CULTURAL
LIAISON COMMISSIONER FOR INDIGENOUS TABOO ENFORCE-
MENT STAAKO NIHI fills up most of the door.

          LIVINGSTONE
This is your office.

Staako looks at the title on the door.

          STAAKO
No need so formal to call me.

The door has no knob; inset into the metal is a pie of colored glass, each slice
a different shade. Staako's fingers dance over the colors. The door OPENS,
silent and automatic. Lights come up.

INT. - STAAKO'S OFFICE - DAY

A single LOHB waits inside, in an office utterly transformed. It is immaculate, and somehow it seems larger than before. There is a desk, several chairs,

all elegant yet alien twist of metal, stark and strange. The walls seem to be
featureless black glass.

> LOHB
> Hello welcome how are you, special
> liaison commissioner for indigenous
> taboo enforcement. I am detailed
> assigned to assist help work for you.

> STAAKO
> A Lohb! Wonderful! Splendid! Who
> loves the infants?

He PINCHES the Lohb on his cheek.

> SWOBODA
> Why does he keep saying that?

Mondragon and Livingstone gape at the office with astonishment.

> MONDRAGON
> What is this place? How...

Staako looks around the office, beaming and grinning. He passes his hand
across a GLOBE on the desk. The black walls suddenly TRANSFORM into
huge floor-to-ceiling "windows," giving Staako a breathtaking view of New
York City's skyscrapers on all sides. Swoboda looks green. Loud TRAFFIC
NOISE swells up.

> STAAKO
> Here, now we listen to the music of
> the city without modesty taboos, yes.
> Roaring honking meanstreets
> jackhammer music of junkies and
> harlots and wild bongo dogs, bracing
> good, right? How do you say? It is
> as sweet as sweet sucking thing, yes?

> LIVINGSTONE
> (unimpressed)
> It's the wrong city.

LOHB
If special liaison commissioner has
further wants requirements needs—

STAAKO
He does! I require beautiful white
talking bird and large peeking glass
and many boxes of round sweet sucking
things. But later! Now there is
great crime to be broken, nai?

Staako sits, folding himself into the odd chair behind the desk, and crossing
his huge legs. He looks at Swoboda.

SWOBODA
Ah. Yes. In that case, we ought to
leave you to your, ah... partners.

Charlie comes through the press at the office door, followed by Stamm. Charlie
is tentative; Stamm has the look of a man contemplating mass murder. Staako
HOPS UP and roars in delight.

STAAKO
My partners! Yes! Who loves the
infants!

Staako PINCHES Charlie's cheek, reaches for Stamm...

STAMM
Just try it, Horny, and you'll eat
those fingers.

Staako freezes, momentarily taken aback. The Lohb SMILES happily at Stamm
and Charlie; he remembers from before in the snack room.

LOHB
Hello greetings Charlie Baker Not Skip.
Hello greetings Freaking Mother Theresa.

SWOBODA
We'll just... leave you to brief Mr.
Nihi on your purse snatcher.

Swoboda, Mondragon, and the others EXIT.

> STAAKO
> I will be great help to you,
> partners. I know much human crime
> science, yes, very long study.

> CHARLIE
> So you said.
> (thoughtful)
> I was wondering... the Starports only
> opened a year and a half ago, so how
> could you have studied us for...

> STAAKO
> ...one hundred six grocheks? Ah, he
> is clever. I learn humanity from
> humans, I drink the electron truth!

> CHARLIE
> (figuring it out)
> The Harmony monitored all of our
> broadcasts for decades...

> STAAKO
> (wags finger, playful)
> Be careful what you say, little
> humans, Staako is listening!

> CHARLIE
> So... everything you know about
> Earth, you learned from our
> television shows.

Now Stamm gets it too.

> STAMM
> Who loves the infants.
> (groaning)
> Oh, crap on a cracker. It's Kojak
> with horns...

EXT. - ZOO PARKING LOT - AFTERNOON

Rutledge and Manning march Greenhair out to their squad car, HAND-
CUFFED. Manning is sullen, angry. Rutledge notes the skimmer.

> RUTLEDGE
> Looks like Nihi is here.

> MANNING
> Another good reason to go.

He SHOVES Greenhair inside the car.

INT. - SQUAD CAR - CONTINUOUS

Aaron is in the back seat, battered and bandaged, wearing HANDCUFFS.
Greenhair is surprised to see him.

> GREENHAIR
> Loverboy. What the hell— ?

> AARON
> Somebody rolled over. Cops hit us at
> the safe house.

> GREENHAIR
> Snake...?

> AARON
> He got clear. I almost made it
> myself. Almost...
> (beat, grin)
> Horseshoes and hand grenades, right?

> GREENHAIR
> You said it. man.

Rutledge and Manning get into the car. Rutledge, behind the wheel, glances back at the prisoners.

> RUTLEDGE
> Don't you two make a darling couple.

> AARON
> Yeah, maybe we can double date with
> you and the nigger.

Manning turns, GRABS Aaron angrily by the collar, and BOUNCES his head off the window.

> MANNING
> I've heard all I want to hear out of
> you. Got it?

Aaron's got it; he shuts up. Rutledge starts the car.

                                                        CUT TO:

TIGHT ON A HOLOGRAM

of the Snatcher. It floats in the air, transparent, yet alive, twisting its neck, unfolding its wings.

> STAAKO (O.S.)
> This is handbag grabbing malefactor,
> yes then?

TNT. - STAAKO'S OFFICE - DAY

The hologram of the Snatcher is being projected from the device on Staako's chest as his fingers manipulate color-coded controls.

> STAMM
> Close enough for government work.

> CHARLIE
> I've been going nuts trying to ID
> this species. The Harmony literature

doesn't mention this species either.

        LOHB
Is not species, Charlie Baker Not
Skip.

        STAMM
        (astonished)
Get out of here!?

Hurt and confused, the Lohb starts to leave the room. Charlie grabs him by
his arm.

        CHARLIE
No, wait… what do you mean?

        STAAKO
What the Lohb means is, this is no
sentient species, no member of the
Harmony of Worlds. This is, how you
say, domesticated companionship
creature, like Baretta white talking
bird and Columbo lazy flop-ears. And
that is the title of that musical
composition, yes!

Stamm and Charlie look at each other as it sinks in.

        STAMM
Our key witness is a freakin' monkey.

        CHARLIE
We just better hope he's a trained
monkey.
                                        CUT TO:

EXT. - CHICAGO STREET - LATE AFTERNOON

The squad car with Rutledge, Manning and the prisoners moves down a busy
street. A SHADOW falls across the speeding car.

WIDEN to reveal the SPIDERHOUND flying directly over the car. People on the street are staring, pointing.

INT. - SQUAD CAR

Rutledge driving. Puzzled by this sudden shadow. She's noticed the people in the street, Can't figure it.

> RUTLEDGE
> Why is everyone staring at us? Are
> my lights on or something?

There's a sudden THUNK as the Spiderhound lands on the back on the squad car, MORPHING. Rutledge gets a glimpse of something terrifying in the rear-view mirror.

> RUTLEDGE
> Jesus Christ!

She SLAMS on the brakes. The car FISHTAILS…and a huge razor-sharp CLAWED HAND comes RIPPING down through the room of the squad car between Rutledge and Manning. The cops go for their guns.

CUT TO:

EXT. - CHICAGO STREET - ON THE SQUAD CAR

As the Spiderhound, standing astride the trunk, RIPS the roof off of the police car as if it were a sardine can. and FLINGS the jagged metal aside. Spectators SHRIEK and dive for cover.
From inside the car, Rutledge and Manning both OPEN UP, firing point blank rounds up at the Spiderhound.

REVERSE ANGLE - FROM INSIDE THE CAR

The Spiderhound SHRIEKS as it takes hits in the head, chest, face…but the bullets just seem to VANISH into its strangely liquid flesh, leaving behind RIPPLES like a stone thrown into a pool of oil, and doing no more damage.

RUTLEDGE   GREENHAIR
Bullets don't hurt it!   Keep it away! No!
                                                 Shoot it! Kill it!
MANNING   No. No, don't! Don't!
I noticed!

Ignoring the cops, the Spiderhound reaches down for Greenhair and Aaron.
Greenhair shrinks down in the back seat, KICKING frantically, but the alien's
huge hands find him nonetheless.
Rutledge FIRES her final shot...no effect. She THROWS her pistol at the
Spiderhound, only to see it SWALLOWED UP in the alien's liquid flesh. Then
she vaults over the seat, trying to free Aaron from the alien's grasp.
With effortless brutality, the Spiderhound BACKHANDS her savagely, knocking her clear out of the car. Her head SLAMS down on the asphalt with a
sickening CRACK.

MANNING
Lisa!

She's unconscious on the ground. Manning jumps out and bends over her as
the Spiderhound tightens its grasp around Aaron and Greenhair and YANKS
them bodily out of the back of the police unit.
It lifts them high in the air, one in each hand, its fingers around their throats,
and HISSES in sudden triumph.

FADE OUT

END OF ACT VI

ACT VII

EXT. - UPTOWN STREET - LATE AFTERNOON

A BIG WOMAN totters down a cracked and broken sidewalk, bent over, leaning on a cane, carrying a heavy purse. She is gray, stooped, feeble. Her progress is painstakingly slow.
We hear a FLAPPING of wings. The woman looks up, startled, as a SHADOW falls across her. She gives a SHRIEK of alarm…and the Snatcher is on her. He BUFFETS her with his wings.

> BIG WOMAN
> Get away! Get away!

She FLAILS at the Snatcher ineffectually with her cane as he RIPS the purse out of her hand and FLIES OFF.
As the sound of wings DWINDLES, the woman hops up, and JOGS across the street to a parked VAN.

INT. - VAN - ON STAAKO

as he yanks the woman unceremoniously inside. Park is behind the wheel. The woman pulls off her GRAY WIG. It's Morello in a dress.

> MORELLO
> So what are we waiting for?

Park puts the truck in gear. A tracking device clutched in Staako's mitt BEEPS. Morello grabs it away.

> MORELLO
> We got him! Left at the corner.

> STAAKO
> Perhaps soon I may pilot the ground
> vehicle. I have made study of
> driving ways of Starsky and Houtch.

> MORELLO
> Right at the next light…

                                                            CUT TO:

TIGHT ON RUTLEDGE

Still and unconscious on a gurney as a pair of PARAMEDICS load her into a
waiting ambulance. WIDEN to reveal

EXT. - CHICAGO STREET - LATE AFTERNOON

A dozen police units surround the ruins of Rutledge's squad car. A POLICE
PHOTOGRAPHER is snapping pictures of the wreckage while cops grill
witnesses. The background crowd includes Buddy Lohb, looking curiously at
everything. Bobbi stands with a shaken Ernie Manning, differences forgotten. A few feet away, Charlie listens.

                    MANNING
          I never saw anything like it. Damn
          thing had to be eight feet tall,
          hands like razors. It kept changing
          shape. We put a dozen bullets in it,
          and it didn't even blink.

Bobbi spots Charlie, gestures him over. Stamm follows.

                    BOBBI
          I have one officer down with a
          fractured skull and another one
          missing. Any idea what we're dealing
          with here, Baker?

                    CHARLIE
          Not really... no...

Bobbi wants answers; her anger explodes out of her.

                    BOBBI
          I thought you knew this stuff,
          damnit.

Buddy Lohb wanders closer to the conversation.

                    CHARLIE
          Look, I don't know if this means

anything, but there are some funny
omissions in the literature the
Harmony provided for translation.
Certain species are never referred
to. Species one, for instance.
Species thirteen and one hundred
eleven. And all the seventies.

                    STAMM
Sounds like Our Friends From the
Stars have a few psycho cousins in
the attic they don't talk about.

                    BOBBI
And one of them has Aaron.
(looking around)
Where the hell is Nihi?

                    STAMM
There's never a consultant around
when you need one.

                    CHARLIE
We sent him off with Park and Morello
to try and nail the purse snatcher.

                    BOBBI
Wonderful. What rocket scientist
thought that was a good idea? I want
to know what the hell did this!

Buddy Lohb steps closer, timidly.

                    BUDDY LOHB
Pardon forgiveness apologies.
(off their looks)
Attacker ravager marauder was
species seven-nine spiderhound.

                    CHARLIE
Seventy-nine! I told you.

Before Bobbi can question the Lohb further, three SKIMMERS scream by overhead, and circle for a landing.

>   BOBBI
>   If that's Topman, I want his head on
>   a stick.

Bobbi strides over as the skimmer's door opens. Manning is right behind her. Stamm looks over at Charlie.

>   STAMM
>   Sweet girl.

ANGLE ON THE SKIMMER

No one is more surprised than Bobbi when Lyhanne is the first one out of the skimmer. A squad of silver cadre angels is right behind him, steel in hand, gleaming. Bobbi stops dead, suddenly at a loss. She has no words for what she'd feeling.

>   BOBBI
>   Lyhanne… I was afraid…

Lyhanne is all urgency.

>   LYHANNE
>   Where is the spiderhound?

>   STAMM
>   You tell us. You're the doofus with
>   the flying car. Hey, the guy's eight
>   feet tall, with wings, and it's
>   flying around with a nazi in one
>   armpit and a cop in the other.
>   Shouldn't be too tough to spot.

Dahrys and her maroons have gotten out of the second skimmer. She comes up to stand beside Lyhanne.

>   MANNING
>   Damn thing ate bullets like they were

M&Ms. Then it grew wings and flew off.

> BOBBI
> With one of my men. Lyhanne, what
> the hell is it? What's it doing
> here? Why did it attack us?

> LYHANNE
> So many questions. Later there may
> be time for answers. Now we must
> find it, and destroy it.

> CHARLIE
> Can you destroy it?

> LYHANNE
> I do not know, Detective Baker. I do
> not know.

CUT TO:

INT. - ATTIC APARTMENT - SUNSET

A cramped walkup in an Uptown tenement. A tiny, elderly munchkin in a
GREEN EYESHADE sits at a child's desk in an apartment full of undersized
furniture. He's counting MONEY, smoothing out bills as he sorts them by
denomination. WALLETS litter the floor beside him.
We hear a FLAPPING. Snatcher LANDS on the sill of the open window behind his TRAINER. The Trainer turns, smiling.

> TRAINER
> Nosash kahae. Astass, astass...

The Snatcher HOPS DOWN and begins plucking wallets from its pockets
and tossing them on the desk. The Trainer SHUTS the window. He sits down
again, scratching the Snatcher on the head. Snatcher WHISTLES with delight. The Trainer begins to empty wallets.

> TRAINER
> Greenpaper greenpaper. Is too much
> green, hard to tell bigmonies out.
> Oo, plastic squares, good...

He PLUCKS OUT several credit cards, pleased... and suddenly the door behind him CRASHES OPEN as Park kicks it in. The Snatcher SHRIEKS and lifts off, Flapping wildly against the ceiling. The Trainer whirls, dropping the cards, his face ashen.

> PARK
> *Police! Get your hands up.*

Morello is right behind Charlie, still in his dress, gun drawn. Staako strolls in after them, ducking under the transom, eager. The Snatcher is still flapping above them, shrieking.

> MORELLO
> *Down,* or it's going to be open season
> on space ducks in here.

> TRAINER
> (to Snatcher)
> *Astass taehna wai.*

The Snatcher LANDS and folds up his wings, docile.

> STAAKO
> We have got you, malefactor.
> (eager, to the cops)
> Should I do it now? May I?

> MORELLO
> (put upon sigh)
> Alright, alright, go ahead.

Staako draws himself proudly up to his full height.

> STAAKO
> You are beneath arrest. You have the right
> to be hushed. If you are not hushed,
> speaking may be used to hurt you in
> tournament of justice. You have the
> right to justice champion. If you have
> not currency sufficient to buy justice
> champion, you will get charity champion
> from topman of tournament...

As Park KNEELS to CUFF the munchkin, we

CUT TO:

EXT. - SEARS TOWER ROOF - SUNSET

as the Spiderhound FLINGS its human captives roughly down atop the Sears Tower, the tallest building in the world. A ferocious wind buffets them. Both men are dazed, half in shock, still wearing handcuffs. Aaron shake his head groggily... looks up at the alien as it MORPHS back from its winged form to its walking shape...

> AARON
> Ah... nanu nanu?

The Spiderhound leans close and HISSES at him. Aaron stumbles backward. The alien reaches for him. Aaron ducks under its grasp, hits the roof, ROLLS. The alien turns, SHRIEKING in frustration... and sees Greenhair, trying to crawl away. He looks less mobile than Aaron. It moves toward him.

> GREENHAIR
> (gibbering with fear)
> No! Stay away! Take him, take him,
> don't, *dooooon't*...

TIGHT ON GREENHAIR

His words turn into a SCREAM as the Spiderhound thrusts its fingers into Greenhair's face, its liquid flesh MELTING through his skin into his brain. Before our eyes, the human starts to WITHER, shrinking, aging, his green hair going white and falling out, his skin wrinkling, spotting, caving in on itself, and finally beginning to SLOUGH OFF with corruption.

ANGLE ON AARON

He drags himself to his feet, horrified, then springs forward, shouting, HAMMERING at the alien form behind with his cuffed fists.

> AARON
> Stop it! Stop it!

The Spiderhound does not even feel the blows. The feeding continues, until Greenhair's withered corpse disintegrates into dust. Only then does the Spiderhound pull away and slowly turn its glowing eyes on Aaron. He steps backward, right to the edge of the roof. Looks behind him. The fall is diz-zying.

> AARON
> One step, and I jump.

> SPIDERHOUND
> Then you will die.

The alien's voice is CHILLING; deep, hollow, all ice and metal, distorted by its inhuman throat.

> AARON
> You... talk...

> SPIDERHOUND
> We drank his mind. His words are our
> words. His knowledge is our
> knowledge.

The Spiderhound slides closer to Aaron.

> SPIDERHOUND
> You are Earthblood-nazi-defined=Enemy
> of Starport.

> AARON
> You're a *machine*...

The Spiderhound reaches out for him. Aaron is right back at the edge of the roof, madly vamping.

> AARON
> It's okay, I like machines, I got a
> microwave, VCR... R2D2 is a close
> personal... *no!*

It's all over but the screaming when suddenly

LYHANNE'S SKIMMER

shoots into frame, a silver blur, and SLAMS into the Spiderhound from the side, KNOCKING it off the roof.

EXT. - SEARS TOWER - ANGLE DOWN

as the Spiderhound FALLS, tumbling, its SHRIEK of fury blending with the wind.

INT. - SKIMMER - SIMULTANEOUS

Lyhanne is at the controls, Bobbi Kelleher beside him.

> BOBBI
> *Yes!*

> LYHANNE
> (grimly)
> No.

EXT. - SEARS TOWER BASE

A half-dozen police cars screech to a halt. The cops pile out, Charlie and Stamm among them, looking up.

> STAMM
> Head up, boys and girls, here he
> comes. It wasn't the damn skimmers,
> it was beauty killed the beast.

Charlie stares upward. He's not so sure.

> CHARLIE
> Save it, Stamm. This monkey can fly.

ANGLE ON THE SPIDERHOUND

Falling, it begins to MORPHS. Manta wings BLOSSOM beneath its arms, its descent slows, and suddenly it banks and begins to CLIMB.

EXT. - SEARS TOWER ROOF

Lyhanne's skimmer lands beside Aaron. Its door opening slowly. Aaron keeps looking over his shoulder, frantic.

> AARON
> Hurry up, damn it, *hurry up!*

He throws himself inside the skimmer a split second before the Spiderhound comes back over the parapet, reaching for him, HISSING.

TNT. - SKIMMER

Aaron stumbles and falls. Lyhanne SLAMS a palm down on a light panel, and the skimmer door CLOSES on the Spiderhound's reaching arm. There is a savage HOWL of pain, the CRUNCH of tearing metal. Black and silver liquids—oil and mercury—SPRAY across the interior, spattering Bobbi and Aaron, but the door closes.

> CUT TO:

EXT. - SEARS TOWER ROOF

Lyhanne's skimmer lurches into the sky again as the Spiderhound ABSORBS its damaged arm, morphing into another shape. Now more skimmers are closing in; Dahrys and the other angels.

INT. - SKIMMER

Bobbi bends over Aaron as Lyhanne pilots.

> BOBBI
> Are you all right?

> AARON
> Oh, great, swell, never been better.
> *Get me out of these damn handcuffs!*

Bobbi looks at Lyhanne as she uncuffs him.

              BOBBI
That thing is growing a new arm down
there. How do you kill something
like that?

              LYHANNE
It is held together by a life
matrix… an energy net. Your guns
are as useless against it as Nhar steel.

              AARON
The Zoo… we have to get back to the
Zoo.
              (off their looks)
Just *do it!*

Lyhanne BANKS the skimmer around hard. They turn.

              AARON
Is it following us?

              LYHANNE
Yes.

              AARON
Then *fly faster!*

                                          CUT TO:

TNT. - ZOO SQUADROOM - DAY

The squadroom is empty except for Sergeant Mondragon when Morello, Park, and Staako Nihi arrive with the purse snatcher and his trainer. Morello looks around. He is still in a dress.

              MORELLO
This place looks like a morgue.
Where is everybody?

Before Mondragon can answer, Bobbi Kelleher and Aaron Stein comes BURST-ING through the doors. Lyhanne is just behind them. He takes up a position blocking the main entrance, a piece of his SHATTERED STEEL in each hand. Aaron grabs Mondragon and SHAKES HIM.

> AARON
> The *keys*. Give me the the keys to
> the evidence locker!

> MONDRAGON
> What? Why? What's wrong, why are—

Aaron looks back over his shoulder, frantic.

> AARON
> *Now!*

Mondragon fumbles out a set of keys. Aaron snatches them and RUNS off. Behind him, Bobbi Kelleher has drawn her gun.

> STAAKO
> This is very exciting police action.

> MORELLO
> Is someone going to tell us what's
> going on?

In reply, the front doors of the Zoo BLOW INWARD, smashed into splinters, and the Spiderhound stalks through.
Staako Nihi dives under the nearest desk, terrified. The Snatcher SHRIEKS and begins flapping against the ceiling, frantic with fear. Park draws his gun. Morello is only a beat behind him. Swoboda steps out of his office.
The Spiderhound SCREAMS its rage. Bobbi begins to PUMP SHOTS into it, with no effect. Park and Morello start FIRING too. The bullets RIPPLE as they punch through the liquid flesh.
Lyhanne darts forward, SLASHING. The Spiderhound reaches for him, and SLAMS a hand right through a brick wall as the angel dances away from the blow, SLASHING again. And then...

REVERSE ANGLE

as Aaron Stein comes rushing back. Around his right arm is a FIRECLAW, alive with energy. Around his left is another.

AARON
Hey! Ugly! I lied. I *hate* machines.

The Spiderhound turns, as Aaron raises his arms and gives it both fists worth. Twin PLASMA BURSTS fly off Aaron's fists and takes the alien square in the chest, hot as the soul of a star.
The Spiderhound EXPLODES, and we

CUT TO:

EXT. - THE ZOO - NIGHT

as the rest of the Zoo crew arrive. Charlie and Stamm are the first up the steps and through the broken doors.

WITH CHARLIE

as he and Stamm enter the squadroom. Lyhanne is climbing unsteadily to his feet. He all but collapses into Bobbi's arms. No one gives them a second look. Staako emerges timidly from under the desk. Stamm looks over the mess and shakes his head.

STAMM
I tell you one thing, I'm not
cleaning up all this crap.

He LIGHTS A CIGAR, looks over at Charlie.

STAMM
Hey, good work, Skippie.

CHARLIE
I didn't do anything.

STAMM
You're still alive. Most of my
partners croak when things get hairy.

Across the squadroom, Aaron is looking at the fireclaws as energy CRACK-LES from one fist to the other. He turns to Swoboda and asks, ever so sweetly...

                    AARON
                (little boy voice)
            Daddy, can I keep them?

                                    DISSOLVE TO:

INT. - ZOO INTERROGATION ROOM - LATER THAT NIGHT

The Trainer sits huddled pathetically, his head barely coming up over the table.
Charlie and Stamm are running Good Cop/Bad Cop with him. Guess who's
playing who.

                    CHARLIE
            We're trying to be reasonable here.
            Just tell us who you sold the credit
            cards to, we'll plead you out, and
            you can be on the next starship home.
            A profit for both houses, nai?

The Trainer SHAKES HIS HEAD, silent, afraid.

                    STAMM
            Screw it, you can't talk to this guy.
            I'm tired and I want to go to bed.
            Put him in the cage with the rats.

                    CHARLIE
                (shocked)
            Jesus, Stamm, look at the size of
            him. He wouldn't stand a chance.
            You know how big those rats are.

                    STAMM
            Like I give a damn? Put him in the
            cage with the rats, they'll teach him
            a couple tunes.

                    TRAINER
                (soft but stubborn)
            Is no rats. Know Earth laws. Want
            defender of publics.

Stamm leans over the table into the Trainer's face.

> STAMM
> The rats *ate* the defender of publics,
> butthole. How's about I twist your
> head off and crap down your neck?

Charlie PULLS Stamm away from the Trainer roughly.

> CHARLIE
> Lay off, Stamm. The guy wants to
> cooperate, damn it, leave him alone.

The Trainer lifts his head, trembling.

> CHARLIE
> You want to say something?

> TRAINER
> (anxious whisper)
> Want lawyer. Want Acey Ellyu.
> Reporting police brutals, shouting,
> kicking, mean-speaking rat-talking.

> STAMM
> Oooh, now you're *really* honking me
> off, junior.

> TRAINER
> Ethnic-slur-speaking too.

> CHARLIE
> All right. I give up. He's too
> smart for us.
> (to Trainer)
> No lawyer, we're cutting you loose.
> You walk.

> STAMM
> You got to be kidding.

                    CHARLIE
          What, we got twenty, thirty
          misdemeanor purse-snatchings? We
          can't hold him on that.
                    (to Trainer)
          Go on, get up. We're shipping you
          back to Starport. After that you're
          Topman's problem.

Tentatively, with an anxious glance at Stamm, the munchkin eases himself off
the chair. Charlie OPENS the door for him.

                    CHARLIE
          The sergeant will give you back your
          stuff when you sign out. Do you want
          us to ship you the body?

The Trainer stops, looks at him, confused.

                    TRAINER
          Body?

                    CHARLIE
          Your flying monkey. Dangerous
          animal, we'll have to put it to
          sleep. You can have the corpse if
          you want, but we don't pay shipping
          charges to other planets.

                    TRAINER
          No, *no,* not to kill friend.

                    CHARLIE
          I'm sorry, it's the law…

The munchkin falls to his knees, WEEPING and pleading.

                    TRAINER
          Please, no, very good friend, not to
          kill, not to kill.
                    (beat, wildly)
          I talk! I talk, I tell stories, I sing and snitch.

DISSOLVE TO:

TNT. - HOSPITAL ROOM - NIGHT

Rutledge's head is swathed in bandages. Manning is there when she opens her eyes, groggy with painkillers.

                RUTLEDGE
    Ernie...

                MANNING
    Right here. Anyone ever tell you,
    you got a hard head, girl.

She smiles up at him, offers a hand. He clasps it.

                RUTLEDGE
    I didn't freeze.

                MANNING
    I noticed that.
      (beat)
    I brought you something.

He takes out a white slip of paper.

                RUTLEDGE
    Your transfer request...

Manning NODS, then TEARS the paper in two.

                RUTLEDGE
    That's good. Things are just getting
    interesting...

                MANNING
    Yeah. That's what I'm afraid of...

CUT TO:

INT. - TOPMAN'S OFFICE - NIGHT

Topman sits behind his desk, half-drunk on orange chocolate liqueur, clearly shaky. Melantha Moore is with him. Across the desk are Lyhanne, Bobbi,

Captain Swoboda.

> TOPMAN
> The spiderhounds began forty thousand
> years ago, by human measuring. There
> was a civilization... proud, wise...
> the star fathers, they called
> themselves... in the annals of Harmony,
> they are species seventy-one

> BOBBI
> Seventy-*one*? I thought—

> LYHANNE
> Let him finish.

> TOPMAN
> Yes. Finish.
> (drinks)
> Species seventy-one were masters of
> biogenetics, like gods they were.
> Theirs was the power to *create* other
> sentient races. They took simple
> animals and raised them to
> consciousness, fashioned new peoples
> from the raw stuff of life...
> beautiful peoples... the wind
> dancers, the builders, the laughing
> fish, all these were children of the
> star fathers...

> LYHANNE
> And species seventy-two through
> seventy-eight to the Harmony of Worlds.

> TOPMAN
> Then... in a moment of vast mad
> folly... the star fathers made a race of warriors...

His voice trails off. He pours another drink.

BOBBI
The spiderhounds.

LYHANNE
Yes. Synthetic organisms. Living
weapons designed to fight and kill.

TOPMAN
(sadly)
The creators lost control of their
creation. Species seven-nine
spiderhounds destroyed star fathers
and all their children, then turned
on each other. When Harmony found them,
only a few were living still.

SWOBODA
But... if all this happened forty
thousand years ago... what the hell
was one of these monsters doing in
the middle of *my precinct?*

A long beat. The humans—even Melantha—are all looking hard at the
Topman. Finally he SIGHS.

TOPMAN
In every Harmony Starport is one
species seven-nine spiderhound,
reprogrammed for obedience, in deep
stasis, to be wakened only in cases
of dire peril. Is our secret
ultimate weapon, should port come
under some fearsome attack.

BOBBI
Reprogrammed for obedience. Right.
Who does your programming?

MELANTHA
Do I understand correctly—there
are two more of these creatures on
Earth, asleep in Starport Copenhagen

and Starport Singapore?
(Topman nods)
They must be removed or destroyed.
Immediately.

TOPMAN
It will be done.

We hear the WHOOSH of the elevator arriving. Lyhanne rises. The door opens. Stamm and Charlie step out. Park and Morello are right behind them.

BOBBI
What are you doing here?

CHARLIE
We know who killed the Skrit.

CUT TO:

INT. - STARPORT BAR - NIGHT

Surrounded by her cadre, Dahrys Nhar-Kql is LAUGHING when Lyhannel and the others enter.

DAHRYS
Lyhanne. Are you still alive? The
crisis is ended, you had best get on
with your *palagar*.

The maroons LAUGH. And suddenly a half-dozen silver cadre angels emerge to stand beside Lyhanne.

LYHANNE
I think not.

Bobbi Kelleher steps up beside him.

BOBBI
Dahrys Nhar-Kql, I'm placing you
under arrest for the murder of the
Skrit trade envoy.

The cops lift their guns. Four revolvers are aimed at the maroon *aryanne,* but Dahrys is only amused.

> DAHRYS
>
> You presume on my patience, human.
> Put away your coward's weapons before
> I take insult.

> LYHANNE
>
> Every breath you draw is an insult to
> the Harmony, to the honor of your
> cadre, to all the children of the
> endless night.

> DANRYS
>
> Is it you who dares accuse me of this
> killing, silver?

> CHARLIE
>
> The facts accuse you.

> DAHRYS
> (scornful)
>
> Be careful, human. To accuse without
> proof is mortal insult. Speak but
> one lie about me and your blood will
> stain the floor this night.

Dahrys pulls her swordstick from her belt, TWISTS it; from both sides of the grip, the long razor-sharp BLADES telescope out.

> CHARLIE
>
> You used a stolen credit card to
> purchase flowers you knew would kill
> the envoy. We have a signed
> statement from the Cheseen thief who
> sold you the plastic.

> DANRYS
>
> The word of a thief is worth less
> than the dark between the stars.

LYHANNE
The dead *aryanne* of Earthblood
boasted to his blademate that he was
getting weapons from a female angel
with hair black as night.

STAMM
Mentioned something about how she was
screwing him blind, too.

DAHRYS
(blazingly angry)
A *lie!* He was weak and stupid. I
would never taint my body with the
seed of—

Then Dahrys realizes what she has said. The admission hangs there in the air.
Stamm SHRUGS.

STAMM
What the hell. I must've heard that
part wrong.

The other angels of the maroon cadre exchange swift glances.

MAROON NAHR
Lyhanne Nhar-Lys, the cadre knew
nothing of these dealings.

Lyhanne NODS stiffly, acknowledging that. The maroon angels BOW as one,
then STEP BACK, leaving Dahrys alone.

TOPMAN
What mad dream is this, Dahrys Nhar-
Kql? What did maroon Nhar care about
Skrits or powercells?

DANRYS
Less than nothing, Chay'ash. Yet only
the bold win the dance, and our
path to glory was blocked by the
silver cadre. What I did, I did to

smash *him* and his silvers.

She gestures at Lyhanne with her swordstick.

> DAHRYS
> It was a close thing. One more step,
> and the *gaharre* was mine, Lyhanne.

> LYHANNE
> The humans have a saying about
> *almost*, Dahrys.

> DAHRYS
> They would do well to remember it,
> then... because you have *almost*
> bested me... yet not quite.
>   (scornful laugh)
> This is not Earth. This is Starport.
> Where human authority ends.

> MELANTHA
>   (to Bobbi)
> She's right, lieutenant. By treaty,
> you have no jurisdiction. You can't
> touch her.

> LYHANNE
> No... but I can.
>   (beat, holds out hand)
> Jhennar, your steel.

Jhennar hands Lyhanne her blades, BOWS.

> JHENNAR
> I am honored, *aryanne*.

> BOBBI
> Lyhanne, no.

He ignores her, advancing lightly on Dahrys, a sword in each hand. She
SMILES, and turns to meet him.

                    DAHRYS
So we dance the *gaharre* at last,
silver.

                    BOBBI
Topman, *do something.*

                    TOPMAN
The Nhar are the Nhar. You cannot
stop them.

And Lyhanne suddenly LEAPS at Dahrys, his swords FLASHING. Her swordstick is a blur at it SPINS in her hands to meet his attack. Steel RINGS on steel.

BOBBI

Unable to look any longer, Bobbi turns away, and finds herself face to face with Charlie. She buries her head on his shoulder; he puts his arms around her. In that moment, Charlie knows.

OFF that knowledge, and the song of the metal, we

                                        DISSOLVE TO:

EXT. - STARPORT FIELD - NIGHT

Outside the dome. The sun has set, and the stars are coming out. The cops are leaving.

ANGLE ON PARK AND MORELLO

Beside one of the cars. Park hesitates as sees several maroon angels carry Dahrys past on a litter, covered by her cloak. He steps close, throws back the cloth, looks down on her face.

                    PARK
What will you do with the body?

                    MAROON NHAR
She was Nhar, child of the endless

night. There we begin and there we
end, in the cold of space.

Park can't help himself. He reaches out, touches her cheek, the beautiful empty
face.

>   PARK
>   She was beautiful. I watched her
>   dance...

>   MAROON NHAR
>   Dahrys will dance forever now, in the
>   dark between the stars.

Park NODS. The maroon covers her face; they carry her away. Park climbs
into the car.

ANGLE ON LYHANNE

Beside a skimmer, Lyhanne stands with Bobbi.

>   LYHANNE
>   I would have given you her eyes, had
>   you wished it.

>   BOBBI
>   Earth girls generally prefer candy or
>   flowers.

>   LYHANNE
>   Anyone can pick a flower. The eyes
>   of an enemy are a rarer gift.

>   BOBBI
>   The only gift I want is you.

Then Bobbi leans over and KISSES him, right on the lips, there in front of
Topman, angels, cops, god, and everyone.

ANGLE ON STAMM AND CHARLIE

Standing together near the Topman as Bobbi kisses Lyhanne. Stamm is so startled that his cigar falls right out of his mouth.

> STAMM
> Will you get a load of that?

> TOPMAN
> I am starting to think that species
> three hundred two Nhar and three
> hundred fifteen human look alike
> after all.

Topman gives a SNORT and stomps off. Lyhanne and Bobbi are still kissing. Stamm turns to Charlie.

> STAMM
> I *knew* these alien sons of bitches
> were here to steal our women.

Charlie doesn't answer. He doesn't even seem to hear. He is looking up, into the star-filled sky. He SMILES.

> CHARLIE
> Look... there's a ship coming down...

Stamm cranes around to look, and we PAN UP to find

A STARSHIP

Bright with light, impossibly beautiful, falling from the zenith as it comes in for a landing.

FADE OUT

THE END

Introduction Blood of the Dragon

In the summer of 1991, there was a lull in my career as a screenwriter. *Beauty and the Beast* had run its course, and I was not interested in taking another staff job. I had written my first feature screenplay and my first pilot by then, but neither one had gone anywhere, and there were no new assignments in the offing.

I welcomed the break, if truth be told, since I saw it as a chance to return to prose. I had not had a novel published since *The Armageddon Rag*, back in 1983. *Wild Cards* mosaics and short story collections, yes; a novel, no. It was past time.

My first impulse was to dust off *Black and White and Red All Over* and continue where I'd left off six years earlier. That would have been the most logical thing to do, certainly. But *Black and White* had gone cold on me, and I had forgotten so much that I would have to redo much of my period research before I could hope to resume.

There were other options. I might have done a *Wild Cards* novel starring the Great and Powerful Turtle, or perhaps a sequel to *Fevre Dream*. Baen Books wanted a follow-up to *Tuf Voyaging*...

Instead I began work on a novel I called *Avalon*.

Despite its title, *Avalon* was not an Arthurian novel. The planet Avalon had been a part of the background of much of my SF, one of the centers of interstellar civilization in the "future history" that provided the background for my first novel, *Dying of the Light*, and many of my best known stories. *Avalon* was to be the story of three students from very different cultures thrown together at Avalon's Academy of Human Knowledge, the opening act of a much larger story that I thought of as an SF *War and Peace*.

I had written thirty pages when a new scene came to me, as vivid as a waking dream. That happens sometimes. It's enough to make a fellow believe in muses. The only problem was, my muse didn't seem to be working on the same novel that I was. The scene she whispered in my ear was from a high fantasy novel, not Avalon. All the same, I knew I had to get it down on paper. One thing I have learned in this business: never mess with the muse.

Thirty pages of *Avalon* went into the file cabinet beside the yellowing manuscript of *Black and White and Red All Over*, while I wrote what turned out to be the first chapter of *A Game of Thrones*. Not the prologue, but the first chapter proper, wherein Bran Stark sees a man beheaded and six direwolf pups are found in the summer snows. By the time I finished, I knew what the second chapter was, and who these characters were, and some of what must follow. I kept writing, and told myself that I would not make the mistake I had made back in 1985; this time I would finish the book before I showed a word of it to anyone.

The lull in my Hollywood career proved to be much shorter than anticipated, however. I had only been at work on the fantasy for six weeks when my energetic Hollywood agent Jodi Levine called to report that she'd gotten pitch meetings for me at NBC, ABC, and Fox. I had been telling Jodi that "The Skin Trade" would make a good TV series, and asking her to get me in to pitch it, and now she had... though I hated the timing. Still, I put the fantasy novel aside and flew out to LA to sell my "Skin Trade" pilot.

It's always best to have more than one string to your bow when fiddling for networks, so I noodled with some other notions on the plane, and found myself remembering the first line of "The Lonely Songs of Laren Dorr," a short fantasy story I'd written in the mid 70s. There is a girl who goes between the worlds...

By the time I got off the plane at LAX, that line from "Laren Dorr" had mutated into a concept for an alternate world series I called *Doors* (later *Doorways*, to avoid confusion with Jim Morrison's band and Oliver Stone's recent film about them). It was *Doors* that ABC, NBC, and Fox all got excited about, not "The Skin Trade," and it was Doors that ABC soon cut me a deal on.

I spent the rest of 1991 writing *Doors*, most of 1992 filming and editing it, and the first part of 1993 supervising the six backup scripts ABC ordered after screening our rough cut. There were other pilots too, *The Survivors* for CBS in 1992, *Starport* for Fox in 1993-1994, and a couple of feature screenplays for Disney. I was still editing and writing *Wild Cards* books as well.

Through all this furious activity, *A Game of Thrones* sat moldering in a file cabinet, beside *Avalon* and *Black and White and Read All Over*. From time to time, I would leaf through the pages I'd done in 1991, and realize how much I wanted to return to the Seven Kingdoms. I found myself thinking about the characters, even when I was up to my neck in some other story. Tyrion in particular haunted me. I had to make the time to tell this story, I realized.

In 1993, in the midst of half a dozen other projects, I resumed work on *A Game of Thrones*.

The story came back to life at once. I had been away from the book for two years, but it felt more like two days. By then I realized that *A Game of Thrones* was only the first part of the story I wanted to tell, the epic I called *A Song of Ice and Fire*. Back then, I thought it was a trilogy...

Before long I was nearing 200 pages, close to the length of *Black and White* when I put it aside... and with so much else on my plate, I knew I would soon have to put this one aside as well. I was writing the fantasy on my own time, for myself, but my various Hollywood projects were all under contract, with built in deadlines and producers, studios, and networks to see that I met them. That meant that whenever I ran short of time, I had to give priority to my film and television work. At this rate, it could be ten years before I managed to complete *A Game of Thrones.*

If I ever did...

The thought that I might lose *A Song of Ice and Fire* as I had lost *Black and White* terrified me. I could not let that happen, but there was only one sure way to prevent it. I had to get the book under contract. That was not a choice I made gleefully, after what had happened the last time, but finally I let the dice fly and sent the first 180 pages of *A Game of Thrones* to my agents with a brief two-page letter sketching out the next two books of the trilogy. Once again I was going to try to sell an unfinished novel.

This time, the dice came up sevens. A dozen publishers responded to the pages, and there was spirited bidding on both sides of the Atlantic. *A Song of Ice and Fire* was soon under contract. I would have that fifth novel after all, it seemed... and a sixth, and a seventh, and more after that. Even so, I could not resume work on *A Game of Thrones* immediately, since I still had several screenplays to finish and deliver. But now at least the books were in the queue.

A Game of Thrones was released in 1996, and *A Clash of Kings* in 1998. *A Storm of Swords* has just been published as I write, but even before I delivered the first book I had come to realize that I would need more than three. *A Song of Ice and Fire* will run to six volumes, I now believe, so I have only reached the halfway point. I'll be spending my next five or six years in the Seven Kingdoms.

As for the novella that follows...

"Blood of the Dragon" exists in large part thanks to the insane persistence of Gardner Dozois, the editor of *Asimov's Science Fiction.* All through my years in Hollywood, Gardner kept badgering me for stories, and I kept telling him that I had no time to write any. But Gargy kept at me, and when I told him I was almost done with a fantasy novel, he said, "Send me an excerpt that can stand on its own. We'll publish it as a novella."

It was Gardner's nagging that made me realize that there was a novella hidden within the larger novel: the tale of a princess in exile, and how a frightened child becomes a queen.

Asimov's published "Blood of the Dragon" in its July, 1996 issue. The next year it made the final Nebula, and at LoneStarCon, the 1997 Worldcon in San Antonio, it won the Hugo for Best Novella.

All Gardner got was a lousy tee-shirt.

Blood of the Dragon

I

Her brother held the gown up for her inspection. "This is beauty. Touch it. Go on. Caress the fabric."

Dany touched it. The cloth was so smooth that it seemed to run through her fingers like water. She could not remember ever wearing anything so soft. It frightened her. She pulled her hand away. "Is it really mine?"

"A gift from the Magister Illyrio," Viserys said, smiling. Her brother was in a high mood tonight. "The color will bring out the violet in your eyes. And you shall have gold as well, and jewels of all sorts. Illyrio has promised. Tonight you must look like a princess."

A princess, Dany thought. She had forgotten what that was like. Perhaps she had never really known. "Why does he give us so much?" she asked. "What does he want from us?" For almost a month, they had lived in the magister's house, eating his food, pampered by his servants. Dany was twelve, old enough to know that such gifts seldom come without their price, here in the free city of Pentos.

"Illyrio is no fool," Viserys said. He was twenty, a gaunt young man with nervous hands and a feverish look in his pale lilac eyes. "The Magister knows that I will not forget my friends when I come into my throne."

Dany said nothing. Magister Illyrio was a dealer in spices, gemstones, dragonbone, and other, less savory things. He had friends in all of the Nine Free Cities, it was said, and even beyond, in Vaes Dothrak and the fabled lands beside the Jade Sea. It was also said that he'd never had a friend he wouldn't cheerfully sell for the right price. Dany listened to the talk in the streets, and she heard these things, but she knew better than to question her brother when he wove his webs of dream. His anger was a terrible thing when roused. Viserys called it *waking the dragon*.

Her brother hung the gown beside the door. "Illyrio will send the slaves to bathe you. Be sure you wash off the stink of the stables. Khal Drogo has a thousand horses; tonight he looks for a different sort of mount." He studied her critically. "You still slouch. Straighten yourself." He pushed back her shoulders with his hands. "Let them see that you have a woman's shape now." His fingers brushed lightly over her budding breasts and tightened on a nipple. "You will not fail me tonight. If you do, it will go hard for you. You don't want to wake the dragon, do you?" His fingers twisted her, the pinch cruelly hard through the rough fabric of her tunic. "*Do you?*" he repeated.

"No," Dany said meekly.

Her brother smiled. "Good." He touched her hair, almost with affection. "When they write the history of my reign, sweet sister, they will say that it began tonight."

When he was gone, Dany went to her window and looked out wistfully on the waters of the bay. The square brick towers of Pentos were black silhouettes outlined against the setting sun. Dany could hear the singing of the red priests as they lit their night-fires, and the shouts of ragged children playing games beyond the walls of the estate. For a moment, she wished she could be out there with them, barefoot and breathless and dressed in tatters, with no past and no future and no feast to attend at Khal Drogo's manse.

Somewhere beyond the sunset, across the narrow sea, lay a land of green hills and flowered plains and great rushing rivers, where towers of dark stone rose amidst magnificent blue-gray mountains, and armored knights rode to battle beneath the banners of their lords. The Dothraki called that land *Rhaesh Andahli*, the land of the Andals. In the Free Cities, they talked of Westeros and the Sunset Kingdoms. Her brother had a simpler name. "Our land," he called it. The words were like a prayer with him. If he said them enough, the gods were sure to hear. "Ours by blood right, taken from us by treachery, but ours still, ours forever. You do not steal from the dragon, oh no. The dragon remembers."

And perhaps the dragon did remember, but Dany could not. She had never seen this land her brother said was theirs, this realm beyond the narrow sea. These places he talked of, Casterly Rock and the Eyrie, Highgarden and the Vale of Arryn, Dorne and the Isle of Faces, they were just words to her. Viserys had been a boy of eight when they fled King's Landing to escape the advancing armies of the Usurper, but Daenerys had been only a quickening in their mother's womb.

Yet sometimes Dany would picture the way it had been, so often had her brother told her the stories. The midnight flight to Dragonstone, moonlight shimmering on the ship's black sails. Her brother Rhaegar battling the Usurper in the bloody waters of the Trident, and dying for the woman he loved. The sack of King's Landing by the ones Viserys called the Usurper's dogs, the lords Lannister and Stark. Princess Elia of Dorne pleading for mercy as Rhaegar's heir was ripped from her breast and murdered before her eyes. The polished skulls of the last dragons staring down sightlessly from the walls of the throne room as the Kingslayer opened father's throat with a golden sword.

She had been born on Dragonstone nine moons after their flight, while a raging summer storm threatened to rip the island fastness apart. They said that storm was terrible. The Targaryen fleet was smashed while it lay at anchor, and huge stone blocks were ripped from the parapets and sent hurtling into the wild waters of the narrow sea. Her mother had died birthing her, and for that her brother Viserys had never forgiven her.

She did not remember Dragonstone either. They had run again, just before the Usurper's brother set sail with his new-built fleet. By then only Dragonstone itself, the ancient seat of their House, had remained of the Seven Kingdoms that had once been theirs. It would not remain for long. The garrison had been prepared to sell them to the Usurper, but one night Ser Willem Darry and four loyal men had broken into the nursery and stolen them both, along with her wet nurse, and set sail under cover of darkness for the safety of the Braavosian coast.

She remembered Ser Willem dimly, a great gray bear of a man, half-blind, roaring and bellowing orders from his sickbed. The servants had lived in terror of him, but he had always been kind to Dany. He called her "Little Princess" and sometimes "My Lady," and his hands were soft as old leather. He never left his bed, though, and the smell of sickness clung to him day and night, a hot, moist, sickly-sweet odor. That was when they had lived in Tyrosh, in the big house with the red door. Dany had slept in her own room there, with a lemon tree outside her window. After Ser Willem had died, the servants had stolen what little money they had left, and soon after they had been put out of the big house. Dany had cried when the red door closed behind them forever.

They had wandered since then, from Tyrosh to Myr, from Myr to Braavos, and on to Qohor and Volantis and Lys, never staying long in any one place. Her brother would not allow it. The Usurper's hired knives were close behind them, he insisted, though Dany had never seen one.

At first the magisters and archons and merchant princes were pleased to welcome the last Targaryens to their homes and tables, but as the years passed and the Usurper continued to sit upon the Iron Throne, doors closed and their lives grew meaner. Years past they had been forced to sell their last few treasures, and now even the coin they had gotten from mother's crown had gone. In the alleys and wine sinks of Pentos, they called her brother "the beggar king." Dany did not want to know what they called her.

"We will have it all back someday, sweet sister," he would promise her. Sometimes his hands shook when he talked about it. "The jewels and the silks, Dragonstone and King's Landing, the Iron Throne and the Seven Kingdoms, all they have taken from us, we will have it back." Viserys lived for that day. All that Daenerys wanted back was the big house with the red door, the lemon tree outside her window, the childhood she had never known.

There came a soft knock on her door. "Come," Dany said, turning away from the window. Illyrio's servants entered, bowed, and set about their business. They were slaves, a gift from one of the magister's many Dothraki friends.

There was no slavery in the free city of Pentos. Nonetheless, they were slaves. The old woman, small and gray as a mouse, never said a word, but the girl made up for it. She was Illyrio's favorite, a fair-haired, blue-eyed wench of sixteen who chattered constantly as she worked.

They filled her bath with hot water brought up from the kitchen and scented it with fragrant oils. The girl pulled the rough cotton tunic over Dany's head, and helped her into the tub. The water was scalding hot, but Daenerys did not flinch or cry out. She liked the heat. It made her feel clean. Besides, her brother had often told her that it was never too hot for a Targaryen. "Ours is the house of the dragon," he would say. "The fire is in our blood."

The old woman washed her long, silver-pale hair and gently combed out the snags, all in silence. The girl scrubbed her back and her feet and told her how lucky she was. "Drogo is so rich that even his slaves wear golden collars. A hundred thousand men ride in his *khalasar*, and his palace in Vaes Dothrak has two hundred rooms and doors of solid silver." There was more like that, so much more, what a handsome man the *khal* was, so tall and fierce, fearless in battle, the best rider ever to mount a horse, a demon archer. Daenerys said nothing. She had always assumed that she would marry Viserys, when she came of age. For centuries the Targaryens had wed brother to sister, since Aegon the Conquerer had taken his sister Rhaenys to bride. The line must be kept pure, Viserys had told her a thousand times; theirs was the kingsblood, the golden blood of old Valyria, the blood of the dragon. Dragons did not mate with the beasts of the field, and Targaryens did mingle their blood with that of lesser men. Yet now Viserys schemed to sell her to a stranger, a barbarian.

When she was clean, the slaves helped her from the water and toweled her dry. The girl brushed her hair until it shone like molten silver, while the old woman anointed her with the spiceflower perfume of the Dothraki plains, a dab on each wrist, behind her ears, on the tips of her breasts, and one last one, cool on her lips, down there between her legs. They dressed her in the wisps that Magister Illyrio had sent up, and then the gown, a deep plum silk to bring out the violet in her eyes. The girl slid the gilded sandals onto her feet, while the old woman fixed the tiara in her hair, and the ruby-studded bracelets around each wrist, and last of all the collar, a heavy golden torc emblazoned with Dothraki glyphs.

"Now you look all a princess," the girl said breathlessly when they were done. Dany glanced at her image in the silvered looking glass that Magister Illyrio had so thoughtfully provided. *A princess*, she thought, but she remembered what the girl had said, how Khal Drogo was so rich even his slaves wore golden collars. She felt a sudden chill, and gooseflesh pimpled the flesh of her bare arms.

Her brother was waiting in the cool of the entry hall, seated on the edge of the pool, his hand trailing in the water. He rose when she appeared and looked her over critically. "Stand there," he told her. "Turn around. Yes. Good. You look…"

"Regal," Magister Illyrio said, stepping through an archway. He moved with surprising delicacy for such a massive man. Beneath loose garments of flame-colored silk, rolls of fat jiggled as he walked. Gemstones glittered on every finger, and his man had oiled his forked yellow beard until it shone like real gold. "May the Lord of Light shower you with blessings on this most fortunate day, Princess Daenerys," the magister said as he took her hand. He bowed his head, showing a thin glimpse of crooked yellow teeth through the gold of his beard. "She is a vision, Your Grace, a vision," he told her brother. "Drogo will be enraptured."

"She's too skinny," Viserys said. His hair, the same silver-blonde as hers, had been pulled back tightly behind his head and fastened with a dragonbone brooch.

It was a severe look that emphasized the hard, gaunt lines of his face. He rested his hand on the hilt of the sword that Illyrio had lent him, and said, "Are you sure that Khal Drogo likes his women this young?"

"She has had her blood. She is old enough for the khal," Illyrio told him, not for the first time. "Look at her. That silver-gold hair, those purple eyes… she is the blood of old Valyria, no doubt, no doubt… and highborn, daughter of the old king, sister to the new, she cannot fail to entrance our Drogo." When he released her hand, Daenerys found herself trembling.

"I suppose," her brother said doubtfully. "The savages have queer tastes. Boys, horses, sheep…"

"Best not suggest this to Khal Drogo," Illyrio said.

Anger flashed in her brother's lilac eyes. "Do you take me for a fool?"

The magister bowed slightly. "I take you for a king. Kings lack the caution of common men. My apologies if I have given offense." He turned away and clapped his hands for his bearers.

The streets of Pentos were pitch dark when they set out in Illyrio's elaborately carved palanquin. A torchbearer went ahead to light their way, while a dozen strong men hoisted the poles to their shoulders. It was warm and close inside behind the curtains. Dany could smell the stench of Illyrio's pallid flesh through his heavy perfumes.

Her brother, sprawled out on his pillows beside her, never noticed. His mind was away across the narrow sea. "We won't need his whole *khalasar*," Viserys said. His fingers toyed with the hilt of his borrowed blade, though Dany knew he had never used a sword in earnest. "Ten thousand, that would be enough, I could sweep the Seven Kingdoms with ten thousand Dothraki screamers. The realm will rise for its rightful king. Tyrell, Redwyne, Darry, Greyjoy, they have no more love for the Usurper than I do. The Dornishmen burn to avenge Elia and her children. And the smallfolk will be with us. They cry out for their king." He looked at Illyrio anxiously. "They do, don't they?"

"They are your people, and they love you well," Magister Illyrio said amiably. "In holdfasts all across the realm, men lift secret toasts to your health while women sew dragon banners and hide them against the day of your return from across the water." He gave a massive shrug. "Or so my agents tell me."

Dany had no agents, no way of knowing what anyone was doing or thinking across the narrow sea, but she mistrusted Illyrio's sweet words as she mistrusted everything about Illyrio. Her brother was nodding eagerly, however. "I shall kill the Usurper myself," he promised, who had never killed anyone, "as he killed my brother Rhaegar. Ani Lannister too, the Kingslayer, for what he did to my father."

"That would be most fitting," Magister Illyrio said. Dany saw the smallest hint of a smile playing around his full lips, but her brother did not notice. Nodding, he pushed back a curtain and stared off into the night, and Dany knew he was fighting the Battle of the Trident once again.

The nine-towered manse of Khal Drogo sat beside the waters of the bay, its high brick walls overgrown with pale ivy. It had been given to the *khal* by the magisters of Pentos, Illyrio told them. The Free Cities were always generous with the horselords. "It is not that we fear these barbarians," Illyrio would explain with a smile. "The Lord of Light would hold our city walls against a million Dothraki, or so the red priests promise… yet why take chances, when their friendship comes so cheap?"

Their palanquin was stopped at the gate, the curtains pulled roughly back by one of Drogo's houseguard. He had the copper skin and dark almond eyes of a Dothraki, but his face was hairless and he wore the spiked bronze cap of the Unsullied. He looked them over coldly. Magister Illyrio growled something to him in the rough Dothraki tongue; the guardsman replied in the same voice, and waved them through the gates.

Dany noticed that her brother's hand was clenched tightly around the hilt of his borrowed sword. He looked almost as frightened as she felt.

"Insolent eunuch," Viserys muttered as the palanquin lurched up toward the manse.

Magister Illyria's words were honey. "Many important men will be at the feast tonight. Such men have enemies. The *khal* must protect his guests, yourself chief among them, Your Grace. No doubt the Usurper would pay well for your head."

"Oh, yes," Viserys said darkly. "He has tried, Illyrio, I promise you that. His hired knives follow us everywhere. I am the last dragon, and he will not sleep easy while I live."

The palanquin slowed and stopped. The curtains were thrown back, and a slave offered a hand to help Daenerys out. His collar, she noted, was ordinary bronze. Her brother followed, one hand still clenched hard around his sword hilt. It took two strong men to get Magister Illyrio back on his feet.

Inside the manse, the air was heavy with the scent of spices, pinchfire and sweet lemon and cinnamon. They were escorted across the entry hall, where a mosaic of colored glass depicted the Doom of Valyria. Beneath an arch of twining stone leaves, a eunuch sang their coming. "Viserys of the House Targaryen, the Third of his Name," he called in a high, sweet voice, "King of the Andals and the Rhoynar and the First Men, Lord of the Seven Kingdoms and Protector of the Realm. His sister Daenerys Stormborn, Princess of Dragonstone. His honorable host Illyrio Mopatis, Magister of the Free City of Pentos."

They stepped past the eunuch into a pillared courtyard overgrown in pale ivy. Moonlight painted the leaves in shades of bone and silver as the guests drifted among them. Most were Dothraki horselords, big men with red-brown skin, their drooping moustachios bound in bronze rings, their black hair oiled and braided and hung with bells. Yet among them moved bravos and sellswords from Pentos and Myr and Tyrosh, a red priest even fatter than Illyrio, hairy men from the Port of Ibben and lords from the Summer Isles with skin as black as ebony. Daenerys looked at them all in wonder... and realized, with a sudden start of fear, that she was the only woman there.

Illyrio whispered to them. "Those three are Drogo's bloodriders, there," he said. "By the pillar is Khal Moro, with his son Rhogoro. The man with the green beard is brother to the Archon of Tyrosh, and the man behind him is Ser Jorah Mormont." The last name caught Daenerys. "A knight?"

"No less." Illyrio smiled through his beard. "Anointed with the seven oils by the High Septon himself."

"What is he doing here?" she blurted.

"The Usurper wanted his head," Illyrio told them. "Some trifling affront. He sold some poachers to a Tyroshi slaver instead of giving them to the Night's Watch. Absurd law. A man should be able to do as he likes with his own chattel."

"I shall wish to speak with Ser Jorah before the night is done," her brother said. Dany found herself looking at the knight curiously. He was an older man, past forty and balding, but still strong and fit. Instead of silks and cottons, he wore wool and leather. His tunic was a dark green, embroidered with the likeness of a black bear standing on two legs.

She was still looking at this strange man from the homeland she had never known when Magister Illyrio placed a moist hand on her bare shoulder. "Over there, sweet princess," he whispered, "there is the *khal* himself."

Dany wanted to run and hide, but her brother was looking at her, and if she displeased him she knew she would wake the dragon. Anxiously, she turned and looked at the man Viserys hoped would ask to wed her before the night was done.

The slave girl had not been far wrong, she thought. Khal Drogo was a head taller than the tallest man in the room, yet somehow light on his feet, as graceful as the panther in Illyrio's menagerie. He was younger than she'd thought, no more than thirty. His skin was the color of polished copper, his moustachios thick and fierce and bound with silver rings.

"I must go and make my submissions," Magister Illyrio said. "Wait here. I shall bring him to you."

Her brother took her by the arm as Illyrio waddled over to the *khal*, his fingers squeezing so hard that they hurt. "Do you see his braid, sweet sister?"

Drogo's braid was black as midnight and heavy with scented oil, hung with a dozen tiny silver bells that rang softly as he moved. It swung well past his belt, below even his buttocks, the end of it brushing against the back of his thighs.

"You see how long it is?" Viserys said. "When Dothraki are defeated in combat, they cut off their braids in disgrace, so the world will know their shame. Khal Drogo has never lost a fight. He is Aegon the Dragonlord come again, and you will be his queen."

Dany looked at Khal Drogo. His face was hard and cruel, his eyes as cold and dark as onyx. Her brother hurt her sometimes, when she woke the dragon, but he did not frighten her the way this man frightened her. "I don't want to be his queen," she heard herself say in a small, thin voice. "Please, *please* Viserys, I don't want to, I want to go home."

"*Home?*" He kept his voice low, but she could hear the fury in his tone. "How are we to go home, sweet sister? They took our home from us!" He drew her into the shadows, out of sight, his fingers digging into her skin. "*How are we to go home?*" he repeated, meaning King's Landing, and Dragonstone, and all the realm they had lost.

Dany had only meant their rooms in Illyrio's estate, no true home surely, but all they had, but her brother did not want to hear that. There was no home there for him. Even the big house with the red door had not been home for him. His fingers dug hard into her arm, demanding an answer. "I don't know..." she said at last, her voice breaking. Tears welled in her eyes.

"I do," he said sharply. "We go home with an army, sweet sister. With Khal Drogo's army, that is how we go home. And if you must wed him and bed him for that, you will." He smiled at her. "I'd let his whole *khalasar* fuck you if need be, sweet sister, all forty thousand men, and their horses too if that was what it took to get my army. Be grateful it is only Drogo. In time you may even learn to like him. Now dry your eyes. Illyrio is bringing him over, and he will *not* see you crying."

Dany turned and saw that it was true. Magister Illyria, all smiles and bows, was escorting Khal Drogo over to where they stood. She brushed away unfallen tears with the back of her hand.

"Smile," Viserys whispered nervously, his hand falling to the hilt of his sword. "And stand up straight. Let him see that you have breasts. Gods know, you have little enough as is."

Daenerys smiled, and stood up straight.

II

"The Dothraki sea," Ser Jorah Mormont said to her, as he reined to a halt beside her on the top of the ridge.

Beneath them, the plain stretched out immense and empty, a vast flat expanse that reached to the distant horizon and beyond. It *was* a sea, Dany thought. Past here, there were no hills, no mountains, no trees nor cities nor roads, only the endless grasses, the tall blades rippling like waves when the winds blew. "It's so green," she said.

"Here and now," Ser Jorah agreed. "You ought to see it when it blooms, all dark red flowers from horizon to horizon, like a sea of blood. Come the dry season, and the world turns the color of old bronze. And this is only *hranna*, child. There are a hundred kinds of grass out there, grasses as yellow as lemon and as dark as indigo, blue grasses and orange grasses and grasses like rainbows. Down in the Shadow Lands beyond Asshai, they say there are oceans of ghost grass, taller than a man on horseback with stalks as pale as milkglass. It murders all other grass and glows in the dark with the spirits of the damned. The Dothraki claim that someday ghost grass will cover the entire world, and then all life will end."

That thought gave Dany the shivers. "I don't want to talk about that now," she said. "It's so beautiful here, I don't want to think about everything dying."

"As you will, *khaleesi*," Ser Jorah said respectfully. The exile had offered her brother his sword the night Dany had been sold to Kahl Drogo; Viserys had accepted eagerly.

She heard the sound of voices and turned to look behind her. She and Mormont had outdistanced the rest of their party, and now the others were climbing the ridge below them. Her handmaid Irri and the young archers of her khas were fluid as centaurs, but Viserys still struggled with the short stirrups and the flat saddle. Her brother was miserable out here. He ought never have come. Magister Illyrio had urged him to wait in Pentos, had offered him the hospitality of his manse, but Viserys would have none of it. He would stay with Drogo until the debt had been paid, until he had the crown he had been promised. "And if he tries to cheat me, he will learn to his sorrow what it means to wake the dragon," Viserys had vowed, laying a hand on his borrowed sword. Illyrio had blinked at that and wished him good fortune.

Dany realized that she did not want to listen to any of her brother's complaints right now. The day was too perfect. The sky was a deep blue, and high above them a hunting hawk circled. The grass sea swayed and sighed with each breath of wind, the air was warm on her face, and Dany felt at peace. She would not let Viserys spoil it.

"Wait here," Dany told Ser Jorah. "Tell them all to stay. Tell them I command it."

The knight smiled. Ser Jorah was not a handsome man. He had a neck and shoulders like a bull, and coarse black hair covered his arms and chest so thickly that there was none left for his head. Yet his smiles gave Dany comfort. "You are learning to talk like a queen, Daenerys."

"Not a queen," said Dany. "A *khaleesi.*" She wheeled her horse about and galloped down the ridge alone.

The descent was steep and rocky, but Dany rode fearlessly, and the joy and the danger of it was a song in her heart. All her life Viserys had told her she was a princess, but not until she rode her silver had Daenerys Targaryen ever felt like one.

At first it had not come easy. The *khalasar* had broken camp the morning after her wedding, moving east toward Vaes Dothrak, and by the third day Dany thought she was going to die. Saddle sores opened on her bottom, hideous and bloody. Her thighs were chafed raw, her hands blistered from the reins, the muscles of her legs and back so wracked with pain that she could scarcely sit. By the time dusk fell, her handmaids would need to help her down from her mount.

Even the nights brought no relief. Khal Drogo ignored her when they rode, even as he had ignored her during their wedding, and spent his evenings drinking with his warriors and bloodriders, racing his prize horses, watching women dance and men die. Dany had no place in these parts of his life. She was left to sup alone, or with Ser Jorah and her brother, and afterwards to cry herself to sleep. Yet every night, some time before the dawn, Drogo would come to her tent, and wake her in the dark, to ride her as relentlessly as he rode his stallion. He always took her from behind, Dothraki fashion, for which Dany was grateful; that way her lord husband could not see the tears that wet her face, and she could use her pillow to muffle her cries of pain. When he was done, he would close his eyes and begin to snore softly and Dany would lie beside him, her body bruised and sore, hurting too much for sleep.

Day followed day, and night followed night, until Dany knew she could not endure a moment longer. She would kill herself rather than go on, she decided one night...

Yet when she slept that night, she dreamt the dragon dream again. Viserys was not in it this time. There was only her and the dragon. Its scales were black as night, wet and slick with blood. *Her* blood, Dany sensed. Its eyes were pools of molten gold, and when it opened its mouth, the flame came roaring out in a hot jet. She could hear it singing to her. She opened her arms and walked into the fire, embraced it, let it swallow her whole, let it cleanse her and temper her and scour her clean. She could feel her flesh sear and blacken and slough away, could feel her blood boil and turn to steam, and yet there was no pain. She felt strong and new and fierce.

And the next day, strangely, she did not seem to hurt quite so much. It was as if the gods had heard her and taken pity. Even her handmaids noticed the change. "*Khaleesi*," Jhiqui said, "what is wrong? Are you sick?"

"I was," she answered, standing over the dragon's eggs that Illyrio had given her when she wed. She touched one, the largest of the three, running her hand lightly over the shell. *Black and scarlet*, she thought, *like the dragon in my dream*. The stone felt strangely warm beneath her fingers...or was she still dreaming? She pulled her hand back nervously.

From that hour onward, each day was easier than the one before it. Her legs grew stronger; her blisters burst and her hands grew callus; her soft thighs toughened, supple as leather.

The *khal* had commanded the handmaid Irri to teach Dany to ride in the Dothraki fashion, but it was the filly who was her real teacher. The horse seemed to know her moods, as if they shared a single mind. With every passing day, Dany felt surer in her seat. The Dothraki were a hard and unsentimental people, and it was not their custom to name their animals, so Dany thought of her only as the silver. She had never loved anything so much.

As the riding became less an ordeal, Dany began to notice the beauties of the land around her. She rode at the head of the *khalasar* with Drogo and his bloodriders, so she came to each country fresh and unspoiled. Behind them the great horde might tear the earth and muddy the rivers and send up clouds of choking dust, but the fields ahead of them were always green and verdant.

They crossed the rolling hills of Norvos, past terraced farms and small villages where the townsfolk watched anxiously from atop white stucco walls. They forded three wide placid rivers and a fourth that was swift and narrow and treacherous, camped beside a high blue waterfall, skirted the tumbled ruins of a vast dead city where ghosts were said to moan amongst blackened marble columns. They raced down Valyrian roads a thousand years old and straight as a Dothraki arrow. For half a moon, they rode through the Forest of Qohor, where the leaves made a golden canopy high above them, and the trunks of the trees were as wide as city gates. There were great elk in that wood, and spotted tigers, and lemurs with silver fur and huge purple eyes, but all fled before the approach of the *khalasar* and Dany got no glimpse of them.

By then her agony was a fading memory. She still ached after a long day's riding, yet somehow the pain had a sweetness to it now, and each morning she came willingly to her saddle, eager to know what wonders waited for her in the lands ahead. She began to find pleasure even in her nights, and if she still cried out when Drogo took her, it was not always in pain.

At the bottom of the ridge, the grasses rose around her, tall and supple. Dany slowed to a trot and rode out onto the plain, losing herself in the green, blessedly alone. In the *khalasar* she was never alone. Khal Drogo came to her only after the sun went down, but her handmaids fed her and bathed her and slept by the door of her tent, Drogo's bloodriders and the men of her *khas* were never far, and her brother was an unwelcome shadow, day and night. Dany could hear him on the top of the ridge, his voice shrill with anger as he shouted at Ser Jorah. She rode on, submerging herself deeper in the Dothraki sea.

The green swallowed her up. The air was rich with the scents of earth and grass, mixed with the smell of horseflesh and Dany's sweat and the oil in her hair. Dothraki smells. They seemed to belong here. Dany breathed it all in, laughing. She had a sudden urge to feel the ground beneath her, to curl her toes in that thick black soil. Swinging down from her saddle, she let the silver graze while she pulled off her high boots.

Viserys came upon her as sudden as a summer storm, his horse rearing beneath him as he reined up too hard. "*You dare!*" he screamed at her. "You give commands to *me? To me?*" He vaulted off the horse, stumbling as he landed. His face was flushed as he struggled back to his feet. He grabbed her, shook her. "Have you forgotten who you are? Look at you. *Look at you!*"

Dany did not need to look. She was barefoot, with oiled hair, wearing Dothraki riding leathers and a painted vest given her as a bride gift. She looked as though she belonged here. Viserys was soiled and stained in city silks and ringmail.

He was still screaming. "You do *not* command the dragon. Do you understand? I am the Lord of the Seven Kingdoms, I will not hear orders from some horselord's slut, do you hear me?" His hand went under her vest, his fingers digging painfully into her breast. "*Do you hear me?*"

Dany shoved him away, hard.

Viserys stared at her, his lilac eyes incredulous. She had never defied him. Never fought back. Rage twisted his features. He would hurt her now, and badly, she knew that.

Crack.

The whip made a sound like thunder. The coil took Viserys around the throat and yanked him backwards. He went sprawling in the grass, stunned and choking. The Dothraki riders hooted at him as he struggled to free himself. The one with the whip, young Jhogo, rasped a question. Dany did not understand his words, but by then Irri was there, and Ser Jorah, and the rest of her *khas*. "Jhogo asks if you would have him dead, *khaleesi*," Irri said.

"No," Dany replied. "No."

Jhogo understood that. One of the others barked out a comment, and the Dothraki laughed. Irri told her, "Quaro thinks you should take an ear to teach him respect."

Her brother was on his knees, his fingers digging under the leather coils, crying incoherently, struggling for breath. The whip was tight around his windpipe.

"Tell them I do not wish him harmed," Dany said.

Irri repeated her words in Dothraki. Jhogo gave a pull on the whip, yanking Viserys around like a puppet on a string. He went sprawling again, freed from the leather embrace, a thin line of blood under his chin where the whip had cut deep.

"I warned him what would happen, my lady," Ser Jorah Mormont said. "I told him to stay on the ridge, as you commanded."

"I know you did," Dany replied, watching Viserys. He lay on the ground, sucking in air noisily, red-faced and sobbing. He was a pitiful thing. He had always been a pitiful thing. Why had she never seen that before? There was a hollow place inside her where her fear had been.

"Take his horse," Dany commanded Ser Jorah. Viserys gaped at her. He could not believe what he was hearing; nor could Dany quite believe what she was saying. Yet the words came. "Let my brother walk behind us back to the *khalasar*." Among the Dothraki, the man who does not ride was no man at all, the lowest of the low, without honor or pride. "Let everyone see him as he is."

"*No!*" Viserys screamed. He turned to Ser Jorah, pleading in the Common Tongue with words the horsemen would not understand. "Hit her, Mormont. Hurt her. Your king commands it. Kill these Dothraki dogs and teach her."

The exile knight looked from Dany to her brother; she barefoot, with dirt between her toes and oil in her hair, he with his silks and steel. Dany could see the decision on his face. "He shall walk, *khaleesi*," he said. He took her brother's horse in hand while Dany remounted her silver.

Viserys gaped at him, and sat down in the dirt. He kept his silence, but he would not move, and his eyes were full of poison as they rode away. Soon he was lost in the tall grass. When they could not see him any more, Dany grew afraid. "Will he find his way back?" she asked Ser Jorah as they rode.

"Even a man as blind as your brother should be able to follow our trail," he replied.

"He is proud. He may be too shamed to come back."

Jorah laughed. "Where else should he go? If he cannot find the *khalasar*, the *khalasar* will most surely find him. It is hard to drown in the Dothraki sea, child."

Dany saw the truth of that. The *khalasar* was like a city on the march, but it did not march blindly. Always scouts ranged far ahead on the main column, alert for any sign of game or prey or enemies, while outriders guarded their flanks. They missed nothing, not here, in this land, the place where they had come from. These plains were a part of them…and of her, now.

"I hit him," she said, wonder in her voice. Now that it was over, it seemed like some strange dream that she had dreamed. "Ser Jorah, do you think…he'll be so angry when he gets back…" She shivered. "I woke the dragon, didn't I?"

Ser Jorah snorted. "Can you wake the dead, girl? Your brother Rhaegar was the last dragon, and he died on the Trident. Viserys is less than the shadow of a snake."

His blunt words startled her. It seemed as though all the things she had always believed were suddenly called into question. "You… you swore him your sword…"

"That I did, girl," Ser Jorah said. "And if your brother is the shadow of a snake, what does that make his servants?" His voice was bitter.

"He is still the true king. He is…"

Jorah pulled up his horse and looked at her. "Truth now. Would you want to see Viserys sit a throne?"

Dany thought about that. "He would not be a very good king, would he?"

"There have been worse… but not many." The knight gave his heels to his mount and started off again.

Dany rode close beside him. "Still," she said, "the common people are waiting for him. Magister Illyrio says they are sewing dragon banners and praying for Viserys to return from across the narrow sea to free them."

"The common people pray for rain, healthy children, and a summer that never ends," Ser Jorah told her. "It is no matter to them if the high lords play their game of thrones, so long as they are left in peace." He gave a shrug. "They never are."

Dany rode along quietly for a time, working his words like a puzzle box. It went against everything that Viserys had ever told her to think that the people could care so little whether a true king or usurper reigned over them. Yet the more she thought on Jorah's words, the more they rang of truth.

"What do *you* pray for, Ser Jorah?" she asked him.

"Home," he said. His voice was thick with longing.

"I pray for home too," she told him, believing it.

Ser Jorah laughed. "Look around you then, *khalessi.*"

But it was not the plains Dany saw then. It was King's Landing and the great Red Keep that Aegon the Conquerer had built. It was Dragonstone where she had been born. In her mind's eye they burned with a thousand lights, a fire blazing in every window. In her mind's eye, all the doors were red.

"My brother will never take back the Seven Kingdoms," Dany said. She had known that for a long time, she realized. She had known it all her life. Only she had never let herself say the words, even in a whisper, but now she said them for Jorah Mormont and all the world to hear.

Ser Jorah gave her a measuring look. "You think not."

"He could not lead an army even if my lord husband gave him one," Dany said. "He has no coin and the only knight who follows him reviles him as less than a snake. The Dothraki make mock of his weakness. He will never take us home."

"Wise child." The knight smiled.

"I am no child," she told him fiercely. Her heels pressed into the sides of her mount, rousing the silver to a gallop. Faster and faster she raced, leaving Jorah and Irri and the others far behind, the warm wind in her hair and the setting sun red on her face. By the time she reached the *khalasar,* it was dusk, and Dany knew what she must do.

The slaves had erected her tent by the shore of a spring-fed pool. She could hear rough voices from the woven grass palace on the hill. Soon there would be laughter, when the men of her *khas* told the story of what had happened in the grasses today. By the time Viserys came limping back among them, every man, woman, and child in the camp would know him for a walker. There were no secrets in the *khalasar.*

Dany gave the silver over to the slaves for grooming and entered her tent. It was cool and dim beneath the silk. As she let the door flap close behind her, Dany saw a finger of dusty red light reached out to touch her dragon's eggs across the tent. For an instant a thousand droplets of scarlet flame swam before her eyes.

The day she had wed Khal Drogo outside the walls of Pentos, the bride gifts had been heaped up about Daenerys in great piles, more gifts than she could possibly imagine, more gifts than she could want or use. The Dothraki had given her slippers and jewels and silver rings for her hair, medallion belts and painted vests and soft furs, sandsilks and jars of scent, needles and feathers and tiny bottles of purple glass, and a gown made from the skin of a thousand mice ("Most lucky," Magister Illyrio told her). Her brother had presented her with her three handmaids, Ser Jorah an old book full of songs and stories from the Seven Kingdoms. The *khal's* bloodriders offered her the traditional three weapons, whip and *arakh* and bow, and Khal. Drogo himself had led forth her filly, grey as the winter sea, with a mane like silver smoke.

Yet it had been Illyrio's gift that made her gasp, the three huge eggs in their bed of velvet. "Dragon's eggs, from the Shadow Lands beyond Asshai," he had told her. "The eons have turned them to stone, yet still they burn bright with beauty."

Stone, she told herself. *They are only stone, even Illyrio said so, the dragons are all dead.* Yet they were most beautiful things Dany had ever seen, each different from the others, patterned in such rich colors that at first she had thought they were crusted with jewels, and so large it took both of her hands to hold one. The shells were covered with tiny scales that shimmered like polished metal in the light. One egg was a deep green with burnished bronze flecks that seemed to come and go as you turned it. Another was pale cream streaked with gold. The last was black, as black as a midnight sea, yet alive with scarlet ripples and swirls.

She put her palm against the black egg, fingers spread gently across the curve of the shell. The stone was warm. Almost hot. "The sun," Dany whispered. "The sun warmed them as they rode."

She commanded her handmaids to prepare her a bath. Doreah built a fire outside the tent, while Irri and Jhiqui fetched the big copper tub—another bride gift—from the packhorses, and carried water from the pool. When the bath was steaming, Irri helped her into it, and climbed in after her to scrub her back and wash the dust from her hair. Dany's skin was flushed and pink when she climbed from the tub. Jhiqui laid her down to oil her body and scrap the dirt from her pores, and afterwards Irri sprinkled her with spiceflower and cinnamon while Doreah brushed her hair until it shone like spun silver. And all the while, Dany watched the dragon's eggs.

"Fetch the brazier," she said when she was clean and sweet-smelling. "I want a fire."

"*Khaleesi,* it is so hot," Jhiqui said.

"Do as I tell you. The brazier."

When the coals were lit, Dany sent her handmaids away and told them she was not to be disturbed. *This is madness,* she told herself, *it will only crack and burn, and it's so beautiful, Viserys will call me a fool if I ruin it,* and yet, and yet...

Gently, she lifted the black-and-scarlet egg from its chest, and carried it with both hands to the fire. She pushed it down amongst the burning coals, and sat crosslegged on her mat to watch. The black scales seem to glow as they drank it the heat. After a moment's thought, she got the other two eggs, and placed them on the brazier as well.

She watched until the coals had turned to ashes. Drifting sparks floated up and out her smokehole. Heat shimmered in waves around the dragon's eggs. And that was all.

Your brother Rhaegar was the last dragon, Ser Jorah had said. Dany gazed at her eggs sadly. What had she expected? A thousand thousand years ago they had been alive, but now they were only pretty rocks. They could not make a dragon. A dragon was air and fire. Living flesh, not dead stone.

Her supper was a simple meal of fruit and cheese and fry bread, with a jug of honeyed wine to wash it down. "Doreah, stay and eat with me," Dany commanded when she sent her other handmaids away. Jhiqui and Irri were Dothraki girls, of an age with her, taken as slaves when Drogo destroyed their father's *khalasar*. They knew only Dothraki ways. Doreah was older, almost twenty. Magister Illyrio had found her in a pleasure house in Lys. Her hair was the color of honey, and she had eyes like the summer sky.

She lowered those eyes when they were alone. "You honor me, *khaleesi*," she said, but it was no honor, only service. Long after the moon had risen, they sat together, talking.

That night, when Khal Drogo came, Dany was waiting for him. He stood in the door of her tent and looked at her with surprise. She rose slowly and opened her sleeping silks and let them fall to the ground. "This night we must go outside, my lord," she told him, for the Dothraki believed that all things of importance in a man's life must be done beneath the open sky.

Khal Drogo followed her out into the moonlight, the bells in his hair tinkling softly. A few yards from her tent was a bed of soft grass, and it was there that Dany drew him down. When he tried to turn her over, she put a hand on his chest. "No," she said. "This night I would look on your face."

There is no privacy in the heart of the *khalasar*. Dany felt the eyes on her as she undressed him, heard the soft voices as she did the things that Doreah had told her to do. It was nothing to her. Was she not *khaleesi?* His were the only eyes that mattered, and when she mounted him she saw something there that she had never seen before. She rode him as fiercely as ever she had ridden her silver, and when the moment of his pleasure came, Khal Drogo called out her name.

They were on the far side of the Dothraki sea when Jhiqui brushed the soft swell of Dany's stomach with her fingers and said, "*Khaleesi,* you are with child."

"I know," Dany told her.

It was her thirteenth name day.

III

The Horse Gate of Vaes Dothrak was made of two gigantic bronze stallions, rearing, their hooves meeting a hundred feet above the roadway to form a pointed arch.

Dany could not have said why the city needed a gate when it had no walls... and no *buildings* that she could see. Yet there it stood, immense and beautiful, the great horses framing the distant buildings and the jagged purple mountain beyond. The bronze stallions threw long shadows across the waving grasses as Khal Drogo led the *khalasar* under their hooves and down the godsway, his bloodriders beside him.

Dany followed on her silver, escorted by Ser Jorah Mormont and her brother Viserys, mounted once more. After the day in the grass when she had left him to walk back to the *khalasar*, the Dothraki had laughingly called him *Khal Rhae Mhar*, the Sorefoot King. Khal Drogo had offered him a place in a cart the next day, and Viserys had accepted. In his stubborn ignorance, he had not even known he was being mocked; the carts were for eunuchs, cripples, women giving birth, the very young and the very old. That won him yet another name: *Khal Rhaggat*, the Cart King. Her brother had thought it was the *khal's* way of apologizing for the wrong Dany had done him. She had begged Ser Jorah not to tell him the truth, lest he be shamed. The knight had replied that the king could well do with a bit of shame...yet he had done as she bid. It had taken much pleading, and all the pillow tricks Doreah had taught her, before Dany had been able to make Drogo relent and allow Viserys to rejoin them at the head of the column.

"Where is the *city?*" she asked as they passed beneath the bronze arch. There were no buildings to be seen, no people, only the grass and the road, lined with ancient monuments from all the lands the Dothraki had sacked over the centuries.

"Ahead," Ser Jorah answered. "Under the mountain."

Beyond the horse gate, plundered gods and stolen heroes loomed to either side of them. The forgotten deities of dead cities brandished their broken thunderbolts at the sky as Dany rode her silver past their feet. Stone kings looked down on her from their thrones, their faces chipped and stained, even their names lost in the mists of time. Lithe young maidens danced on marble plinths, draped only in flowers, or poured air from shattered jars. Monsters stood in the grass beside the road; black iron dragons with jewels for eyes, roaring griffins, manticores with their barbed tails poised to strike, and other beasts she could not name. Some of the statues were so lovely they took her breath away, others so misshapen and terrible that Dany could scarcely bear to look at them. Those, Ser Jorah said, had likely come from the Shadow Lands beyond Asshai.

"So many," she said as her silver plodded slowly onward, "and from so many lands."

Viserys was less impressed. "The trash of dead cities," he sneered. He was careful to speak in the Common Tongue, which few Dothraki could understand, yet even so Dany found herself glancing back at the men of her *khas*, to make certain he had not been overheard. He went on blithely. "All these savages know how to do is steal the things better men have built... and kill." He laughed. "They do know how to kill, for certes. Otherwise I'd have no use for them at all."

"They are my people now," Dany said. "You should not call them savages, brother."

"The dragon speaks as he likes," Viserys said… in the Common Tongue. He glanced over his shoulder at Aggo and Rakhrao, riding behind them, and favored them with a mocking smile. "See, the savages lack the wit to understand the speech of civilized men." A moss-eaten stone monolith loomed over the road, fifty feet tall. Viserys gazed at it with boredom in his eyes. "How long must we linger amidst these ruins before Drogo gives me my army? I grow tired of waiting."

"The princess must be presented to the *dosh khaleen*…"

"The crones, yes," her brother interrupted, "and there's to be some mummer's show of a prophecy for the whelp in her belly, you told me. What is that to me? I'm tired of eating horsemeat and I'm sick of the stink of these savages." He sniffed at the wide, floppy sleeve of his tunic, where it was his custom to keep a sachet. It could not have helped much. The tunic was filthy. All the silk and heavy wools that Viserys had worn out of Pentos were stained by hard travel and rotted from sweat.

Ser Jorah Mormont said, "The Western Market will have food more to your taste, Your Grace. The traders from the Free Cities come there to sell their wares. The *khal* will honor his promise in his own time."

"He had better," Viserys said grimly. "I was promised a crown, and I mean to have it. The dragon is not mocked." Spying an obscene likeness of a woman with six breasts and a ferret's head, he rode off to inspect it more closely.

Dany was relieved, yet no less anxious. "I pray that my sun-and-stars will not keep him waiting too long," she told Ser Jorah when her brother was out of earshot.

The knight looked after Viserys doubtfully. "Your brother should have bided his time in Pentos. There is no place for him in a *khalasar*. Illyrio tried to warn him."

"He will go as soon as he has his ten thousand. My lord husband promised a golden crown."

Ser Jorah grunted. "Yes, *khaleesi*, but… the Dothraki look on these things differently than we do in the west. I have told him as much, as Illyrio told him, but your brother does not listen. The horselords are no traders. Viserys thinks he sold you, and now he wants his price. Yet Khal Drogo would say he had you as a gift. He will give Viserys a gift in return, yes… in his own time. You do not *demand* a gift, not of a *khal*. You do not demand anything of a *khal*. There," he announced, pointing. "Vaes Dothrak. The city of the horselords."

Cohollo came to Dany as Irri and Jhiqui were helping her down off her silver. He was the oldest of Drogo's three bloodriders, a squat bald man with a crooked nose and a mouth full of broken teeth, shattered by a mace twenty years before when he saved the young *khalakka* from sellswords who hoped to sell him to his father's enemies. His life had been bound to Drogo's the day her lord husband was born.

"*Khaleesi*," Cohollo said to her, in Dothraki. "Drogo, who is blood of my blood, commands me to tell you that he must ascend the Mother of Mountains this night, to sacrifice to the gods for his safe return."

Only men were allowed to set foot on the Mother, Dany knew. The *khal's* bloodriders would go with him, and return at dawn. "Tell my sun-and-stars that I dream of him, and wait anxiously for his return," she replied, thankful. Dany tired more easily as the child grew within her; in truth, a night of rest would be most welcome. Her pregnancy only seemed to have inflamed Drogo's desire for her, and of late his embraces left her exhausted.

Doreah led her to the hollow hill that had been prepared for her and her *khal.* It was cool and dim within, like a tent made of earth. "Jhiqui, a bath, please," she commanded, to wash the dust of travel from her skin and soak her weary bones. It was pleasant to know that they would linger her for a while, that she would not need to climb back on her silver on the morrow.

The water was scalding hot, as she liked it. "I will give my brother his gifts tonight," she decided, as Jhiqui was washing her hair. "He should look a king in the sacred city. Doreah, run and find him and invite him to sup with me." Viserys was nicer to the Lysene girl than to her Dothraki handmaids, perhaps because Magister Illyrio had let him bed her back in Pentos. "Irri, go to the bazaar, and buy fruit and meat. Anything but horseflesh."

"Horse is best," Irri said. "Horse makes a man strong."

"Viserys hates horsemeat."

"As you say, *khaleesi*."

She brought back a haunch of goat and a basket of fruits and vegetables. Jhiqui roasted the meat with sweetgrass and firepods, basting it with honey as it cooked, and there were melons and pomegranates and plums and some queer eastern fruit Dany did not know. While her handmaids prepared the meal, Dany laid out the clothing she'd had made to her brother's measure: a tunic and leggings of crisp white linen, leather sandals that laced up to the knee, a bronze medallion belt, a leather vest painted with fire- breathing dragons. The Dothraki would respect him more if he looked less a beggar, she hoped, and perhaps he would forgive her for shaming him that day in the grass. He was still her king, after all, and her brother. They were both blood of the dragon.

She was arranging the last of his gifts—a sandsilk cloak, green as grass, with a pale grey border that would bring out the silver in his hair—when Viserys arrived, dragging Doreah by the arm. Her eye was red where he'd hit her. "How *dare* you send this whore to give me commands," he said. He shoved the handmaid roughly to the carpet.

The anger took Dany utterly by surprise. "I only wanted...Doreah, what did you say?"

"*Khaleesi*, pardons, forgive me. I went to him, as you bid, and told him you commanded him to join you for supper."

"No one commands the dragon," Viserys snarled. "*I am your king!* I should have sent you back her head!"

The Lysene girl quailed, but Dany calmed her with a touch. "Don't be afraid, he won't hurt you. Sweet brother, please, forgive her, the girl mispoke herself, I told her to *ask* you to sup with me, if it please Your Grace." She took him by the hand and drew him across the room. "Look. These are for you."

Viserys frowned suspiciously. "What is all this?"

"New raiment. I had it made for you." Dany smiled shyly.

He looked at her and sneered. "Dothraki rags. Do you presume to dress me now?"

"Please… you'll be cooler and more comfortable, and I thought… maybe if you dressed like them, the Dothraki…" Dany did not know how to say it without waking his dragon.

"Next you'll want to braid my hair."

"I'd never…" Why was he always so cruel? She had only wanted to help. "You have no right to a braid, you have won no victories yet."

It was the wrong thing to say. Fury shone from his lilac eyes, yet he dared not strike her, not with her handmaids watching and the warriors of her *khas* outside. Viserys picked up the cloak and sniffed at it. "This stinks of manure. Perhaps I shall use it as a horse blanket."

"I had Doreah sew it specially for you," she told him, wounded. "These are garments fit for a *khal.*"

"I am the Lord of the Seven Kingdoms, not some grass-stained savage with bells in his hair," Viserys spat back at her. He grabbed her arm. "You forget yourself, slut. Do you think that big belly will protect you if you wake the dragon?"

His fingers dug into her arm painfully and for an instant Dany felt like a child again, quailing in the face of his rage. She reached out with her other hand and grabbed the first thing she touched, the belt she'd hoped to give him, a heavy chain of ornate bronze medallions. She swung it with all her strength.

It caught him full in the face. Viserys let go of her. Blood ran down his cheek where the edge of one of the medallions had sliced it open. "You are the one who forgets himself," Dany said to him. "Didn't you learn *anything,* that day in the grass? Leave me now, before I summon my *khas* to drag you out. And pray that Khal Drogo does not hear of this, or he will cut open your belly and feed you your own intestines."

Viserys scrambled back to his feet. "When I come into my kingdom, you will rue this day, slut." He walked off, holding his torn face, leaving her gifts behind him.

Drops of his blood had spattered the beautiful sandsilk cloak. Dany clutched the soft cloth to her cheek and sat crosslegged on her sleeping mats.

"Your supper is ready, *khaleesi,*" Jhiqui announced.

"I'm not hungry," Dany said sadly. She was suddenly very tired. "Share the food among yourselves, and send some to Ser Jorah, if you would." After a moment, she added, "Please, bring me one of the dragon's eggs."

Irri fetched the egg with the deep green shell, bronze flecks shining amidst its scales as she turned it in her small hands. She curled up on her side, pulling the sandsilk cloak across her and cradling the egg against her, in the hollow between her swollen belly and small, tender breasts. She liked to hold them. They were so beautiful, and sometimes just being close to them made her feel stronger, braver, as if somehow she was drawing strength from the stone dragons locked within.

She was lying there, holding the egg, when she felt the child move within her... as if he were reaching out, brother to brother, blood to blood. "*You* are the dragon," Dany whispered to him, "the *true* dragon. I know it. I know it." And she smiled, and went to sleep dreaming of home.

IV

The silk tenting that roofed Khal Drogo's high-timbered hall had been rolled back this night, so her son's naming feast might be celebrated beneath the open sky. The moon had followed Dany and her women back from the house of the *dosh khaleen*, and now it seemed to follow them inside. It was the seventh full moon since Drogo had planted his seed, the night she had looked upon his face, and their child grew heavy inside her.

Dany rode beneath the arched entry and up the center aisle, every eye on her. Flames leapt ten feet in the air from three huge stone-lined firepits. The air was thick with the smells of roasting horsemeat and curdled, fermented mare's milk, the cushions crowded. The sounds of drums and horns swirled up into the night. Half-clothed women spun and danced on the low tables, amid joints of meat and platters piled high with plums and dates and pomegranates. Many of the men were drunk, yet no *arakh*s would clash tonight, not here in the sacred city, where blades and bloodshed were forbidden.

The Dothraki shouted out comments on her belly and her breasts as she passed, hailing the prince within her. She could not understand all they said, but one phrase came clear. "*The stallion that mounts the world,*" they bellowed.

She had heard it first from the oldest crone, a bent and shriveled stick of a woman with a single black eye, the voice of the *dosh khaleen*. "Khalakka dothrae!" she had shrieked, arms raised high. *The prince is riding!* "He shall be the stallion who mounts the world!" And with that she had peered at Dany, her eye dark as polished flint in her wrinkled face. "What shall he be called, the stallion who mounts the world?"

"He shall be called Rhaego," she had answered, as bells rang all around her, a sudden clangor of bronze birds. A deep-throated war horn had sounded its long low note, and a roar had gone up from the Dothraki. "*Rhaego,*" they chanted. "*Rhaego, Rhaego!*"

Khal Drogo was waiting on the high bench, and he nodded as Irri helped her down off her silver. Khal Jommo and Khal Ogo, who had been in Vaes Dothrak with their *khalasars* when they arrived, had been given seats of high honor to Drogo's right and left. The bloodriders of the three *khals* sat below them, and further down, Khal Jommo's four wives.

As Doreah and Irri arranged her cushions, Dany searched for her brother. Even across the length of the crowded hall, Viserys should have been conspicuous with his pale skin, silvery hair, and beggar's rags, but she did not see him anywhere. Her glance roamed the crowded tables near the walls, where men whose braids were even shorter than their manhoods sat on frayed rugs and flat cushions around the low tables, but all the faces she saw had black eyes and copper skin. She spied Ser Jorah Mormont near the center of the hall, close to the middle firepit. It was a place of respect, if not high honor; the Dothraki esteemed the knight's prowess with a sword. Dany sent Jhiqui to bring him to her table. Mormont came at once, and went to one knee before her. "*Khaleesi,*" he said, "I am yours to command."

She patted the stuffed horsehide cushion beside her. "Sit and talk with me."

"You honor me." The knight seated himself cross-legged on the cushion. A slave knelt before him, offering a wooden platter full of ripe figs. Ser Jorah took one and bit it in half.

"Where is my brother?" Dany asked. "He ought to have come by now, for the feast."

"I saw His Grace this morning," he told her. "He told me he was going to the Western Market, in search of wine."

"Wine?" Dany said doubtfully. Viserys could not abide the taste of the fermented mare's milk the Dothraki drank, she knew that, and he was oft at the bazaars these days, drinking with the traders who came in the great caravans from east and west. He seemed to find their company more congenial than hers.

"Wine," Ser Jorah confirmed, "and he has some thought to recruit men for his army from the sellswords who guard the caravans." A serving girl laid a blood pie in front of him, and he attacked it with both hands.

"Is that wise?" she asked. "He has no gold to pay soldiers. What if he's betrayed?" Caravan guards were seldom troubled much by thoughts of honor, and the Usurper in King's Landing would pay well for her brother's head. "You ought to have gone with him, to keep him safe. You are his sworn sword."

"We are in Vaes Dothrak," he reminded her. "No one may carry a blade here, or a shed a man's blood."

"Yet men die," she said. "Jhogo told me. Some of traders have eunuchs with them, huge men who strangle thieves with wisps of silk. That way no blood is shed and the gods are not angered."

"Then let us hope your brother will be wise enough not to steal anything." Ser Jorah wiped the grease off his mouth with the back of his hand and leaned close over the table. "He had planned to take your dragon's eggs, until I warned him that I'd cut off his hand if he so much as touched them."

For a moment Dany was so shocked she had no words. "My eggs... but they're *mine*, Magister Illyrio gave them to me, a bride gift, why would Viserys want... they're only stones..."

"The same could be said of rubies and diamonds and fire opals, princess... and dragon's eggs are rarer by far. Those traders he's been drinking with would sell their own manhoods for even one of those *stones*, and with all three Viserys could buy as many sellswords as he might need."

Dany had not known, had not even suspected. "Then... he should have them. He does not need to steal them. He had only to ask. He is my brother... and my true king."

"He is your brother," Ser Jorah acknowledged.

"You do not understand, ser," she said. "My mother died giving me birth, and my father and my brother Rhaegar even before that. I would never have known so much as their names if Viserys had not been there to tell me. He was the only one left. The only one. He is all I have."

"Once," said Ser Jorah. "No longer, *khaleesi*. You belong to the Dothraki now. In your womb rides the stallion who mounts the world." He held out his cup, and a slave filled it with fermented mare's milk, sour-smelling and thick with clots.

Dany waved her away. Even the smell of it made her feel ill, and she would take no chances of bringing up the horse heart she had forced herself to eat. "What does it mean?" she asked. "What is this stallion? Everyone was shouting it at me, but I don't understand."

"The stallion is the *khal* of *khals* promised in ancient prophecy, child. He will unite the Dothraki into a single *khalasar* and ride to the ends of the earth, or so it was promised. All the people of the world will be his herd."

"Oh," Dany said, in a small voice. Her hand smoothed her gown down over the swell of her stomach. "I named him Rhaego."

"A name to make the Usurper's blood run cold."

Suddenly Doreah was tugging at her elbow. "*My lady*," the handmaid whispered urgently, "your brother..."

Dany looked down the length of the long, roofless hall and there he was, striding toward her. From the lurch in his step, she could tell at once that Viserys had found his wine…and something that passed for courage.

He was wearing his scarlet silks, soiled and travel stained. His cloak and gloves were black velvet, faded from the sun. His boots were dry and cracked, his silver-blond hair matted and tangled. A longsword swung from his belt in a leather scabbard. The Dothraki eyed the sword as he passed; Dany heard curses and threats and angry muttering rising all around her, like a tide. The music died away in a nervous stammering of drums.

A sense of dread closed around her heart. "Go to him," she commanded Ser Jorah. "Stop him. Bring him here. Tell him he can have the dragon's eggs, if that is what he wants." The knight rose swiftly to his feet.

"Where is my sister?" Viserys shouted, his voice thick with wine. "I've come for her feast. How dare you presume to eat without me? No one eats before the king. Where is she? The whore can't hide from the dragon."

He stopped beside the largest of the three firepits, peering around at the faces of the Dothraki. There were five thousand men in the hall, but only a handful who knew the Common Tongue. Yet even if his words were incomprehensible, you had only to look at him to know that he was drunk.

Ser Jorah went to him swiftly, whispered something in his ear, and took him by the arm, but Viserys wrenched free. "Keep your hands off me! No one touches the dragon without leave."

Dany glanced anxiously up at the high bench. Khal Drogo was saying something to the other *khals* beside him. Khal Jommo grinned, and Khal Ogo began to guffaw loudly.

The sound of laugher made Viserys lift his eyes. "Khal Drogo," he said thickly, his voice almost polite. "I'm here for the feast." He staggered away from Ser Jorah, making to join the three *khals* on the high bench.

Khal Drogo rose, spat out a dozen words in Dothraki, faster than Dany could understand, and pointed. "Khal Drogo says your place is not on the high bench," Ser Jorah translated for her brother. "Khal Drogo says your place is there."

Viserys glanced where the *khal* was pointing. At the back of the long hall, in a corner by the wall, deep in shadow so better men would not need to look on them, sat the lowest of the low; raw unblooded boys, old men with clouded eyes and stiff joints, the dim-witted and the maimed. Far from the meat, and further from honor. "That is no place for a king," her brother declared.

"Is place," Khal Drogo answered, in the Common Tongue that Dany had taught him, "for Sorefoot King." He clapped his hands together. "A cart! Bring cart for *Khal Rhaggat!*"

Five thousand Dothraki began to laugh and shout. Ser Jorah was standing beside Viserys, screaming in his ear, but the roar in the hall was so thunderous that Dany could not hear what he was saying. Her brother shouted back and the two men grappled, until Mormont knocked Viserys bodily to the floor.

Her brother drew his sword.

The bared steel shone a fearful red in the glare from the firepits. "*Keep away from me!*" Viserys hissed. Ser Jorah backed off a step, and her brother climbed unsteadily to his feet. He waved the sword over his head, the borrowed blade that Magister Illyrio had given him to make him seem more kingly. Dothraki were shrieking at him from all sides, screaming vile curses.

Dany gave a wordless cry of terror. She knew what a drawn sword meant here, even if her brother did not.

Her voice made Viserys turn his head, and he saw her for the first time. "There she is," he said, smiling. He stalked toward her, slashing at the air as if to cut a path through a wall of enemies, though no one tried to bar his way.

"The blade... you must not," she begged him. "Please, Viserys. It is forbidden. Put down the sword and come share my cushions. There's drink, food... is it the dragon's eggs you want? You can have them, only throw away the sword."

"Do as she tells you, fool," Ser Jorah shouted, "before you get us all killed."

Viserys laughed. "They can't kill us. They can't shed blood here in the sacred city... but *I* can." He laid the point of his sword between Daenerys' breasts, and slid it downward, over the curve of her belly. "I want what I came for," he told her. "I want the crown he promised me. He bought you, but he never paid for you. Tell him I want what I bargained for, or I'm taking you back. You and the eggs both. He can keep his bloody foal. I'll cut the bastard out and leave it for him." The sword point pushed through her silks and pricked at her navel. Viserys was weeping, she saw; weeping and laughing, both at the same time, this man who had once been her brother.

Distantly, as from far away, Dany heard her handmaid Jhiqui sobbing in fear, pleading that she dared not translate, that the *khal* would bind her and drag her behind his horse all the way up the Mother of Mountains. She put her arm around the girl. "Don't be afraid," she said. "I shall tell him."

She did not know if she had enough words, yet when she was done Khal Drogo spoke a few brusque sentences in Dothraki, and she knew he understood. The sun of her life stepped down from the high bench. "What did he say?" the man who had been her brother asked her, flinching.

It had grown so silent in the hall that she could hear the bells in Khal Drogo's hair, chiming softly with each step he took. His bloodriders followed him, like three copper shadows. Daenerys had gone cold all over. "He says you shall have a splendid golden crown that men shall tremble to behold."

Viserys smiled and lowered his sword. That was the saddest thing, the thing that tore at her afterwards... the way he smiled. "That was all I wanted," he said. "What was promised."

When the sun of her life reached her, Dany slid an arm around his waist. The *khal* said a word, and his bloodriders leapt forward. Qotho seized the man who had been her brother by the arms. Haggo shattered his wrist with a single, sharp twist of his huge hands. Cohollo pulled the sword from his limp fingers. Even now Viserys did not understand. "No," he shouted, "you cannot touch me, I am the dragon, the *dragon*, and I will be *crowned!*"

Khal Drogo unfastened his belt. The medallions were pure gold, massive and ornate, each one as large as a man's hand. He shouted a command. Cook slaves pulled a heavy iron stew pot pulled from the firepit, dumped the stew onto the ground, and returned the pot to the flames. Drogo tossed in the belt and watched without expression as the medallions turned red and began to lose their shape. She could see fires dancing in the onyx of his eyes. A slave handed him a pair of thick horsehair mittens, and he pulled them on, never so much as looking at the man.

Viserys began to scream the high, wordless scream of the coward facing death. He kicked and twisted, whimpered like a dog and wept like a child, but the Dothraki held him tight between them. Ser Jorah had made his way to Dany's side. He put a hand on her shoulder. "Turn away, my princess, I beg you."

"No." She folded her arms across the swell of her belly, protectively.

At the last, Viserys looked at her. "Sister, please... Dany, tell them... make them... sweet sister..."

When the gold was half-melted and starting to run, Drogo reached into the flames, snatched out the pot. "Crown!" he roared. "Here. A crown for Cart King!" And upended the pot over the head of the man who had been her brother.

The sound Viserys Targaryen made when that hideous iron helmet covered his face was like nothing human. His feet hammered a frantic beat against the dirt floor, slowed, stopped. Thick globs of molten gold dripped down onto his chest, setting the scarlet silk to smoldering... yet no drop of blood was spilled.

He was no dragon, Dany thought, curiously calm. *Fire cannot kill a dragon.*

V

When the battle was done, Dany rode her silver through the fields of the dead. Her handmaids and the men of her *khas* came after, smiling and jesting among themselves.

Dothraki hooves had torn the earth and trampled the stands of beans and rye into the ground, while *arakhs* and arrows had sown a terrible new crop and watered it with blood. Dying horses lifted their heads and screamed at her as she rode past. Wounded men moaned and prayed. *Jagga rhan* moved among them, the mercy men with their heavy axes, taking a harvest of heads from the dead and dying alike. After them would scurry a flock of small girls, pulling arrows from the corpses to fill their baskets. Last of all the dogs would come sniffing, lean and hungry, the feral pack that was never far behind the *khalasar*.

The sheep had been dead longest. There seemed to be thousands of them, black with flies, arrow shafts bristling from each carcass. Khal Ogo's riders had done that, Dany knew; no man of Drogo's *khalasar* would be such a fool as to waste his arrows on sheep when there were shepherds yet to kill.

The town was afire, black plumes of smoke roiling and tumbling as they rose into a hard blue sky. Beneath broken walls of dried mud, riders galloped back and forth, swinging their long whips as they herded the survivors from the smoking rubble. The women and children of Ogo's *khalasar* seemed to walk with a sullen pride, even in defeat and bondage; they were slaves now, but they seemed not to fear it. It was different with the townfolk. Dany felt pity for them; she remembered what terror felt like. Mothers stumbled along with blank, dead faces, pulling sobbing children by the hands. There were only a few men among them, cripples and cowards and grandfathers.

Ser Jorah said the people of this country named themselves the Lhazareen, but the Dothraki called them *haesh rakhi*, the Lamb Men. Once Dany might have taken them for Dothraki, for they had the same copper skin and almond-shaped eyes. Now they looked alien to her, squat and flat-faced, their black hair cropped unnaturally short. They were herders of sheep and eaters of vegetables, and Khal Drogo said they belonged south of the river bend. The grass of the Dothraki sea was not meant for sheep.

Dany saw one boy bolt and run for the river. A rider cut him off and turned him, and the others boxed him in, cracking their whips in his face, running him this way and that. One galloped behind him, lashing him across the buttocks until his thighs ran red with blood. Another snared his ankle with a lash and sent him sprawling. Finally, when the boy could only crawl, they grew bored of the sport and put an arrow through his eye.

Ser Jorah met her outside the shattered gate. He wore a dark green surcoat over his mail. His gauntlets, greaves, and greathelm were dark grey steel. The Dothraki had mocked him for a coward when he donned his armor, but the knight had spit insults right back in their teeth, tempers had flared, longsword had clashed with *arakh*, and the rider whose taunts had been loudest had been left behind to bleed to death.

Ser Jorah lifted the visor of his flat-topped greathelm as he rode up. "Your lord husband awaits you within the town."

"Drogo took no harm?"

"A few cuts," Ser Jorah answered, "nothing of consequence. He slew two *khals* this day. Khal Ogo first, and then the son, Fogo, who became *khal* when Ogo fell. His bloodriders cut the bells from their hair, and now Khal Drogo's every step rings louder than before."

Ogo and his son had shared the high bench with her lord husband at the naming feast where Viserys had been crowned, but that was in Vaes Dothrak, beneath the Mother of Mountains, where every rider was a brother and all quarrels were put aside. It was different out in the grass. Ogo's *khalasar* had been attacking the town when Khal Drogo caught him. She wondered what the Lamb Men had thought, when they first saw the dust of their horses from atop those cracked-mud walls. Perhaps a few, the younger and more foolish who still believed that the gods heard the prayers of desperate men, took it for deliverance.

Across the road, a girl no older than Dany was sobbing in a high thin voice as a rider shoved her over a pile of corpses, face down, and thrust himself inside her. Other riders dismounted to take their turns. That was the sort of deliverance the Dothraki brought the Lamb Men.

I am the blood of the dragon, Daenerys Targaryen reminded herself as she turned her face away. She pressed her lips together and hardened her heart and rode on toward the gate.

"Most of Ogo's riders fled," Ser Jorah was saying. "Still, there may be as many as ten thousand captives."

Slaves, Dany thought. Khal Drogo would drive them downriver to one of the towns on Slaver's Bay. She wanted to cry, but she told herself that she must be strong. *This is war, this is what it looks like, this is the price of the Iron Throne.* This was what she was bringing home with her.

Drogo had sworn it to her as they stood beside the Womb of the World, back in Vaes Dothrak. "I will give my son the iron chair his mother's father sat in. I will give him the Seven Kingdoms. I, Drogo, *khal,* I will do this thing," he had vowed. "I will take my *khalasar* west to where the world ends, and ride the wooden horses across the black salt water as no khal has done before. will kill the men in the iron suits, tear down their stone houses, and bring their broken gods back to Vaes Dothrak. So swears Drogo son of Bharbo, before the Mother of Mountains, as the stars look down in witness." They had left Vaes Dothrak two days later, striking south and west across the plains. Khal Drogo led the *khalasar* on his great red stallion, with Daenerys beside him on her silver. She had carried the child for eight moons now, but Dothraki women rode almost up until the day they gave birth.

"I've told the *khal* he ought to make for Meereen," Ser Jorah said. "He'll get a better price there than he would from a slaving caravan. Illyrio writes that they had a plague last year, and now the brothels are paying double for healthy young girls, and triple for boys under ten. If enough children survive the journey, the gold will buy us all the ships we need, and hire men to sail them."

Behind them, the girl being raped made a heartrending sound, a long sobbing wail that went on and on and on. Dany's hand clenched hard around the reins, and she turned the silver's head. "Make them stop," she commanded Ser Jorah.

"*Khaleesi?*" The knight sounded perplexed.

"You heard my words," she said. "Stop them." She spoke to her *khas* in the harsh accents of Dothraki. "Jhogo, Quaro, you will aid Ser Jorah. I want no rape."

The warriors exchanged a baffled look.

Jorah Mormont spurred his horse closer. "Princess," he said, "you have a gentle heart, but you do not understand. This is how it has always been. Those men have shed blood for the *khal*. Now they claim their reward."

Across the road, the girl was still crying, her high singsong tongue strange to Dany's ears. The first man was done with her now, and a second had taken his place.

"She is a lamb girl," Quaro said in Dothraki. "She is nothing, *khaleesi*. The riders do her honor. The Lamb Men lay with sheep, it is known."

"It is known," her handmaid Irri echoed.

"It is known," agreed Jhogo, astride the tall grey stallion that Drogo had given him. "If her wailing offends your ears, *khaleesi*, Jhogo will bring you her tongue." He drew his *arakh*.

"I will not have her harmed," Dany said. "I claim her. Do as I command you, or Khal Drogo will know the reason why."

"*Ai, khaleesi*," Jhogo replied, kicking his horse. Quaro and the others followed his lead, the bells in their hair chiming.

"Go with them," she commanded Ser Jorah.

"As you command." The knight gave her a curious look. "You are your brother's sister, in truth."

"Viserys?" She did not understand.

"No," he answered. "Rhaegar." He galloped off.

Dany heard Jhogo shout. The rapers laughed at him. One man shouted back. Jhogo's *arakh* flashed, and the man's head went tumbling from his shoulders. Laughter turned to curses as the horsemen reached for weapons, but by then Quaro and Aggo and Rakharo were there. She saw Aggo point across the road to where she sat upon her silver. The riders looked at her with cold black eyes. One spat. The others scattered to their mounts, muttering.

All the while the man atop the lamb girl continued to plunge in and out of her, so intent on his pleasure that he seemed unaware of what was going on around him. Ser Jorah dismounted and wrenched him off with a mailed hand. The Dothraki went sprawling in the mud, bounced up with a knife in hand, and died with Aggo's arrow through his throat. Mormont pulled the girl off the pile of corpses and wrapped her in his blood-spattered cloak. He led her across the road to Dany. "What do you want done with her?"

The girl was trembling, her eyes wide and vague. Her hair was matted with blood. "Doreah, see to her hurts. You do not have a rider's look, perhaps she will not fear you. The rest, with me." She urged the silver through the broken wooden gate.

It was worse inside the town. Many of the houses were afire, and the *jagga rhan* had been about their grisly work. Headless corpses filled the narrow, twisty lanes. They passed other women being raped. Each time Dany reined up, sent her *khas* to make an end to it, and claimed the victim as slave. One of them, a thick-bodied, flat-nosed woman of forty years, blessed Dany haltingly in the Common Tongue, but from the others she got only flat black stares. They were suspicious of her, she realized with sadness; afraid that she had saved them for some worse fate.

"You cannot claim them all, child," Ser Jorah said, the fourth time they stopped, while the warriors of her *khas* herded her new slaves behind her.

"I am *khaleesi*, heir to the Seven Kingdoms, the blood of the dragon," Dany reminded him. "It is not for you to tell me what I cannot do." Across the city, a building collapsed in a great gout of fire and smoke, and she heard distant screams and the wailing of frightened children.

They found Khal Drogo seated before a square windowless temple with thick mud walls and a bulbous dome like some immense brown onion. Beside him was a pile of heads taller than he was. One of the short arrows of the Lamb Men stuck through the meat of his upper arm, and blood covered the left side of his bare chest like a splash of paint. His three bloodriders were with him.

Jhiqui helped Dany dismount; she had grown clumsy as her belly grew larger and heavier. She knelt before the *khal*. "My sun-and-stars is wounded." The *arakh* cut was wide but shallow; his left nipple was gone, and a flap of bloody flesh and skin dangled from his chest like a wet rag.

"Is scratch, moon of life, from *arakh* of one bloodrider to Khal Ogo," Khal Drogo said in the Common Tongue. "I kill him for it, and Ogo too." He turned his head, the bells in his braid ringing softly. "Is Ogo you hear, and Fogo his *khalakka*, who was *khal* when I slew him."

"No man can stand before the sun of my life," Dany said, "the father of the stallion who mounts the world."

A mounted warrior rode up and vaulted from his saddle. He spoke to Haggo, a stream of angry Dothraki too fast for Dany to understand. The huge bloodrider gave her a heavy look before he turned to his *khal.* "This one is Mago, who rides in the *khas* of Ko Jhaqo. He says the *khaleesi* has taken his spoils, a daughter of the lambs who was his to mount."

Khal Drogo's face was still and hard, but his black eyes were curious as they went to Dany. "Tell me the truth of this, moon of my life," he commanded, in Dothraki.

Dany told him what she had done, in his own tongue so the *khal* would understand her better, her words simple and direct.

When she was done, Drogo was frowning. "This is the way of war. These women are our slaves now, to do with as we please."

"It pleases me to hold them safe," Dany said, wondering if she had dared too much. "If your warriors would mount these women, let them take them gently and keep them for wives. Give them places in the *khalasar* and let them bear you sons."

Qotho was ever the cruelest of the bloodriders. It was he who laughed. "Does the horse breed with the sheep?"

Something in his tone. reminded her of Viserys. Dany turned on him angrily. "The dragon feeds on horse and sheep alike."

Khal Drogo smiled. "See how fierce she grows!" he said. "It is my son inside her, the stallion who mounts the world, filling her with his fire. Ride slowly, Qotho... if the mother does not burn you where you sit, the son will trample you into the mud. And you, Mago, hold your tongue and find another lamb to mount. These belong to my *khaleesi.*" He started to reach out a hand to Daenerys, but as he lifted his arm Drogo grimaced in sudden pain, and turned his head.

Dany could almost feel his agony. The wounds were worse than Ser Jorah had led her to believe. "Where are the healers?" she demanded. The *khalasar* had two sorts; barren women and eunuch slaves. The herbwomen dealt in potions and spells, the eunuchs in knife, needle, and fire. "Why do they not attend the *khal?*"

"The *khal* sent the hairless men away, *khaleesi,*" old Cohollo assured her. Dany saw the bloodrider had taken a wound himself; a deep gash in his left shoulder.

"Many riders are hurt," Khal Drogo said stubbornly. "Let them be healed first. This arrow is no more than the bite of a fly, this little cut only a new scar to boast of to my son."

Dany could see the muscles in his chest where the skin had been cut away. A trickle of blood ran from the arrow that pierced his arm. "It is not for Khal Drogo to wait," she proclaimed. "Jhogo, seek out these eunuchs and bring them here at once."

"Silver Lady," a woman's voice said behind her, "I can help the Great Rider with his hurts."

Dany turned her head. The speaker was one of the slaves she had claimed, the heavy, flat-nosed woman who had blessed her.

"The *khal* needs no help from women who lie with sheep," barked Qotho. "Aggo, cut out her tongue."

Aggo grabbed her hair and pressed a knife to her throat.

Dany lifted a hand. "No. She is mine. Let her speak."

Aggo looked from her to Qotho. He lowered his knife.

"I meant no wrong, fierce riders." The woman spoke Dothraki well. The robes she wore had once been the lightest and finest of woolens, rich with embroidery, but now they were mud-caked and bloody and ripped. She clutched the torn cloth of her bodice to her heavy breasts. "I have some small skill in the healing arts."

"Who are you?" Dany asked her.

"I am named Mirri Maz Duur. I am godswife of this temple."

"*Maegi*," grunted Haggo, fingering his *arakh*. His look was dark. Dany remembered the word from a terrifying story that Jhiqui had told her one night by the cookfire. A *maegi* was a woman who lay with demons and practiced the blackest of sorceries, a vile thing, evil and soulless, who came to men in the dark of night and sucked life and strength from their bodies.

"I am a healer," Mirri Maz Duur said.

"A healer of sheeps," sneered Qotho. "Blood of my blood, I say kill this *maegi* and wait for the hairless men."

Dany ignored the bloodrider's outburst. This old, homely, thick-bodied woman did not look like a *maegi* to her. "Where did you learn your healing, Mirri Maz Duur?"

"My mother was godswife before me, and taught me all the songs and spells most pleasing to the Great Shepherd, and how to make the sacred smokes and ointments from leaf and root and berry. When I was younger and more fair, I went in caravan to Asshai by the Shadow, to learn from their mages. Ships from many lands come to Asshai, so I lingered long to study the healing ways of distant peoples. A moonsinger of the Jogos Nhai gifted me with her birthing songs, a woman of your own riding people taught me the magics of grass and corn and horse, and a maester from the Sunset Lands opened a body for me and showed me all the secrets that hide beneath the skin."

Ser Jorah Mormont spoke up. "A maester?"

"Marwyn, he named himself," the woman replied, in the Common Tongue. "From the sea. Beyond the sea. The Seven Lands, he said. Sunset Lands. Where men are iron and dragons rule. He taught me this speech."

"A maester in Asshai," Ser Jorah mused. "Tell me, godswife, what did this Marwyn wear about his neck?"

"A chain so tight it was like to choke him, Iron Lord, with links of many metals."

The knight looked at Dany. "Only a man trained in the Citadel of Oldtown wears such a chain," he said, "and such men do know much of healing."

"Why should you want to help my *khal*?"

"All men are one flock, or so we are taught," replied Mirri Maz Duur. "The Great Shepherd sent me to earth to heal his lambs, wherever I might find them."

Qotho gave her a stinging slap. "We are no sheep, *maegi*."

"Stop it," Dany said angrily. "She is mine. I will not have her harmed."

Khal Drogo grunted. "The arrow must come out, Qotho."

"Yes, Great Rider," Mirri Maz Duur answered, touching her bruised face. "And your breast must be washed and sewn, lest the wound fester."

"Do it, then," Khal Drogo commanded.

"Great Rider," the woman said, "my tools and potions are inside the god's house, where the healing powers are strongest."

"I will carry you, blood of my blood," Haggo offered.

Khal Drogo waved him away. "I need no man's help," he said, in a voice proud and hard. He stood, unaided, towering over them all. A fresh wave of blood ran down his breast, from where Ogo's *arakh* had cut off his nipple. Dany moved quickly to his side. "I am no man," she whispered, "so you may lean on me." Drogo put a huge hand on her shoulder. She took some of his weight as they walked toward the great mud temple. The three bloodriders followed. Dany commanded Ser Jorah and the warriors of her *khas* to guard the entrance, and make certain no one set the building afire while they were still inside.

They passed through a series of anterooms, into the high central chamber under the onion. Faint light shone down through hidden windows above. A few torches burnt smokily from sconces on the walls. Sheepskins were scattered across the mud floor. "There," Mirri Maz Duur said, pointing to the altar, a massive blue-veined stone carved with images of shepherds and their flocks. Khal Drogo lay upon it. The old woman threw a handful of dried leaves onto a brazier, filling the chamber with fragrant smoke. "Best if you wait outside," she told the rest of them.

"We are blood of his blood," Cohollo said. "Here we wait."

Qotho stepped close to Mirri Maz Duur. "Know this, wife of the Lamb God. Harm the *khal* and you suffer the same." He drew his skinning knife and showed her the blade.

"She will do no harm." Dany felt she could trust this old, plain-faced woman with her flat nose; she had saved her from the hard hands of her rapers, after all.

"If you must stay, then help," Mirri told the bloodriders. "The Great Rider is too strong for me. Hold him still while I draw the arrow from his flesh." She let the rags of her gown fall to her waist as she opened a carved

chest, and busied herself with bottles and boxes, knives and needles. When
she was ready, she broke off the barbed arrowhead and pulled out the shaft,
chanting in the singsong tongue of the Lhazareen. She heated a flagon of wine
to boiling on the brazier, and poured it over his wounds. Khal Drogo cursed
her, but he did not move. She bound the arrow wound with a plaster of wet
leaves, and turned to the gash on his breast, smearing it with a pale green
paste before she pulled the flap of skin back in place. The *khal* ground his
teeth together and swallowed a scream. The godswife took out a silver needle
and a bobbin of silk thread and began to close the flesh. When she was done
she painted the skin with red ointment, covered it with more leaves, and bound
the breast in a ragged piece of lambskin. "You must say the prayers I give you
and keep the lambskin in place for ten days and ten nights," she said. "There
will be fever, and itching, and a great scar when the healing is done."

Khal Drogo sat, bells ringing. "I sing of my scars, sheep woman." He
flexed his arm and scowled.

"Drink neither wine nor the milk of the poppy," she cautioned him.
"Pain you will have, but you must keep your body strong to fight the poison
spirits."

"I am *khal*," Drogo said. "I spit on pain and drink what I like. Cohollo,
bring my vest." The older man hastened off.

"Before," Dany said to the ugly Lhazareen woman, "I heard you speak
of birthing songs..."

"I know every secret of the bloody bed, Silver Lady, nor have I ever lost
a babe," Mirri Maz Duur replied.

"My time is near," Dany said. "I would have you attend me when he
comes, if you would."

Khal Drogo laughed. "Moon of my life, you do not ask a slave, you tell
her. She will do as you command." He jumped down from the altar. "Come,
my blood. The stallions call, this place is ashes. It is time to ride."

Haggo followed the *khal* from the temple, but Qotho lingered long
enough to favor Mirri Maz Duur with a stare. "Remember, *maegi*, as the *khal*
fares, so shall you."

"As you say, rider," the woman answered him, gathering up her jars and
bottles. "The Great Shepherd guards the flock."

VI

The flies circled Khal Drogo slowly, their wings buzzing, a low thrum at
the edge of hearing that filled Dany with dread. The sun was high and pitiless.
Heat shimmered in waves off the stony outcrops of the lows hills around them.
As she rode, a thin finger of sweat trickled down slowly between Dany's swol-

len breasts. The only sounds were the steady clop of their horses' hooves, the rhythmic tingle of the bells in Drogo's hair, and the distant voices behind them. Dany watched the flies.

They were as large as bees, gross, purplish, glistening. The Dothraki called them *bloodflies*. They lived in marshes and stagnant pools, sucked blood from man and horse alike, and laid their eggs in the dead and dying. Drogo hated them. Whenever one came near him, his hand would shoot out quick as a striking snake to close around it. She had never seen him miss. He would hold the fly inside his huge fist, long enough to hear its frantic buzzing. Then his fingers would tighten, and when he opened his hand again, the fly would be only a red smear on his palm.

A fly crept across the rump of his stallion, and the horse gave an angry flick of its tail and brushed it away. The others flitted around Drogo, closer and closer. The *khal* did not react. His eyes were fixed on distant brown hills, the reins loose in his hands. Beneath his painted vest, a plaster of fig leaves and caked blue river mud covered the wound on his breast. The herbwomen had made it for him. The poultice Mirri Maz Duur had made had itched and burned, and he had torn it off six days ago, cursing her for a *maegi*. The mud plaster was much more soothing, and the herbwomen made him poppy wine as well. He had been drinking it heavily these past three days, and when it was not poppy wine, it was fermented mare's milk or pepper beer.

Yet he scarcely touched his food, and he thrashed and groaned in the night. Dany could see how drawn his face had become. Rhaego was restless in her belly, kicking like a stallion, yet even that did not stir Drogo's interest as it had. Every morning her eyes found fresh lines of pain on his face when he woke from his troubled sleep. And now this silence. It was making her afraid. Since they had mounted up at dawn, he had said not a word. When she spoke, she got no answer but a grunt, and not even that much since midday.

One of the bloodflies landed on the bare skin of the *khal's* shoulder. Another, circling, touched down on his neck, and crept up toward his mouth. Khal Drogo said nothing, did nothing. His body swayed in the saddle, bells ringing, as his stallion kept onward at a steady walking pace.

Dany pressed her heels into her silver and rode closer. She must do something, she knew. She could not let him go on like this. "My lord," she said softly. "Drogo. My sun-and-stars."

He did not seem to hear. His eyes were open and staring. The bloodfly crawled up under his drooping mustache and settled on his cheek, in the crease beside his nose. Dany gasped. Terror made her heart beat faster. "*Drogo*," she cried, loudly. Clumsily, she reached over and touched his arm.

Khal Drogo reeled in the saddle, tilted slowly, and fell heavily from his horse. The flies scattered for a heartbeat, and then circled back to settle on him where he lay.

"No," Dany said, reining up. Heedless of her belly for once, she scrambled off her silver and ran to him.

The grass beneath him was brown and dry. Drogo cried out in pain as Dany knelt beside him. His breath rattled harshly in his throat, and he looked at her without recognition. "My horse," he gasped. Dany brushed the flies off his chest, smashing one as he would have. His skin burned beneath her fingers.

The *khal's* bloodriders had been following just behind them. He heard Haggo shout, and then they were there. Cohollo vaulted from his horse to land beside her. "Blood of my blood," he said as he dropped to his knees. The other two kept to their mounts.

"No," Khal Drogo groaned, struggling in Dany's arms. "Must ride. Ride. No."

"He fell from his horse," Haggo said, staring down. His broad face was impassive, but his voice was leaden.

"You must not say that," Dany told him. "We have ridden far enough today. We will camp here."

"Here?" Haggo looked around them. The land was brown and sere, inhospitable. "This is no camping ground."

"It is not for a woman to bid us halt," said Qotho, "not even a *khaleesi*."

"We camp here," Dany repeated. "Haggo, tell them Khal Drogo commanded the halt. If any ask why, say to them that my time is near and I could not continue. Cohollo, bring up the slaves, they must put up the khal's tent at once. Qotho—"

"You do not command me, *khaleesi*," Qotho said.

"Find Mirri Maz Duur," she told him. The godswife would be walking among the other Lamb Men, in the long column of slaves. "Bring her to me, with her chest."

Qotho glared down at her, his eyes hard as flint. "The *maegi*." He spat. "This I will not do."

"You will," Dany said, "or when Drogo wakes, he will hear why you defied me."

Furious, Qotho wheeled his stallion around and galloped off in anger... but Dany knew he would return with Mirri Maz Duur, however little he might like it. The slaves erected Khal Drogo's tent beneath a jagged outcrop of black rock whose shadow gave some relief from the heat of the afternoon sun. Even so, it was close and warm under the sandsilk as Irri and Doreah helped Dany walk Drogo inside. Thick patterned carpets had been laid down over the ground, and pillows scattered in the corners. Eroeh, the timid girl Dany had rescued outside the mud walls of the Lamb Men, set up a brazier. They lay Drogo down on a woven mat. "No," he muttered, in the Common Tongue. "No, no." It was he said, all he seemed capable of saying.

Doreah unhooked his heavy medallion belt and stripped off his vest and leggings, while Jhiqui knelt by his feet to undo the laces of his riding sandals. Irri wanted to leave the door flaps open to let in the breeze, but Dany forbade it. She would not have them see Drogo this way, in delirium and weakness. When her *khas* came up, she posted them around the tent to stand at guard. "Admit no one without my leave," she told Jhoqo. "No one."

Eroeh stared fearfully at Drogo where he lay. "He dies," she whispered. Dany slapped her. "The *khal* cannot die. He is the father of the stallion who mounts the world. His hair has never been cut. He still wears the bells his father gave him."

"*Khaleesi,*" Jhiqui said, "he fell from his horse."

Trembling, her eyes full of sudden tears, Dany turned away from them. *He fell from his horse!* It was so, she had seen it, and the bloodriders, and no doubt her handmaids and the men of her *khas* as well. And how many more? They could not keep it secret, and Dany knew what that meant. A *khal* who could not ride could not rule, and Drogo had fallen from his horse.

"We must bathe him," she said, stubbornly. She must not allow herself to despair. "Irri, have the tub brought at once. Doreah, Eroeh, find water, cool water, he's so hot." He was a fire in human skin.

The slaves set up the heavy copper tub in the corner of the tent. When Doreah brought the first jar of water, Dany wet a length of silk to lay across Drogo's brow, over the burning skin. His eyes looked at her, but he did not see. When his lips opened, no words escaped them, only a moan. "Where is Mirri Maz Duur?" she demanded, her patience rubbed raw with fear.

"Qotho will find her," Irri said.

Her handmaids filled the tub with tepid water that stank of sulfur, sweetening it with jars of bitter oil and handfuls of crushed mint leaves. While the bath was being prepared, Dany knelt awkwardly beside her lord husband, her belly great with their child within. She undid his braid with anxious fingers, as she had the night he'd taken her for the first time, beneath the stars. His bells she lay aside carefully, one by one. He would want them again when he was well, she told herself.

A breath of cool air entered the tent as Aggo poked his head through the silk. "*Khaleesi,*" he said, "the Andal is come, and begs leave to enter."

"The Andal" was what the Dothraki called Ser Jorah. "Yes," she said, rising clumsily, "send him in." She trusted the knight. He would know what to do if anyone did.

Ser Jorah Mormont ducked through the door flap and waited a moment for his eyes to adjust to the dimness of the tent. In the fierce heat of the south, he wore loose trousers of mottled sandsilk and open-toed riding sandals that laced up to his knee. His scabbard hung from a twisted horsehair belt. Under a bleached white vest, he was bare-chested, skin reddened by the sun. "Talk goes from mouth to ear, all over the *khalasar*," he said. "It is said Khal Drogo fell from his horse."

"Help him," Dany pleaded. "For the love you say you bear me, help him now."

The knight knelt beside her. He looked at Drogo long and hard, and then at Dany. "Send your maids away."

Wordlessly, her throat tight with fear, Dany made a gesture. Irri herded the other girls from the tent.

When they were alone, Ser Jorah drew his dagger. Deftly, with a delicacy surprising in such a big man, he began to scrape away the black leaves and dried blue mud from Drogo's chest. The plaster had caked hard as the mud walls of the Lamb Men, but like those walls, it cracked easily. Ser Jorah broke the dry mud with his knife, pried the chunks from the flesh, peeled off the leaves one by one. A foul, sweet smell rose from the wound, so thick it almost choked her. The leaves were crusted with blood and pus, Drogo's breast black and glistening with corruption.

"No," Dany whispered, as tears ran down her cheeks. "No, please, gods hear me, *no*."

Khal Drogo moaned, and thrashed where he lay, fighting some unseen enemy. Black blood ran slow and thick from his open wound.

"Your *khal* is good as dead, princess."

"No, he can't die, he *mustn't*, it was only a cut." Dany took his large, callused hand in her own small ones, and held it tight between them. "I will not let him die..."

Ser Jorah gave a bitter laugh. "*Khaleesi* or queen, that command is beyond your power. Save your tears, child. Weep for him tomorrow, or a year from now. We do not have time for grief. We must go, and quickly, before he dies."

Dany was lost. "Go? Where should we go?"

"Asshai, I would say. It lies far to the south, at the end of the known world, yet men say it is a great port. We will find a ship to take us back to Pentos. It will be a hard journey, make no mistake. Do you trust your *khas*? Will they come with us?"

"Khal Drogo commanded them to keep me safe," Dany replied uncertainly, "but if he dies..." She touched the great swell of her belly. "I don't understand. Why should we flee? I am *khaleesi*. I carry Drogo's heir. He will be *khal* after Drogo..."

Ser Jorah frowned. "Princess, hear me. The Dothraki will not follow a suckling babe. Drogo's strength was what they bowed to, and only that. When he is gone, Jhaqo and Pono and the other kos will fight for his place, and this *khalasar* will devour itself. The winner will want no more rivals. The boy will be taken from your breast the moment he is born. They will give him to the dogs..."

Dany hugged herself. "But *why?*" she cried plaintively. "Why should they kill a little baby?"

"He is Drogo's son, and the crones say he will be the stallion who mounts the world. It was prophesied. Better to kill the child than to risk his fury when he grows to manhood."

The child kicked inside her, as if he had heard. Dany remembered the story Viserys had told her, of what the Usurper's dogs had done to Rhaegar's children. His son had been a babe as well, yet they had ripped him from his mother's breast and dashed his head against a wall. That was the way of men. "They must not hurt my son!" she cried. "I will order my *khas* to keep him safe, and Drogo's bloodriders will—"

Ser Jorah held her by the shoulders. "A bloodrider dies with his *khal*. You know that, child. They will take you to Vaes Dothrak, to the crones, that is the last duty they owe him in life… when it is done, they will join Drogo in the night lands."

Dany shivered. She did not want to go back to Vaes Dothrak and live the rest of her life among those terrible old woman, yet she knew that the knight spoke only the truth. Drogo had been more than her sun and stars; he had been the shield that kept her safe. "I will not leave him," she said stubbornly, miserably. She took his hand again. "I will not."

A stirring at the tent flap made Dany turn her head. Mirri Maz Duur entered, bowing low. Days on the march, trailing behind the *khalasar*, had left her limping and haggard, with blistered and bleeding feet and hollows under her eyes. Behind her came Qotho and Haggo, carrying the godswife's chest between them. When the bloodriders caught sight of Drogo's wound, the chest slipped from Haggo's fingers and crashed to the floor of the tent, and Qotho swore an oath so foul it seared the air.

Mirri Maz Duur studied Drogo, her face still and dead. "The wound has festered."

"This is your work, *maegi*," Qotho said. Haggo laid his fist across Mirri's cheek with a meaty *smack* that drove her to the ground. Then he kicked her where she lay.

"*Stop it!*" Dany screamed.

Qotho pulled Haggo away, saying, "Kicks are too merciful for a *maegi*. Take her outside. We will stake her to the earth, to be the mount of every passing man. And when they are done with her, the dogs will use her as well. Weasels will tear out her entrails and carrion crows feast upon her eyes. The flies off the river shall lay their eggs in her womb and drink pus from the ruins of her breasts…" He dug iron-hard fingers into the soft, wobbly flesh under the godswife's arm and hauled her to her feet.

"No," Dany said. "I will not have her harmed."

Qotho's lips skinned back from his crooked brown teeth in a terrible mockery of a smile. "No? You say me *no?* Better you should pray that we do not stake you out beside your *maegi.* You did this, as much as the other."

Ser Jorah stepped between them, loosening his longsword in its scabbard. "Rein in your tongue, bloodrider. The princess is still your *khaleesi.*"

"Only while the blood-of-my-blood still lives," Qotho told the knight. "When he dies, she is nothing."

Dany felt a cold fire inside her, burning away her fear. "Before I was *khaleesi,* I was the blood of the dragon. Ser Jorah, summon my *khas.*"

"No," said Qotho. "We will go. For now... *khaleesi.*" Haggo followed him from the tent, scowling.

"That one means you no good, princess," Ser Jorah said. "The Dothraki say a man and his bloodriders share one life, and Qotho sees it ending. A dead man is beyond fear."

"No one has died," Dany said. "Ser Jorah, I may have need of your blade. Best go don your armor." She was more frightened than she dared admit, even to herself.

The knight bowed. "As you say." He strode from the tent.

Dany turned back to Mirri Maz Duur. The woman's eyes were wary. "So you have saved me once more."

"And now you must save him," Dany said. "Please..."

"You do not ask a slave," Mirri replied sharply, "you tell her." She went to Drogo burning on his mat, and gazed long at his wound. "Ask or tell, it makes no matter. He is beyond a healer's skills." The *khal's* eyes were closed. She opened one with her fingers. "He has been dulling the hurt with milk of the poppy."

"Yes," Dany admitted.

"I made him a poultice of firepod and sting-me-not and bound it in a lambskin."

"It burned, he said. He tore it off. The herbwomen made him a new one, wet and soothing."

"It burned, yes. There is great healing magic in fire, even your hairless men know that."

"Make him another poultice," Dany begged. "This time I will make certain he wears it."

"The time for that is past, my lady," Mirri said. "The poison spirits have tasted of his heart. All I can do now is ease the dark road before him, so he might ride painless to the night lands. He will be gone by morning."

Her quiet words were a knife through Dany's breast. What had she ever done to make the gods so cruel? She had finally found a safe place, had finally tasted love and hope. She was finally going home. And now she must lose it all...

"No," she pleaded. "Save him, and I will free you, I swear it. You must know a way... some magic, some..."

Mirri Maz Duur sat back on her heels and studied Daenerys through eyes as black as night. "There is a spell." Her voice was quiet, scarcely more than a whisper. "But it is hard, lady, and dark. Some would say that death is cleaner. I learned the way in Asshai, and paid dear for the lesson. My teacher was a bloodmage from the Shadow Lands."

Dany went cold all over. "Then you are *truly* a *maegi*..."

"Am I?" Mirri Maz Duur smiled. "Only a *maegi* can save your rider now, Silver Lady."

"Is there no other way?"

"No other."

Khal Drogo gave a shuddering gasp.

"Do it," Dany blurted. She told herself she must not be afraid; she was the blood of the dragon. "Save him."

"There is a price," the godswife said softly.

"You'll have gold, horses, whatever you like."

"It is not a matter of gold or horses. This is bloodmagic, lady. Only death may pay for life."

Dany's breath caught in her throat. "Death?" She wrapped her arms around herself protectively, rocked back and forth on her heels. "My death?" She told herself she would die for him, if she must. She was the blood of the dragon, she would not be afraid. Her brother Rhaegar had died for the woman he loved.

"No," Mirri Maz Duur promised. "Not your death, *khaleesi*."

Dany trembled with relief. "Do it."

The *maegi* nodded solemnly. "As you speak, so it shall be done. Call your servants."

Khal Drogo writhed feebly as Rakharo and Quaro lowered him into the bath. "No," he muttered, "no. Must ride." Once in the water, all the strength seemed to leak out of him.

"Bring his horse," Mirri Maz Duur commanded, and so it was done. Jhogo led the great red stallion into the tent. When the animal caught the scent of death, he screamed and reared, rolling his eyes. It took three men to subdue him.

"What do you mean to do?" Dany asked her.

"We need his blood," Mirri answered. "That is the way."

Jhogo edged back, his hand on his hilt of his *arakh*. He was youth of sixteen years, whip-thin, fearless, quick to laugh, with the faint shadow of his first mustache on his upper lip. He fell to his knees before her. "*Khaleesi*," he pleaded, "you must not do this thing. Let me kill this *maegi*."

"Kill her and you kill your *khal*," Dany said.

"This is bloodmagic," he said. "It is forbidden."

"I am *khaleesi*, and I say it is not forbidden. In Vaes Dothrak, Khal Drogo slew a stallion and I ate his heart, to give our son strength and courage. This is the same. The *same*."

The stallion kicked and reared and snorted as Rakharo, Quaro, and Aggo pulled him close to the tub where the *khal* floated like one already dead, pus and blood seeping from his wound to stain the bathwaters. Mirri Maz Duur chanted words in a tongue that Dany did not know, and a knife appeared in her hand. Dany never saw where it came from. It looked old; hammered red bronze, leaf-shaped, its blade covered with ancient glyphs. The *maegi* drew it across the stallion's throat, under the noble head, and the horse kicked and shuddered as the blood poured out of him in a red rush. He would have collapsed, but the men of her *khas* held him up. It took all four. "Strength of the mount, go into the rider," Mirri sang as horse blood swirled into the waters of Drogo's bath. "Strength of the beast, go into the man."

Jhogo looked terrified as he struggled with the stallion's weight, afraid to touch the dead flesh, yet afraid to let go as well. Dany was faint with relief. *Only a horse,* she thought. If they could buy Drogo's life with the death of a horse, she would pay the price a thousand times over.

When they let the stallion fall, the bath was a dark red, and nothing showed of Drogo but his face. Mirri Maz Duur had no use for the carcass. "Burn it," Dany told them. It was what they did, she knew. When a man died, his mount was killed as well and placed beneath him on the funeral pyre, to carry him to the night lands. The men of her *khas* dragged the carcass from the tent. The blood had gone everywhere. Even the sandsilk walls were spotted with red, and the rugs underfoot were black and wet.

The braziers were lit. Mirri Maz Duur tossed a pale red powder onto the coals. It gave the smoke a sharp, spicy scent, a pleasant enough smell, yet Eroeh fled sobbing, and Dany was filled with a strange fear. But she had gone too far to turn back now. She sent her other handmaids away.

"Go with them, Silver Lady," Mirri Maz Duur told her.

"I will stay," Dany said. "The man took me under the stars and gave life to the child inside me. I will not leave him."

"You must. Once I begin to sing, no one must enter this tent. *No one,* do you understand? My song will wake powers older and darker than you know. The dead will dance here this night. No living man must look on them."

Dany bowed her head, helpless. "No one will enter." She bent over the tub, over Drogo in his bath of blood, and kissed him lightly on the brow. *"Bring him back to me,"* she whispered to Mirri Maz Duur before she fled.

Outside the sun was low on the horizon, the sky a bruised red. The *khalasar* had made camp. Tents and sleeping mats were scattered as far as the eye could see. A hot wind blew. Jhogo and Aggo were building a pyre beneath the dead stallion. A crowd had gathered. They stared at Dany with hard black eyes, their faces closed and unsmiling, like masks of beaten copper. She saw Ser Jorah Mormont, wearing mail and leather now, sweat beading on his broad, balding forehead. He pushed his way through the Dothraki to Dany's side. When he saw the scarlet footprints her boots had left on the ground, the color seemed to drain from his face. "What have you done, you little fool?" he asked hoarsely.

"I had to save him."

"We could have fled," he said. "I would have seen you safe to Asshai, princess. There was no need…"

"Am I truly your princess?" she asked him.

"You know you are, gods save us both."

"Then help me now."

Ser Jorah grimaced. "Would that I knew how."

Mirri Maz Duur's voice rose to a high, ululating wail that sent a shiver down Dany's back. Some of the Dothraki began to mutter and back away from her. The tent was aglow with the light of braziers within. Through the blood-spattered sandsilk, she glimpsed shadows moving.

Mirri Maz Duur was dancing, and not alone.

Dany saw naked fear on the faces of the Dothraki. "This *must not be*," Qotho thundered.

She had not seen the bloodrider return. Haggo and Cohollo were with him. They had brought the hairless men, the eunuchs who healed with knife and needle and fire.

"I say this *will* be," Dany replied.

"*Maegi*," Haggo growled. And old Cohollo—Cohollo who had bound his life to Drogo's on the day of his birth, Cohollo who had always been kind to her—Cohollo looked at her with loathing and spat full in her face.

"You will die, *maegi*," Qotho promised, "but the other must die first." He drew his *arakh* and made for the tent.

"No," she shouted, "you *musn't*." She caught him by the shoulder, but Qotho shoved her aside. Dany fell to her knees, crossing her arms over her belly to protect the child within. "Stop him," she commanded her *khas*, "kill him."

Rakharo and Quaro stood beside the flap of the tent. Quaro took a single step forward, reaching for the handle of his whip, but Qotho spun graceful as a dancer, the curved *arakh* rising. It caught Quaro low under the arm, the bright sharp steel biting up through leather and skin, through muscle and rib bone. Blood fountained as the young rider reeled backward, gasping. Qotho wrenched the blade free.

"*Horselord*," Ser Jorah Mormont called. "Try me." His longsword slid from its scabbard.

Qotho charged, cursing. The *arakh* moved so fast that Quaro's blood flew from it in a fine spray, like rain in a hot wind. The longsword caught it a foot from Ser Jorah's face, and held it quivering for an instant as Qotho howled in fury. The knight was clad in chainmail, with gauntlets and greaves of lobstered steel and a heavy gorget around his throat, but he had not thought to don his helm.

Qotho danced backwards, *arakh* whirling around his head in a shining blur, flickering out like lightning as the knight came on in a rush. Ser Jorah parried as best he could, but the slashes came so fast that it seemed to Dany that Qotho had four *arakhs* and as many arms. She heard the crunch of sword on mail, saw sparks fly as the long curved blade glanced off a gauntlet. Suddenly it was Mormont stumbling backwards, and Qotho leaping to the attack. The left side of the knight's face ran red with blood, and a cut to the hip opened a gash in his mail and left him limping. Qotho screamed taunts at him, calling him a craven, a milk man, a eunuch in an iron suit. "You die now!" he promised, *arakh* shivering through the red twilight. Inside Dany's womb, her son kicked wildly. The curved blade slipped past the straight one and bit deep into the knight's hip where the mail gaped open.

Mormont grunted, stumbled. Dany felt a sharp pain in her belly, a wetness on her thighs. Qotho shrieked triumph, but his *arakh* had found bone, and for half a heartbeat it caught. It was enough. Ser Jorah brought his longsword down with all the strength left him, through flesh and muscle and bone, and Qotho's forearm dangled loose, flopping on a thin cord of skin and sinew. The knight's next cut was at the Dothraki's ear, so savage that Qotho's face seemed almost to explode.

The Dothraki were shouting, Mirri Maz Duur wailing inside the tent like nothing human, Quaro pleading for water as he died. Dany cried out for help, but no one heard. Rakharo was fighting Haggo, *arakh* dancing with *arakh*, until Jhogo's whip cracked, loud as thunder, the lash coiling around Haggo's throat. A yank, and the bloodrider stumbled backwards, losing his feet and his sword. Rakharo sprang forward, howling, swinging his *arakh* down with both hands through the top of Haggo's head. The point caught between his eyes, red and quivering. Someone threw a stone, and when Dany looked, her shoulder was torn and bloody. "No," she wept, "no, please, stop it, it's too high, the price is too high." More stones came flying. She tried to crawl toward the tent, but Cohollo caught her. Fingers in her hair, he pulled her head back and she felt the cold touch of his knife at her throat. "My baby," she screamed, and perhaps the gods heard her, for as quick as that, Cohollo was dead. Aggo's arrow took him under the arm, to pierce his lungs and heart.

When at last Daenerys found the strength to raise her head, she saw the crowd dispersing, the Dothraki stealing silently back to their tents and sleeping mats. Some were saddling their horses and riding off. The sun had set. Fires burned throughout the *khalasar*, and they seemed to burn hotter and angrier than any fires she had ever known, great orange blazes that crackled with fury and spit embers at the sky.

She tried to rise, and agony seized her and squeezed her like a giant's fist. The breath went out of her; it was all she could do to gasp. The sound of Mirri Maz Duur's voice was like a funeral dirge. Inside the tent, the shadows whirled.

An arm went under her waist, and then Ser Jorah was lifting her off her feet. His face was sticky with blood, and Dany saw that half his ear was gone. She convulsed in his arms as the pain took her again, and as if from far away she heard the knight shouting for her handmaids to help him. *Are they all so afraid?* she wondered silently, and knew the answer. Another pain took her, and Dany bit back a scream. It felt as if her son had a knife in each hand, as if he hacking at her to cut his way out.

"Doreah, curse you," Ser Jorah roared. "Come here. Fetch the birthing women."

"They will not come. They say she is accursed."

"They'll come, or I swear I'll have their heads."

Doreah wept. "They are gone, my lord."

"The *maegi*," someone else said. Was that Aggo? "Take her to the *maegi*."

No, Dany wanted to say, no, not that, you mustn't, but when she opened her mouth, a long wail of pain escaped, and she doubled over in Ser Jorah's arms, the sweat breaking over her skin. *What was wrong with them, couldn't they see?* Inside the tent the shapes were dancing, circling the brazier and the bloody bath, dark against the sandsilk, and some did not look human. She glimpsed the shadow of a great wolf, and another like a man wreathed in flames.

"The Lamb Woman knows the secrets of the birthing bed," Irri said. "She said so, I heard her."

"Yes," Doreah agreed, "I heard her too."

No, she shouted, or perhaps she only thought it, for no whisper of sound escaped her lips. She was being carried. Her eyes opened to gaze up at a flat dead sky, black and bleak and starless. *Please, no.* The sound of Mirri Maz Duur's voice grew louder, until it filled the world. *The shapes!* she screamed. *The dancers!*

Ser Jorah carried her inside the tent.

VII

Wings shadowed her fever dreams.

"You don't want to wake the dragon, do you?"

She was walking down a long hall beneath high stone arches. She could not look behind her, *must* not look behind her. There was a door ahead of her, tiny with distance, but even from afar, she saw that it was painted red. She walked faster, and her bare feet left bloody footprints on the stone.

"You don't want to wake the dragon, do you?"

She saw sunlight on the Dothraki sea, the living ocean of the plain, rich with the smells of earth and death. Wind stirred the grasses, and they rippled like water. Drogo was there, and he held her in strong arms, and his hand stroked her sex and opened her and woke that sweet wetness that was his alone, and the stars smiled down on them, stars in a daylight sky. "Home," she whispered, as he entered her and filled her with his seed, "home." But suddenly the stars were gone, and across the blue sky swept the great wings, and the world took flame.

"...don't want to wake the dragon, do you?"

Ser Jorah's face was drawn and sorrowful. "Rhaegar was the last dragon," he told her, his words echoing off the walls of cold stone. One moment he was there and the next he was fading, his flesh pale and colorless, less substantial than the wind. "The last dragon," he whispered, thin as a wisp, and he was gone. She felt darkness behind her, and the red door seemed further away than ever. Dany began to run.

"...don't want to wake the dragon, do you?"

Viserys stood before her, screaming. "The dragon does not beg, slut. You do not command the dragon. I am the dragon, and I will be crowned." The molten gold trickled down his face like wax, burning deep channels in his flesh. *"I am the dragon and I will be crowned!"* he shrieked, and his fingers snapped like snakes, biting at her nipples, pinching, twisting, even as his eyes burst and ran like jelly down seared and blackened cheeks.

"...don't want to wake the dragon..."

The red door was so far ahead of her, and she could feel the icy breath behind, sweeping up on her. If it caught her she would die a death that was more than death, howling forever alone in the darkness. She began to run.

"...don't want to wake the dragon..."

She could feel the heat inside her, a terrible burning in her womb. Her son was standing there, so tall and proud, with Drogo's copper skin and her own silver-gold hair, violet eyes shaped like almonds. And he smiled for her and began to lift his hand toward hers, but when he opened his mouth the fire poured out. She saw his heart burning through his chest, and in an instant he was gone, consumed like a moth by a candle, turned to ash. She wept for her child, the promise of a sweet mouth on her breast, but her tears turned to steam as they touched her skin.

"...want to wake the dragon..."

Ghosts lined the hallway, dressed in the faded rainment of kings. In their hands were swords of pale fire. They had hair of silver and hair of gold and hair of platinum white, and their eyes were opal and amethyst, tourmaline and jade. "Faster," they cried, "faster, faster." She raced, and her feet melted the stone wherever they touched. *"Faster!"* the ghosts cried as one, and she screamed and threw herself forward. A great knife of pain ripped down her back, and she felt her skin tear open and smelled the stench of burning blood and saw the shadow of wings. And Daenerys Targaryen flew.

"...*wake the dragon*..."

The door loomed before her, the red door, so close, so close, the hall was a blur around her, the cold receding behind. And now the stone was gone and she flew across the Dothraki sea, high and higher, the green rippling beneath, and all that lived and breathed fled in terror from the shadow of her wings. She could smell home, she could see it, there, just beyond that door, green fields and great stone houses and arms to keep her warm, *there*. She threw open the door.

"...*the dragon*.."

And saw her brother Rhaegar, tall and strong, mounted on a stallion as black as his armor. Fire glimmered red through the narrow eyeslit of his helm. "The last dragon," Ser Jorah's voice said faintly. "The last, the last." Dany lifted his polished black visor. The face within was her own.

After that, for a long time, there was only the pain, the fire within her, and the whisperings of stars.

She woke to the taste of ashes. "No," she moaned, "no, please."

"*Khaleesi?*" Jhiqui hovered over her, a frightened doe.

The tent was drenched in shadow, still and close. Flakes of ash drifted upwards from a brazier, and Dany followed them with her eyes through the smoke hole above. *Flying,* she thought. *I had wings, I was flying.* But it was only a dream. "Help me," she whispered, struggling to rise. "Bring me..." Her voice was raw as a wound, and she could not think what she wanted. Why did she hurt so much? It was as if her body had been torn to pieces and remade from the scraps. "I want..."

"Yes, *khaleesi.*" Quick as that Jhiqui was gone, bolting from the tent, shouting. Dany needed... something... someone... what? It was important, she knew. It was the only thing in the world that mattered. She rolled onto her side and got an elbow under her, fighting the blanket tangled about her legs. It was so hard to move. The world swam dizzily. *I have to...*

They found her on the carpet, crawling toward her dragon eggs. Ser Jorah Mormont lifted her in his arms and carried her back to her sleeping silks, while she struggled feebly against him. Over his shoulder she saw her three handmaids, Jhogo with his little wisp of mustache, and the flat broad face of Mirri Maz Duur. "I must," she tried to tell them, "I have to..."

"...sleep, princess," Ser Jorah said.

"No," Dany said. "Please. Please."

"Yes." He covered her with silk, though she was burning. "Sleep and grow strong again, *khaleesi*. Come back to us." And then Mirri Maz Duur was there, the *maegi*, tipping a cup against her lips. She tasted sour milk, and something else, something thick and bitter, and almost gagged. Warm liquid ran down her chin. Somehow she swallowed. The tent grew dimmer, and sleep took her again. This time she did not dream. She floated, serene and at peace, on a black sea that knew no shore.

After a time—a night, a day, a year, she could not say—she woke again. The tent was dark, its silken walls flapping like wings when the wind gusted outside. This time Dany did not attempt to rise. "Irri," she called, "Jhiqui. Doreah." They were there at once. "My throat is dry," she said, "so dry," and they brought her water. It was warm and flat, yet Dany drank it eagerly, and sent Jhiqui for more. Irri dampened a soft cloth and stroked her brow. "I have been sick," Dany said. The Dothraki girl nodded. "How long?" The cloth was soothing, but Irri seemed so sad, it frightened her. "*Long*," she whispered. When Jhiqui returned with more water, Mirri Maz Duur came with her, eyes heavy from sleep. "Drink," she said, lifting Dany's head to the cup once more, but this time it was only wine. Sweet sweet wine. Dany drank, and lay back, listening to the soft sound of her own breathing. She could feel the heaviness in her limbs, as sleep crept in to fill her up once more. "Bring me..." she murmured, her voice slurred and drowsy. "Bring... I want to hold..."

"Yes?" the *maegi* asked. "What is it you wish, *khaleesi?*"

"Bring me... dragon's egg... please..." Her lashes turned to lead, and she was too weary to hold them up.

When she woke the third time, a shaft of golden sunlight was pouring through the smoke hole of the tent, and her arms were wrapped around a dragon's egg. It was the pale one, its scales the color of buttercream, veined with whorls of gold and bronze, and Dany could feel the heat of it. Beneath her bedsilks, a fine sheen of perspiration covered her bare skin. *Dragondew,* she thought. Her fingers trailed lightly across the surface of the shell, tracing the wisps of gold, and deep in the stone she felt something twist and stretch in response. It did not frighten her. All her fear was gone, burned away.

Dany touched her brow. Under the film of sweat, her skin was cool to the touch, her fever gone. She made herself sit. There was a moment of dizziness, and the deep ache between her thighs. Yet she felt strong. Her maids came running at the sound of her voice. "Water," she told them, "a flagon of water, cold as you can find it. And fruit, I think. Dates."

"As you say, *khaleesi.*"

"I want Ser Jorah," she said, standing. Jhiqui brought a sandsilk robe and draped it over her shoulders. "And a warm bath, and Mirri Maz Duur, and..." Memory came back to her all at once, and she faltered. "Khal Drogo," she forced herself to say, watching their faces with dread. "Is he—?"

"The *khal* lives," Irri answered quietly... yet Dany saw a darkness in her eyes when she said the words, and no sooner had she spoken than she rushed away to fetch water.

She turned to Doreah. "Tell me."

"I... I shall bring Ser Jorah," the Lysene girl said, bowing her head and fleeing the tent.

Jhiqui would have run as well, but Dany caught her by the wrist and held her captive. "What is it? I must know. Drogo... and my child." Why had she not remembered the child until now? "My son... Rhaego... where is he? I want him."

Her handmaid lowered her eyes. "The boy... he did not live, *khaleesi*." Her voice was a frightened whisper.

Dany released her wrist. My son is dead, she thought, as Jhiqui left the tent. She had known somehow. She had known since she woke the first time to Jhiqui's tears. No, she had known *before* she woke. Her dream came back to her, sudden and vivid, and she remembered the tall man with the copper skin and long silver-gold braid, bursting into flame. Small wonder she had not asked for him.

She should weep, she knew, yet her eyes were dry as ash. She had wept in her dream, and the tears had turned to steam on her cheeks. *All the grief has been burned out of me,* she told herself. She felt sad, and yet... she could feel Rhaego receding from her, as if he had never been.

Ser Jorah and Mirri Maz Duur entered a few moments later, and found Dany standing over the other dragon's eggs, the two still in their chest. It seemed to her that they felt as hot as the one she had slept with, which was passing strange. "Ser Jorah, come here," she said. She took his hand and placed on the black egg with the scarlet swirls. "What do you feel?"

"Shell, hard as rock." The knight was wary. "Scales."

"Heat?"

"No. Cold stone." He took his hand away. "Princess, are you well? Should you be up, weak as you are?"

"Weak? I am strong, Jorah." To please him, she reclined on a pile of cushions. "Tell me how my child died."

"He never lived, my princess. The women say..." He faltered, and Dany saw how the flesh hung loose on him, the way he limped when he moved.

"Tell me. Tell me what the women say."

He turned his face away. His eyes were haunted. "They say the child was..."

She waited, but Ser Jorah could not say it. His face grew dark with shame. He looked half a corpse himself.

"Monstrous," Mirri Maz Duur finished for him. The knight was a powerful man, yet Dany understood in that moment that the *maegi* was stronger, and crueler, and infinitely more dangerous. "Twisted. I drew him forth myself. He was scaled like a lizard, blind, with the stub of a tail and small leather wings like the wings of a bat. When I touched him, the flesh sloughed off the bone, and inside he was full of graveworms and the stink of corruption. He had been dead for years."

Darkness, Dany thought. The terrible darkness sweeping up behind to devour her. If she looked back she was lost. "My son was alive and strong when Ser Jorah carried me into this tent," she said. "I could feel him kicking, fighting to be born."

"That may be as it may be," answered Mirri Maz Duur, "yet the creature that came forth from your womb was as I said. Death was in that tent, *khaleesi*."

"Only shadows," Ser Jorah husked, but Dany could hear the doubt in his voice. "I saw, *maegi*. It saw you, alone, dancing with the shadows."

"The grave casts long shadows, Iron Lord," Mirri said. "Long and dark, and in the end no light can hold them back."

Ser Jorah had killed her son, Dany knew. He had done what he did for love and loyalty, yet he had carried her into a place no living man should go and fed her baby to the darkness. He knew it too; the grey face, the hollow eyes, the limp. "The shadows have touched you too, Ser Jorah," she told him. The knight made no reply. Dany turned to the godswife. "You warned me that only death could pay for life. I thought you meant the horse."

"No," Mirri Maz Duur said. "That was a lie you told yourself. You knew the price."

Had she? Had she? *If I look back I am lost.* "The price was paid," Dany said. "The horse, my child, Quaro and Qotho, Haggo and Cohollo. The price was paid and paid and paid." She rose from her cushions. "Where is Khal Drogo? Show him to me, godswife, *maegi*, bloodmage, whatever you are. Show me Khal Drogo. Show me what I bought with my son's life."

"As you command, *khaleesi*," the old woman said. "Come, I will take you to him."

Dany was weaker than she knew. Ser Jorah slipped an arm around her and helped her stand. "Time enough for this later, my princess," he said quietly.

"I would see him now, Ser Jorah."

After the dimness of the tent, the world outside was blinding bright. The sun burned like molten gold, and the land was seared and empty. Her handmaids waited with fruit and wine and water, and Jhogo moved close to helped Ser Jorah support her. Aggo and Rakharo stood behind. The glare of sun on sand made it hard to see more, until Dany raised her hand to shade her eyes. She saw the ashes of a fire, a few score horses milling listlessly and searching for a bite of grass, a scattering of tents and bedrolls. A small crowd of children had gathered to watch her, and beyond she glimpsed women going about their work, and withered old men staring at the flat blue sky with tired eyes, swatting feebly at bloodflies. A count might show a hundred people, no more. Where the other forty thousand had made their camp, only the wind and dust lived now.

"Drogo's *khalasar* is gone," she said.

"A *khal* who cannot ride is no *khal*," said Jhogo.

"The Dothraki follow only the strong," Ser Jorah said. "I am sorry, my princess. There was no way to hold them. Ko Pono left first, naming himself Khal Pono, and many followed him. Jhaqo was not long to do the same. The rest slipped away night by night, in large bands and small. There are a dozen new *khalasars* on the Dothraki sea, where once there was only Drogo's."

"The old remain," said Aggo. "The frightened, the weak, the sick."

"And we who swore," Jhogo added. "We remain."

"They took Khal Drogo's herds, *khaleesi*," Rakharo said. "We were too few to stop them. It is the right of the strong to take from the weak. They took many slaves as well, the *khal*'s and yours, yet they left some few."

"Eroeh?" asked Dany, remembering the frightened child she had saved outside the city of the Lamb Men.

"Mago seized her, who is Khal Jhaqo's bloodrider now," said Jhogo. "He mounted her high and low and gave her to his *khal*, and Jhaqo gave her to his other bloodriders. They were six. When they were done with her, they cut her throat."

"It was her fate, *khaleesi*," said Aggo.

If I look back I am lost. "It was a cruel fate," Dany said, "yet not so cruel as Mago's will be. I promise you that, by the old gods and the new, by the lamb god and the horse god and every god that lives. I swear it by the Mother of Mountains and the Womb of the World. Before I am done with them, Mago and Ko Jhaqo will plead for the mercy they showed Eroeh."

The Dothraki exchanged uncertain glances. "*Khaleesi*," the handmaid Irri explained, as if to a child, "Jhaqo is a *khal* now, with twenty thousand riders at his back."

She lifted her head. "And I am Daenerys Stormborn, Daenerys of House Targaryen, of the blood of Aegon the Conquerer and Maegor the Cruel and old Valyria before them. I am the dragon's daughter, and I swear to you, these men will die screaming. Now bring me to Khal Drogo."

He was lying on the bare red earth, staring up at the sun.

A dozen bloodflies had settled on his body, though he did not seem to feel them. Dany brushed him away and knelt beside him. His eyes were wide open but did not see, and she knew at once that he was blind. When she whispered his name, he did not seem to hear. The wound on his breast was as healed as it would ever be, the scar that covered it grey and red and hideous.

"Why is he out here alone, in the sun?" she asked them.

"He seems to like the warmth, princess," Ser Jorah said. "His eyes follow the sun, though he does not see it. He can walk after a fashion. He will go where you lead him, but no further. He will eat if you put food in his mouth, drink if you dribble water on his lips."

Dany kissed her sun-and-stars gently on the brow, and stood to face Mirri Maz Duur. "Your spells are costly, *maegi*."

"He lives," said Mirri Maz Duur. "You asked for life. You paid for life."

"This is not life, for one who was as Drogo was. His life was laughter, and meat roasting over a firepit, and a horse between his legs. His life was an *arakh* in his hand and his bells ringing in his hair as he rode to meet an enemy. His life was his bloodriders, and me, and the son I was to give him."

Mirri Maz Duur made no reply.

"When will he be as he was?" Dany demanded.

"When the sun rises in the west and sets in the east," said Mirri Maz Duur. "When the seas go dry and mountains blow in the wind like leaves. When your womb quickens again, and you bear a living child. Then he will return, and not before."

Dany gestured at Ser Jorah and the others. "Leave us. I would speak with this *maegi* alone." Mormont and the Dothraki withdrew. "You *knew*," Dany said when they were gone. She ached, inside and out, but her fury gave her strength. "You knew what I was buying, and you knew the price, and yet you let me pay it."

"It was wrong of them to burn my temple," the heavy, flat-nosed woman said placidly. "That angered the Great Shepherd who herds us all."

"This was no god's work," Dany said coldly. *If I look back I am lost.* "You cheated me. You murdered my child within me."

"The stallion who mounts the world will burn no cities now. His *khalasar* shall trample no nations into dust."

"I spoke for you," she said, anguished. "I saved you."

"*Saved* me?" The Lhazareen woman spat. "Three riders had taken me, not as a man takes a woman but from behind, as a dog takes a bitch. The fourth was in me when you rode past. How then did you save me? I saw my god's house burn, where I had healed good men beyond counting. My home they burned as well, and in the street I saw piles of heads. I saw the head of a baker who made my bread. I saw the head of a boy I had saved from deadeye fever, only three moons past. I heard children crying as the riders drove them off with their whips. Tell me again what you saved."

"Your life."

Mirri Maz Duur laughed cruelly. "Look to your *khal* and see what life is worth, when all the rest is gone."

Dany could hear no more, not another word. She called out for Ser Jorah and the men of her *khas* and bid them take Mirri Maz Duur and bind her hand and foot and hold her close, but the *maegi* smiled at her as they carried her off, as if they shared a secret. A word, and Dany could have her head off... yet then what would she have? A head? If life was worthless, what was death?

They led Khal Drogo back to her tent, and Dany commanded them to fill a tub, and this time there was no blood in the water. She bathed him herself, washing the dirt and the dust from his arms and chest, cleaning his face with a soft cloth, soaping his long black hair and combing the knots and tangles from it till it shone again as she remembered. It was well past dark before she was done, and Dany was exhausted. She stopped for drink and food, but it was all she could to nibble at a fig and keep down a mouthful of water. Sleep would have been a release, but she had slept enough... too long, in truth. She owed this night to Drogo, for all the nights that had been, and yet might be.

The memory of their first ride was with her when she led him out into the darkness, for the Dothraki believed that all things of importance in a man's life must be done beneath the open sky. She told herself that there were powers stronger than hatred, and spells older and truer than any the *maegi* had learned in Asshai. The night was black and moonless, but overhead a million stars burned bright. A comet hung low in the east, its long red banner spread across a third of the sky like a dragon's tail. She took that for an omen.

No soft blanket of grass welcomed them here, only the hard dusty ground, bare and strewn with stones. No trees stirred in the wind, and there was no stream to soothe her fears with the gentle music of water. Dany told herself that the stars would be enough. "Remember, Drogo," she whispered, as she made him comfortable. "Remember our first ride together, the day we wed. Remember the night we made Rhaego, with the *khalasar* all around us and your eyes on my face as you took me. Remember how cool and clean the water was in the Womb of the World. Remember, my sun-and-stars. Remember, and come back to me."

The birth had left her too raw and torn to take him inside of her, as she would have wanted, but Doreah had taught her other ways, and Dany remembered. She used her hands, her mouth, her breasts. She raked him with her nails and covered him with kisses and whispered and prayed and told him stories. She tried once, and twice, and half a hundred times, and by the end she had bathed him with her tears. Yet Drogo did not feel, or speak, or rise.

And when a bleak dawn broke over an empty horizon, Dany knew that he was truly lost to her. "When the sun rises in the west and sets in the east," she whispered sadly. "When the seas go dry and mountains blow in the wind like leaves. When my womb quickens again, and I bear a living child. Then you will return, my sun-and-stars, and not before."

Never, the darkness cried, *never never never.*

Inside the tent Dany found a cushion, soft silk stuffed with feathers. She clutched it to her breasts as she walked back out to Drogo, to her sun-

and-stars. *If I look back I am lost.* It hurt even to walk, and she wanted to sleep, to sleep and not to dream.

She knelt, kissed Drogo on the lips, and pressed the cushion down across his face.

VIII

The land was red and dead and parched, and good wood was hard to come by. Her foragers returned with gnarled cottonwoods, purple brush, sheaves of brown grass. They took two of the tallest and straightest trees, hacked the limbs and branches from them, skinned off the bark, and split them, laying the logs in a rough square. Its center they filled with straw, brush, bark shavings, and bundles of dry grass. Rakharo chose a stallion from the small herd that remained to them; he was not the equal of Khal Drogo's red, but few horses were. In the center of the square, Aggo fed him a withered apple and dropped him in an instant with an axe blow between the eyes.

Mirri Maz Duur, bound hand and foot, watched from the dust with disquiet in her black eyes. "It is not enough to kill a horse," she told Dany. "By itself, the blood is nothing. You do not have the words to make a spell, nor the wisdom to find them. Do you think bloodmagic is a game for children? You call me *maegi* as if it were a curse, but all it means is *wise.* You are a child, with a child's ignorance. Whatever you mean to do, it will not work. Loose me from these bonds and I will help you."

"I am tired of the *maegi's* braying," Dany told Jhogo. He took his whip to her, and after that the godswife kept silent.

Over the carcass of the horse, they build a platform of hewn logs; trunks of smaller trees and limbs from the greater, and the thickest straightest branches they could find. They laid the wood east to west, from sunrise to sunset. On the platform they piled Khal Drogo's treasures: his great tent, his painted vests, his saddles and harness, the whip his father had given him when he came to manhood, the *arakh* he had used to slay Khal Ogo and his son, a mighty dragonbone bow. Aggo would have added the weapons Drogo's bloodriders had given Dany for bride gifts as well, but she forbade it. "Those are mine," she told him, "and I mean to keep them." Another layer of brush was piled about the *khal's* treasures, and bundles of dried grass scattered over them.

Ser Jorah Mormont drew her aside as the sun was creeping toward its zenith. "Princess…" he began.

"Why do you call me that?" Dany challenged him. "My brother Viserys was your king, was he not?"

"He was, my lady."

"Viserys is dead. I am his heir, the last blood of House Targaryen. Whatever was his is mine now."

"My... queen," Ser Jorah said, going to one knee. "My sword that was his is yours, Daenerys. And my heart as well. That never belonged to your brother. I am but a knight, and I have nothing to offer you but exile, but I beg you, hear me. Let Khal Drogo go. You shall not be alone. I promise you, no man shall take you to Vaes Dothrak unless you wish to go. You need not join the *dosh khaleen*. Come east with me. Yi Ti, Qarth, the Jade Sea, Asshai by the Shadow. We will see all the wonders yet unseen, and drink what wines the gods see fit to serve us. Please, *khaleesi*. I know what you intend. Do not. Do not."

"I must," Dany told him. She touched his face, fondly, sadly. "You do not understand. You cannot understand."

"I understand that you loved him," Ser Jorah said, in a voice thick with despair. "I loved my lady wife once, yet I did not die with her. You are my queen, my sword is yours, but do not ask me to stand aside as you climb on Drogo's pyre. I love you too dearly to watch you burn."

"Is that what you fear?" Dany kissed him lightly on his broad forehead. "I am not such a child as that, sweet ser."

"You do not mean to die with him? You swear it, my queen?"

"I swear it," she said, in the Common Tongue of the Seven Kingdoms that by rights were hers.

The third level of the platform was woven of branches no thicker than a finger, and covered with dry leaves and twigs. They laid them north to south, from ice to fire, and piled them high with soft cushions and sleeping silks. The sun had begun to lower toward the west by the time they were done. Dany called the Dothraki around her. Fewer than a hundred were left. How many had Aegon started with, she wondered? It did not matter.

"You will be my *khalasar*," she told them. "I see the faces of slaves. I free you. Go if you wish, no one shall harm you. Stay if you will, as brothers and sisters, husbands and wives." The black eyes watched her, wary, expressionless. "I see the faces of children, women's faces, the wrinkled faces of the aged.

"I was a child yesterday. Today I am a woman. Tomorrow I will be old. To each of you I say, give me your hands and your hearts, and there will always be a place for you." She turned to the three young warriors of her *khas*. "Jhogo, to you I give the silver-handled whip that was my bride gift, and name you *ko*, and ask your oath, that you will live and die as blood of my blood, riding at my side to keep me safe from harm."

Jhogo took the whip from her hands, but his face was lost and confused. "*Khaleesi*," he said hesitantly, "this is not done. It would shame me, to be bloodrider to a woman."

"Aggo," Dany called, paying no heed to Jhogo's words. *If I look back I am lost*. "To you I give the dragonbone bow that was my bride gift." It was double-curved, shiny black and exquisite, taller than she was. "I name you *ko*, and ask your oath, that you should live and die as blood of my blood, riding at my side to keep me safe from harm."

Aggo accepted the bow with lowered eyes. "I cannot say these words. Only a man can lead a *khalasar* or name a *ko*."

"Rakharo," Dany said, turning away from the refusal, "you shall have the great *arakh* that was my bride gift, with hilt and blade chased in gold. And you too I name my *ko*, and ask that you live and die as blood of my blood, riding at my side to keep me safe from harm."

"You are *khaleesi*," Rakharo said, taking the *arakh*. "I shall ride at your side to Vaes Dothrak beneath the Mother of Mountains, and keep you safe from harm until you take your place with the crones of the *dosh khaleen*. No more can I promise."

She nodded, as calmly as if she had not heard his answer, and turned to the last of her champions. "Ser Jorah Mormont," she said, "first and greatest of my knights, I have no bride gift to give you, but I swear to you, one day you shall have from my hands a longsword like none the world has ever seen, dragon-forged and made of Valyrian steel. And I would ask for your oath as well."

"You have it, my queen," Ser Jorah said, kneeling and laying his sword at her feet. "I vow to serve you, to obey you, to die for you if need be."

"Whatever may come?"

"Whatever may come."

"I shall hold you to that oath. I pray you never regret the giving of it." Dany lifted him to his feet. Stretching on her toes to reach his lips, she kissed the knight gently and said, "You are the first of my Queensguard."

She could feel the eyes of the *khalasar* on her as she entered her tent. The Dothraki were muttering to themselves and giving her strange sideways looks from the corners of their dark almond eyes. They thought her mad, Dany realized. Perhaps she was. She would know soon enough. *If I look back I am lost.*

Her bath was scalding hot when Irri helped her into the tub, but Dany did not flinch or cry aloud. She liked the heat. It made her feel clean. Jhiqui had scented the water with the oils she had found in the market in Vaes Dothrak; the steam rose moist and fragrant. Doreah washed her hair and combed it out, workingloose the mats and tangles. Irri scrubbed her back. Dany closed her eyes and let the smell and the warmth enfold her. She could feel the heat soaking through the soreness between her thighs. She shuddered when it entered her, and her pain and stiffness seemed to dissolve. She floated.

When she was clean, her handmaids helped her from the water. Irri and Jhiqui fanned her dry, while Doreah brushed her hair until it fell like a river of liquid silver down her back. They scented her with spiceflower and cinnamon; a touch on each wrist, behind her ears, on the tips of her milk-heavy breasts. The last dab was for her sex. Irri's finger felt as light and cool as a lover's kiss as it slid softly up between her lips.

Afterwards, Dany sent them all away, so she might prepare Khal Drogo for his final ride into the night lands. She washed his body clean, and brushed and oiled his hair, running her fingers through it for the last time, feeling the weight of it, remembering the first time she had touched it, the night of their wedding ride. His hair had never been cut. How many men could die with their hair uncut? She buried her face in it, and inhaled the dark fragrance of the oils. He smelled like grass and warm earth, like smoke and semen and horses. He smelled like Drogo. *Forgive me, sun of my life,* she thought. *Forgive me for all I have done and all I must do. I paid the price, my star, but it was too high, too high...*

Dany braided his hair and slid the silver rings onto his mustache and hung his bells one by one. So many bells, gold and silver and bronze. Bells so his enemies would hear him coming and grow weak with fear. She dressed him in horsehair leggings and high boots, buckling a belt heavy with gold and silver medallions about his waist. Over his scarred chest she slipped a painted vest, old and faded, the one Drogo had loved best. For herself she chose loose sandsilk trousers, slippers that laced halfway up her legs, and a vest like Drogo's.

The sun was going down when she called them back to carry his body to the pyre. The Dothraki watched in silence as Jhogo and Aggo bore him from the tent. Dany walked behind him. They lay him down on his cushions and silks, his head toward the Mother of Mountains far to the northwest.

"Oil," she commanded, and they brought forth the jars, and poured them over the pyre, soaking the silks and the brush and the bundles of dry grass, until the oil trickled from beneath the logs and the air was rich with fragrance.

Dany called for her handmaids. "Bring my eggs," she commanded them. Something in her voice made them run.

"The dragon's eggs?" Ser Jorah took her arm. "My queen, Drogo will have no use for dragon's eggs in the night lands. Better to sell them in Asshai. Sell one and we can buy a ship to take us back to the Free Cities, Sell all three and you will be a wealthy woman all your days."

"They were not given to me to sell," Dany told him.

She climbed the pyre herself to place the dragon's eggs around her sun-and-stars. The black beside his heart, under his arm. The green beside his head, his braid coiled around it. The cream-and-gold down between his legs. When she kissed him for the last time, Dany could taste the sweetness of the oil on his lips.

As she climbed down off the pyre, she noticed Mirri Maz Duur watching her. "You are mad," the godswife said hoarsely.

"Is it so far from madness to wisdom?" Dany asked. "Ser Jorah, take this *maegi* and bind her to the pyre."

"To the...? My queen, you cannot mean..."

"Do as I say." Still he hesitated, until her anger flared. "You swore to obey me, whatever might come. Rakharo, help him."

The godswife did not cry out as they dragged her to Khal Drogo's pyre and staked her down amidst his treasures. Dany poured the oil over the woman's head herself. "I thank you, Mirri Maz Duur," she said, "for the lessons you have taught me."

"You will not hear me scream," Mirri responded, as the oil dripped from her hair and soaked her clothing.

"I will," Dany said, "but it is not your screams I want, only your life. I remember what you told me. Only death can pay for life." Mirri Maz Duur opened her mouth, but made no reply. As she stepped away, Dany saw that the contempt was gone from the *maegi*'s flat black eyes; in its place was something that might have been fear.

Then there was nothing to be done but watch the sun, and look for the first star.

When a horselord dies, his horse is slain with him, so he might ride proud into the night lands. The bodies are burned beneath the open sky, and the *khal* rises on his fiery steed to take his place among the stars. The more fiercely the man burned in life, the brighter his star will shine in the darkness.

Jhogo spied it first. "*There*," he said in a hushed voice. Dany looked and saw it, low in the east. The first star was her comet, burning red. Blood red; fire red; the dragon's tail. She could not have asked for a stronger sign. She called for the torch. Aggo brought it to her. "*Khaleesi,* are you—"

"Yes." Dany took the torch from his hand, and thrust it down between the logs at the base of the pyre. The oil took the fire at once, the brush and dried grass a heartbeat later. Tiny flames went darting up the fire like swift red mice, skating over the oil and leaping from bark to branch to leaf. A rising heat puffed at her face, soft and sudden as a lover's breath, but in seconds it had grown too hot to bear.

Dany stepped backwards. The wood crackled, louder and louder. Mirri Maz Duur began to sing in a shrill, ululating voice. The flames whirled and whithed, racing each other up the platform. The dusk shimmered as the air itself seemed to liquify from the heat. Dany heard wood spit and crack. The fires swept over Mirri Maz Duur. Her song grew louder, shriller...then she gasped, again and again, and her song became a shuddering wail, thin and high and full of agony.

And now the flames reached Khal Drogo, and now they were all around him. His clothing took fire, and for an instant he was clad in wisps of floating orange silk and tendrils of curling smoke, grey and greasy. Dany's lips parted and she found herself holding her breath. Part of her wanted to go to him as Ser Jorah had feared, to rush into the flames to beg for his forgiveness and take him inside her one last time, the fire melting the flesh from their bones until they were as one, forever.

She could smell the odor of burning flesh, like horseflesh roasting in a firepit. The pyre roared in the deepening dusk like some great beast, drowning out of fainter sound of Mirri Maz Duur's screaming and sending up long tongues of flame up to lick at the belly of the night. As the smoke grew thicker, the Dothraki began to back away, coughing and muttering. Huge orange gouts of fire unfurled their banners in the hellish wind, the logs hissing and cracking, glowing cinders rising on the smoke to float away into the dark like so many new-born fireflies. The heat beat at the air with great red wings, driving the Dothraki back, driving off even Mormont, but Dany stood her ground. She was the blood of the dragon, and the fire was in her blood.

She had sensed the truth of it long ago, Dany thought as she took a step closer to the conflagration, but the brazier had not been hot enough. The flames flickered and writhed before her like the women who had danced at her wedding. whirling and singing and spinning their yellow and orange and crimson veils, fearsome to behold, yet lovely, so lovely, alive with heat. Dany opened her arms to them, her skin flushed and glowing. Mirri Maz Duur had fallen silent. The godswife thought her a child, but children grow, and children learn. *Only death can pay for life.*

Another step, and Dany could feel the heat of the sand on the soles of her feet, even through her sandals. Sweat ran down her thighs and between her breasts and in rivulets over her cheeks, where tears had once run. Ser Jorah was shouting behind her, but he did not matter any more, only the fire mattered, The flames were so beautiful, the loveliest things she had ever seen, each one a sorcerer robed in yellow and fire and pale blue, swirling their long smoky cloaks. She saw burning lions and great yellow serpents and unicorns made of air and fire, fish and foxes and monsters, each more beautiful than the last. She saw a horse, a great grey stallion made of smoke, its flowing mane a nimbus of blue flame. *Yes, my love, my sun-and-stars, yes, mount now, ride now.*

Her vest had begun to smolder, so Dany shrugged it off and let it fall to the ground. The painted leather burst into sudden flame as she skipped closer to the fire, her breasts bare to the blaze, streams of milk flowing from her red and swollen nipples. *Now,* she thought, *now,* and for an instant, just an instant, she glimpsed Khal Drogo before her, mounted on his stallion of smoke, a flaming lash in his hand. He smiled at her, and the great whip snaked down at the pyre, hissing.

And from somewhere behind the smoke there came a *crack*, as of shattering stone. The platform of wood and brush and grass began to shift and collapse in upon itself. Bits of burning wood slid down at her, and she was showered with ash and cinders. And something else came crashing down, bouncing and rolling, to land at Dany's feet. It was a chunk of curved rock, pale and veined with gold, broken and smoking. The roaring filled the world, yet dimly through the firefall Dany heard women shriek and children cry out in wonder.

And there came a second *crack*, loud and sharp as thunder, and the smoke stirred and whirled around her and the pyre shifted, the blackened logs exploding as the fire touched their secret hearts. She heard the terrified screams of frightened horses, and the voices of the Dothraki raised in shouts of fear and terror, and Ser Jorah calling her name and cursing. *No,* she wanted to shout to him, *no, my good knight, do not fear for me. The fire is mine. I am Daenerys Stormborn, daughter of dragons, mother of dragons, don't you see? Don't you SEE?*

With a tremendous roar and a belch of flame and smoke that reached thirty feet into the sky, the pyre collapsed and came down around her. Unafraid, Dany strode forward, into the firestorm, calling to her children. The third *crack* was as loud and sharp as the breaking of the world.

When the fire died at last and the ground became cool enough to walk upon, Ser Jorah Mormont found her amidst the ashes, surrounded by blackened logs and bits of glowing ember and the burnt bones of a stallion. She was naked, covered with soot, her clothes turned to ash, her beautiful hair all crisped away… yet she was unhurt.

The cream-and-gold dragon was suckling at her left breast, the green-and-bronze at the right. Her arms cradled them close. The black-and-scarlet beast was draped across her shoulders, its long sinuous neck coiled under her chin. When it saw Jorah, it raised its head and looked at him with eyes as red as coals.

Wordless, the knight fell to his knees. The men of her *khas* came up behind him. Jhogo was the first to lay his *arakh* at her feet. "Blood of my blood," he murmured, pushing his face to the smoking earth. "Blood of my blood," she heard Aggo echo. "Blood of my blood," Rakharo shouted.

And after them came her handmaids, and then the others, all the Dothraki, men and women and children, and Dany had only to look at their eyes to know that they were hers now, today and tomorrow and forever, hers as they had never been Drogo's.

As Daenerys Targaryen rose to her feet, her black *hissed*, pale smoke venting from its mouth and nostrils. The other two pulled away from her breasts and added their voices to the call, their wings stirring the air, and for the first time in hundreds of years, the night was alive with the music of dragons.

Editor's Acknowledgments

The editor wishes to acknowledge the proofreader Brad Ackerman who took on that task willingly. Tony Lewis for his advice and for his expert eyes looking over this, any mistakes that have been made are my fault and not theirs! Rick Katze for scanning the manuscript. Mark Olson for all the hand holding that he did for a first time editor. Deb Geisler for talking with the artist Charles Vess, about his wonderful cover art and helping me put the dustjacket together.

And lastly I thank the husband, Russell, who put up with my staring at a computer far too much, editing this book and neglecting him.

Quartet was set in Adobe Garamond and printed by Sheridan Books, Chelsea, MI.

The New England
Science Fiction Association (NESFA)
and NESFA Press

Recent books from NESFA Press:

Find details and many more books on our web page: www.nesfa.org/press

Books may be ordered by writing to:
NESFA Press
PO Box 809
Framingham, MA 01701

We accept checks, Visa, or MasterCard. Please add $2.50 postage and handling per order.

The New England Science Fiction Association:

NESFA is an all-volunteer, non-profit organization of science fiction and fantasy fans. Besides publishing, our activities include running Boskone (New England's oldest SF convention) in February each year, producing a semi-monthly newsletter, holding discussion groups relating to the field, and hosting a variety of social events. If you are interested in learning more about us, we'd like to hear from you. Write to our address above!